**Lucien lo**

"'

"Why, Majo_____ _____ ____ with an arched brow. "Are we no longer continuing the pretense you're here on business?"

From behind him, Ethan pointed an accusatory finger. "You knew! You knew General Jackson sent us to find La Venganza."

Her laughter washed over him like a hot bath. "Of course I knew. Do I look like an idiot?"

Now he leaned forward, his face a breath away from hers. "I want the villain's name."

Taking a step back, Marisa folded her arms over her chest. "What villain?"

"You know exactly what villain." His tone grew deadly, each soft syllable laced with a hard edge. "Who is La Venganza, señorita?"

"Ask your questions elsewhere. You'll get nothing from me." She waved a hand as if to shoo him away.

In one smooth arc, Lucien grabbed her flying hand in his right fist. His left hand cupped her chin, forcing her to look into his eyes. The velvet of her skin, like a rose petal, seeped into his fingers. He'd never touched her bare flesh before now. Never felt her warmth or known such incredible softness in anyone.

But the anger that blazed in her eyes reminded him of stable fires, alligators, and blood streaming from a comrade's forehead. Besides, she had a lover. A lover who was a criminal.

"I will find La Venganza."

With a shake of her head, she simultaneously broke out of his grasp and his gaze. "You'll find nothing." She flashed a superior smile. "You don't even know where to look. La Venganza could be standing before you, and you wouldn't know."

## Praise for Katherine Brandon / Gina Ardito

### KISMET'S ANGEL

"Rich in emotion, romance, and adventure.... The author's melodic voice adds elegance and weight to the stormy tale of a woman's hidden destiny."
~*Shelby Reed, author of The Fifth Favor* and *Seraphim*

"Ms. Brandon swept me away to a gilded land of Indian royalty and British occupation, then out to sea to battle pirates on the way to New Orleans and the War of 1812. Epic historical romance with just a touch of Kismet—perfect!"
~*Kelly McCrady, author of The Empire's Edge*

### KISMET'S REVENGE
"Katherine Brandon is an author to watch out for in the future! Her stories flow with excitement and heart-touching moments. They are definite keepers!"
~*Judith Leger, author, Love's True Enchantment*

### THE BONDS OF MATRI-MONEY

"[An] extraordinary tale."
~*Coffee Time Romance*

"A rare treat for fans of cute romances, it leaves you wanting more, more, more."
~*Romance Weblog*

### A LITTLE SLICE OF HEAVEN
"I literally read this book straight through. I read all night. I could not put it down."
~*The Romance Studio*

"A great style..." ~*Fallen Angel Review*

# Kismet's Revenge

## Kismet Series, Book Two

## by

# Katherine Brandon

*Happy Reading!*

*Katherine Brandon*

*2010*

This is a work of fiction. Names, characters, places, and incidents either are the product of the author's imagination or are used fictitiously, and any resemblance to actual persons living or dead, business establishments, events, or locales, is entirely coincidental.

**Kismet's Revenge: Kismet Series, Book Two**

Cover Art by *Tamra Westberry*

The Wild Rose Press
PO Box 708
Adams Basin, NY 14410-0706
Visit us at www.thewildrosepress.com

Publishing History
First English Tea Rose Edition, 2010
Print ISBN 1-60154-794-3

Published in the United States of America

*"Pandemonium, the high capital of Satan and his peers."*
*- John Milton (Paradise Lost)*

PROLOGUE

Fort Mims, Mississippi Territory
August 30, 1813

Marisa Álvarez would remember this day the rest of her life. Today the man she loved would ask her to be his wife. Last evening, he confessed he had something of great importance to discuss with her. What else could he mean but a marriage proposal?

Excitement danced in her veins, and she forced her feet to root in the dirt floor while she chopped vegetables for this evening's chicken burgoo. Still, her mind serenaded her with songs of a golden future. She and Tomás would have a wonderful life together. She'd already chosen the plot of land where they'd build their home, *El Castillo de Cielo,* the Castle of Heaven. An idyllic place, with plenty of pasture for the horses they'd raise. And of course, their children. Lots of children—tall, handsome boys and pretty, petite girls.

A broad arm snaked around her waist, rousing her from the daydream, and she flinched.

Her brother's amused face leaned close to hers. "There's a strange look to you today, *Montesita.* Do you think, perhaps, Tomás is finally ready to ask for your hand?"

Happiness burst from her in sparks. "I hope so, 'Lando."

"'Tis long past time." He squeezed her midriff tighter than an overlaced corset. "You've been walking out for more than a year now."

"Bah!" her father grumbled from the head of the dining table. "There'll be no marriage until this cursed war is ended."

Struggling from her brother's embrace, Marisa stamped a foot. "But, Papa—"

Papa's glower cut off her argument more cleanly than her knife cut the turnips. "I won't have my daughter a widow before she's scarcely a wife. If Tomás intends to wed you, he must agree to wait until there is peace in this land again."

Resentment bubbled, and she chopped the vegetables with renewed vigor. "Then I'll never marry. Tomás will tire of waiting and wed another."

Mama stirred the large black pot on the open hearth and clucked her tongue. "Tomás will wait, *mi hija*. In the meantime, you must practice patience."

"Patience." Orlando snorted. "Asking our *montesita* to practice patience is akin to asking the Red Sticks to practice forgiveness."

Laughter erupted from the family, and Marisa's face burned. "Fine for you to say, 'Lando. You didn't have to wait to wed Juanita." She gestured at her heavily pregnant sister-in-law who sat near the crackling fire, embroidering yellow flowers on a tiny white gown.

Her mother strode to her side, and shooed 'Lando when his finger poised over a carrot slice. "Surely you don't wish to wed in this makeshift fort, *querida*, when you might have a much grander affair at home with all your friends and family in attendance."

"No," she admitted, eyes downcast. "But it is so hard to wait."

"Well." Mama kissed her forehead. "Since Tomás has not asked you yet, I fear you must continue to wait a bit longer."

A rhythmic knock on their cabin door sent Marisa's heart into spasms.

"I believe her waiting has come to an end," Orlando quipped and pulled the apron over her head. "Go. Capture your suitor's heart. Juanita and I will help Mama finish the meal."

Suddenly breathless, Marisa stole a glance at Juanita and caught her nod. "Of course we will. Go. And return to us a betrothed lady."

On a delighted squeal, she hugged 'Lando, and then raced to open the door. Tomás Marquez stood on the other side, resplendent in his military uniform. Her heart fluttered. Oh, he was so handsome!

"*Buenos días*, Marisa." He stooped to duck inside the low doorway and greeted the other occupants.

"Why, Tomás," Juanita said with a sly grin. "What a surprise to see you today."

Ruddy color filled the sharp angles of his cheeks. "I thought Marisa would like to walk with me before the noon meal."

Marisa turned pleading eyes to her father.

Don Carlos waved his hand. "Go, but don't tarry. There's work to be done."

She stifled another squeal and ran to her father to kiss his roughly whiskered cheek. "*Gracias*, Papa."

"*De nada, Montesita*." He placed a gentle kiss behind her earlobe. "May God grant you happiness."

Hand-in-hand with Tomás, she stepped outside the dark house and waited for her eyes to adjust to the bright sunshine. Around her, a normal day at Fort Mims unfolded. Laughing children skirted cabins near fields that once grew tall stalks of golden corn. Their mamas hung wet laundry on ropes strung from wall to wall while they kept watch.

Tomás led her through the opened gate into the woods and along the edge of Tensaw Lake. Senses heightened to record every moment of today's events, she drank in the heat of a summer afternoon. The tinge of chimney smoke stung her nostrils. Songbirds scampered over tree branches, chirping love calls to their mates. Through the leafy canopy, sunlight dappled the water. The same sparkle glistened in her veins as they strode over mossy ground. Tomás's hand, large and strong, fit perfectly around her smaller dainty fingers.

At last, he stopped and indicated she sit on a large, flat rock at the lake's edge. Eyes intense with liquid fire, he knelt and clasped her fingers within his. She tensed with unbridled excitement as pulses jumped through her bones.

"*Montesita*, you know I adore you. I'm not a wealthy man, but if you'd be my wife, I'd be richer than all the kings in this world. Will you be mine, *querida*?"

*Kaboom! Kaboom! Kaboom!* A warning drum roll from the fort drowned out Marisa's answer. She had no time to speak again.

Hundreds of savages streamed from the woods, brandishing red-painted clubs. Red Stick Indians!

Their angry whoops chilled her blood as they raced toward the fort.

A flash of blue caught her eye. Militia leader, Major Beasley, struggled to close the gate against the horde. Piles of sand, which had built up due to neglect, prevented the gate from budging more than a mere inch. On raucous cries, at least a dozen savages overpowered the major. They struck him with their clubs again and again and again. Marisa blinked back tears, and when next she looked toward the fort, the Red Sticks scurried over a fallen body to gather inside.

Bile rose in her throat. Horror turned her feet to lead.

"*Montesita.*" Tomás grabbed her wrist, yanking her upright. "Hurry!"

He dragged her through dense foliage and deeper into the forest. Branches whipped her face. Pebbles pierced her soles. Tears streamed from her eyes. Her lungs burned for air, and her legs screamed with pain.

At last, Tomás stopped before a wall of rocks with a narrow breach. "Hide yourself!" He shoved her sideways into the stone fortress, then reached inside his jacket and pulled out a knife. "Don't make a sound. Stay here until I return. Do you understand?"

"My family," she managed to gasp.

"I'll find your family," he vowed. "You must remain here where it's safe. Promise me."

Panic stole her voice, and she nodded.

Hastily, Tomás cut several branches from nearby trees and draped them across her hiding place. "I love you, *Montesita.*"

"I love you," she replied, but had no way of knowing if he'd heard her before he plunged into the woods.

Time crawled on a snail's shell. Trapped, Marisa could do nothing but breathe…and wait. Outside her niche, terrible screams rent the air. The pleasant cooking smells turned acrid. Blood's metallic scent singed her nostrils and coated her tongue. Before long, her limbs numbed. She didn't know how long she stood, eyes squeezed shut against heavy smoke. Helpless to do anything else while her ears rang with tortured cries, she let her lips move in prayer.

*Madre de Dios, keep my family safe. Protect our neighbors. Tomàs. Stay with Tomàs. Help them all, por favor.*

Finally, the world fell silent. Still, no one came.

What had happened to Tomás, to her family? Why had no one come for her?

*Por Dios, they cannot be dead. Please.*

Acid burned her parched throat. With her heart thundering against her ribs, she dredged up enough courage to slip from the rock wall. On shaky legs, she raced toward the fort.

Thick black smoke obscured her vision, and she stumbled into several rabbit holes in her haste. Yet every time she fell, she picked herself up and pushed forward. She ignored the pain in her chest, in her ankles, in her head. Only her family mattered. As she neared the fort, waves of heat bathed her in smoky sweat. Every building inside lay engulfed in flames.

Major Beasley slumped against the gate, lifeless, bloody, and broken. She made a quick sign of the cross and moved on. Where was Tomás? Had he found her family in time? Were they all safe? Waiting for a signal to come out of hiding?

Inside the stockade, hundreds of bodies littered the ground like old dolls in a child's neglected nursery. They bore no faces. The children she'd seen earlier now sat stacked against the fence, mounds of bloodied pulp. The Red Sticks had smashed them there, splattering their brains on the wood and sand. The adults had all been scalped, skin and hair ripped away to reveal stark white bone. A maelstrom of dizziness engulfed her, but she shook off the waves and ran toward her family's crude cabin in the fort's center. Her feet stumbled over limp hands, torn limbs, a dog's carcass.

Near the place she'd left so happily a few hours earlier, a woman lay on her stomach, motionless. Her black hair remained intact. Marisa inched closer to examine the woman's head, but saw no wounds or blood. "Juanita? Can you hear me?" No reply. "Please, Juanita, wake up! Where is everyone?

Juanita, please!"

With growing impatience, she rolled over her sister-in-law. And screamed.

Juanita's belly, sliced open, glistened in the orange light. A well-formed boy, removed from his sac of waters, lay lifeless beneath his dead mother. Sinking to the blood-soaked ground, Marisa vomited the acid that had roiled her stomach.

Out of the smoky gloom a man appeared and grabbed her around the waist. She flailed against him. She screamed. She punched. She kicked.

"*Montesita*, hush!"

The moment she recognized his voice, she collapsed into his embrace. "W-we h-have to find—"

"No." He pulled her against his chest, shielding her eyes from the carnage. "It's too late. Only God can help them now."

Numb, she allowed him to pull her away from the mutilated corpses that littered Fort Mims.

Marisa Álvarez would remember this day the rest of her life.

# PART I

*"Vengeance, deep brooding o'er the slain*
*Had locked the source of softer woe;*
*And burning pride and high disdain*
*Forbade the rising tear to flow."*
*- Sir Walter Scott (The Lay of the Last Minstrel)*

## CHAPTER 1

*The Hermitage, Tennessee*
*October 1817*

"By the eternal, this scoundrel shall pay!" Major General Andrew Jackson stormed around the charred remains of his stables. The building, only completed to his satisfaction yesterday, now lay in pieces of blackened wood, soot, and cooling embers.

Major Lucien St. Clair stared at the wreckage, and his heart sank. *Not again.* "At least we hadn't moved the horses into their new quarters yet."

Jackson shook his head. "I had the horses moved last evening. Someone must have removed them before setting the fire."

Lucien stroked a hand across his chin. Months of work and a considerable amount of money...gone in a night's dastardly action. "Are we supposed to be grateful the villain has a consideration for animals?"

Jackson shot him an impatient look and held out his hand. "Where is it?"

With a sigh, Lucien reached into his pocket and removed a folded slip of paper. He didn't need to read the words written inside. He knew them by heart.

The incidents had begun nearly a year earlier when Jackson had called his men to military drills in the yard. Dozens of soldiers leaped into their saddles, but slid beneath their mounts' bellies to land in the dirt, flat on their backs. The cinch knots of every saddle had been cut. A note sealed with red wax and pinned to the shirt of the sleeping stable boy read, "*La venganza es mía.*" Vengeance is mine. An elaborate 'V,' entwined with a rosebud through the center, embellished the wax.

After that one event, the pranks appeared with increasing frequency. One morning, the soldiers awakened to discover every left boot missing from the camp. The right boots still sat beneath the cots. They found the lefts a few hours later when a boot parade floated downstream in muddied waters. The following week, while readying weapons for target practice, the soldiers couldn't load their ammunition. Cotton stuffed the barrel of every gun.

Five days later, shortly before midnight, loud screeches awakened the Hermitage's residents. Chickens, released from the hen house, skittered about the yard. Beneath the light of a new moon, thirty soldiers in their underwear, led by their incensed general, were forced to chase the squawking hens in the dusty barnyard.

Months passed with nothing amiss. The general and his men relaxed. All believed the culprit had given up his games. Until the pranks recurred. Canteens were spiked with heavy doses of pepper. Someone dressed three bulls in Mrs. Jackson's nightgowns. Mrs. Jackson discovered a family of skunks and their nest thrust into the pantry. After each incident, the cryptic message would be found, signed with the same blood red 'V.'

*La venganza es mía.* No one knew what the

writer avenged, or how he managed to arrange his pranks and escape discovery time and time again.

Two days ago, the general had wagered a great deal of money in a well-publicized horse race. At the onset of the race, a mare in season cantered behind the starting line. Jackson's stallion caught the scent, unseated his rider, and sprinted from the lineup to chase after the female. The General forfeited the race and lost a tidy sum. When the handlers finally caught up to the stallion and mare, the paper flew from the female's tail, tied with a pretty pink ribbon.

Major General Andrew Jackson, the Hero of New Orleans and the War of 1812, found himself a laughingstock in his hometown.

"Where was this one found?" He shook the paper in Lucien's face.

"Inside the pocket of the gown your wife wears today. The scoundrel must have placed it there during the night while everyone slept. Mrs. Jackson informed me she'd hung the gown on the back of her door last evening, as is her normal habit."

The general's eyes narrowed to dangerous slits. "The villain was in my house?" He kicked a smoldering remnant of beam.

Fiery sparks shot into the air, and Lucien flinched.

"It is my fault," a deep voice said.

Lucien whirled. A light-skinned Indian stood behind him, his face a solemn mask.

William Weatherford circled the smoky ruins. "My fault. This man seeks me."

"We've discussed this," Jackson growled. "I granted you a pardon for Fort Mims. I've accepted your surrender. No one under my command would dare defy my orders."

Lucien bit back a smile. "With all due respect, sir, I doubt the culprit considers himself under your command."

Jackson glowered. "Nevertheless, no one tells me who can live at my home."

"Yes, but I must return to *my* home." Weatherford shook his head. "I've taken advantage of your hospitality too long. I dishonor your generosity by remaining while you lose face with your friends and neighbors. I shall leave here before sunrise."

Would the chief's departure slake the villain's thirst? A niggle of doubt wormed Lucien's brain, but he kept his counsel and allowed the man to walk away without an argument.

*"Shall thy grave with rising flowers be dress'd,*
*And the green turf lie lightly on thy breast;*
*There shall the morn her earliest tears bestow,*
*There the first roses of the year shall blow."*
*— Alexander Pope (Elegy to the Memory of an*
*Unfortunate Lady)*

CHAPTER 2

*Pensacola, Florida*

*"Feliz Navidad,* Tía Rosa."

Marisa placed a nosegay of white roses on the well-tended grave. The wind kicked up and blew dirt across this noble site. With a shaky hand, she brushed the particles away. So much death. Too much death. When would the dark angel torment someone else for a change? Even the roses' edges had already browned. White roses, like the people Marisa loved, lived too-short lives.

Sighing, she stood and dusted off her gown. "I must go. Tío might need me. Wish my family a Merry Christmas, *por favor.*"

On the sign of the cross, she turned from the grave and walked toward her uncle's inn, *El Castillo de Plata.* After a foray into the cellar, she entered the kitchen, her arms laden with vegetables. She dropped her burden atop the scarred oaken table with a plop. Poor Tío could no longer chew solid food and breathe at the same time. Thus, she planned a soothing broth for Christmas dinner.

She left the vegetables for Santos to peel and strode upstairs to the last bedchamber in the hall. When she opened the door, gloom surrounded her like fog. Sickness stifled the air. Beneath a window overlooking the woods beyond, her uncle lay in the wrought-iron bed, nearly swallowed whole by a mound of homespun quilts.

"*Montesita?*" Tío's voice, thick with the exhaustion of labored breath, cut her heart to ribbons.

"*Sí*, Tío." Turning the oil lamp's flame higher, she forced a smile to disguise her concern. He looked so frail. Surely Death planned to pay another visit to her family soon.

Tío Miguel had always resembled her father, don Carlos—big and burly with radiant skin, a full head of gilt hair, and snapping green eyes. Now, he'd faded to skeletal with a waxy pallor, his hair reduced to wisps of gray.

"Come." He patted the bedside. "You visited your tía for Christmas?"

"Yes." She sat on the edge of the mattress and took his clammy hand to kiss the upraised veins beneath his bony fingers. Icy flesh chilled her lips.

"Did you tell her I'll join her soon?"

Tears welled, but she sniffed them away. "I told her."

"Don't cry, *Montesita*. I must return to the dust I once was." The bed swayed as he struggled to sit up.

Quickly, she braced an arm around his waist to assist him. Her fingers found his ribs through the bedclothes, and she shuddered. Death hovered nearer than she'd realized.

"Before I leave this realm," he said, "we must speak of La Venganza."

She stiffened, but widened her eyes in a look of endless surprise. "Why would you wish to speak to me about that scoundrel?"

His brow pleated in deep, censorious lines, and she flushed.

"My time is short, *querida*. Don't play the innocent with me. I knew La Venganza's identity from the cinch knots." He smirked, a ghoulish smile in his drawn face. "You pulled the same antic when you were six years of age. Do you remember?"

Misty memory floated into her head, a time when life held more joy than misery. "Papa planned to take 'Lando hunting," she said softly. "When I begged to go along, 'Lando said I should stay home to help Mama in the kitchen."

"Your brother gained the saddle only to slide under the horse's belly and land on his backside."

She smiled. "I told him he should help Mama in the kitchen while I hunted with Papa."

Tío leaned against the pillows and shook a finger of chastisement. "Your papa was at his wits' end with you. He knew you dressed his bull in your mother's nightgown. He caught you sinking Manuel de Valde's shoes in the river."

"Only after Manuel blackened Orlando's eye," she retorted.

Her uncle's lips quirked. "What about *Señor* Lopez?"

"*Señor* Lopez was a bitter old man. When Papa asked if I might attend school with 'Lando, he said, 'An intelligent woman is more dangerous than a nest of asps among your bedclothes.' I gave him a chance to experience such a nightmare."

His flinty gaze probed her soul. "Hiding snakes in his bed only confirmed his opinion that you were beyond redemption and should remain ignorant for your own good."

"They weren't poisonous," she argued. "And Papa educated me himself. So my prank had the perfect outcome."

"Only because your papa didn't thrash you," Tío said sternly. "Your tía and I spent many an evening with your father's letters, chuckling over your escapades. But now, you play a dangerous game. You must forget General Jackson and the Seminoles before you come to harm."

Anger spiked, and she shot to her feet. "Forget? I can't forget. The nightmares still haunt me. After Horseshoe Bend, Chief Red Eagle surrendered to General Jackson. But the general pardoned him and allowed him to stay *as an honored guest* at the Hermitage. Have you forgotten what the Red Sticks did to my parents? To Juanita? And 'Lando?"

Visions of gore raced through her mind like wildfire. Screams echoed in her brain, and she shook her head to banish the memories.

"I know my words won't sway you," he said. "But I beg you to give up this game of vengeance and find someone to love."

Love? No. Love brought pain. And death. "You know I'll never seek out love again."

"Ah, *querida*. What else is worthwhile in life? Your papa would say, 'Love comforteth like sunshine after rain.'"

Brushing a fingertip over his brow, she pushed errant wisps of hair into place. "You're desperate to win this argument if you resort to Shakespeare."

His eyes crinkled. "And what would be your reply?"

"*A Midsummer Night's Dream*. 'And yet, to say the truth, reason and love keep little company together nowadays.'"

He sighed, and the air in his chest rattled. "You win."

She pressed her lips to his brittle forehead and murmured, "I always do."

The sigh became a series of loud, wet coughs, and she quickly reached for the bucket stowed at the bedside.

But he waved her off and gasped, "Go make us a fine Christmas dinner, *Montesita*. I do believe it will be my last."

*"She walks in beauty, like the night*
*Of cloudless climes and starry skies;*
*And all that's best of dark and bright*
*Meet in her aspect and her eyes."*
*— Lord Byron (Hebrew Melodies)*

## CHAPTER 3

The following spring, General Jackson ordered his men to advance, once again, on Pensacola. Within hours, he had arrested the governor, Colonel Masot, and taken control of the territory. But his victory came at great cost. Unaccustomed to the heat and insects of Florida, more than one hundred soldiers became so ill they couldn't sit upright. In order to transport them home, Jackson ordered Major St. Clair to acquire twenty-five wagons from a local wheelwright.

On the day of their departure, however, Lucien counted only eleven wagons in the encampment. "What happened to the other fourteen wagons?"

Red-faced, the wheelwright dropped his gaze to the ground and mumbled, "They have square wheels."

The heat must have affected Lucien. He would have wagered a year's salary he'd heard the man say… *No. Ridiculous.* He leaned closer. "I beg your pardon."

"Last night." The man's voice grew stronger. "Someone outfitted the other wagons with square wheels."

"The devil you say!" Jackson leaped between the two men, his expression murderous. "Who would place square wheels on my wagons?"

The man cowered behind a bent, filthy arm. "Not all the wheels, *señor*. One wheel on each wagon."

"Replace them," Lucien ordered. "We'll get a later start, but at least we'll be able to transport our soldiers home."

But the man shook his head. "Someone took an axe to all the other wheels."

"Who...?" Unease flickered in Lucien's belly and flared to life when the wheelwright waved the familiar folded paper. "La Venganza?"

The general's face mottled. "La Venganza? Here? How did he know to find me in Pensacola? By Jupiter, I won't tolerate these pranks one moment longer." With the force of a hurricane, he whirled to whip all his fury on Lucien. "St. Clair, you will find La Venganza. Do whatever you have to, go where the trail leads. Leave no stone unturned. Find him, and I'll reward you handsomely."

"Yes, sir." His gut twisted.

How on God's earth could he find this blackguard?

As if he read Lucien's mind, the general clapped his shoulder. "You'll need help in discovering such a clever villain." He turned to the assembled troops. "Sergeant Greene, to me!"

An eager young man with dark hair and wide-set eyes stepped forward and offered a crisp salute. "Sir?"

"You will assist Major St. Clair in his endeavors."

The young man's face glowed with excitement. "Yes, sir, General!"

With a nod, Jackson grabbed his roan's reins

and swung into the saddle. "Remember, boys. Leave no stone unturned. Track him down, and you'll be richly rewarded." One hand upraised, he gave the signal for his men to prepare for their return to Tennessee.

Lucien stepped in front of the steed. "Sir? What about the sick? Will they stay behind?"

"No." On a sigh, the general alit from his horse and returned his gaze to his troops. "Those too ill to sit shall have the wagons. Those well enough to sit but too ill to walk shall ride. All who are healthy enough to walk will do so, including myself."

Envy pinched Lucien behind the eyes. He'd rather walk from Pensacola to Tennessee than stay behind and seek out La Venganza. But he had his orders, and he'd follow them, no matter how impossible the task might prove.

Jackson's hand clapped his shoulder again. "You're a good man, St. Clair. My wife's favorite, as a matter of fact. If anyone can discover the identity of this scoundrel, you can. 'Tis why I chose you."

Such high praise should have elated Lucien, but in fact, only depressed him more. He might as well have been ordered to capture fog. La Venganza was a phantom who wreaked havoc, and then disappeared, leaving no earthly trail.

Still, he saluted the general. "Thank you, sir. We won't disappoint you." He gained his saddle, signaled Sergeant Greene to do the same, and forced a confident air far from the doubt that hovered over him like a storm cloud. "Shall we begin our quest, Sergeant?"

"Yes, sir." The dark-haired greenhorn glanced around, eyes wide in confusion. "But how? And where?"

"Since the last place the villain struck was the wheelwright's yard, I assume he's still near Pensacola. We'll begin our questions here."

\*\*\*\*

Above Lucien, the orange sun burned, broken only by the sporadic appearance of palm fronds, which offered precious little protection from the unbearable heat. Against the bright blue sky, flamingoes squawked and sought fare. On the streets, red-skinned Indians clustered in groups, hatred obvious in their stony glares.

Sergeant Greene's gaze swerved left to right, and his posture stiffened in the saddle. "You don't suppose they know we're with General Jackson's Volunteers, do you?"

Lucien caught the edge of fear in the sergeant's voice, but didn't reprimand him. Based on the general's high-handed actions of the last several days, they'd probably gain more cooperation if they distanced themselves from the Tennessee Volunteers.

"Doubtful." Since the general and his militia did not subscribe to any military uniform, their civilian garb gave them an edge over Pensacola's residents. "They're more likely suspicious because we're strangers here. We need a reasonable explanation for our presence."

Why would two men, two *American* men, come to Spanish Florida? What business could they possibly...?

Business! Of course.

"My family owns a trading company," he said suddenly. "We'll say we're considering a business here. Which means, we must dispense with military formality. You will call me Lucien and I will call you...?"

"Ethan, sir—er, Lucien." The young man flushed scarlet.

*Wonderful. The kid's greener than spring grass.*

With a reason for their visit confirmed, they now needed a suspect to follow. More questions tumbled inside Lucien's skull. How could they draw the scoundrel from his lair? How had La Venganza found them in Pensacola? Was it possible La Venganza was someone close to the general? Or at the very least, a member of the Volunteers?

He shook his head. The villain might be somehow tied to the general, but not through the militia. These were men they all relied upon, men who'd vowed to give their lives in service if necessary. La Venganza's actions made a mockery of such noble sacrifice.

La Venganza was a braggart and a coward who skulked behind his folded papers and enigmatic messages. A braggart would no doubt want to remain in town long enough to hear tales of his exploits. Surely the villain's arrogance demanded public accolades. Which meant La Venganza still hovered near Pensacola. So, where would a man in Pensacola go for gossip?

"We should find a tavern. Or a meeting hall. Somewhere with a lot of local residents."

"A few of the boys found an inn on the outskirts of town," Ethan replied. "Near the army garrison, with a tavern inside."

Excellent. A perfect location for scoundrels to bask in drunken glory. "Is it crowded?"

"We couldn't find a seat when we were there two nights ago." A broad grin spread over Ethan's face. "Of course, the innkeeper might have something to do with the site's popularity."

"Generous with the drinks, eh?" He removed a handkerchief from his pocket and wiped the sweat from his brow. The air lay thick and humid, a steamy soup. "Lead the way, Ethan."

While Ethan prodded his mount ahead, Lucien kept alert to their surroundings. On the south end of town, the tranquil bay shimmered turquoise. West Indies blacks strode the streets with various goods piled upon their turbaned heads. Spanish seamen and soldiers, resplendent in crisp uniforms of crimson, blue, and white, eyed them with narrowed gazes.

At last, Ethan pulled his mount to a halt before a dove-gray, two-story building at the edge of a deep forest. With a discerning eye, Lucien studied the radiant windows and white shutters. A high-pitched roof over an expansive porch shielded the sun's harsh rays.

"*El Castillo de Plata*." Ethan read the hand-painted sign posted near a winding path. "What do you suppose that means?"

"The Silver Castle," Lucien said. "Do they have a stable?"

"Oh, yes, sir, Lucien. Quite a fine one." Ethan pointed beyond the main building. "In the back there."

They rode to a clapboard paddock with immaculate stalls, fresh hay, and a lush pasture. Approving the conditions, Lucien dismounted and tossed his reins to a nearby stable boy.

"See that Boreas is given a good rubdown." He patted the gelding's rump. "And some clean water. He's earned it in this heat."

The boy bobbed his head. "*Sí, señor*, our horses receive the best of care. The *señorita* would not have it any other way."

Another boy came forward to take Ethan's reins, and the two men strode the circular path toward the establishment's front door.

The moment they stepped inside, Lucien's eyes went black. The vibrant sunshine outside didn't allow for the inn's dim interior. Unable to discern more than ephemeral shadows, he followed raucous shouts and clinks of tankards. Surely, the noise would lead to a tavern.

Even after his vision cleared, he stood in the

doorway for several minutes, convinced he still suffered sun blindness. But she shined brighter than a thousand suns. In the crowded room, she sparkled like a diamond surrounded by coal. A gilt-haired goddess leaned over an elderly gentleman's shoulder, placing a tankard in his hand.

Ethan's snort cut through the haze. "I told you the crowds were due to the innkeeper. She's lovely, isn't she?" His sharp elbow poked Lucien's ribs. "I don't know about you, but I'm hoping La Venganza stays in Pensacola for a long time."

More to clear the fog than to disagree with Ethan's wish, Lucien shook his head.

"Marisa!" a man boomed from the other side of the room. "Have you heard what La Venganza did this morning?"

Lucien's ears perked up.

"No, Pablo," the goddess said, her voice clearer than a mountain stream. "I haven't heard about the rascal's latest escapade. What has he done now?"

At that exact moment, three men rose from a table, scraping their chairs along the floor. Quickly, Lucien signaled Ethan to grab the seats before someone else reached them first.

Meanwhile, the burly, bearded man named Pablo extolled the tale of the square-wheeled wagons—with some embellishment—to the delight of the crowd.

But the goddess shook her head. "*El General* is a dangerous man."

"*El General* is an arrogant ass!" Pablo retorted.

A group of soldiers in the corner stomped their boots and hooted with laughter.

"With four thousand armed men at his beck and call," the lady shouted over the noise, "even an arrogant ass can be deadly. Mark my words, friends, we've not seen the last of Major General Andrew Jackson."

"She's quite a woman," a hoarse voice whispered in Lucien's ear.

Lucien turned. The elderly gentleman he'd noticed earlier hunched over their table. By God, the man looked wizened and weathered to frailty. Lucien kicked the empty chair beside him and gestured for the old man to sit.

"*Gracias, señor.*" He groaned and stretched out his legs. "At my age, standing has become a mortal enemy."

Lucien offered his hand. "Lucien St. Clair."

"Ramon Santiago." The old man shook with a clasp firmer than his appearance suggested. "*Buenos días.*" Ramon looked toward Ethan.

To Lucien's embarrassment, the young man's gaze remained fixed on the woman who filled and delivered tankards from one table to another. "This is my business partner, Ethan Greene," Lucien said. He tried to kick the sergeant, but his toe slammed the table leg instead.

If the old man heard the sudden thud, he didn't react. "What brings you and *Señor* Greene to Pensacola?"

"We represent a shipping company based in New Orleans." The lie flowed smoothly off his tongue. "We're hoping to establish business here."

Ramon nodded. "Pensacola is an excellent choice. This town provides the best harbor on the Gulf of Mexico."

"As well as a host of glorious creatures," Ethan exclaimed with a wistful sigh.

Ramon smiled. "Ah, I see you've fallen under the spell of Pensacola's most beautiful citizen."

Head on a bent elbow, Ethan finally turned his attention to Ramon. "Who is she?"

"Marisa Álvarez," the older gentleman said. "The owner of this inn."

"Does she have a husband?"

Despite the question ringing in his own head, Lucien shot his subordinate a glare of disapproval.

"Not yet." Ramon leaned forward and shielded his mouth behind a shaky hand. "But if you're thinking of pursuing her yourselves, there's something you should know."

Lucien raised a brow. "What makes you think we might be interested in pursuing her?"

Ramon threw back his head and laughed. "Why do you think this inn is so crowded in the middle of the day? Every man here would gladly give his life for the opportunity to steal a kiss from Marisa Álvarez."

"So, what should we know about Marisa Álvarez before we decide to pursue her heart?" Ethan pressed.

"Marisa Álvarez is La Venganza's woman."

*"O what a tangled web we weave,*
*When first we practise to deceive!"*
*— Sir Walter Scott (Marmion)*

CHAPTER 4

The lady neared their table, two tankards in hand. Ramon beckoned her with the crook of a gnarled finger.

Poisoned honey, Lucien thought. For all her sweetness in face and form, a lady as immoral as this one could destroy a man if she crept into his veins. But, oh, how she tempted! Her hair draped her face in silver mist. Apple green eyes danced with amusement. She wore a plain cotton gown spotted with colorful stains of various shapes and sizes. Regardless of her shabby apparel, she walked with the carriage of royalty.

She smiled, warm and indulgent, and Lucien's groin sat up to take notice.

"What are you about now, Ramon?" Her soft, lyrical voice only enhanced her ethereal qualities.

In truth, she had the features and stature of a delicate fairy. Yet, if he believed Ramon, this charming sprite spent her nights as mistress to a villain.

Ramon drew her forward, one hand cradling her slender waist. "*Señores*, may I present *Señorita* Marisa Álvarez, the proprietor of *El Castillo de Plata?*"

27

She placed the tankards on the table with an echoed thud. "*Buenos días, señores. Bienvenido al Castillo de Plata.*"

Swallowing his distaste, Lucien rose. He bent only enough to show manners, but no approval. "*Muchas gracias.*"

Ethan's chair crashed to the floor as he scrambled to rise and take her hand. "I'm Ethan Greene, dear lady." He kissed her fingertips. Hooded eyes simpered over her knuckles. "I do hope you speak English since I'm completely ignorant of your lovely tongue."

The goddess exchanged a glance of impatience with Ramon, who shrugged. "And you, sir?" she asked Lucien in English.

"Lucien St. Clair." Each barbed syllable stung his lips.

"The gentlemen have come from New Orleans on business," Ramon said.

Her gaze settled on Lucien. "You'll need rooms?"

"Yes." In order to break the spell cast by her sultry eyes, he lifted a tankard and sipped cool ale. "If you have any available."

"Of course." She turned to a brawny bald man behind the counter. "Santos, *ven aquí!*"

On a series of eager nods, the brute strode around the bar. His heavy footfalls shook the tables and sloshed ale before he came to a halt beside her. "*Sí?*"

Lucien bit back a smile at the contrast. The giant and the diminutive fairy.

"Would you show these gentlemen two rooms upstairs?"

"Marisa!" a drunken voice slurred. "Come be my good luck charm."

"Excuse me." She flashed an indulgent smile at a circle of soldiers dicing in the nearest corner and floated away as gracefully as she'd appeared.

"I leave you in capable hands, *señores*." Ramon rose stiffly. "Santos will take care of your needs and see you're made comfortable." With one last smirk, he added, "La Venganza is a very lucky man, is he not?"

His guffaws trailed behind as he hobbled back to his own table.

****

Over the cluster of dark heads crouched in the corner with their dice, Marisa's attention refocused on Ramon. He grinned, winked, and tossed a subtle nod at the two strangers. From the corner of her eye, she watched them drain their tankards while Santos waited to escort them upstairs.

With a wicked grin, Ramon shouted, "Marisa! My ale is warm. Fetch me another, *por favor*."

She straightened and quirked an eyebrow. "Next time you leave your table to gossip, bring your tankard with you. I'm not in the habit of supplying free ale to careless men."

His right hand flew to cover his heart. "You wound me! I wasn't gossiping. I merely took the time to make two strangers feel welcome. Besides, I don't come to this place for the ale. I come for your company."

"You come for ale." She set her hands on her hips. "My company is the price you pay for your wants."

"I come because it does this old heart good to see such beauty walking the earth." His normally shaky voice resounded strong and clear. A hush rose in the crowded room. Every man halted conversation to listen.

Ramon flung his arms wide as if he knew he had the crowd's complete attention. "I come to see a goddess who deigns to live among mere mortals. I come because one glimpse of your loveliness outshines the brilliance of the noonday sun."

"*Sí,*" resounded from the circles of patrons, accompanied by vigorous nods.

So many eyes burned into her. Perspiration rolled down her back and drenched her chemise. On an exasperated breath, she tossed her head.

"*Es la verdad,* Marisa." Ramon's hand encompassed the room of suddenly awestruck men. "We all come for the same reason."

Another wave of nods and agreements ensued.

Heat hurtled into her cheeks. When he shot a glance to where the two strangers stood watching the exchange, her gaze naturally followed. The taller, more handsome of the two, froze her feet to the floor with an icy glare. With his thick mane of honey hair and sharp golden gaze, he resembled a lion ready to pounce. Hands fisted at her sides, she prodded her legs to move toward the casks behind the counter.

"I'll fetch you another ale," she muttered.

As if her capitulation offered some secret signal, the soldiers returned to their own pursuits.

Once she'd filled a tankard, she settled beside Ramon and placed the ale on the table. Shivers tickled her spine when Santos walked past with the strangers in tow, and she frowned.

Ramon leaned forward and poked her nose. "Is something amiss, *querida?*"

She sighed and seated her chin in her hand. "That man? St. Clair? He hates me."

"Why should that bother you?"

"I don't know." She shrugged. "All I know is he stared at me with so much disapproval I felt dirty. The dark one with his leers didn't bother me at all. I know how to handle such a man, but the fair one…"

"Ah, well." Ramon's smile snared her suspicions before he dropped his gaze to his tankard. "I might be able to explain the stranger's cool reaction."

"Oh?" Fine hairs danced on her nape. What had

he done now?

"While Pablo recounted our rascal's latest escapade, Antonio Gutierrez ran into the inn as if the hounds of hell snapped at his heels."

"Antonio? The wheelwright's son?" Surprise shot her upright. "You don't think the general demanded proof of the square wheels, do you?"

Ramon shook his head. "*Gracias a Dios,* he believed what the wheelwright told him. However, the prank angered General Jackson so much he left two additional officers behind when he headed home. They've been charged with seeking out the identity of La Venganza. A Major St. Clair and a Sergeant Greene, both of the Tennessee Volunteers."

Realization struck, and she held up a hand. "Do not tell me. One had dark hair and dark eyes, while the other was taller with golden hair and eyes." Alarms rang in her head. "How do you suppose they found their way here?"

"I already told you why men flock to this inn." He nudged his elbow against her ribs. "No doubt they heard of the beautiful *señorita* and came to make her acquaintance."

Her cheeks flamed anew, and she swigged a healthy gulp from his tankard to ease the burn. "So, what did you tell them about me?"

"I told them you were La Venganza's woman."

The ale reversed direction and she choked. As she struggled to clear her throat, she slammed the tankard on the table. "You told them what?!"

Several heads turned in their direction again. Fresh embarrassment crawled up her throat, but she waved off the curious looks.

When the soldiers once again returned to their own conversations, she confronted Ramon. "How could you? No wonder the man looked at me as if I were dirt. What were you thinking?"

"Ah, now, how better for you to know what

they're about?" He traced a scar in the oaken tabletop. "They will watch you very carefully in the hope you'll lead them to La Venganza. And, while they're watching you, you'll be able to watch them without arousing their suspicions. It is a perfect plan, no?"

Indeed. A perfect plan. Marisa giggled. "You're spending far too much time in my company, Ramon. Why, you've become quite devious these days."

He placed a hand atop hers and squeezed. "Merely following your fine example. Now, sing for me, *Montesita*. You know how I love to hear you sing."

****

Once settled in their separate bedchambers, Ethan sat in the lone chair in the corner of Lucien's room.

Lucien paced the narrow space between the wrought-iron bed and the open window. His mind swirled. "Did you hear the applause and cheers of the crowd when Pablo revealed the prank of the square wheels?"

Ethan shrugged. "Apparently, La Venganza is considered a hero among the people of Pensacola."

"But why?" he persisted. "How do they know La Venganza?"

"Perhaps General Jackson isn't La Venganza's only target. Or maybe he's avenging himself for some Spanish wrong. The notes alone point to a Spaniard. *La venganza es mia.* That's Spanish, yes?"

"Yes. It means, 'Vengeance is mine.' But, if La Venganza is harassing others besides General Jackson, who?" Each footstep raised another question. "Who are La Venganza's targets? Other generals? Men of power? Americans? What is the common thread among the victims? And what is Marisa's link? Why did Ramon delight in telling us she is La Venganza's woman? For that matter, how did he know two strangers would know about La Venganza?"

"You don't think Ramon is one of La Venganza's men?"

Lucien paused near the window to look out over the grounds below. "The thought has occurred to me."

A shadowy figure appeared below, a woman who strode with purpose toward the stable. The serving girl? Miss Álvarez? Too far away for Lucien to be certain. He turned from the window, and his feet took up the familiar to and fro pattern again.

Ethan snorted. "Ramon is an infirm. I've seen oak trees less gnarled and bent than he. His spectacles are thick as planks of wood, and his limp is quite pronounced. What possible use could a feeble, myopic old man be to La Venganza?"

"He couldn't remove wagon wheels or replace them." Lucien's pace grew frenetic while his mind jumped from idea to idea. "At his age, he couldn't move swiftly enough to catch a snail. I doubt he leaves the notes where they're found. And with his penchant for spirits and idle chitchat, he wouldn't be the sort of man in whom you'd confide secrets."

"Ramon is a man who seems to like three things in life." Ethan held up a hand and counted on his fingers. "A pretty girl, cold ale, and gossip."

Lightning struck, and Lucien stopped. "Unless, he is used for precisely that reason."

A frown creased Ethan's boyish features. "I don't understand."

"Think about it! Ramon is a harmless old man. Even better, he's a drunkard and a rumormonger. Who better to keep La Venganza informed of the comings and goings in town? Ramon fits in anywhere. Every town and every tavern has a man like Ramon among its patrons. He'd be forgotten before he'd even left the premises. A man like

Ramon is as common and nondescript as paper."

Bitterness filled Lucien's mouth. He cast another glance out the window where the grounds lay silent and unoccupied once again.

*Unlike a certain woman with the face of an angel, but the morals of a viper.*

\*\*\*\*

At seven o'clock that evening, Lucien and Ethan entered a nearly empty tavern. All remnants of the soldiers had vanished. The chairs and tables sat neatly on the swept floor. Tabletops gleamed from lemon oil. Opened windows allowed the evening breeze to air out stale odors of smoke and ale.

Santos remained behind the bar, polishing tankards. Meanwhile, a pretty, buxom girl with a freckled face and bright red hair set a table in the center of the room. She must have spotted them in the doorway because she gestured for them to enter.

"Where are the crowds?" Ethan surveyed the room with a casual glance. "The soldiers, the others who were here earlier? Everyone has disappeared."

"Dinner is only served to those residing above stairs," the girl said as she placed two silver wine goblets on the table. "The soldiers must return to their barracks."

Lucien pointed to the two chairs, two plates, and two goblets. "What of Miss Álvarez? Won't she join us?"

He hated himself for asking, but at the moment, he didn't have control of his tongue. Nor could he help but notice how plain the tavern looked without her presence, as if she'd taken the soul of the room when she left.

"Marisa left on an errand nearly an hour ago." Anita set a plate of red snapper and sliced onions before each man. The scent of fresh tomatoes and vinegar filled the air. "I doubt she'll return until late this evening."

"Anita!" Santos shouted from his place behind the bar. "Enough talk. More work."

Ducking her head, she offered them an apologetic smile. "Santos thinks I talk too much." With a quick curtsey, she left the table and hurried out of the room.

"I wonder what errand would take hours to complete." Ethan cast a sideways glance at Santos who watched them through narrowed eyes. He leaned closer to whisper to Lucien. "Do you suppose Marisa's errand has something to do with La Venganza?"

"With La Venganza's bed, no doubt." Lucien scooped up a forkful of fish, but his stomach twisted, and he dropped the food back to the plate. His appetite had disappeared, replaced by a violent need to throttle the lovely innkeeper.

Hours later, the tavern sat near-bursting with soldiers. Every square inch of space held a drunken man. In one corner, a group of soldiers sang off-key ditties. A circle of men around the bar laughed at ribald jokes. The farthest corner, beneath an open window, held the dicing group. Still, the innkeeper made no appearance.

Another hour elapsed when, tankard halfway to his lips, Lucien paused. Lightning crackled in the air around him, and the fine hairs on his nape danced.

Through the press of bodies, he caught sight of tousled gilt hair dotted with dry leaves and bits of grass. His surroundings melted. The noises and odors drifted away. Only Marisa Álvarez existed in that moment, his senses acute to nothing but her.

She stood in a dark corner of the hall. Her breasts heaved as if she'd run a great distance. Obviously, she'd hoped to escape anyone's notice. When she swirled off her dark blue cloak, his gaze locked on a large tear that wended up the back of the garment. The gown underneath drooped, sodden and muddy at the hem. Despite the condition of her clothing, her eyes sparkled with delight, and her cheeks flushed a pale pink. To all outward appearances, she looked like a woman who'd just made wild and passionate love in a meadow.

Steam rose from Lucien's collar, and he gulped ale to cool the burn. He shot up from the chair, prepared to question her. "The whore has returned."

Ethan's startled gaze drank in her dishabille, and he grinned. "So she has."

"Wait here." He pushed his way past the circle of men blocking the doorway, but in the hall, he stopped. Nothing remained but a pair of mud-encrusted boots.

Marisa had vanished.

*"A councilor ought not to sleep the whole night through, a man to whom the populace is entrusted, and who has many responsibilities."*
— Homer (The Iliad)

## CHAPTER 5

Shortly after sunrise the following morning, Lucien pounded on Ethan's door. "Ethan, wake up, dammit!"

At last, the door creaked open a sliver. One sleepy eye peered from the slight space. "What the hell? Lucien? The birds aren't even up yet."

"Get dressed," he barked. "We're expected at Government House within the hour."

The sliver became a chasm as Ethan flung the door wide and folded his arms over his bare chest. "Why?"

"Because Colonel King wants to see us. I'll be outside the stables, horses saddled and ready. You have ten minutes to make yourself presentable and meet me there." Without awaiting a reply, he turned and headed for the staircase.

Exactly eight minutes later, Lucien stood outside the stables as promised. One hand held an open pocket watch. The other, two sets of reins. Ethan turned the corner, rumpled and unshaven, but awake. Well, if the colonel wanted punctuality *and* cleanliness in the future, he'd have to give them more advance notice. More fastidious than his counterpart, Lucien always appeared crisp and clean-shaven. This morning was no exception.

Still, he forgave Ethan the lapse and gestured for him to gain his mount's saddle. Once Lucien sat astride Boreas, he led them away from *El Castillo de Plata*.

They rode through the city while fishmongers attracted customers with plaintive cries. Sweet yeasty odors from the bakers' shops filled the air. Pretty girls displayed ripe fruits and vegetables on the streets.

"Only the vendors are up and about at this hour," Ethan muttered.

Lucien shot him a glare of disapproval, and the younger man flushed. No other words passed between them until they arrived at their destination.

Government House, an imposing two-story building with massive carved granite columns, reigned over a lush landscape of crystal clear waters and colorful gardens. Long the residence of the territory's governor, Colonel King had quickly moved in when assigned the prestigious position by General Jackson.

Upon their arrival, a liveried footman led Lucien and Ethan into a vast room filled with mahogany furniture and shelves of books. The colonel sat behind the massive desk, which only served to dwarf his already unimposing posture. Sweat dripped from his chalk-white face, and his hands trembled visibly.

Lucien offered a crisp salute, and Ethan followed. "You sent for us, Colonel?" Lucien asked.

King fanned his face with the back of his hand. Several times, he opened his mouth, but no words issued forth. Finally, he handed over a folded paper with a red seal. Dread chilled Lucien's flesh, and he took the item with all the enthusiasm of a man passed a dead fish.

Ethan leaned closer to peer over Lucien's

shoulder. "La Venganza?"

At King's nod, Lucien's heart plummeted. "When?"

"Last night," King managed. "The bastard put an alligator in my privy."

Questions swirled, but he went with the obvious first. "How did he manage to fit—"

"The thing was a baby," King interjected. "But in the middle of the night, I couldn't tell. All I saw was a hell of a lot of teeth aimed right for my arse. I screamed like a bloody banshee. Half my company's probably laughing in their breakfast dishes this morning." His eyes narrowed and aimed displeasure directly at Lucien. "Didn't General Jackson order you two to find La Venganza?"

After several deep breaths, Lucien forced a calm tone and relaxed stance. "He did, sir. But we've searched for less than a day. We need more time."

"Time?" While his whitened knuckles gripped the desk's hand-carved edge, King rose to glower over his underlings. "For what, Major St. Clair? Time for the bastard to find a fire-breathing dragon to place in my bed? If I give you enough time, La Venganza will make me look like a buffoon before the entire city!"

And heaven forbid the public should ridicule him. Lucien bit his tongue to keep the sarcasm in check. "I give you my word. We'll deliver La Venganza to you shortly."

Colonel King glared and his chest heaved with the effort to maintain his bluster. "You have one month. If you haven't caught the villain by then, I'll report your failure to General Jackson."

A month's time? For two strangers? Against a town of suspicious residents who considered La Venganza a folk hero? Impossible. Surely, the colonel would see reason.

"I appreciate your discomfort, sir," Lucien said,

"but we may need more than one month to catch—"

"One month, Major!"

He sighed. "Yes, sir."

"Dismissed, gentlemen." With an imperious wave, King regained his seat.

After a crisp salute, Ethan and Lucien walked out of the office. In silence they strode down the hall to the front door of Government House where Ethan finally halted. "One month?" he mumbled. "How the hell are we to find La Venganza in one month?"

"Damned if I know," Lucien replied. "But I suggest we keep a closer eye on *Señorita* Álvarez. Sooner or later, she is bound to lead us directly to the villain."

****

"General Jackson returned to Tennessee, but not before leaving several men behind." Marisa knelt at the graves of her *tía* and *tío* while dawn streaked pink across the cerulean sky. "Colonel King is our new governor, and Captain Gadsden is in charge of collecting revenue. Most amazing of all? Ramon informed me a Sergeant Greene and Major St. Clair have been ordered to find La Venganza."

A cool breeze rustled the palm fronds overhead. "Don't grumble, *Tío*. These two will have no better luck than the others who've come here seeking La Venganza." A pair of leonine eyes rose in her mind, and she shivered. "I admit Major St. Clair plagues me. He studies me too closely. And his eyes! I imagine if they looked at me with something other than suspicion, I might find them beautiful. They're such a pure golden color, with tiny green sparks. But when he turns his gaze toward me, he strips me bare."

Thoughts of the major's animosity raised bumps on her arms. In an attempt to lighten the mood, she turned to the second headstone. "Did you think I forgot your flowers, *Tía*?" She placed a small bouquet of roses atop the grave. "Six red today."

Rising, she dusted the soil from her knees, and then made the sign of the cross. "I must go before *El General's* toadies seek me out. Tell my family I'm well and think of them every day. I miss you all. Until we're together again, may God keep me in your thoughts."

Her heart heavier yet lighter at the same time, she walked away from the gravesite, intent on a direct return to the inn. Somehow, her conversations with *Tío* and *Tía* always left her with this imbalance. Work, however, distracted her from morose thoughts—and today, a certain major's unsettling eyes.

For several hours, she kept busy with daily tasks. She reviewed the account ledgers, stocked kitchen supplies, ordered ale and rum brought into the tavern from the cellar. Once certain Anita had thoroughly cleaned the guests' rooms, she entered the kitchen. Santos stirred the contents of a large pot over the fire. The aroma of vegetable stock tinged the air.

"I thought we'd have *arroz con pollo* tonight." He nodded toward the large table where several hens lay.

Marisa plopped onto a stool beside him and set to work preparing the evening meal. For the next two hours, she plucked the feathers off chickens, chopped vegetables, kneaded bread dough, boiled rice, and pitted cherries for a dessert. She and Santos worked in complete silence, a comfortable silence between two people who knew each other well.

"Go, Marisa," Santos said after a while. "I'll see to the rest of the meal."

With a nod of thanks, she rose and left the kitchens.

She trudged to the gravesite once more. The

roses she'd placed in the morning no longer sat in their place of honor. *All is well...*

Well pleased, she returned to the inn. Passing the tavern doors, she espied the two gentlemen seated at a table while Anita served their supper. As expected, the dark-haired one ogled her while the golden man scowled.

The major's smoldering façade sent shudders across her flesh, and she sped past the tavern and staircase. Once inside her office in the rear of the building, she locked the door with a loud click and leaned her back against the wood. Only then did she feel truly safe from the major's intense scrutiny.

****

The soldiers returned to the tavern later that evening. Lucien and Ethan, seated at the same table they'd held since dinner, scanned the crowds with open curiosity. One man, however, failed to appear this particular night. Lucien noted Ramon's absence with keen insight.

"If your theory is correct," he told Ethan, "our friend, Ramon, wouldn't miss tonight's evening of cold ale, pretty girls, and gossip."

Ethan grimaced. "Come now, Lucien. Are you still considering Ramon a spy sent by La Venganza?"

"Merely exploring the possibility," he replied with a casual shrug. "Think on it. If my suspicions are closer to the truth than yours, Ramon has no need to come to the tavern tonight. Whatever task La Venganza set him upon was probably accomplished last evening."

"And you think Ramon's disclosure of Marisa's relationship with the scoundrel was part of La Venganza's scheme?"

"I can't say just yet." Lucien scrubbed a hand over his chin. "If La Venganza ordered Ramon to reveal Marisa's duplicity to us, I can only assume he did so because he discovered our identity and purpose here."

Ethan shook his head. "But that makes no sense. Why would any man toss Marisa into the fray? To distract us?" He turned to glance at Marisa on the other side of the room, then flashed Lucien a lewd smile. "Although I admit, she's a hell of a distraction."

Marisa stood behind the bar with Santos, a far enough distance that Lucien should have no trouble ignoring her. Yet his senses remained on alert to her every motion, every sound. Despite the noise of the crowd, he would swear her breathing echoed his own.

"Everyone here treats her with respect and deference," Ethan added.

Lucien jerked his head at the bartender. "I'd wager Santos's constant presence has a lot to do with the way everyone treats her. The man could probably break bones with a handshake. Would you risk his wrath?"

While Ethan shivered in reply, an idea circled Lucien's brain. Santos was big, brawny, and not too bright. Could he be one of La Venganza's merry men? Quite possibly. And the way he hovered around Marisa only added more credence to the thought.

A man like La Venganza, who lived in the shadows, would want to be certain his beloved was well protected. Particularly if his beloved was as beautiful as Marisa.

"Good evening, gentlemen." As if conjured up by his thoughts, the innkeeper stood at their table. Her smile dazzled. "I hope you had a pleasant day."

Ethan immediately shot to his feet. "Please, Marisa, sit with us for a while."

"Thank you, but I cannot." She looked over their empty tabletop, and her smile faded. "Shall I fetch you something to drink?"

"No need." Lucien waved a hand and then pointedly scanned the room. "Where is Ramon this evening?"

Although he studied her carefully, she gave away nothing in her eyes or expression. "He lives too far away to visit every night. I trust you are finding your stay with us pleasant?"

"I fear our business has not gone as planned," Lucien replied with a frown. "Unless circumstances change significantly, we may need to remain for quite a while. I hope that our continued stay won't inconvenience you, Marisa."

The soldier named Pablo managed to find an empty chair and dragged it to their table. "What's this you say? The residents of Pensacola have not welcomed you properly? What blackguards have mistreated you, *señores*? Tell me their names, and I shall personally see them punished for their rudeness."

Lucien waved a hand. "That won't be necessary."

"Oh, but it is necessary! Tell me. Are any of the villains here tonight?"

Lucien allowed his gaze to travel around the many men clustered at their various interests. The gamblers rolled their dice in the corner. The inebriated still sang their ditties, and the lascivious continued to laugh at their ribald jests. Over them all, Santos filled fresh tankards, which Anita carried from table to table.

At last, he let his attention settle on Marisa. "I doubt the villains would dare to show themselves here tonight. Villains are, by and large, cowards at heart."

"I find it hard to imagine," Marisa interjected, eyes wide with doe innocence, "that any villainy exists in Pensacola."

Pablo patted her hand in a comforting manner. "Of course you do, *querida*. You are far too delicate a flower to know the treachery of dishonest men."

"Yet, I'm sure the *señorita* is well versed in the perfidy of women," Lucien remarked.

The barb struck. Her eyes flinched, although she gave no other reaction to the obvious insult. Sly vixen, but for Lucien, her lack of outrage told the true tale. An innocent lady would have gasped or cried foul at such aspersions to her character.

In this case, however, Pablo leaped to Marisa's defense by pounding his tankard on the tabletop. Droplets of ale splashed like rain on Ethan's surprised face.

"Defile the lady's character again," Pablo growled, "and you'll explain your sins to St. Peter this very evening."

The room grew deathly quiet, and dozens of suspicious glares focused on Lucien.

Ethan wiped his wet face with the back of his sleeve. "Lucien," he hissed. "Have you gone mad? Apologize at once."

Lucien made no move whatsoever.

A contingent of soldiers, hands poised on their sword hilts, converged behind Pablo to create a wall of sullen faces. The air thickened with silent animosity. Still, Lucien remained silent and waited.

"Gentlemen!" Marisa's shout broke the hypnotic spell of violence brewing in the tavern. Despite her tiny stature, she commanded attention from every man in the room. "I won't have brawls in my inn, and well you know it. Many of you are far too deep in your cups to realize what you're saying right now. Therefore, I'm closing up for the night. All of you, get out!"

To help punctuate her statement, Santos stepped from behind the bar, arms folded over his massive chest. He stopped before Marisa, and once again, Lucien was struck by the contrast of light and dark, mountainous and petite. Both, however, wore expressions which would brook no argument. With a few low grumbles, the men straightened and made their way to the door.

When only Marisa, Santos, Pablo, Ethan and Lucien remained, the lovely but angry innkeeper nodded her satisfaction. Around her, chairs were overturned, tankards littered tabletops, and a growing stench of stale ale and vomit lingered in the air.

"Santos," she said on a sigh, "see the rest of our guests out while Anita and I take care of the mess in here."

The giant nodded and clamped a heavy paw on Lucien's shoulder. "You leave now."

Pablo staggered to his feet with a wobbly grin. "We're leaving, Santos." His uneven gaze traveled between Ethan and Lucien. "Aren't we, gentlemen?"

With one last glance at Marisa who gathered tankards onto a round tray, Lucien led the men into the hall. They milled there for a moment until Pablo poked a bony elbow into Lucien's ribs.

"Well, *señor*, you now owe Marisa more than an apology."

"Oh?" Lucien's brow arched in the man's direction. "I don't believe I owe Marisa anything."

In the darkened hall, Pablo's grin gleamed white. "I beg to differ. After all, she just saved your life."

*"The grave is the general meeting-place."*
*— Thomas Fuller (Gnomologia)*

## CHAPTER 6

Several days later, when *El General's* toadies entered the inn, Marisa crouched on her hands and knees as she scrubbed the floors with a soapy horsehair brush. Rising onto her haunches, she blew a wisp of hair from her eyes. "Have a care, gentlemen. The tiles are slick when they're wet."

Hands up, Sergeant Greene retreated toward the door. "Forgive us, Marisa. We'll return when the floor is dry."

"Nonsense." She waved them through. "Go on."

A flush crept up the sergeant's face and neck, but he tiptoed past. "I'm so sorry."

The major showed no such qualms. He stalked across the wet tiles, leaving a trail of muddy boot prints behind him.

"*Bastardo!*" Marisa's eyes stabbed daggers at his broad back as he ascended the stairs. His shoulders stiffened.

He'd heard her. Good. She watched his ramrod posture disappear abovestairs. Someone would have to teach the major his manners.

The sergeant paused, however, halfway up the stairs, his hand on the banister. "May I tender my apologies? I fear Mr. St. Clair is a bit preoccupied at the moment."

Marisa said nothing, but folded her arms over her chest. When both men were gone, she returned her attention to the muddied tiles. While she scrubbed, she imagined a dozen dire punishments for the major. At last, she settled on her favorite.

When the floors finally gleamed to her satisfaction, she headed to her greenhouse. There, she cut twelve perfect scarlet blooms from one of the many rosebushes inside. Flowers in hand, she strode to the gravesite for a talk with her aunt and uncle.

**** 

By seven o'clock, Lucien and Ethan sat at their usual table. The same serving girl, Anita, brought them their meals. The same emptiness struck Lucien at Marisa's absence from the room, but he swallowed the bitter taste of regret with a grimace.

Not so, Ethan, who flashed hopeful eyes at Anita. "Perhaps Miss Álvarez will join us this evening?"

Someone should kick the puppy dog out of that boy. Unfortunately, Lucien had more pressing worries at the moment. Like La Venganza. And a certain green-eyed witch.

"Marisa never eats here." The girl pulled the chairs from the table so the men could seat themselves.

"Oh?" Ethan tilted his head. "Where does she eat?"

"In the kitchen with Santos and me." Lowering her voice to a whisper, she leaned close. "Poor Marisa! Since don Miguel passed away last Christmas, she's been so alone. She pretends to be happy with her life. But she's experienced so much tragedy. I often wonder she can still smile at all..."

"Anita!" Santos cut in. "See to the gentlemen's dinner."

"Coming, Santos." With a quick head bob, she hurried to the kitchen.

At that moment, the air charged with static electricity. Acute awareness tingled Lucien's flesh, and he turned to see the topic of their discussion in the hall. He glared at her with undisguised contempt, but his body belied his disgust. Breath refused to leave his lungs. Desire stirred.

Her wide green eyes fluttered beneath sooty lashes and reflected surprise. When her cheeks filled with bright pink color, he fixed on that blush to trap her in his gaze. His brain called her to come inside, to sit beside them, almost daring her to enter the lion's den.

Instead, she turned and walked past the open doors. Somewhere farther down the hall, a door squeaked open, and then slammed shut.

"St. Clair?" Ethan's voice, paired with a firm hand on his shoulder, shook Lucien from his dark thoughts.

"'I feel sorry for her.'" He mimicked the serving girl's words. "'She's been so alone.' Bah! The woman's lover is a criminal. She's an immoral whore."

"Those are the best kind, Lucien. Those are the very best kind."

A full week had elapsed. He and Ethan had casually questioned soldiers, shopkeepers, and serving girls up and down the streets of Pensacola. But, they'd come no closer to learning the identity of La Venganza. Any mention of Marisa's name resulted in tightened lips and orders to go away.

Time to confront the lady—and he used the term loosely—herself.

Tonight, he planned to stay in the tavern as long as necessary. He'd find out about her connection with La Venganza if he had to shake the truth from her.

And so, he waited. And waited. And waited.

His eyes grew heavy with exhaustion, and he

blinked several times to clear his blurring vision.

Suddenly, she was there.

He didn't see her, but her soft voice wafted above the din and sang in his ears.

Slowly, he rose, ready to seek her out among the throng.

"Mr. St. Clair!" Ramon Santiago elbowed his way through the crowd.

Dammit.

"Mr. Santiago. Good to see you again." Lucien pushed his chair closer to the feeble old man. "Please, sit. I was just leaving."

"Good evening, Mr. Greene." Ramon sank into the offered seat, his face breaking into a wide grin. "You're too late, you know, Mr. St. Clair. She's already gone."

With a muffled curse, he pushed drunken soldiers out of his way and strode from the tavern. But the hum he'd sensed had evaporated. Once again, Marisa had managed to elude him.

Returning to the tavern, he stalked to where Ramon sat beside Ethan, with his sallow cheek atop a shaky fist. "How did you know...?"

The old man snorted. "You stare at her with such intensity, this place could burn down around you and you'd never notice."

Annoyance itched his skin, and he bent so his face aligned with Ramon's. "I stare at her because you told me she was La Venganza's woman. And I wonder why she'd sell herself to a criminal."

Pablo popped his bushy head into their conversation so quickly, Lucien jumped back. "Who said La Venganza's a criminal?"

Ramon pointed an index finger in Lucien's direction.

"Have a care, gentlemen." Pablo's murderous gaze took in Lucien and Ethan. "La Venganza is the only man brave enough to stand up to the villains bent on destroying Pensacola. He alone takes on the likes of General Jackson and those damned Seminoles."

Eyes wide, Ethan leaned forward. "So La Venganza hasn't only targeted General Jackson?"

Ramon and Pablo exchanged an amused glance, and then burst out laughing.

"Of course not," Ramon said. "*El General* is only one of La Venganza's enemies."

"Who are the others?" Ethan pressed. "Are they all men of power? Men of wealth?"

Lucien sighed. If the boy didn't pull back quickly, every man in this place would know their real objective.

Ramon shook his head. "Power and wealth hold no sway with him. Only actions matter. La Venganza avenges the innocent. He's quite good at exploiting an enemy's weakness."

"Tread softly, *amigos*," Pablo added in his usual grumble, "lest you draw his displeasure."

Once again, Ramon rested his cheek in his hand, this time on a sigh filled with wonder. "La Venganza is a hero. He makes me proud to be a Spaniard."

Pablo lifted his tankard above his shaggy head. "To La Venganza!"

"La Venganza!" chorused the crowd of men.

On the wave of goodwill he'd created with his toast, Pablo floated away.

Ramon's gaze grew soft and dreamy as he stared at the doorway. "Ah, here she is now."

When Lucien's focus veered toward the object of Ramon's interest, he discovered Marisa entering the tavern. Her lovely hair lay in a thick silver braid wrapped in ivory ribbon. She wore a clean but old gown of brown muslin.

Bitterness danced on Lucien's tongue. How could someone so sullied appear to be so innocent?

"Come, *querida*." Ramon rose from his chair and

gestured to the empty seat with a sweeping hand. "Join us."

Ethan nearly fell over himself to stand. "Please, Marisa, do."

As she glided forward, her eyes locked on Lucien's, caught the light of a nearby wall sconce, and glowed like peridots.

Although his body tightened with desire, he refused to show her any favor outwardly. Instead, he offered her a terse nod. "Madam."

She allowed Ramon to lead her to his empty chair before responding in kind to Lucien. "Mr. St. Clair. Mr. Greene. How was your dinner this evening? I hope the custard was to your liking."

"I found the custard especially delightful," Ethan enthused. "And Mr. St. Clair seemed to enjoy it, as well."

Lucien stifled the urge to punch the stars out of the sergeant's eyes. Instead, he folded his hands on the table.

Marisa simply offered Ethan a wide smile. "I'm so glad. My *tía* taught me the recipe when I was a child. It was always one of my favorite treats."

"Then thank your *tía* for us." Lucien didn't have to study her too closely to notice the change in her demeanor.

Her face clouded with pain, and her tone grew harsh. "I will." She rose and bobbed her head slightly. "*Buenas noches, señores.*"

She floated away on a tide of sadness. No surprise, Ramon followed her.

With her departure, conversation lulled. All too soon, Lucien noticed Ethan's wide yawns and realized he, himself, struggled to remain awake. The heat, and the week's fruitless activities, had no doubt exhausted them both.

"We may as well seek our beds." He staggered to his feet and swayed slightly.

By Jove, he was more tired than he'd realized. He'd be lucky to reach his room before giving in to his need for sleep. "I doubt we'll learn anything more tonight."

*"Careless she is with artful care,*
*Affecting to seem unaffected."*
— *William Congreve (Amoret)*

## CHAPTER 7

Lucien slowly awoke to strange noises and a raging headache. Unpleasant odors, ripe and foul, stung his nostrils. He tried to open his eyes, but his lids refused to lift, as if some sticky substance sealed them shut.

A horse's soft whinny shot him upright. His palms flattened against scratchy straw. What the—?

When he finally pried his eyes open, he didn't see his room at *El Castillo de Plata*. Instead, four primitive wooden walls met his gaze. One wall held a large crude window with a flip up wooden sash. The other three held bridles, bits, and stirrups, hanging on hooks. Rather than the wrought-iron bed he'd sunk into last night, he reclined upon mounds of hay.

He was in a horse's stall! In a stable!

A shadow loomed overhead, and he glanced up to find Boreas, who snorted and shook his jet black mane at this invasion of his private space. The gelding's hooves, thank God, never moved.

By the devil, what was he doing here? He scrambled to the corner of the stall and suddenly realized his troubles had just begun.

Not only had he awakened in Boreas's stall, he

was nude. And he reeked of horse dung.

On unsteady legs, he rose to peer out the window that overlooked the pasture. The sun already sat high above the trees.

A woman walked past the window, the red-haired serving girl, and Lucien ducked against the wall to be certain she didn't see him. Inaudible conversation reached his ears. On a deep breath, he slipped closer to the window. How many people were in the pasture today?

Dozens milled about the grounds outside his little box. A dark-skinned woman with a blue and gold turban wrapped around her head held a large basket of fruit, and Anita examined each piece with careful consideration. Several stable boys tended to two horses in the paddock. On the outskirts of the pasture, a troop of Spanish soldiers from the nearby fort loitered, some watching the horses, a few ogling the women. Of course, should Lucien choose to leave his hiding place, they'd have a new outrage to ogle.

He slammed a fist against the wall. "Damn her!"

Marisa was responsible for this. He didn't know how or why, but whether directly or not, she had orchestrated this horrendous situation.

"*Señor* St. Clair?" a hesitant voice called from the walkway outside the stall. "Are you awake?"

"Yes," he ground out. "Who's out there?"

"It's me, sir. Roberto." A familiar stable boy stopped by the low wall, a folded slip of paper in his filthy fist. His eyes focused first on Lucien's naked torso, but then quickly looked away. "I was told to give you this when you woke up."

Gaze still fixed on some distant corner, he thrust the item forward.

But Lucien's attention focused on the paper's red seal, which blazed like a flame. "Who told you to give this to me?"

The boy shook his head. "I never saw the man's

face."

Of course he didn't. La Venganza would never be so careless. And even if Roberto had seen the villain, Lucien suspected he'd never admit it.

Anger consumed him as he yanked the paper from the boy's grip. "Get out of here."

Roberto quickly backed away, eyes closed. "*Sí, señor.*"

Alone again, Lucien broke the seal and read the familiar message. *La venganza es mía.*

Never a personal target of the villain's vendetta before now, he simmered with righteous indignation. How dare this scoundrel humiliate him in such a way? And why? Was this what Pablo meant with his warning about drawing La Venganza's displeasure? Because he'd dared to insult Marisa?

Well, he'd have to confront the devil's mistress to get at the truth of this puzzle. Now, more than ever, he wanted answers.

But first, he needed to get out of this stall. And he'd require a bath. Along with some clean garments. Which meant he'd need the blasted stable boy again.

"Roberto!" he shouted. "Are you still there, lad?"

"*Sí?*"

"Fetch me a blanket."

"*Sí, señor.*" The stable boy reappeared a moment later with an old, scratchy horse blanket.

Lucien winced at the condition of the shabby cover. Still, given the choice of striding from this stable completely naked or with some kind of shield between himself and a dozen curious onlookers, he'd take the shield, regardless of its sorry condition.

When he strode into the inn a few minutes later, he cursed Marisa anew. His feet were still bare, and now they bled, thanks to the rock-strewn grounds he'd trod to slip past his possible witnesses without being seen.

Marisa was not in the hall. Rage heated his blood one degree for every minute that elapsed before he might confront her. He strode to the kitchen and pushed open the door. Only Santos stood behind the long table, a dozen conch shells spread out before him.

"Where is she?" he demanded.

Santos looked up. "Who?"

"Marisa."

"Marisa's at the markets. She ordered a bath prepared in your room."

Lucien couldn't keep the sarcasm in check a moment longer. "How considerate of her. How do you suppose she knew I'd need a bath?" A louder question resounded in Lucien's head. Why had she arranged a bath for him? Guilty conscience? Or to subtly drop the hint she knew where he'd spent the night?

Santos shrugged and slammed a hammy fist onto one of the shells, which shattered beneath the onslaught. "Don't know. Ask Marisa. She's at the markets."

Lucien surrendered, the lure of a hot bath and clean clothes stronger than his desire to continue battling with a halfwit.

****

When he returned downstairs a while later, Lucien discovered Marisa sweeping the porch. Since she hummed while she worked, she never turned at his quiet approach. All the better to startle her.

"Ahem!" He expected a flinch or gasp or some other surprised reaction to his sudden throat-clearing from behind her.

But she turned slowly to face him and offered a smile meant to dazzle seraphim. "Good day, Mr. St. Clair. I trust you slept well?"

"I slept deeply," he replied. "And for far longer than is my normal habit."

Her finger wagged near his nose. "I should have warned you not to drink with Pablo and Ramon. Their consumption of ale could bring a *horse* to its knees."

Any doubts Lucien harbored about her participation in last night's events disappeared when he heard the emphasis she placed on that one word.

Her smile turned sympathetic as she set the broom against the wall and added, "No doubt your head aches this morning. Well, Anita has the perfect remedy for a night of overindulgence. She makes the most wonderful *plátanos*. I'll fetch her right away."

She strode past, but he gripped her arm and pulled her against him. "Oh, no, Marisa. I have no need of anything save information. Information *you* will provide."

In an attempt to intimidate her, he lowered his head closer, mere breaths from hers, and glowered. The gasp she emitted drew his gaze to her lush lips.

"How dare you!" She wriggled like a fish, but her struggles only pressed her deeper into his chest.

There would be no easy escape for the *señorita* this time. Lucien wrapped both arms around her waist until they stood in what others might consider a lovers' embrace. Yet, despite the heat burgeoning in his core, his need for answers far surpassed any other desires.

"Release me at once," she hissed. Thick lashes fluttered, but couldn't shadow the hatred blazing in her eyes.

Once again, his mind sought answers for the eternally baffling question. How could anyone so incredibly lovely be so duplicitous?

"Santos!" Her chest heaved with her shouting and her efforts to pull away. With each inhalation, her bodice rubbed his shirtfront until the telltale darts of her nipples pierced the thin fabric separating their flesh.

His groin stirred more forcefully, ready to override logic in a quest for satisfaction. For the sake of honor and sanity, he loosened his grip enough for her to break free without stumbling.

The moment an inch of space appeared between them, she raced for the door and hurried inside. He followed, but halted when she ran headlong into her giant bodyguard.

"Marisa?" Santos mumbled. "*Qué pasa?*"

The concern in Santos's tone apparently had magical qualities for her. The panic disappeared from her expression, and she reverted to the calm, efficient innkeeper. "Has Anita begun peeling the vegetables yet?"

The behemoth's brows drew together, and his brow furrowed with confusion. "*Sí.* She is in the kitchen. Shall I fetch her?"

"No," she said hastily. On a shaky breath, she added, "I'll need your help with something after Mr. St. Clair and I finish our conversation. Would you stay here, please?"

Lucien hid a smile. Did she think he'd draw back because of Santos? "Perhaps Santos can help me as well," he said smoothly.

The giant looked at him, curiosity puckering his large forehead. "*Sí?*"

"I'm wondering how I woke up in the stable next to my horse today."

"You did?" A giggle escaped, and Marisa belatedly raised her fingers to her lips as if to stop her mirth. On Lucien's growl, she sobered. "Forgive me, *señor.* I'm sure you found no humor in your circumstances."

"Particularly since I did not drink ale last night. In fact, I distinctly remember reaching my room upstairs and getting into bed." No need to comment on his state of undress. Why humiliate himself any further with these two?

True to form, Santos said nothing and his expression remained impassive.

But Marisa's eyes widened in doe-like innocence. "How odd. And yet, you woke in the stable? Do you walk in your sleep, perchance?"

"No." Before she might continue to feign ignorance, he pulled out the paper with the familiar red seal and waved it in her face. "Apparently, your lover is angry with me."

Her cheeks flushed scarlet. "I have no lover, Mr. St. Clair."

"But you know why La Venganza decided to rearrange my sleeping quarters last evening, don't you?"

She didn't reply.

The room grew oppressive as a wall of stubborn silence built up between the occupants. Marisa's gaze remained locked on Lucien, and he refused to even blink. He wanted her to break, to collapse beneath the weight of her secrets.

Unfortunately, Santos broke first. "Marisa, do you need my help or not?" His innocuous question eased the tension too soon.

She shook her head. "No, Santos. Go back to the kitchen and help Anita. I have work to do in my office." Turning on her heel, she tossed over her shoulder, "By the by, Mr. St. Clair, my *tía* always said the biggest difference between men and animals is that men can be taught to wipe their feet. Perhaps La Venganza thought you might feel more comfortable sleeping with your own kind last evening."

Realization slapped his face like a dueler's challenge. "Would this be the same *tía* who taught you the custard recipe?"

"Of course," she replied. "Whenever I was ill, *Tía* would make her special custard to help me sleep."

By God. Somehow this angelic-looking woman had drugged him—and Ethan, judging by his absence thus far today. Once he'd succumbed to the effects of her special custard, she'd had La Venganza haul him into the stables. As punishment for muddying her floors yesterday. Regardless of the humiliation still burning inside him, he chuckled. No doubt his mother would have done something similar had he disrespected his childhood home in such a way.

Since he could appreciate the clever message she'd communicated, he allowed her to walk away, the victor. This time.

Besides, he had his own work to do. He needed proof regarding his suspicions of the identity of La Venganza. Marisa's lover.

Like an invisible fist, the image of Marisa wrapped in a faceless man's arms punched him in the gut. Through sheer force of will, he remained perfectly staid and focused his thoughts on visions of flaming stables, exhausted compatriots walking from Pensacola to Tennessee, and an incensed General Jackson demanding Lucien's head for his failure. With his emotions once again under control, he headed to Ethan's room to rouse him from his stupor.

*"When there is an income tax, the just man will pay
more and the unjust less on the same amount of
income."*
— *Plato (The Republic)*

## CHAPTER 8

Inside her uncle's old office, Marisa reviewed
receipts and bills, copying figures into the leather-
bound ledger. She loved this room, still sensed Tío's
presence in the dark, heavy furnishings. A tin of
tobacco sat in a place of honor within easy reach.
Sometimes, like now, when the doldrums choked her
spirit, she'd remove the lid and inhale the sweet-
smoky scent.

Memories flooded back, days of laughter and
innocence. Days before Tío took ill with
consumption, before they lost Tía to the fever. Before
Fort Mims...

Eyes closed, she leaned back and listened
carefully.

*Papa quotes Shakespeare in their sitting room at
home.'"Discomfort guides my tongue and bids me
speak of nothing but despair.' The Tragedy of King
Richard II."*

*'Lando, sitting cross-legged on her right, chimes
in, "'He who has never hoped can never despair.' The
Winter's Tale."*

*Mama's laughter echoes from the chair above her
head. "Come now, Montesita. Surely you won't allow
the men to best you. What say you?"*

*A little girl's voice lisps, "'Do not repent these things for they are heavier than all thy woes can stir. Therefore betake thee to nothing but despair.' Also The Winter's Tale."*

*"Marisa wins again." Papa's chortles fill her head.*

*"I always do," she crows.*

*"Ah, but someday," Papa replies, "a man will outwit you with Shakespeare. And you will know he is meant to hold your heart for a lifetime. Never marry a man you can best in any battle of wits, Montesita. Love needs respect to grow."*

A violent pounding erupted outside and shattered the daydream into colorful pieces. Her eyelids shot up as the door burst open.

Santos strode in with a wide-eyed, dirty-cheeked boy in his wake. "Doña Isabella," he said. "Jackson's soldiers are demanding taxes. They have threatened to throw her and the children out of their home."

"Damn *El General*, his henchmen, and his revenues!" Marisa slammed the ledger closed and shot to her feet. When the boy flinched in reaction, she softened her tone. "Go with Santos, Benito. Tell Roberto to saddle Tormenta. I'll be along shortly."

Santos held out a hand. "Come, Benito."

The door closed behind them with a snick. Alone again, she pulled a set of keys from her gown pocket, unlocked the lowest drawer of Tío's desk, and removed a cedar chest.

"These villains are no better than Colonel Masot's revenue collectors," she muttered. "Another group of spoilt boys who pretend to be men by bullying a woman. What do they care if we have nothing left to feed our children? So long as they receive their money."

Hastily, she stuffed her pocket with coins, replaced the chest, and relocked the drawer. Pockets weighed down, she stalked out of the office, down the hall, and outside. She didn't stop until she reached the stables where Santos and Roberto stood with her favorite mare.

Santos offered her a leg up, and she gained the saddle.

"Where's Benito?" She scanned the path. The child tossed pebbles near the pasture. "Benito!"

He turned, and she patted her lap. "Let's go rescue your mama."

While Santos grabbed the boy, Marisa yanked her skirts to one side. After Benito was settled before her in the saddle, she took the reins from Santos's fat fist. "I'll be back soon."

With a snap of the reins, horse and riders galloped off to doña Isabella's house.

Every thunder of hooves jarred her temper higher. Don Marco Quincero had fought alongside the Americans in the Battle of Mobile Bay and lost his life. He'd left behind a wife with six children dependent on her dressmaking skills to prevent the family's starvation. And how did the American army repay don Marco for his bravery? They sent a contingent of soldiers to harass his widow.

*Thank you, General Jackson, War Hero.*

Her grasp on the boy's waist tightened. "I promise, Benito," she whispered in his ear. "Someone will let these men know they cannot intimidate all of us. Someone will avenge the innocent..."

****

On their way back from a useless round of questions-with-no-answers at the army garrison, Lucien and Ethan spotted Marisa flying out of the stables on the dappled gray mare.

"Now, where is she going with such haste?" Ethan whispered.

"I don't know, but I intend to find out," Lucien replied in the same hushed tone. "Return to the inn.

64

I'll follow the harlot. Perhaps she'll lead me to La Venganza's hideout."

"Let's hope so," Ethan said. "Remember Colonel King's threat. I don't wish for my military record to be blemished by this conundrum that is La Venganza."

"Nor I." Lucien turned his horse around while Ethan continued on toward the stable. He kept off the path and stayed hidden within the forest. The travel was treacherous, but he maintained this route to be certain she wouldn't notice him.

Not that she showed any awareness of her surroundings. A small boy sat with her in the saddle, yet she rode headlong and swift, as if Satan nipped her heels. Branches raked her face, leaves scattered in her hair, but she drove her mare onward toward some destination only she knew.

Boreas showed more intelligence than Marisa. The beast picked his way around the edge of the forest in careful steps while Marisa urged her mare to dangerous speeds, heedless of ruts or rabbit holes. All too soon, the horse and riders pulled far ahead, but the steady echo of hooves kept Lucien on their trail.

At last, he found her stopped before a small, well-kept cottage. In the front yard where chickens squawked, eight armed men shouted obscenities at a bedraggled woman. In addition to the noise from the hens, five children clung to the woman's skirts, and their overwrought screeches rent the air.

Anger coursed through Lucien's veins. What kind of monster would treat a woman with children so cruelly? Fists at the ready, he inched forward. Before he reached the clearing, however, Marisa leapt out of the saddle. Once on the ground, she reached for the child and set him down beside her. Thankfully, the well-trained mare remained still, despite the noise and the ire of her mistress.

"Mama!" On a heartbreaking cry, the boy raced to the woman at the center of the circle of men.

"Benito! *Gracias a Dios!*" The woman pulled him into the cluster of terrified children. After a quick hug, she sent all six children into the safety of the house behind her.

When all the little ones hovered in the doorway, the leader of the wolf pack advanced on the older woman.

From his vantage point at the edge of the melee, Lucien recognized several men from Captain Gadsden's unit, including the leader of this sorry band. Lieutenant Henry Spenser, a smarmy rat with no respect for anyone, took another step forward.

"Enough!" Marisa launched herself between the woman and Spenser, arms spread as a shield. "Leave her be, you filthy cowards!"

"Go back to your inn, *señorita*," Spenser sneered. "Your ale isn't needed here."

"I'm here to pay her fines, *puerco,*" Marisa retorted.

"With what?" His gaze raked her from head to toe. "Unless there's gold beneath those skirts, peddle your wares elsewhere."

Lucien didn't know what he expected, but her pulling a handful of coins from her pocket certainly had never entered his mind. "I have gold, but you won't find it beneath my skirts." She hurled the money at Spenser's head. Several coins struck him above the eyebrow and sliced an open wound that drew blood.

"Payment in full," she shouted. "Now, get out of here and don't return!"

Spenser brushed a hand across his forehead. His eyes narrowed at the blood upon his finger. "You'll pay for this," he said in a low growl. Hands curled into fists, he took a step toward her.

Time for Lucien to make his presence known.

"That will do, Lieutenant Spenser," he announced and stepped into the fray.

Marisa whirled, eyes ablaze like a hungry tigress about to pounce.

"But, Major," Spenser sputtered, "the bitch—"

"The *lady* defended her friend," Lucien amended. "Now, take your gold, and your soldiers, and return to Captain Gadsden at once."

Lieutenant Spenser's posture crumbled, but the expression in his eyes hurled daggers at Marisa. "Yes, sir."

The hair on Lucien's nape danced, a signal to stay alert for possible retribution. His gaze swerved from one unfriendly face to another. The soldiers glared with undisguised hostility.

"That's an order, Lieutenant."

On a quick whistle from Spenser, the rest of the unit gathered the scattered coins. Within minutes, they saddled up, and rode away.

Lucien waited to be certain no sudden retaliatory action would occur. Only when he deemed them safe did he return his focus to the other players in this drama. Fury sparked around Marisa like fireworks. The older woman raced into her home to comfort the crying children.

He attempted to approach Marisa first, to warn her of the danger of confronting men like Spenser without a man to keep her from harm.

But she turned away and strode to where her mare still waited. "Cowards," she muttered and swung into the saddle unassisted.

One kick of her heels, and the mare cantered toward home.

Lucien watched Marisa depart with a secret smile. She hadn't even bothered to acknowledge his presence, much less thank him for his interference.

From inside the cottage, the older woman peered at him, head tilted as if she tried to discern his identity while he did the same. Her dark hair, streaked silver, hung disheveled to her shoulders. Tears stained her cheeks. Around her, the children still sniffled and whined.

Clicking his heels, he bowed to the group. "Forgive me, lady. I am Lucien St. Clair, a guest at the *señorita's* inn. I mean you and your children no harm."

She took a step closer to the door. "I am Isabella Quincero."

Silence ensued, broken only by the occasional bird call or a squirrel that scurried along a tree branch. Now what should he do? Should he apologize for Spenser and his cohorts? Logic told him to follow Marisa. After all, she still might lead him to La Venganza's hideaway if he caught up with her now. But the lady and her brood seemed to require reassurance, and he wouldn't leave her if she might still be in distress.

"Well," he said at last. "I hope you are unharmed?"

The lady nodded, and her features softened. "May I offer you tea, *señor*?"

He grinned. Finally, a chink in Pensacola's armor. With a nod, he strode to the edge of the clearing to retrieve Boreas. "I'd like that, *señora. Gracias.*"

**\*\*\*\***

In his room at *El Castillo*, Lucien described the scene for Ethan. "Marisa is a spitfire. I can't imagine what Spenser would have done to her if I hadn't intervened."

"I can't imagine what *she* would have done to Spenser if you hadn't intervened," Ethan rejoined with a chuckle.

He laughed. "Either way, I couldn't allow the two of them to come to blows. After I ordered Spenser and his men to return to Captain Gadsden,

Marisa stormed off without ever acknowledging my presence. But doña Isabella appreciated my interference."

"Oh?" Ethan raised a lascivious eyebrow.

"Get your mind out of the gutter, Ethan," Lucien retorted. "Doña Isabella is a gentle lady. What I mean is she told me a few interesting things about our lovely innkeeper."

Ethan folded his arms behind his head and stretched his legs out before him. "Such as?"

Impatience propelled Lucien into his normal routine. He paced as he considered all he'd learned in the last few hours. "Such as, doña Isabella is not the only person in Pensacola treated to Marisa's generosity. Three months ago, a farmer's home was burned to the ground by Seminoles. Marisa gave the family, the Salinas, shelter at the inn until they rebuilt. She took no payment. She claimed they'd suffered a grave injustice and someone would gain retribution on their behalf. Within a week, the Seminoles involved were found imprisoned in the calaboose. They'd locked themselves inside to escape the wrath of the spirits."

Ethan's brow wrinkled. "The spirits? What spirits?"

"According to the tribe's chief, spirits visited their camp and wreaked havoc. Supposedly, they were angry at the Seminoles for their role in the Salinas' fire." With each to and fro step, he counted on his fingers. "They found a dead crow in the middle of the village at sunset. Horses disappeared from camp only to reappear in the same location hours later. Crops were cut down and harvested in the middle of the night. Pottery was smashed and sunk into the creek. One evening, an angry god visited the chief. The god said the only way the chief could save his people was to lock them in the calaboose."

"Sounds like La Venganza's usual antics." Ethan frowned.

"And this is not the first time the Quincero family has narrowly avoided eviction with help from Marisa, either. Two years ago, the same event played out with Colonel Masot's revenue collectors. Afterward, Isabella approached Marisa to arrange repayment. She offered Marisa a new wardrobe for her assistance, but Marisa declined."

Ethan snorted. "I don't know many ladies who would turn down new garments."

"Marisa did. Claimed she had a responsibility to protect the innocent from injustice."

His words gained the expected reaction. Ethan sat bolt upright. "What did Pablo and Ramon say about La Venganza?"

"He uses an enemy's weakness against him."

Ethan scratched his head as if awakening a memory. "No. Something more."

"La Venganza avenges the innocent," Lucien reminded him.

"Which means Marisa is not only La Venganza's mistress. The two see themselves as the saviors of the oppressed."

Lucien nodded. Ethan had easily connected the thoughts in the same way he had.

"They work together," Lucien concluded.

****

With a fresh bouquet from the greenhouse, Marisa visited the gravesite. As she knelt before the headstones, a series of high-pitched screeches rang out. A flock of flamingoes flew above, headed for the shoreline. Their bright wings spread across the clear blue sky like feathery pink clouds.

She sighed. "It's already mid-July. Soon I will leave again. But don't worry. Santos and Anita will care for you while I'm away."

Perspiration beaded her forehead, and she

dabbed a lemon-scented handkerchief to blot the moisture. "Forgive me for saying so, but I hate the heat and dampness of this city." A gray insect buzzed near her eyes, and she waved a hand in front of her face. "And the mosquitoes! *Dios*! They're the most bloodthirsty creatures."

As a fond memory floated into her consciousness, she closed her eyes and smiled. "Did Papa ever write to you about the day I fell in the swamp? Timmy Pendleton told 'Lando I was ugly and I should be fed to the alligators. I decided to put an alligator in his bed while he slept."

The misty memories became real in her imagination. "I only wanted a baby, nothing that would hurt Timmy. I spotted a little beastie swimming in the bog and stepped on a log to reach for it, but the log turned out to be the beastie's mama. She rolled, and I lost my footing. If 'Lando hadn't fished me out, I might have granted Timmy's wish and fed the alligators. When he carried me home, Papa wanted to thrash me, but he took one look at me and said I'd punished myself. I didn't realize what he meant until the next morning."

She opened her eyes and blinked to return the memories to their rightful place—the past.

"The bog had more than alligators. I think there must have been thousands of mosquitoes, as well. Poor Mama! For days she fretted I would contract yellow fever. But Papa said God had a special angel who watched over the foolish. He was right. I itched from head to toe, but I never became ill."

A movement near the forest's edge caught her eye. She froze. Someone had followed her here. The sun glinted off golden hair. St. Clair. Of course. She sighed. Even in this somber place, the major and his cohort refused to grant her peace.

She touched her index finger to a single rose petal. The bloom, soft as velvet, only hardened her heart and resolve. "Luckily," she announced as she got to her feet, "I've learned to take greater care around dangerous creatures since then."

With angry strides, she approached the major's hiding place. "You might as well come out from behind the trees. I know you're there, Mr. St. Clair."

To his credit, he didn't bother to continue his subterfuge and immediately stepped into the clearing at the edge of the graveyard.

Despite the resentment which bubbled in her veins, she offered him a slick smile. "Are you lost, *señor*? Have a care. These woods can be confusing for visitors. Only last month, a little boy wandered away from his parents, and we had to gather a group of soldiers to search for him. It was already after dark when Pablo found him far too close to the swamp. I'd hate to have an alligator snatch you."

The only reaction he showed to her barb was in that irksome arched brow. "As a matter of fact," he replied in the same deceptive banter, "I was looking for you."

"To apologize for muddying my floor?" She shook her head and turned toward the inn. "I assure you, it isn't necessary."

"I had no intention of apologizing."

"Oh? Then I don't understand what you could possibly want from me." A lump the same size as the lie rose in her throat, and she swallowed. She fisted her hands and studied him until his return scrutiny sped up her heartbeat and hurled heat into her cheeks. She'd managed to keep the tremor from her voice, but not from her legs. Only one way to prevent him from noticing his proximity unnerved her. With a toss of her hair, she sped toward the inn.

He gripped her arm and pulled her closer, so close his breath brushed her neck in a warm caress. "I want to meet your lover, Marisa."

His rough words scraped her nerves, and she

yanked her arm from his grasp. "I have no lover, Mr. St. Clair."

Spotting Santos as he exited the root cellar, she picked up her skirts and ran toward him. Relief lent her wings, and she fairly flew to his protection so he might accompany her inside. Even then, she never slowed her pace until she'd reached her office and safely locked the door behind her.

*"Power, like a desolating pestilence, pollutes whatever it touches."*
*— Percy Bysshe Shelley (Queen Mab)*

## CHAPTER 9

Immediately after breakfast the next morning, a soldier arrived with a summons for Lucien and Ethan. General Jackson's aide-de-camp, Captain James Gadsden, required their presence at once.

Captain Gadsden lived in a private residence large enough to accommodate himself and his unit of soldiers. When Lucien entered with Ethan on his heels, a dour-faced servant led them into a large ballroom, which had been converted into a barracks. Gadsden and his men waited there, mouths twisted into grim scowls of resentment.

The soldiers wore nothing but their underdrawers. And Gadsden, attired in a white nightshirt at least three sizes too big, paced like a madman while the tails of the shirt slapped against his ankles. As he paced, he waved a paper in the air. Colorful curses streamed from his thin lips.

Lucien sighed. Damn. La Venganza had excelled at his games last evening. The culprit had not only targeted Captain Gadsden, but his unit of soldiers as well.

"He cut all of our pants legs at the knees," Gadsden announced. "My entire brigade has a wardrobe of short pants and knickers fit for a troop of young boys."

He threw his hands in the air, and La Venganza's note floated to the floor. Ethan bent to retrieve the paper and tucked it into his pocket while Gadsen continued his tirade.

"Oh, but that's not all. Every one of our uniform shirts is painted with a yellow line down the middle of the back. Even my nightshirts are branded with the stripe of a coward!" With outstretched arms, he indicated the billowy nightshirt. "I was forced to borrow this from one of the servants. I want this man caught, gentlemen. And I want him caught today!"

"We're trying, Captain," Lucien replied, fighting to hide a smile.

Captain Gadsden looked like a boy playing dress-up in his father's clothing. And his soldiers resembled nothing more intimidating than irate sheep in their gray, woolen drawers.

Lucien would never admit the idea aloud, but he admired La Venganza's style. Although considered one of General Jackson's most trusted men, as well as a brilliant engineer, Colonel Gadsden had earned a reputation as a terrible leader and a tyrant. And the men in his company behaved as the very cowards Marisa had designated them yesterday.

La Venganza must have sensed these faults and painted the men with a stripe of cowardice for their actions toward doña Isabella. Lucien saw the fine hand of a woman in this insult. Not just any woman's hand, the hand of Marisa Álvarez.

"The culprit won't get away, Captain," Lucien promised.

"You'd best hope he doesn't, Major," Gadsden growled in reply. "General Jackson has given me complete autonomy here, you know. Another such incident, and I won't rest until I see that you and Sergeant Greene are discharged from service and publicly humiliated."

****

Teeth gritted against the outraged shouts that sat on his tongue, Lucien rode to *El Castillo*. With every bounce of the saddle, his temper simmered another degree closer to boil.

For the last few weeks, he'd allowed Marisa's beauty to distract him from his duty. No more. She would tell him her lover's identity, or he'd toss her in the calaboose until she cooperated.

When he pulled up outside the inn, he left Boreas tied to the hitching post out front. Once he'd dismounted, he scaled the steps and kicked open the inn's door. "Marisa!"

Behind him, like a pesky mosquito, Ethan buzzed. "Lucien, slow down."

He waved off the sergeant and bellowed her name loud enough to shake the roof. "Marisaaaaa!"

A white-faced Anita raced down the staircase, one finger pressed to her lips. "She's in the kitchen, *señores*. Is something wrong?"

"Damn right," Lucien muttered. With ground-eating strides, he headed for the kitchen, shoved open the door and found Marisa inside.

Her head bent, she stood over a long wooden table and rolled out a lump of dough.

"Give me his name, Marisa."

"Oh!" Obviously startled by his intrusion, her head shot up, and she slammed the rolling pin onto the table.

Flour flew into his face and onto his crisp, clean shirt. Did she know how much the miniscule spots annoyed him? Her smile and luminous eyes suggested she'd known exactly how her sudden action would result. He prided himself on his impeccable state of dress at all times. But she'd managed to gain the upper hand at an opportune moment. Again. Well, not for long...

He brushed the flour from his clothing with a flick of his fingers, then lowered his tone and his head. "Who is La Venganza?"

"Why, *Major*." She fixed him with an arched brow. "Are we no longer continuing the pretense you're here on business?"

From behind him, Ethan pointed an accusatory finger. "You knew! You knew General Jackson sent us to find La Venganza."

Her laughter washed over him like a hot bath. "Of course I knew. Do I look like an idiot?"

Now he leaned forward, his face a breath away from hers. "I want the villain's name."

Taking a step back, Marisa folded her arms over her chest. "What villain?"

"You know exactly what villain." His tone grew deadly, each soft syllable laced with a hard edge. "Who is La Venganza, *señorita*?"

"Ask your questions elsewhere. You'll get nothing from me." She waved a hand as if to shoo him away.

In one smooth arc, Lucien grabbed her hand in his right fist. His left hand cupped her chin, forcing her to look into his eyes. The velvet of her skin, like a rose petal, seeped into his fingers. He'd never touched her bare flesh before now. Never felt her warmth or known such incredible softness in anyone.

But the anger that blazed in her eyes reminded him of stable fires, alligators, and blood streaming from a comrade's forehead. Besides, she had a lover. A lover who was a criminal.

"I *will* find La Venganza."

With a shake of her head, she simultaneously broke out of his grasp and his gaze. "You'll find nothing." She flashed a superior smile. "You don't even know where to look. La Venganza could be standing before you, and you wouldn't know."

"Oh, but La Venganza isn't standing before me," he drawled. "La Venganza's whore stands before me. And I shall use the whore to catch the villain."

Her face colored as rosy as her skin had felt in his hand. "I'm not a whore, Major St. Clair. Have a care, or you might incur La Venganza's wrath once again. I promise you, this time you won't appreciate the consequences."

"Again?" Ethan whispered. "What does she mean, 'again'?"

Lucien ignored the question and locked his gaze on the blush staining her cheeks. "I want your lover's name."

Palms flat, her fingers curled around the table's edge, she leaned toward him. "I…have…no…lover." Each word left her lips in succinct rhythm. While he digested her denial, she straightened. "As for La Venganza, you'll never find him. Go to your General and confess your failure to your duty. Perhaps he'll take pity on you and treat you with kindness, although I doubt the man has a sympathetic thought for anyone who isn't red-skinned."

"I've never failed in my duty before. I will not fail now," he said. "You'll cooperate with me, whether you wish to or nay."

She tossed her head. "I would sooner help the Devil than align myself with you."

"Why, Marisa," he replied silkily. "If you're in league with La Venganza, you're already the Devil's whore."

She fisted her hands at her sides, no doubt to keep from slapping him. "You're wasting your time, and I'm tired of your insults."

He admired her fortitude, if not her loyalty. "Tell me the identity of La Venganza."

"Never!"

"Tell me or by God, I'll—"

"What will you do? Haul me off to the calaboose?

Clap me in irons?" She shifted her posture to one hip and folded her arms over her chest. "Do what you wish, I'll tell you nothing! If you believe I'm so disloyal I would abandon La Venganza merely because you ask, then you know nothing about me!"

"I know you well enough. I know you're a traitorous whore with some idea of misguided loyalty."

Her smile became cold enough to freeze the Mississippi in August. "Even whores have honor, Major."

"Whores have no honor. That's what makes them whores." From the corner of his eye, he spotted a sudden motion.

Santos lumbered toward them, but Ethan took a step in the giant's direction. One quick shove, and the young man stumbled toward the door. Fathomless eyes pierced Lucien's soul as the ogre placed a hand upon Marisa's shoulder to lend her support.

"Now," she said firmly. "If you are going to arrest me, do so. If not, leave me. I have work to do."

Since the formidable bulk of Santos barred him from further contact, Lucien had no choice but to let her return to preparing the meal. But satisfaction rippled down his spine when she pushed the rolling pin over the dough in an almost violent manner.

*"You are a woman, you must never speak what you think; your words must contradict your thoughts, but your actions may contradict your words."*
— *William Congreve (Love for Love)*

## CHAPTER 10

Lucien and Ethan hovered outside the kitchen for over an hour. At last, Marisa stormed past, headed toward the rear of the building. Although she must have seen them, she never acknowledged their presence. Instead, she slammed the office door, a physical barrier to any additional arguments.

At the deafening sound, Ethan flinched. "Now what?"

"Now," Lucien said with a shrug. "We wait."

"Wait? For what? And how long?"

"For Marisa to make a move," he replied. "Surely she'll try to warn her lover that we're looking for him. And we'll wait as long as it takes for her to lead us to him."

They took up sentry posts near the tavern doors for the rest of the day, which turned slowly into night.

Dinner came and went. Still, Marisa remained locked in her office. Lucien and Ethan sat at their usual table and listened to the soldiers' usual trivial gossip.

After more than seven hours, Ethan rose. When his chair screeched over the floor, the grating noise shot pain directly through Lucien's eyes, straight into his brain.

"You can stay if you like, Lucien. But if you ask me, this is getting us nowhere." He glanced over the crowd and scowled. "Time is running out. I think we should start questioning the other patrons. Someone's bound to know something."

Another hour elapsed while Ethan moved around the room, from one cluster of soldiers to the next. The same show replayed over and over. The group would start out friendly, shake his hand, invite him into their conversations. But Lucien could always tell the exact moment Ethan turned the topic to La Venganza. The change was never subtle. Postures stiffened, brows drew together angrily, and an invisible wall of resentment popped up. After dozens of cold shoulders, Ethan returned to their table on a defeated sigh.

"The general should inspire as much loyalty as La Venganza," he grumbled.

"No luck then?" Lucien hid a smile. Ethan's lack of success didn't surprise him in the slightest.

"No. And I'm off to bed."

Lucien bade him good night, but stubbornly remained. Tonight, he nursed an ale quickly grown warm in the room's close confines. His eyes grew heavy, yet he refused to give in. The moment he let down his guard, he knew Marisa Álvarez would take advantage.

Yet another hour passed.

Santos finally tapped him on the shoulder. "Out," the giant said. "I close up now."

"Sorry." He rose and left the tavern, but loitered in the hallway to watch while Santos finished cleaning, and then locked the tavern door. Without a backward glance, the barkeeper ascended the stairs to seek his bed.

Lucien had just decided to do the same when a

sharp sound from the front porch pierced his sleepy brain.

Damn! Marisa had somehow left the inn without his notice, and he cursed himself for playing into her hands. Quickly, he hid himself in a darkened alcove near the front door.

Her blue cloak's hood covered her telltale hair when she slipped inside. But he couldn't mistake her size or the way she moved. The scent of her skin, like roses, wafted to him. He stiffened, ready to confront her, but she turned to look around her with haunted eyes.

"Santos?" She tiptoed closer to his hiding place, and he shrank back against the wall. "Anita?"

As if she shrugged off apprehension with her cloak, she relaxed her stance and sighed. On her sigh, she pulled a ring of keys from her pocket and unlocked the tavern door.

A heartbeat later, yellow light spilled. A glass tinkled and slapped onto wood. His location in the shadows prevented him from seeing her actions, but he recognized the sound of a bottle uncorked and the splash of liquid. Curiosity overrode common sense, and he leaned out into the light.

She stood near the bar, a glass of amber liquid held in the air. "*Feliz cumpleaños*, 'Lando."

'Lando? Who was 'Lando? Had someone slipped inside with her? Impossible. She'd come into the inn alone. Still, he inched closer, in time to see her toss the alcohol down her throat.

Before she'd barely swallowed, she choked.

He bit back a laugh.

"*Dios!*" she rasped. "You never told me whiskey tasted so horrid! Why would anyone intentionally drink this liquid fire?" She slammed the glass on the counter. Her shadow paced to and from as the clock in the hall ticked off time. "Major St. Clair is far more clever than we originally thought."

Well, that certainly piqued his curiosity. Another stealthy step gained him a fuller view of the room. Her cloak lay draped over one chair, a bottle of whiskey and a single glass sat on the bar. She paced near an open window and wrung her hands. No one else cast a shadow. So where was this 'Lando she spoke with? Was he a phantom? A figment of her imagination? Was she drunk?

"Oh, the major still believes I'm La Venganza's mistress," she said to thin air. "But if he stays here much longer, he may learn the truth."

*You may count on it, señorita.*

She whirled then, and the light caught tears glistening on her cheeks. Guilt pierced his heart.

"I'm so tired," she whispered. "Tired of vengeance, tired of death. I want to go home."

She sank into the nearest chair and dropped her head on an outstretched arm atop the table. A hum filled the air. Lucien's ears prickled. Had someone answered her? No. The sound came from Marisa as she sang. Perhaps the liquor had taken effect, or perhaps her arm muffled her voice. For though he caught a few sporadic words, the lyrics and their meaning escaped him.

When her song ended, silence reigned. Lucien assumed she'd fallen asleep, but uncertainty forced him to remain unnoticed. The clock continued to tick, and he finally decided to wake her. Before he took a step, however, a squeal pierced his ears. While his attention had swerved to the clock, she must have roused herself. She stood now, hands braced on the window she'd just closed. Quickly, he ducked back into the dark.

Her movements were soundless as she scooped up her cloak and exited the tavern, locking the door behind her. A familiar scent tickled his nostrils when she passed his hiding place, completely oblivious to his presence.

Alone in the hall, he waited several long minutes. Still his lungs inhaled the perfume of crisp, fresh air on rose-kissed skin. When the scent dissipated, he headed for the staircase. And stopped. Near the door, her boots, soles scraped clean and leather gleaming, caught his eye. A far cry from the last time he'd seen them, caked with mud. Realization struck like a hammer.

The evening Colonel King had his encounter with the alligator in the privy, Marisa had returned to the inn quite late. Leaves littered her hair, and black mud coated her boots and gown. Black mud, which no doubt came from a swamp. A swamp filled with alligators.

She and her lover hadn't romped in a meadow that night. They'd hunted alligators in a swamp.

His heart sank. Damn her! Pieces of the La Venganza puzzle were quickly clicking into place. And he'd sacrifice his commission, if only he could be mistaken.

*"The same energy of character which renders a man
a daring villain would have rendered him useful to
society, had that society been well organized."*
— *Mary Wollstonecraft*

## CHAPTER 11

"Have you had any luck in your search,
gentlemen?" Marisa's derisive voice echoed through
the tavern. She stood near their table, a smug smile
on her face. "Have you found La Venganza yet?"

"No." Lucien folded his arms over his chest. Let
her think she had the upper hand. At least a while
longer. "Nevertheless, I will find him."

"Ha! You couldn't find a rose among a field of
daisies."

As she turned, he grabbed her hand. "Why not
give me the man's name? If you trust me, I might
help your lover avoid a hangman's noose."

"If I trust you?" She yanked her hand from his.
"Why should I trust you?"

Leaning back, he shrugged. "I haven't given you
a reason not to trust me." *Unlike you, who have
played me for a fool since our first meeting.*

A silver brow arched. "No? You lied to me, *Major*
St. Clair! You lied to me about who you are and why
you came to Pensacola."

Ethan shifted in his seat. "Marisa, please. No
one need ever know how we came to learn his
identity, but you simply must tell us his name."

She turned her questioning gaze to the pup. "Must I? Why?"

"Why?" he repeated.

"Yes, *Sergeant Greene*, why? Simply because you demand it? Do you think you are the only men here seeking La Venganza? Look around you." She bent, voice lowered to a mere whisper. "The dark-haired gentleman sitting alone in the corner? Cuba's foreign minister sent him to discover La Venganza's whereabouts. The two men dicing with Pablo represent a British envoy intent upon finding La Venganza. Last week a man arrived from Germany. Two months ago, an angry Seminole threatened to burn down the inn unless I divulged La Venganza's location. Every soldier in this room wishes to know La Venganza's identity. Some wish to join his band, others wish to shake his hand. Some, like you, merely wish to hang him. Now if I won't share his secrets with any of them, why would I tell you?"

"Because he can't continue along this path," Lucien argued. "If you care for him, save him from destruction."

She gazed at the ceiling as if sharing a secret joke with heaven. "If you'll excuse me, I have work to do."

"Dammit, Marisa," he called after her retreating back. "Have you no honor that you'd protect your lover from the law?"

Once more she whirled. This time her eyes blazed. "Sometimes, the law must be circumvented to protect the innocent."

He nearly laughed aloud, but stifled his humor at her naïveté. Surely she didn't believe such nonsense. "Laws are enacted to protect the innocent and punish the guilty."

"Do not dare to lecture me about the law!" she shouted. A dozen patrons turned from their conversations to stare, and she ducked her head as if in penance. "One day, Major," she murmured, "you may learn what I learned long ago. One day you may be forced to choose between one you love and the law you so revere. I pray to God when that day comes, you will be able to live with the consequences of your decision."

Should he push her? Perhaps if he prodded her temper, she'd blurt out her lover's name in a fit of pique. Or if the man sat here already, he might fly to her defense. "You wouldn't know God, madam, if He came down from heaven and shook your hand. Only the virtuous know God."

Nothing. No reaction at all. Except a slow smile. "Mary Magdalene knew God."

"Only after she repented."

"As will you one day," she replied. "I look forward to seeing you beg my pardon, Major. Until then, I'll strive to remember your ignorance makes you believe yourself superior to those who haven't had your good fortune."

While she stalked off, he watched carefully. Did she seek out any particular man in the crowd? Did anyone go to her? No. She headed behind the bar and filled several tankards while around them, the soldiers continued their games and gossip.

"You may as well surrender," a woman whispered in his ear. "She won't tell you anything."

He turned and found himself face to face with Anita who grinned like a cat with a fat mouse trapped in her paws.

She jerked her head toward the door leading outside. "I need a bit of fresh air. What about you two?"

He and Ethan nearly upended their chairs in their haste.

Outside, she sat on the porch swing and patted the space beside her. Lucien declined. When Ethan made a move, he shot the young man a disapproving look until he hung back.

With a careless shrug, she pushed the swing on the toes of her outstretched foot. "The more you harangue Marisa, the less you'll get from her. Now, me? I'm not so stubborn. So tell me. What do you wish to know about my *montesita*?"

"*Montesita*?" Ethan asked.

"Marisa," she told him. "*Montesita* is her family's name for her."

"'Little wild one,'" Lucien automatically translated. "Fitting."

"*Sí*." She tilted her head back and chuckled. "She was always tiny, but full of mischief. Her brother gave her the name when she was about five years of age. 'Lando meant it as an insult, but—"

"'Lando!" At Lucien's outburst, Anita flinched. He mumbled a quick apology for his outburst, then added, "'Lando is her brother?"

"He was."

"Was?" Lucien frowned. That explained why Marisa spoke to thin air when holding her discussion with him the other evening.

"Was," Anita repeated more firmly. "He is gone now." She crossed herself. "May God have mercy on his soul."

"What happened to him?" Ethan asked.

"He died." She sighed. "Such a waste of an elegant man! He resembled Marisa, with the same silver hair and bright green eyes. A bit less of a rascal as an adult. But as a child, he often outfoxed Marisa with his naughty games."

"Forgive me, *señorita*," Ethan interrupted. "But how do you know all this?"

She tilted her head. "Do you know how old I am, *señor*?"

"If I were to guess," he replied smoothly, "I'd say no more than one score and five."

"Ha!" Anita cackled. "I shall be two score and

eight on my next birthday." Her foot sent the swing moving faster. "I was *Montesita's dueña*, her nursemaid, from the day of her birth until we came to Pensacola."

Excitement rippled down Lucien's spine. At last—someone who knew Marisa. Truly knew her. Not idle rumor or speculation. Facts.

"When did you come to Pensacola?" he asked.

"During the Creek War. When the militia attacked Burnt Corn, Marisa's father, don Carlos, sent Santos and me here to stay with his brother to keep us safe."

"And Marisa came with you?"

Anita shook her head and counted on her fingers. "Don Carlos, doña Maria, *Montesita*, Orlando, and his wife, Juanita, who was eight months along with child, all moved to Fort Mims."

"Fort Mims?" Excitement chilled to dread. He remembered the fate of those poor people. The idea of Marisa so close to death rocked him. Regardless of her current life, she was far too fragile for such a place. "How long did the family remain there?"

The swing stopped all forward motion. Anita's somber expression drained the last vestiges of gratitude from Lucien's heart.

"Until the very end," she replied. "On the day of the attack, Marisa left the fort with a young man, Tomás Marquez, shortly before noon. They were near Tensaw Lake when the Red Sticks swarmed the fort. Tomás, who had just asked her to marry him, hid her in a cave of some sorts and returned to help the family escape. He never came back for her. When she finally left her hiding place, they were all dead. Even poor Juanita and her unborn babe did not escape the butchery." She clucked her tongue. "My poor *montesita*. To have to see what she saw that day..."

While shivers racked her slender frame, Lucien

knelt to take her hands in his. Her icy fingers chilled his palms. For several long moments, she said nothing, merely stared at the air around her.

"Afterwards," she said at last, "Marisa found her way to Pensacola."

Dear God.

"How?" Lucien pressed. How on earth could she have endured the horrors of that day and then traveled for weeks to reach this inn?

"They walked," Anita replied simply. "How else?"

Lucien leaped on the telling pronoun. "They?"

Anita nodded. "Another survivor accompanied her."

Another survivor? La Venganza perhaps?

Lucien could barely control the interest in his tone. "Who was this other survivor?"

"I don't know." Anita shrugged. "He disappeared after leaving her at the inn. Marisa has lived here since then."

"By God!" Ethan sank onto the railing as if his legs could no longer support him.

Little wonder. Lucien's limbs trembled like fig pudding. "She's lucky to be alive!" he remarked.

Anita grimaced. "Don't tell her that. She'd never believe you."

"Anita!" Santos stepped out onto the porch, his moon face twisted into a murderous expression. "Come inside. Now."

With a wink, she rose. "I told you. Santos thinks I talk too much."

****

Lucien watched from atop a hill while Marisa tended the graves. Hoping to avoid notice, he hung back. Sympathy warred with his sense of duty. Knowing her past gained him insight into her loyalty to La Venganza. Still, such loyalty was misguided, and not to be tolerated.

When she stood, her gaze caught his immediately. "Have you nothing better to do than follow me about all day? Can't I even mourn the dead without your loathsome presence?"

He feigned nonchalance with a careless shrug. "Tell me how to find La Venganza, and you'll never see me again."

Her lips twisted. "Tempting." Increasing her pace, she strode past him, tossing over her shoulder, "Sadly, I must decline."

"Why?" he called after her. "Was La Venganza with you at Fort Mims?"

She stopped, posture ramrod straight. But when she faced him, her expression held no anger, only a bleak sadness that nearly broke his heart. Tears glistened, and her voice shook. "Do not ever speak of Fort Mims to me. You, who've never known the pain of such a place. You have no right. Why won't you go away and leave me be?"

"Because it's my duty to bring La Venganza to justice."

"Justice?" She shook her head. "Tell me, Major. Are you familiar with William Shakespeare's *Measure for Measure*? 'The jury, passing on the prisoner's life, may in the sworn twelve have a thief or two guiltier than him they try.'"

"I like to think our justice system is better than that of Shakespeare's day."

With a careful eye, she scanned his immaculate shirt and crisp trousers. A flicker of unease ran through him. For the first time in his life, his pristine clothing embarrassed him.

"Judging by your manner of dress, you've had an easy life, no doubt living in a grand house with servants and privileges that other men only dare to dream of. You've never known hardship or sorrow, have you?"

Lucien thought fleetingly of his long dead sister

and the deaths of his parents. "On the contrary. I've had my share of sorrow."

"Oh?" She raised an eyebrow. "Was your sorrow due to the hatred and brutality of others? Would you so blithely accept sorrow if your law had done nothing to prevent it? And how bitter would you become to discover the law will never atone for its neglect to those you loved and lost?"

"That's still no reason for a man to take the law into his own hands."

"Was it not your Thomas Jefferson who wrote that when governments become destructive, it is the right of the people to alter or abolish them and institute new governments?"

He shook his head. "Not through vengeance, Marisa. Even you must see that such acts are the deeds of a coward."

She folded her arms over her chest as if to protect herself from his barbs. "So now it's cowardice to demand justice for the wrongs committed against you?"

Lord, she had a quick and clever mind. No wonder she charmed so many of Pensacola's residents. She had plenty to recommend her: beauty, intelligence, humor. Everything but chastity. He frowned. "Why not give me the man's name? Why not unburden your conscience?"

"'Conscience is but a word that cowards use, devis'd at first to keep the strong in awe.'"

Her second use of Shakespeare. Clearly the playwright had some significance to her. Very well. "'Richard III,'" he said. "'And thus I clothe my naked villany with odd old ends stol'n forth of holy writ, and seem a saint when most I play the devil.'"

****

No one had ever defeated her with Shakespeare before.

Marisa dug her fingernails into her palm to keep

from scratching the major's handsome face. Instead, she nodded and ground out, "I wish you a good day, Major St. Clair."

Nearly tripping over her feet in her haste to get away from the sanctimonious major, she raced to *El Castillo*.

But he caught up to her in a heartbeat. "Perhaps I should ask Ramon about La Venganza."

"Ramon?" She cocked her head. "You think Ramon works for La Venganza? As what? A gossip?" Lucien flushed, and she laughed. "Oh, Major, you're a fool!"

"Be careful." He shot up a hand.

She ignored his warning. "Bah! You don't frighten me."

Her strides lengthened, growing more hurried as the inn's safe haven came into view. She gained strength from *El Castillo*, found her thirst for justice burning in her heart and belly.

"You wish to know of Ramon? I'll tell you of Ramon."

"Who is he?" Lucien demanded, keeping pace beside her.

"He's an old man who had only one joy in life, his family. The Red Sticks took that joy from him."

"I wasn't speaking of Ramon," Lucien growled.

"Well, I was," she retorted. "During the Creek War, the Red Sticks attacked his village. They killed his wife and only child, and then set fire to his house. He survived because the savage who clubbed him didn't notice Ramon still breathed before he left." Reaching *El Castillo's* porch, she whirled to look down on the major. "Ramon lost everything he held dear in one day. He lives alone in a small farmhouse about a mile from *El Castillo*. Occasionally, his loneliness becomes too much for him to bear. When that happens, he comes here for a pint of ale and some companionship. He's nothing more than a lonely old man, Major. He is *not* a criminal!"

Without waiting for a reply, she strode inside, down the hall and into her office, where she slammed the door. With a loud and emphatic click she slid the bolt home, ending their discussion.

*Oh, could you view the melody*
*Of every grace*
*And music of her face,*
*You'd drop a tear;*
*Seeing more harmony*
*In her bright eye*
*Than now you hear."*
*— Richard Lovelace (Lucasta)*

## CHAPTER 12

That evening, the crowd inside the tavern spilled into the hall and out onto the porch. Civilians outnumbered soldiers among the revelers. Hundreds of people swarmed the inn, cheering, laughing, and singing. Music played on the grounds outside while children raced in circles.

Speechless, Lucien stood in the middle of the staircase, eyes drinking in the spectacle. He recognized several of the children from *doña* Isabella's house. His sharp gaze even caught a few Indians among the throngs.

"What do you suppose...?" Ethan nudged an elbow in his ribs.

Shaking his head, Lucien descended and shouldered through the press of people into the tavern.

"Why, 'tis *El General's* spies!" Pablo shouted from his usual table. "I'm surprised you're still here."

"Oh?" Lucien arched a brow as he approached

95

the soldier and his cronies. "Why is that?"

"Haven't you heard?" another soldier asked.

"Heard what?" Ethan chimed in over Lucien's left shoulder.

"Your Colonel King has been sent packing from Government House and that miserable Captain Gadsden with him," Pablo replied with a broad grin. "Cuba dispatched a new governor, and your general's men are no longer welcome in Pensacola. You must be out of the city within the next five days, or you'll be cooling your heels in the calaboose."

Which meant he'd failed in his duty to the general. La Venganza still eluded him. Fine hairs danced on Lucien's nape, but not due to Pablo's announcement.

The reason for the sensation became clear when someone behind him yelled, "Marisa!"

She strolled through the crowds, and they parted for her as if royalty approached. While she flitted from guest to guest, bestowing a smile here and a greeting there, every graceful movement of her hands prickled his skin. In the middle of the room, she stopped, eyes alight with emerald fire. Did her delight have to do with the fact she knew he'd have to leave before fulfilling his vow to find La Venganza?

No. When he followed her line of vision, his gaze locked on a grinning Ramon Santiago seated at a table not far away. So her joy was for the old man, not for his failure.

Well, he still had five days to catch the villain. And he'd use every minute available until the new governor's men ran him out of town. With a nudge in Ethan's side, he said goodbye to Pablo and the others, and then strode toward the old man.

"Major St. Clair!" Ramon greeted him as if they were old friends, hand outstretched. "I suppose you and Sergeant Greene will leave us now that Spain is back in control here."

Lucien recalled Marisa's comments regarding the old man's loneliness and shook the trembling hand warmly. "*Señor* Santiago. I haven't seen you here in quite a while."

"Ah, well, it's a long walk from my home to this inn." Tankard held high, he gestured to Marisa. "*Querida*! Fetch two more pints for our friends."

Hands on hips, she called back, "Are you paying for their pints?"

In two strides, Lucien stood beside her. He grasped her wrist, and a spark flew. With a gasp, she pulled away. So...she'd felt the heat as well. Gaze locked on her perfect rosebud lips, he bent toward her like a puppet on strings. They stood so close they shared the same breath.

Ramon cleared his throat, and the magic around them disintegrated.

As if he'd awakened from a stupor, he shook himself. "I'll pay for our pints. And for Ramon's as well."

"Well, *muchas gracias*, Major," Ramon exclaimed.

Marisa blinked several times. No doubt she needed to clear the fog in her brain, an action Lucien understood perfectly. At last, she sighed. "Very well."

As she headed for the bar, Lucien stumbled into the nearest empty chair. *Too many people in here.* The crush of so many bodies caused the heat coursing through his veins. Nothing more.

Once she'd filled two tankards, she meandered through the crowd to their table. Slamming them down, she turned away.

But Ramon halted her by clasping her hand. "Stay with us."

Her gaze narrowed on Lucien. "No, thank you. I don't care for the company you're keeping tonight."

"Perhaps you're not accustomed to the company of gentlemen," he said.

She stiffened, but then she melted her skeletal hardness with a warm smile. "A true gentleman would not insult a lady."

"When I see a lady," Lucien murmured, "I'll be certain to mend my ways."

Sergeant Greene sputtered on his ale. "Lucien, you owe Marisa an apology."

She waved a hand. "No, Sergeant. An apology now would not hold the weight required to atone for the insults he's heaped on me these last few weeks. But I'm a patient woman. I prefer to wait until he must come to me on his knees, begging forgiveness for every slur he's cast my way."

Completely at ease with his conscience, Lucien leaned back in his chair. "I fear you'll have a long wait."

Challenge flashed in her eyes. "I've already told you, I'm a patient woman."

"Marisa, *querida*." Ramon raised her fingers to his lips. "I'm feeling morose tonight. Will you sing for me, *por favor*?"

A booming voice erupted behind her. "Quiet! Marisa is going to sing!"

Cheers and boot heels thundered in the tavern.

"I don't suppose I might decline now," she shouted over the noise.

Laughing, Ramon jerked a head at Lucien. "Listen. I don't believe you've ever heard anything as glorious."

"Santos?" she said, her gaze locked on the giant behind the bar.

Nodding like an eager puppy, he pulled a guitar from beneath the counter. One quick strum silenced the room.

Hands clasped in Ramon's, she sang.
*"When dawn comes, I shall fly to you*

*And on golden wings we will soar to our home.*
*We will abide one for the other,*
*And no longer will we feel the need to roam.*

*For far too long have we been torn asunder.*
*I've missed the beating of your heart.*
*But soon we will be together again*
*And know that we shall never part.*

*To a castle you will take me,*
*A castle in the skies.*
*And though others may forsake me*
*I will always see the love shining in your eyes.*

*For far too long have we been torn asunder.*
*I've missed the beating of your heart.*
*But soon we will be together again*
*And know that we shall never part.*
*Never again shall we part..."*

Lucien's heart sighed inside his chest. By God, her voice could rival the angels'. She held the last note until the walls shook, and when she finally ended the song, tears shimmered in her eyes. But he couldn't tell if emotion or the strain affected her.

While the soldiers broke into thunderous applause, she broke from Ramon's hold and elbowed her way out of the room.

Struck dumb, Lucien stared through the mass of people until she'd disappeared. No wonder Ramon and the others grew silent at the prospect of hearing her sing. Thinking of her loveliness, her clever wit, her magnificent talent, he suffered another stab of pity.

What must her life have been like before Fort Mims? If he'd met her before the Creek War, before the existence of La Venganza, would he have fallen in love with her?

Foolish thought. Because despite her finer

qualities, she was also immoral, childish, and bitter. And despite all he knew about her—her vices and virtues—he'd already allowed her to carve a piece of his heart for her very own.

Like a man who had walked across the desert, he wanted to reach out and drink her into his soul. He tossed back his head and laughed at the absurdity. Ethan and Ramon stared at him, but he didn't bother to explain.

*Farewell, Montesita. Perhaps, if we'd met at another time...*

# PART II

*"There is something in a woman beyond all human delight; a magnetic virtue, a charming quality, an occult and powerful motive."*
*— Robert Burton (Anatomy of Melancholy)*

## CHAPTER 13

Belle Monde, New Orleans
August 1820

"Lucien, the children must have their naps."

At the sound of that lyrical voice, Lucien looked up from the shell game he played with his niece and nephew. Their doting mama, Antoinetta St. Clair, beamed down upon them brighter than sunlight. For some reason he couldn't fathom, his sister-in-law reminded him of Marisa Álvarez.

Odd, since the women shared no resemblance. Perhaps, the idea came from Marisa's accusation he'd never known sorrow. True enough, he'd led a fairly sheltered life. He was a child when his father and sister died. And while his mother's death had struck a blow, she'd lain ill for so long, her end had been a blessing. When compared to Marisa's ordeal at Fort Mims, his sorrow paled.

Antoinetta, however, had survived more than her share of sorrows. Raised in India by her Uncle Ahmed, she'd spent her childhood in relative peace. The day after her eighteenth birthday, her world turned upside-down. Betrothed to a vicious monster, she'd survived horrors no human, much less a woman, should have to endure. Only his brother, Darian, who rescued Antoinetta, healed her. With love.

"You're thinking of her again," Antoinetta accused with a smile.

"No, I'm not," he denied a little too quickly. "I was thinking about you."

"Me?" Stormy eyes widened. "Why me?"

He glanced at the children who watched the exchange from their blanket under the pecan trees. "Later." As Antoinetta lifted Armand, he bent to pick up Corinne. "Well, imps, Mama says you must take your naps, and so you shall."

"But we're not sleepy," Corinne argued. The statement might have made a bigger impact if she didn't yawn immediately after making it.

"Nevertheless, you'll take your nap now," Antoinetta announced but she softened her demand with a gentle kiss pressed upon the child's forehead.

Lucien and Antoinetta carried the children past the orchards and back into the house. They walked through the foyer in silence. Both children had already surrendered to their need for sleep. He followed Antoinetta up the circular staircase to the nursery on the third floor where their nursemaid waited. After tucking the children into their beds, Antoinetta closed the door and signaled him to follow her downstairs to the sitting room where they could speak privately.

Once there, Antoinetta leaned against the settee and folded her arms over her chest. "So?"

"What?" Lucien asked.

"What were you thinking about me in the orchard?"

"You might as well tell her, Lucien," a voice drawled from the doorway. "She won't let it rest until she has her answer."

"Darian!" Antoinetta whirled, eyes wide. "That is *not* true."

"Really?" Darian St. Clair raised an elegant eyebrow as he sauntered into the room.

Before she could reply, he wrapped his arm around her waist and pulled her down beside him on the settee. When he picked up her hand and kissed her fingertips, her purr carried promises of passion to be explored later. The easy camaraderie of husband and wife kicked Lucien in the gut. Not jealousy, more a longing for the same contentment in his life. Since leaving Pensacola, restlessness ruled his days and nights. And he knew where to lay the blame for the unease that overwhelmed his mind. Marisa Álvarez.

"Lucien?" Antoinetta's prompt broke his reverie of apple green eyes, gilt hair, and an angel's song. "What were you thinking about me in the garden?"

Curiosity danced in her expression, but a pang of guilt struck him. "Perhaps I shouldn't..."

"Tell her, Lucien," Darian said. "There will be no living with her until she finds out what you're hiding. Tell her so we might all sleep easily."

With a playful slap on her husband's forearm, she giggled. "It is true. So now you *must* tell me, Lucien."

"Marisa once told me I didn't really know sorrow."

"I knew it was about *her*," she crowed.

"Let him finish, sweet," Darian replied.

A flush crept up Lucien's neck, and he stared at the sunlight streaming onto the polished oaken planks at his feet. That day, when he'd stalked over Marisa's newly-washed floor with his muddy boots, what had his childish behavior cost her in time on her knees, her petal-soft hands immersed in scalding water? He shook his head. "Antoinetta, forgive me, but you know sorrow better than either of us."

Darian's expression darkened. "And you know better than to bring up the subject—"

"No, darling." She ran a gentle finger down his scarred cheek. "It was a long time ago. Let him ask his questions. Go on, Lucien. What do you wish to know?"

A lump rose in his throat, and he swallowed hard. "Have you ever been forced to choose between someone you love and doing what you know is right?"

Her face paled, and Lucien yanked his collar away from his tightening throat. He'd give anything to turn back time, even briefly, to avoid causing her pain. But Darian murmured some soothing phrase Lucien couldn't decipher, and Antoinetta nodded. She tilted her head onto Darian's shoulder, and he brushed a hand over her hair. Within the blink of an eye, her complexion refreshed to that of ripe peaches.

"I've made that choice more times than I care to recall," she said on a sigh.

"What did you do? How did you know when to follow your head and when to follow your...?" The lump reappeared and this time refused to settle down. "Your heart?"

Her icy blue eyes focused solely on him as she sat up. "Ahmed often said life is a road with many forks. Sometimes you take the right path, sometimes the wrong. The trouble is, you're never certain which path is the right path until long after you've passed the crossroads. All you can do is place your faith in Kismet, the goddess of fate. She alone knows where your path will lead, and will guide your way." She took his hand and clasped tightly. "So what does your heart tell you about your innkeeper?"

The lump in his throat heated, drying his mouth to dust. How could he possibly explain what he felt? How could he rationalize the dreams, the memories, and the way his heart constricted every time he thought about her? To say the words aloud would mean he'd have to face the truth, accept what he'd suspected for far too long.

Then again, he'd chosen to divulge his secrets to Antoinetta because if anyone might understand his twisted emotions, his sister-in-law would. With her boundless love and past experience, only she would listen and counsel without mockery or judgment.

On a deep inhale for courage, he gave her the one answer he could, the truth. "I don't know how to explain my feelings about Marisa except to say she's in my thoughts constantly."

Her hand squeezed his. "Then you must return to Pensacola. If Kismet wishes you and Marisa to be together, she'll not help you from here."

Antoinetta had only finished her statement when a familiar dark-haired soldier raced into the room with a footman on his heels.

"Sir! Wait! I haven't announced you yet!"

Sergeant Ethan Greene came to a halt before Lucien and offered a crisp—if breathless—salute. "Major."

Instantly, Lucien rose. "What is it, Sergeant? What's happened?"

"The General's son has been kidnapped," Ethan replied, "by La Venganza."

****

Faster than a hurricane, Lucien changed his clothes, packed a saddlebag, and returned to the sitting room to grab Ethan by the wrist and drag him out of the house.

"Talk!" he ordered as he stalked to the stables.

Ethan raced to keep up. "Do you remember Lyncoya?"

"Of course."

Andrew and Rachel Jackson had never had children of their own. But the Hermitage always burgeoned with little ones, mostly relatives of Rachel's who became wards to the Jacksons for one reason or another.

Lyncoya, an orphaned Red Stick, came to Jackson after the Battle at Tallushatchee in 1813. When soldiers discovered an Indian woman's body, the ten-month-old was pinned beneath her. Taking pity on the child, Jackson sent him to his wife at the Hermitage.

But Lyncoya still retained some semblance of his native background. By the age of five, he'd fashioned a bow and arrow, and then began smearing paint on his face. As he grew older, he loved to hide behind trees and leap out unexpectedly to frighten the other children.

"Lyncoya was in the woods, playing with his homemade bow," Ethan told Lucien.

"Did anyone see La Venganza take the boy?"

Ethan shook his head. "No. One moment the boy was playing in the bushes, and the next he was gone."

He halted outside the stables. "The note? Where did you find the note?"

"Well, at first, we didn't realize he'd been taken. We assumed he was playing hide-and-seek. Then I found the note pinned to the boy's pillow."

Anger pumped Lucien's blood, and he strode forward, hands fisted to maintain control. "Have any demands been made for the boy's return?"

"Not yet."

"Excellent." Inside the stable, Lucien headed straight for Boreas's stall and tack. "Then there's still time."

"Time for what, Major?"

He tossed the saddle on the gelding's back. "Time for me to get the truth out of *Señorita* Álvarez."

"Major, shouldn't we concentrate on finding La

Venganza instead of his mistress?"

"We are, Sergeant," Lucien said as he tightened the cinch knot in place. "Marisa Álvarez isn't La Venganza's mistress. She *is* La Venganza!"

*"I am a woman! nay, a woman wrong'd!*
*And when our sex from injuries take fire,*
*Our softness turns to fury-and our thoughts*
*Breathe vengeance and destruction."*
— *Richard Savage (Sir Thomas Overbury)*

## CHAPTER 14

"Are you certain Marisa is La Venganza?" Ethan asked as they rode headlong to Pensacola. "I can't believe such a goddess could be capable—"

"Don't be swayed by a pair of pretty green eyes, Sergeant," Lucien snapped. "She's no goddess. She is La Venganza."

"Yes, but," Ethan argued. "How can you be sure?"

A squirrel skittered across their path, bushy tail twitching.

Lucien tightened his grip on the reins. "Put the pieces together. First, there's the name. *La Venganza*, a feminine article."

"But that's due to the genders of the Spanish language. Even I know that much, and I don't speak the damned tongue."

"Add in the timing. La Venganza began harassing the general shortly after William Weatherford's arrival at the Hermitage."

Ethan shook his head. "The general wasn't the scoundrel's only victim, remember?"

"Let's take this one step at a time, Sergeant.

Weatherford was responsible for the greatest tragedy in Marisa's life. She lost her family and betrothed, all brutally cut down, in one afternoon at Fort Mims. And I'd wager she has no idea that Weatherford did not lead that attack. So when General Jackson pardoned the chief and transported him to the Hermitage to protect him from retaliation, La Venganza targeted the general to avenge the deaths of so many innocents."

"Pablo said that!" Ethan's excitement scattered birds in the trees overhead.

"Yes, he did. Now we move on, briefly, to Colonel King and Captain Gadsden. Both became targets when they allowed their positions of power to corrupt their sense of justice." His gaze skimmed over the trees that dripped leafy branches into mud dark as pitch. "In fact, the alligator in Colonel King's privy confirmed my suspicions. Do you remember the evening before we were summoned to Government House? Marisa came into the inn late with leaves in her hair?"

"You said she'd been out with her lover."

"I reconsidered that thought a long time ago. She was more likely hunting alligators. Her gown and boots were coated in black mud that night. Mud from the swamps. I'm fairly certain Marisa caught the beastie the colonel discovered in his privy."

Doubt still shadowed Ethan's eyes. "Pensacola's a long way from Tennessee. At least a month's journey riding hard, as we are. For a woman, the trip would take longer."

"The fact she's a woman only makes me more certain. Consider the methods of this so-called vengeance. Loosened cinch knots, released chickens, spiked canteens, cut breeches, and yellow-striped shirts."

His memory called up his own brush with La Venganza, waking in Boreas's stall, after he'd muddied her floors. Even now, he flushed with guilt at his rudeness and silently saluted La Venganza for getting her message across in such a clever, non-threatening way.

"All the pranks were fairly harmless, meant to embarrass or teach the victims a lesson. The alligator was a baby. If La Venganza had wanted to hurt the colonel, she might have found a young adult alligator. Their teeth are fairly sharp by the time they're a year old."

"Perhaps she was afraid that an adult would bite her before she could get it into Government House," Ethan suggested.

While the sun dipped into the horizon on the west, he considered the idea, but quickly dismissed it. "No, Ethan. The baby was intentional. Women are far more clever than men, but less bloodthirsty."

The sergeant's eyes narrowed to suspicious slits. "Why didn't you tell anyone what you knew?"

"Because I had no real proof," he said.

"Still, you might have confided in me."

Lucien stiffened. "Why? We'd been ousted from Pensacola. I'd hoped with Spain once again in control, La Venganza would disappear. I didn't think she'd continue to be a nuisance. That's all she really was, a nuisance. The pranks, while humiliating for their victims, were harmless."

Ethan's face darkened. "Until now."

Lyncoya. An innocent boy, now a vengeful woman's pawn. "Until now."

\*\*\*\*

For days on end, Lucien rode them hard. When they finally reached *El Castillo de Plata*, he barely halted Boreas before he dismounted. Without waiting for Ethan, he scaled the gray steps two at a time and strode inside.

Even before his eyes adjusted to the dim interior, his senses told him Marisa wasn't here.

Empty air slapped his cheeks and desolation swept through him.

"Marisaaaaaaaaa!" His bellow could shake the timbers from the ceiling.

No reply.

His boots stomped like thunder in the empty inn as he sped to the tavern.

Fury rose when he found Santos alone, sweeping the floor. Surely, the man had heard his shouts. Well, the giant would hear him now, by God. "Santos!"

The man had the gall to look up in surprise. "The inn is closed. Come back next week."

"Never mind that," Lucien retorted. "Where is she?"

Santos's dark eyes widened in newborn innocence. "Who?"

A breathless Ethan stopped short at Lucien's back. "Where is everyone?"

"The inn is closed," Santos repeated in monotone. "Come back next week."

Lucien's patience, which had dangled by a hair for the last week, snapped. "Dammit, Santos, where is she?"

"Who?" The man never paused in the sweep of the broom across the planked floor.

"Marisa! Where is Marisa?"

"She's gone home," Santos replied. "The inn is closed. Come back next week."

His brain sizzled, a lit fuse ready to explode. "She lives here."

Looking up from the floor, Santos blinked. "Not in August."

"Why not in August?"

"Because that's when she goes home."

Lucien scrubbed a hand over his face and inhaled deeply to gain control of his twitching emotions. Clearly, Santos needed a more patient touch. "Where is her home in August?"

"*El Castillo de Oro.*"

At last. Progress. "Is that nearby?

The giant simply shrugged.

Oh, how his fingers itched to plunge a knife between those shoulder blades. Santos couldn't possibly be that simple-minded. Perhaps he played a part? A part scripted by La Venganza?

"Where is *El Castillo de Oro*?" He kept his tone even, as if speaking to a child—his niece or nephew. "How far from here?"

Another shrug. "Somewhere in Alabama. Come back next week."

On a frustrated growl, Lucien exited the tavern with Ethan.

La Venganza had managed, once again, to slip through their fingers.

At least until Anita breezed past them, shouting, "She's home, Santos. Our *montesita's* home!"

*"Stone walls do not a prison make,*
*Nor iron bars a cage;*
*Minds innocent and quiet take*
*That for an hermitage;*
*If I have freedom in my love,*
*And in my soul am free,*
*Angels alone that soar above*
*Enjoy such liberty."*
— *Richard Lovelace (To Althea: From Prison)*

CHAPTER 15

An exhausted Marisa returned to *El Castillo de Plata*. After so many days of travel, she wanted only to climb into a soft bed for a long sleep. Outside the stables, she handed Tormenta's reins to Roberto and then stumbled to the front of the inn.

A few more steps...

In a few more steps, she'd collapse in her bed where, as she always did after this journey, she'd sleep a full day away. And when she finally woke, Anita and Santos would help her reassemble her shattered pieces.

As if summoned by her thoughts, Anita and Santos appeared on the porch, faces wreathed in smiles. Her tension melted like heated butter. Until she spotted the two men who hovered like vultures. She stopped short.

"Major St. Clair?" Yes. The ghost who haunted her dreams had returned. In the flesh. She pushed her lips into a thin smile. "Welcome back to Pensacola. Will you and Sergeant Greene want rooms again?"

"No, *señorita*," he replied, his voice like chips of ice that pelted her weary brain.

Relief and disappointment warred within her. With the inn closed these last two months, she could use the money renting the rooms would fetch. Still, she didn't relish having these two men with their suspicious minds and constant presence under her roof again.

"Well, then, I wish you gentlemen a pleasant day." Calling on her last stores of energy, she climbed the stairs toward the front porch. Before she reached the top step, Anita met her to wrap a supporting arm around Marisa's waist. "If you'll excuse me, I've only returned home from a long journey and I'd like—"

"We've come for Lyncoya," the sergeant called.

Between the top step and the porch, Marisa stopped and turned toward the angry faces peering up at her. "Lyncoya?" Her exhausted mind scanned the catalog of languages she spoke, but came up with nothing familiar in the term. "What's a Lyncoya?"

"General Jackson's son," Major St. Clair replied, each word clipped and curt.

The chill in his tone rippled the hair on her nape. Running a palm over her goosed skin, she smiled blandly. "So *El General* has returned to Pensacola again? Does Colonel Callava know about his arrival yet? You may wish to warn your general our new governor is nothing like Colonel Masot. He won't run to Fort Carlos, giving us up so easily."

In three strides, the major stood at the bottom of the stairs, golden eyes level with hers. "Where is he, Marisa?"

"Colonel Callava?" By now, her eyelids weighed more than full tankards, and she stifled a yawn. "I should think he's at Government House."

"Where is Lyncoya?" he said through gritted teeth.

"I've no idea." A sudden thought struck like a flint, sparking new energy inside her. "Is he lost? Santos, catch up with Ramon. I left him on the main road not more than a few minutes ago."

With an eager nod, Santos stepped forward, but the major cut his hand across the air, halting him in mid-stride.

Marisa's mind already raced to various hiding places near the inn. "Don't worry, gentlemen. Between us, we'll find your Lyncoya soon enough. How old is he? Not too young, I hope. The swamps here can be terrifying to little ones. How long has he been missing? What does he look like? Where was he last seen?"

"I would think you'd know the answers better than I." The major scaled the last step and towered over her. In one fluid motion, his rough grip clamped her wrist and yanked her from Anita's buffeting embrace.

Pain shot up her arm, and she gasped. "What are you doing? Let me go!"

Anita reached for Marisa, but the major hauled her up against his side. "How dare you! Release her at once!"

"Not until she tells us what she's done with Lyncoya." His eyes blazed with unholy rage, riveted to hers.

Was he mad?

"I've done nothing with Lyncoya!" She struggled to pull free, but he only squeezed his fingers like a vise. Any tighter and he'd snap her bones. "I don't even know Lyncoya!"

"Don't lie to me."

Anita turned to Santos. "Do something, you half-wit!"

"I'm not lying!" Marisa cried. The major's fingers left whitened imprints on her skin. Tears of pain filled her eyes. "Please, would you let me go? You're hurting me."

Instead of releasing her, he grasped both wrists and wrenched them behind her back. Muscles already abused screamed in silent agony. "I'm arresting you for the kidnapping of General Jackson's son." His hot breath filled her ear, "Let's see you wriggle out of this trap, *La Venganza.*"

She stiffened. La Venganza? He still chased La Venganza? And what was this about a kidnapping? Her brain swam, and she nearly swooned.

"Marisa?" Santos took a step forward. *"Qué pasa?"*

A loud click sounded, and her gaze swerved to Sergeant Greene, pistol aimed directly at Santos's chest.

*"Nada,* Santos," she urged. *"Haz nada!"* Do nothing! She turned to St. Clair. "Please, don't shoot him. He's done nothing wrong."

To her relief, he agreed. "Put the gun away, Ethan. Our *señorita* is ready to cooperate now, isn't she?"

Her heart slid into her throat, and she nodded.

"Where is Lyncoya?" he repeated.

What nightmare had she come home to? Why didn't he believe her? Her eyes filled with tears that blurred her vision, and she blinked them away. "On the soul of my sainted mother, I do not know."

"Very well." He pulled her toward the stairs. "Let's go."

Lines of surprise etched Anita's face. "Wait! Where are you taking her?"

"To the calaboose," the major replied as he prodded her toward the hitching posts where the horses waited. "Don't fret, madam. A few days in prison, and she'll tell us where Lyncoya is."

"And then she'll stand trial for her crimes against the general," the sergeant added. "Your Marisa is really La Venganza."

"No!" Santos turned to her, hands stretched outwards. "Tell them, Marisa. *Madre de Dios*, tell them the truth!"

"No!" Marisa's shout nearly shook the birds from the trees, but she inhaled several deep breaths to regain control.

She'd always known this day might come. And while she'd prepared for the eventuality, perhaps Anita and Santos had not. If she kept calm, forced an air of serenity, they wouldn't worry.

"*Haz nada*," she said softly. "All will be well. Santos, come to me."

Santos approached, round eyes wet with tears. He stopped just out of arm's length when the major shook his head.

She ignored his growl of chastisement and gestured with a crooked finger. "Come to me," she repeated in a tone that would coax a frightened toddler to her side. Santos bent toward her, and she stood on tiptoe to kiss his bald pate. Her lips trembled, and she hoped the poor man never noticed. "Say nothing, do nothing. All will be well."

Straightening, he nodded.

Despite the tumble of emotions that pitched her stomach, she pasted on a reassuring smile. "Go with Anita. All will be well."

Once Santos backed away, the major hauled her against his side. "You'll ride with me. May I assume there will be no attempts to escape?"

Marisa shook her head. "Help me up," she managed to croak through her fear-ridden throat.

St. Clair gave her a boost, sidesaddle, and quickly settled beside her. His arm wrapped her waist, pinning her to his hard chest. When his cohort sat astride his own mount, he jerked his head.

"Make the arrangements."

"Yes, sir!"

The sergeant's horse thundered off. The hoof beats echoed her heart's rapid pulse rhythm.

"Try to escape, *lady*, and things will go far worse for you."

Worse? A hangman's noose popped into her imagination, and she shivered.

With a tug of the reins, they set off.

As they rode away, Marisa sought one last look at the people she loved. Over the major's stiff shoulder, she spotted Anita on the porch, hugging a weepy Santos.

She raised a hand in farewell, but the major pushed her arm back down to her side.

"All will be well," she whispered.

If only she believed her own words.

****

Outside the calaboose, Sergeant Greene waited to help Marisa off the major's steed. When she reached for him, he grasped her waist and tossed her to the ground. Fear and exhaustion had sapped her, and she stumbled to her knees in the dirt.

The charming sergeant with the indulgent smile and appreciative glances had disappeared. In his place stood a man who looked at Marisa as if she were a creature from the swamps. "Whore."

He spat, but she managed to roll away before his spittle landed on her.

"Ethan." The major's disapproval resonated with deadly calm. "I will not tolerate cruelty to a lady." He bent and offered his hand. "I'm sorry, Marisa."

Finding some inner wall of strength, she pulled herself upright without his help. With her hands fisted, she faced the monsters. The daughter of don Carlos Ramon Orlando Álvarez would not cower. Over the years, she had survived more horror, more death than either of these two scoundrels. Let them do their worst. She would face her fate with courage, honor intact until the moment darkness enveloped her forever. Best of all, no matter what they did to her, La Venganza would live on. And that was the greatest revenge.

The major arched a brow. "I appreciate your cooperation thus far, *señorita*. Will you continue to be so accommodating, or shall we carry you inside?"

If he meant to intimidate her, he'd find she didn't frighten easily. Nails digging into her palms, she brought her trembling limbs under control. Now if only her voice would stay steady. "Despite what you may think of me, sir, I'm an honorable lady. Lead on, and I will follow."

No hesitation, not a tremor belied the terror that spread like wildfire in her veins. Pride straightened her spine, and she swept a hand before the men.

The major frowned. "Ethan, take the lead. I'll follow behind the *prisoner*." He laced the words with malice.

No doubt he expected her to whimper and beg. Well, he'd never see such weakness from her. She fell into step behind the sergeant. The major strode so close to her back, his breath wafted over her nape. Nerves danced in her bones.

When the sergeant yanked open the door, a wall of fetid odor nearly knocked her to her knees. Sweat, human waste, and the desperate smell of fear assailed her nostrils. Hoisting her head high, she walked inside. Rows of filthy cells lined the gray stone walls.

Revulsion rose, but she forced her gaze straight ahead. She would not look at the iron bars and squalid boxes, would not weaken. Her captors greeted the prison's captain, a man she recognized from the inn. Captain Herrera rose and picked up a large ring of keys. With a quick nod, he indicated they follow him. He walked to the farthest end of the building and stopped at the very last cell. While Marisa kept her eyes focused on the captain's shaky hands, he unlocked and opened the door. The hinges, old and rusted from dampness, squealed in protest.

Eyes downcast, he murmured, "This cell gives you a small measure of privacy, *señorita*. It is the best I might offer you."

"*Gracias, Capitan.*" She struggled to dig up one last smile, but found her reserves sorely lacking. Abandoning hope, she walked into the cell with as much poise as she could pull together.

The door squealed shut behind her, and the key turned in the lock with a loud click that echoed in her broken heart. She stared at the damp walls and the tiny, barred window. Beside her sat a low, narrow bed of wooden planks. In the corner, a bucket of stagnant water served as a privy. This cell held no mattress, no blankets, none of the comforts she'd looked forward to when walking those last few steps to the inn.

Melancholy cloaked her shoulders. She would die in this hole.

"Someone must sign the papers," Captain Herrera said.

"I'll do it." The eagerness in Sergeant Greene's tone raised her hackles.

*Bastardo.*

Still wearing the travel-stained dress she'd donned two days ago, she sank onto the wooden bed and buried her face in her hands.

"You might save us a great deal of time and trouble if you tell us where Lyncoya is."

Fanning her fingers, she peered at the major on the other side of the bars. "I do not know where Lyncoya is. I have never seen Lyncoya."

"As you wish," he said on a sigh and turned away.

"Major?" she called. When he stopped, she swallowed hard. "What will happen to me?"

He edged closer, eyes alight with a promise she could not fulfill. "If you tell us what happened to Lyncoya and we find him alive and safe, the General might be persuaded to judge you with mercy."

An icy hand grabbed her heart, squeezed. "And if not?"

"If Lyncoya is not found," he said, his tone flat. "Or if he dies, your punishment will be death."

The breath left her lungs and refused to return. Death. Since she couldn't produce the child, her death was imminent. "How soon?" she managed to eke from her tight throat.

"Marisa." He held out his hand. "Just tell us what we wish to know. Please?"

"How soon, Major? Do you suppose I'll be hanged? Shot? Or will *El General* allow me the privilege of choosing my own method of execution? I wager he won't allow me a death by old age." An invisible yoke weighted down her neck, and she ran her hands over her face to shield her eyes from the dirty straw on the floor.

"I'm sorry, *Montesita.*"

Her head came up with a snap. Liquid pain trickled down her spine. "Don't call me that! Only those who love me call me *Montesita.* You, who bring me here to await death, do not have the right!"

He stalked forward and gripped the bars in his fists. "I didn't bring you here! You did."

"Oh?" She slapped a palm on the bench. "I dragged myself into this hole?"

"Yes, dammit! You should have left the general and his family alone. This time, you went too far. You kidnapped an innocent child."

Indignation sprang her to her feet. "I didn't kidnap anyone!"

He sighed again. "I'll return tomorrow."

"Come tomorrow." Defeat and exhaustion had worn her down, and she sank to the bench, with no energy left to fight. "Come as many times as you wish, but my words will always be the same. I don't know where Lyncoya is. When you execute me, my words will still be the same."

"Perhaps tomorrow, you'll reconsider."

She shook her head. "There is nothing to reconsider. Tell Santos to give you your old rooms at *El Castillo*. You shouldn't be forced to live in filth while you're here."

Lucien had the grace to flush. She treated him more kindly than he treated her, and they both knew it.

"Thank you," he murmured.

"*De nada.*"

*"Trust not him with your secrets, who, when left
alone in your room, turns over your papers."*
— *Johann Kasper Lavater (Aphorisms on Man)*

## CHAPTER 16

Lucien waited until the middle of the night.
Assured the other occupants of the inn slept soundly,
he crept from his room and down the stairs. The
floorboards creaked when he hit the first floor.
Sucking in a breath, he flattened against the wall.

Nothing moved. No one came.

Tension drained from his pores, and he inched
his way to the office in the back. He tried the latch.
Locked, of course. Foolish to think Marisa might
have suffered a momentary lapse. He'd need to find
another way into the room. Once again, he slipped
through the dark, barren hall to the front door. On
the way, he grabbed the fireplace bellows. With the
door open, he placed the bellows near the jamb to
block the hinges, and then wandered onto the porch.
Down the stairs and around the inn's side, he
stopped at the large window that looked in on the
office. Finding a nice-sized rock beside the path, he
picked it up and hurled it through the glass. Crash!

Again, he shrank back, this time in the nearby
hedgerow. All remained still. No cry of alarm
sounded, no sudden spill of lamplight flooded the
room, no shadows lurked inside.

After he brushed the shards aside with a sweep

of his jacketed arm, he crawled through the opening. He didn't bother to light a lamp. Rather, he felt around—the walls, the desk, the chair—until he gained his bearings.

When his eyes grew accustomed to the darkness, he headed for the desk's drawers. Locked. Ever careful, Marisa wouldn't leave anything open. But there had to be a key somewhere.

He felt along the desktop, rifled through papers, all to no avail. The bookshelves revealed nothing. Finally, he dropped to the floor and ran his fingers along the rough boards. Near the closet, a plank popped up unevenly. Using his fingernails, he pried up the board and discovered a deep niche beneath. When he shoved his hand inside, his fingers brushed something cold and metallic, a ring of keys.

Smug satisfaction rippled through him when he pulled the ring out of hiding. The weight in his hand, however, didn't prolong the feeling. The ring contained at least fifty keys!

Here in the dark, he'd need hours to try each one to find the right fit for the desk. He'd have to risk lighting a lamp. After he lit the wick, the room blazed, and he turned down the flame until he had barely enough light to see. Measuring the keyhole in the desk to the various keys on the ring took attempts with several possibilities, but he managed to open the top drawer.

Nothing important leaped out at him. The drawer held receipts for rum and ale, sealing wax, and writing paper. While he looked through the receipts and odds and ends, unease slithered in his bones. Never before had he invaded someone's privacy. His actions tonight besmirched his honor. Still, Marisa had left him no choice.

He searched the drawer thoroughly, but found nothing. The second drawer held the same amount of relevant information.

The bottom drawer, however, required another key to open. Again, Lucien inserted different keys until the proper key clicked into place. He slid open the drawer and found a small oaken chest with brass straps. Naturally, when his fingers pried at the lid, he found the chest locked. Opting to check the rest of the drawer's contents before he fumbled with yet another key on the crowded ring, he set the box aside. Beneath the chest sat a pile of papers tied with a scarlet ribbon. Curiosity stirred.

After untying the ribbon, he removed the topmost paper and held it to the lamp. Damn. An old letter, nothing more.

And then the word '*aligator*' caught his eye. His knees buckled, and he sank into the chair. Surprise rose as he read the letter from start to finish.

*Dear Miguel,*

*Our montesita has been up to her old tricks again. Do you recall the little boy named Timmy on the neighboring farm…?*

The letter told in full detail of an escapade involving Marisa, a boy named Timmy Pendleton, and a baby alligator. Curious at what else he might find, Lucien chose another letter from the pile.

\*\*\*\*

He read for over an hour. Amazement grew with each escapade he discovered. As her nickname reflected, the girl who looked as innocent and fragile as a newborn angel, raised hell from the time she could walk. Every prank executed by La Venganza resembled an incident from Marisa's childhood.

He read about Manuel de Valde's shoes in the creek, the mare at the horserace, the baby alligator, and the cut cinch knot on her brother's saddle. There were tales of bulls dressed in women's clothes, dead fish stuffed into boots, live snakes placed among bedding, and buckets of cold water perched above doorways for unsuspecting passersby. But the final letter in the pile, written in don Carlos' hand, broke Lucien's heart.

> *...There has been a violent incident at the village of Burnt Corn Creek, not more than twenty miles from here. I believe it would be best for us to flee the area lest the Red Sticks retaliate.*
>
> *I'm sending Anita and Santos to you until this cursed war is over, Miguel. You know how fond we are of them. Santos may be simple-minded, but surely you'll find a way to employ him at the inn. Our other servants reside with their own relatives until the danger has passed.*
>
> *We'll be heading to Mr. Mims's home within a few days time. He has built a stockade fence around his land and invited the neighboring residents to band together until this threat passes. It was my intention to send the children to you as well, but our Juanita is too far along with child to make the journey safely. She and Orlando must remain with Maria and me.*
>
> *As for Montesita, she's become rather attached to a dashing young man named Tomás Marquez. The two refuse to be separated, regardless of the dangers. Ah, to be young and in love, eh, Little Brother?*
>
> *Maria and I couldn't be happier. Tomás is a lieutenant in*

*the Mississippi Territorial Militia. He fully understands my concerns regarding his current occupation and has agreed to my request that he complete his term of service before any wedding occurs. Although he adores Marisa, he is not so taken with her that he'll brook any of her antics. He is a very sensible and reliable young man. I've no doubt he will be an ideal husband for our girl. He might even be able to make a respectable woman of her.*

*Poor Maria had despaired of our wildcat ever becoming a young lady. Until Tomás came along, I feared Maria might be right, especially since you and I know of her many adventures.*

*Once the danger is over and we've returned home, I'll write again and tell you the date of the coming nuptials. You know how much our montesita loves you and Rosa. I know she'll want you at El Castillo de Oro to share in her happiness on her wedding day. Until then, dear Brother, may God keep us safe in His hands.*

*Carlos.*

Finished at last, Lucien sighed and ran a hand through his hair. Poor Marisa, witness to her family's brutal execution, and now facing her own. What might have become of her if she'd never gone to Fort Mims? If don Carlos had not moved his family there, if they'd remained at their *Castillo de Oro*, they might have all survived.

128

Pity overwhelmed him, and his hands grew slick with sweat. Kismet hadn't been very kind to the Álvarez family.

The letter slid away and floated gently to the floor. When he knelt to retrieve the paper, the red wax blared like a beacon. The Álvarez family seal was a large A entwined with a single rose. When he turned the paper upside-down and looked again, the A became a V with the stem of the rose cutting directly across the middle before entwining about each arm of the letter.

Damn. Lucien now had all the proof he needed.

To hang the woman he loved.

*"Foolish men who accuse a woman mindlessly-*
*you cannot even see you cause what you abuse."*
*— Juana Ines de la Cruz (Hombres Necios)*

CHAPTER 17

Early the following morning, Lucien returned to the calaboose alone. Since Ethan learned the truth of La Venganza's identity, he burned animosity stronger than a bonfire. While Lucien understood the blow the sergeant's pride had suffered, bested by a mere slip of a girl, that understanding didn't stretch far enough to allow abusive retaliation.

When he entered the dank, gloomy prison, he nodded at the captain in charge, a gray-haired, gray-complexioned man who spooned slimy beans from a steaming bowl on the table. The soldier looked up, and the food slid off the spoon to land on his pot belly.

Lucien stifled a shudder of revulsion. "I'm here to see *Señorita* Álvarez."

Using the empty spoon, the man pointed to the last cell, and then returned his attention to his dish of green leaves and dirt-colored legumes.

As he walked down the bleak corridor, Lucien studied the cells. None held an occupant. But for how long would Marisa remain the calaboose's only prisoner? All the more reason to gain her cooperation and a confession, and then get her the hell out of here as soon as possible. Provided her exit didn't come at the end of a rope.

Silent as a cat, he approached her cell. He preferred not to wake her if she still slept.

A night in prison had not treated her kindly. She sat on the edge of the narrow bed, one elbow resting on her lap, chin cupped in her hand. Her matted hair, lacking any silver luster, snarled around her shoulders. The rumpled and filthy dress wrapped her frame in a mountain of greasy tatters.

"What news, Major?" she asked.

Compassion stirred in Lucien's hardened soul. The once-beautiful goddess now resembled an angel imprisoned in hell.

"Have you reconsidered, *señorita*? Would you like to tell me what you've done with Lyncoya?"

With a heavy sigh, she turned in his direction. Huge purple hollows rimmed her dirty cheeks below her eyes. "I've told you a hundred times, Major. I don't know where Lyncoya is."

Frustration pounded his skull. Didn't she realize the longer she held her tongue, the closer she put her neck to the hangman's noose?

"Marisa, please. I understand your resentment toward the general and the Red Sticks. But you cannot use that anger to harm an innocent child. Tell me where I might find Lyncoya."

Her dim eyes narrowed. "I...don't...know." She enunciated each word as if speaking to Santos. "I did not take the child."

All patience disintegrated, and he grabbed the cool cell bars hard enough to yank them out of the wall. "Dammit, I know you took the boy!"

The bitter sound of her laughter smacked the stone walls and rippled his spine. "Do you honestly believe I would harm a child?"

God, he hoped not. "I don't believe you'd intentionally harm Lyncoya. I think you saw him playing alone and seized an opportunity for one last jest at the general's expense. But this is no jest, Marisa. This is kidnapping."

Face ashen, she flung her arms wide, encompassing her cell. "Look around you. *This* is kidnapping. Why do you keep insisting I took this child? I didn't even know General Jackson and his family were in Pensacola."

"The general is still in Tennessee, waiting for word regarding his son's whereabouts." He took a breath and allowed her a chance to recant her feigned ignorance. Nothing. She didn't even blink.

"Well, then, ask anyone, Major," she snapped. "You'll discover I haven't been in Pensacola for nearly eight weeks now."

"Plenty of time to travel to Tennessee, snatch the boy and hide him before your return yesterday."

Now she blinked—several times. "Are you saying the boy disappeared in Tennessee?" At his nod, she shot to her feet. "Then why are you looking for him in Pensacola? Why do you assume I'm the culprit?"

"Because we found your note."

"Note?" Her fingers rolled over her temples. "What note?"

"The note you left pinned to his pillow. *La venganza es mía.* Sound familiar to you?"

"La Venganza?" Confusion etched her brow. Her eyes widened. Thick lashes batted furiously against her bruised cheekbones. "You think La Venganza kidnapped the general's son? Why? La Venganza protects the innocent. He would never take a child from his mother. That would hurt the very two people he is charged with safeguarding. Such an act goes against everything La Venganza stands for."

He waved a hand. "Stop the pretense, Marisa. I know you're La Venganza."

"You do?" Her pale face split into a grin that reached both ears. "My, what a clever man you are,

Major! Well then, let me begin again." In two steps, she stood before him. Nothing separated them but iron bars and opposing wills. "*I* did not kidnap anyone. I was not in Tennessee. I have never been in Tennessee."

"That's a lie and we both know it."

She sniffed. "Then we have nothing more to say to one another. Good day, Major."

Before he could argue, she settled on the wooden bed, this time her rigid back facing him.

Anger pulsed beneath his flesh, and he turned from the cell. "Perhaps some more time here will change your mind."

****

*Bam! Bam! Bam!*

Lucien bolted upright in the middle of the night. The door. Someone pounded on his door. Senses shot to full alert, he tossed off the bedcovers and padded across the floor. When he turned the lock, Ethan's whitened face popped into the open space.

"Sergeant? What is it? What's wrong?"

"I think you'd better come with me to the calaboose."

He stifled a yawn. "Now? What time is it?"

"It's after one. And yes, sir, I think we should go immediately!"

"I'll meet you in the stable in five minutes."

When Lucien closed the door, hope flourished. Only one event could have Ethan eager to ride to the prison in the middle of the night. Marisa must have confessed. Thank God. After he dressed quickly, he met Ethan at the stable, and the two set off with all due haste.

As Boreas galloped the short distance to the calaboose, Lucien prodded his brain for ideas how to help Marisa out of the morass in which she'd entangled herself.

The general would be furious. Only the calmest

of arguments would sway him from personally wrapping the noose around her pretty neck. Which meant Lucien would have to win over the general's wife. Rachel Jackson could often press her husband to leniency, particularly in the pursuit of justice for women. Since the couple had never received a ransom request, Lucien might persuade them Lyncoya had never been in danger. And if Mrs. Jackson learned of Marisa's experience at Fort Mims, she might champion the young woman's cause out of pity.

Noises of revelry broke his musings, and he glanced around. The nearer they came to the prison, the louder and more merry the sounds became.

"Is there a celebration at the garrison this evening?" he asked Ethan.

The sergeant frowned, black brows drawn together in a grim line. "No." He shot out his arm, finger pointing to the crowds surrounding the calaboose.

Dozens of soldiers staggered over the grounds. Some held tankards of ale, others smoked cigars. Still others stood arm-in-arm, while they caterwauled to rival a crowd of feral cats.

Beneath a swaying palm tree, Santos strummed his guitar. And to his right, Anita danced with Pablo. From the farthest corner of the prison, a slender white hand bounced to the rhythm of the music.

"What the hell...?" Lucien dismounted and tossed Boreas's reins to Ethan. "Stay here."

With angry strides, he stalked to the prison and flung open the door. No guard stopped him. Apparently, the sentry on duty reveled among the merrymakers. Blood simmering, he headed for the rear cell.

Marisa had her back to him. Her hand still floated through the barred window, and her hips swayed to the music. Desire rose in Lucien's core, but rage cooled the embers before they might spark.

"Marisa!" a gravelly voice called from outside. "Will you sing for us this evening?"

"Of course I will, Enrique," she shouted. "Don't you know a caged bird sings the sweetest songs?"

Boisterous laughter erupted.

"There will be no songs for this caged bird to sing tonight," Lucien announced coldly.

She jumped back, and the goblet she'd held sloshed red liquid over her frayed bodice.

"Blast it all, Major!" With the back of her hand, she brushed the liquid down, spreading the stain like blood from an open wound.

When she looked up, a sliver of moonlight framed her glassy eyes. Was she drunk?

As if to answer his unasked question, she raised the goblet. "Would you care for some claret? It's quite de...licious." Her tongue stumbled over the last few syllables

Hell, yes. She was drunk. "No, thank you," he managed through gritted teeth.

She shrugged. "As you wish."

"Damn it all, Marisa." He clamped a hand on his skull to keep his brain from exploding. "Don't you realize the trouble you're in? A little boy is missing, and you invite the soldiers to join you in a celebration?"

"I had nothing to do with that little boy," she exclaimed. "Nor did I encourage anyone to congregate outside tonight."

"While I cannot attest to the former, I will confirm the latter," a smooth voice announced from behind him.

Lucien whirled and found himself face-to-face with an aristocratic man garbed in a pristine Spanish Army uniform. Bright blue eyes studied him from beneath a mane of golden hair.

"I do not believe we've been properly introduced," the stranger said and frowned. "A lapse of protocol on your part. I am Colonel Jose Callava, governor of Pensacola. You should have presented yourself at Government House upon your arrival in our city, Major."

A guilty flush crept up Lucien's neck. "I apologize for my discourtesy, Colonel, but my business here is quite urgent."

The governor's lips twisted in a grimace. "Yes, I've heard. But the kidnapping of your general's son is no excuse for bad manners."

"Perhaps not, but it's no cause for a celebration either," he retorted.

The governor jerked his head at the window and folded his arms over his chest. "The people gathered to soothe the *señorita's* fears, to relieve her loneliness. Do you have a valid reason for imprisoning this city's most loved citizen within the calaboose?"

"The *señorita* kidnapped General Jackson's son."

The goblet fell to the floor with a clatter, and Marisa flung herself at the bars. "I did no such thing."

The governor's frown deepened. "This is a serious charge, sir."

Lucien arched a brow at Marisa. "Would you care to tell the governor about your clandestine activities?"

Hatred spewed from her eyes like venom. But she kept her lips closed and shook her head. So be it. The tale would have to come from him.

"The reason I believe she is the culprit, Colonel, is because your city's most loved citizen is, in fact, the cunning villain, La Venganza."

Eyes wide with surprise, the governor turned to Marisa. "Is this true?"

She didn't reply, merely dropped her gaze to the

goblet and the spilled red wine soaking the straw. But the colonel's scrutiny diminished her. Already petite, she now shrank into herself. Pity stabbed Lucien, but he reminded himself that he was not dealing with an innocent young lady, but a cunning saboteur.

The governor sighed in defeat. "I wish to be kept informed of your investigation, Major."

*"For in the silent grave, no conversation,
No joyful tread of friends, no voice of lovers!
No careful father's counsels, nothing's heard
For nothing is, but all oblivion,
Dust and an endless darkness."*
— *Beaumont and Fletcher (Tragedy of Thierry and
Theodoret)*

## CHAPTER 18

Lucien returned to the calaboose the next day with a large wicker basket, which he placed on the floor outside her cell. The sweet aroma had intoxicated him all the way here, and he hoped the contents would have the same effect on Marisa.

Today she reclined on the planked bed. One arm tossed over her head revealed a gaping tear in her worn sleeve. If she stayed here much longer, her clothing would disintegrate. His stomach twitched, and he pushed the thought away.

She twisted to stare at him through one eye. "You may as well turn around, Major. I still don't know what happened to Lyncoya."

"What say we forget about Lyncoya for a while?" He pushed the basket forward until the wicker brushed the iron bars. "Anita made you something to eat."

With a low groan, she rolled onto her side and drew her knees against her chest. "No, thank you."

"I believe she called them *plátanos.*" In an effort

to entice her, he took one from the basket. "She said they're your favorite. She also said they'd soothe your stomach after last night's indulgences."

Slowly, she sat up and reached for the food. Pink circled her chalk cheeks. "I don't normally drink..."

He remembered the night he heard her choking on the whiskey and bit back a smile as he passed her the fried plantain. "Eat. Then we'll talk."

While he watched her bite into the crispy treat, he dragged a chair toward the cell. Her eyes closed, this time in an expression of rapture, and then she swallowed.

"What do you want, Major?" she asked. "I've already told you I had nothing to do with what happened to Lyncoya. No matter how many times you visit me, I can't tell you what I don't know."

He ignored the question and sprawled in the chair, legs outstretched on the slimy floor. He had to fight to keep his disgust masked. But if she could bear this hell, he would do no less. He pasted a bland expression on his face. "Have you ever been to New Orleans?"

She took another small bite, chewed, and swallowed. "No."

"My brother and his wife live there with their four children."

Her face screwed up as if she'd tasted something sour. "How wonderful. I lost my brother and his wife at Fort Mims. Their first child would have been born a few weeks later—if he'd been allowed to survive."

Lord, she did know how to make things difficult, didn't she? With a sigh, he pressed on. "My sister-in-law is an amazing woman. She has survived the most horrific experiences life can bestow upon a mere mortal."

"Oh?" Another bite, another sour look. "Was she at Fort Mims?"

"Fort Mims is *your* tragedy," he replied. "But

you are not the only person who's ever suffered misfortune in life. Like you, Antoinetta survived a horrific past. But she didn't let her pain eat away her future. And of course, my brother, Darian, helped see her through her hardships. When two people trust each other, there is no problem they can't solve together."

He gave her a moment to digest what he told her along with her *plátanos*. She seemed to do just that, chewing slowly.

Finally she swallowed and sighed. "Your sister-in-law is a very lucky woman, Major. But I still can't tell you where Lyncoya is."

Dammit. He straightened in the chair and scrubbed a hand over his face. How could someone so clever be so foolish? "Marisa, you must realize the longer you hold onto the boy, the less I'll be able to help you."

Her exasperation exploded in a load wail. "Why won't you believe me? If I knew where Lyncoya was, I'd gladly tell you. But I don't."

"All right then," he replied. "If you didn't kidnap Lyncoya, where have you been the last two months?"

She crumpled before his eyes. One finger twirled into a filthy hank of hair, round and round and round. "Are your parents alive, Major?"

Questions flooded his head, but he gave her the opportunity to drive this conversation wherever she felt comfortable. "No. My father died when I was three. My mother passed away more than ten years ago."

She rose from the bench and leaned against the bars of her cage. Tears rolled in silver streams down her dirty cheeks. A dart of remorse shot his chest. He couldn't catch his breath, and each inhale filled his lungs with damp despair. God, how could she bear staying in this hell? All she had to do was tell him the truth and he'd release her. She had to know that. So why did she continue to cling to the same lie?

"When I escaped from Fort Mims," she said, her voice a mere whisper, "there was no time to see to the dead. We feared the Red Sticks might return to capture us. We were forced to run for our lives. Before we could see to a decent burial." The tears became a flood, and her shoulders shook violently with her sobs. "I left my family to rot in the dirt that day. As carrion for the vultures. I have no crypt, no gravesite, no headstone to mark where they lived or where they died."

"I'm sorry," he murmured. "I understand your pain—"

"You couldn't possibly understand!" Her forehead bent to the bars. "I never gave my family the burial they deserved. Dogs, wolves, and birds of prey have picked through their bones and strewn them wherever they may."

Lucien winced. No wonder she spent so much time at her aunt and uncle's graves. They represented the only marking place for all she'd lost.

"*El Castillo de Oro* stands as proof my family lived and loved before they were slaughtered. *That* is where I've been, Major. I was nowhere near Tennessee. I was at *El Castillo de Oro* and Fort Mims. I go there every year to pay my respects."

With no other choice, he rose. "That's a touching story, Marisa, but it's not the tale I want to hear from you."

He walked away then, leaving her sick and vulnerable. Self-hatred flared inside him. Bile ate his insides. But he needed to know about Lyncoya. Until she told him where to find the boy, he refused to listen to anything else she might say, no matter how pitiable.

**\*\*\*\***

Outside the calaboose, Ethan lounged against

the wall, arms folded over his chest. "Has she told you anything yet?"

Lucien shook his head. "She still insists she knows nothing about Lyncoya."

Ethan's lips drew into a grim line. "She'd better sing a new tune quickly. While you were with her, the general's messenger arrived. The Jacksons received a ransom note. La Venganza is demanding five thousand dollars for Lyncoya's safe return. General Jackson doesn't wish to wait any longer. He wants her to release the boy. If she doesn't release Lyncoya by the end of the week, the general has ordered us to execute her."

An icy chill passed through him. No. Surely they'd grant him more time. He'd need to find this messenger, tell him to ask the general for patience. Marisa couldn't hold out much longer. She was already so fragile. A few more days might break her. But he needed the luxury of time.

Frantic, Lucien surveyed the grounds. Although several Spanish uniforms clustered near the calaboose, no one he recognized from the Volunteers lingered nearby. "Where's the messenger?"

Ethan's face flamed red. "I...er...I sent him back to Tennessee."

Grabbing Ethan by his shirt collar, he shook the younger man until his teeth rattled. "You did what?"

"I sent him back to Tennessee."

"Why in the hell would you do that?"

Ethan pried at Lucien's fists to remove his grip. "I...I didn't think."

"You didn't think?" Lucien released his hold, and Ethan stumbled against the stone wall. "What was there to think about? You simply accepted a strange man's word that the general wants us to execute a young woman? How does he even know about Marisa?"

"He doesn't." Ethan shook his head as if to clear

fog. "The general's order was to discover La Venganza's identity and then execute him as a war criminal."

Disbelief rose in waves. "Did he give you any written orders?"

"Well, no, but—"

Lucien paced the dusty ground, and he raked his hands through his hair. "By God! Do you honestly believe the general would order us to hang a woman? Hell, she's barely a woman. She's a young girl in way over her head and scared to death."

Ethan blocked him, hands on his hips. "She kidnapped Lyncoya. She's asking for a ransom from Major General Andrew Jackson for the boy's return."

"I'm well aware of the charges against her, Sergeant. You don't need to remind me."

"Apparently, someone must," Ethan snapped.

"I'm in charge of this investigation. The general entrusted me to bring his son home safely, and I will do so, but it will be done my way!"

"Your way of handling this is getting us nowhere. You're no closer to finding La Venganza now than you were a year ago. Lyncoya has been missing for more than three months. If threatening to execute Marisa forces her to release him, I'm all for it. 'Don't be swayed by a pair of pretty green eyes.' Isn't that what you told me?"

Lucien shook his head. "I won't follow such drastic orders without written proof from General Jackson."

"If you won't," Ethan replied, eyes as inscrutable as a snake's. "I will. La Venganza has six days to release Lyncoya into our custody. If she doesn't, on the seventh day she dies. And if I have to, I'll personally tighten the rope around her neck."

\*\*\*\*

Boot heels thudded near her cell, and Marisa peered through the bars as the shadow loomed closer. Accustomed to the major's lighter, steadier gait, she suspected these boots belonged to his cohort. No surprise then when Sergeant Greene's dark scowl came into view.

Brimstone smoldered behind his eyes, and she wrapped her arms around herself to ward off the chill that seeped into her bones. "Where is Major St. Clair?" She strained to look behind the sergeant's broad shoulder.

He kicked the chair beside her cell, and it tumbled into the corner. The resounding crash made her flinch.

"Since your pretty face tends to distract him from his objectives, he's seeking answers elsewhere while I take over your interrogation."

At her tallest, she couldn't look him squarely in the eye. Nevertheless, she straightened her spine and offered him a level gaze. "It wouldn't matter if God demanded answers. I didn't take the boy. I have no idea where he is or what happened to him."

Greene snorted. "You may have been able to bat your lashes and play the innocent with Major St. Clair, but I'm not so easily led. The general received your ransom request, *señorita*. Now where is Lyncoya?"

"Ransom?" Her heart plummeted. A ransom request was akin to her death decree. Unless someone found the boy soon, they'd execute her. "H-how...?" Her voice cracked, and she swallowed hard. "How long?"

"You have until Sunday evening to reveal the boy's whereabouts."

Sunday. Six days. Dread rose in a ball of bile, scorching her throat. "And if I cannot?"

"You'll be hanged at sunrise on Monday."

Hanged! Her mind blanked, and she gripped the bars to keep from sinking onto the lice-infested straw at her feet. Hysteria claimed her. Seven years ago, she'd eluded death when she'd been at Fort Mims. Now death would take his due because she'd been at Fort Mims. Again. She erupted in maniacal laughter. How absurd!

The sergeant's expression turned icy. "This is no jest, Marisa. Do you think it will be funny when your pretty little neck snaps like a twig as you dangle in the air? You find humor in the idea you'll gasp for breath, writhing in agony at the end of a rope?"

His vivid reminder sobered her. "No, I do not. But I think you should know you plan to hang an innocent woman. I hope you can live with yourself after my death."

He smirked. "My conscience is quite clear. General Jackson sent an order for your execution. By this afternoon, Colonel Callava will have been advised and will have no choice but to concede to the General's request."

"*Debo rogar. Madre de Dios, ayúdeme. Encuentra al niño antes de que sea demasiado atrasado.*" I must pray. Mother of God, help me. Find the child before it is too late.

Taking solace in the prayers of her childhood, she recited Spanish litanies learned so many years ago. At a happier time, in an idyllic place.

"Forget your prayers for the boy," the sergeant told her in kind. "Better you pray for entry into heaven. God alone can help you now."

Only after his boots retreated from the prison did her mind grasp the improbable. Sergeant Greene had spoken to her in flawless Spanish.

*"Each Morn a thousand Roses brings, you say;*
*Yes, but where leaves the Rose of Yesterday?"*
*— Omar Khayyam (Rubaiyat)*

## CHAPTER 19

The next five days crawled on a tortoise of endless boredom. With nothing but four stone walls and personal demons to face day in and day out, little wonder many prisoners went mad. Despite Marisa's pleas for the comfort of their company in her final hours, the major refused to allow Santos or Anita to visit the calaboose.

Outside her cell, the scaffold stood. Its shadow creased the slice of sunlight piercing through her window. At night, skeletal hands reached for her in her dreams. Icy bones wrapped around her throat, drew the breath from her lungs. Desolation became her only nighttime companion. Death hovered. And she could not stop the progress.

Only one person did not abandon her. The major came to her every day. He always brought her food from Anita, and he always left minutes after she insisted she knew nothing about Lyncoya. Part of her burned to tell him her suspicions regarding the sergeant, but unsure on which side of this tragedy he sat, she didn't dare. Her one hope lay in a priest. Even the odious Sergeant Greene could not deny her the last rites before her death. And once he'd heard her confession and cleansed her immortal soul, she would reveal what she'd learned about the sergeant.

On the morning before her execution, the major sank into the chair outside her cell, his stubbled face drawn, deep shadows beneath his eyes.

"You look tired, Major," she greeted him.

He offered her a sad smile and pointed an index finger in her direction. "You don't look so well-rested yourself."

Her hands trembled, and she hid them inside the folds of her shredded gown. "By tomorrow, I'll have eternal rest."

"Let's not talk about tomorrow."

Relief coursed through her veins. Too many reminders of tomorrow prevented her from serenity. Too many reminders of tomorrow summoned the dread she'd struggled to keep at bay all week. The gray stone walls closed in on her. How many others had spent time in this cramped, filthy box before taking that last walk to their deaths? Had anyone received a pardon at the last moment? Would she? Would Lyncoya be found alive and well before they hanged her?

Feet too itchy to stand still, she paced before the bars. "What shall we talk about? The weather? Has it rained recently? Or is it still hot as Hades outside?"

"Let's talk about La Venganza."

Surprise halted her in mid-step. "La Venganza? Why?"

He shrugged. "Why not?"

"Because there is nothing to say about La Venganza. You already know all there is to know about La Venganza. Everyone who felt his sting only did so after abusing the innocent. Even your general and those Seminoles. They allowed the victims of Fort Mims to be forgotten. Your general's pride means a great deal to him. To lose face in front of his neighbors must have caused him some distress."

"You were responsible for all of it? The boots? The alligator? The mare?"

"Every last prank."

"Even what happened to me?"

Despite her grim circumstances, she smiled at the memory. "Especially what happened to you."

He leaned back in the chair. "How did you manage to carry me down to the stables?"

"Santos helped." She swiftly raised her right hand. "But I swear it was the only time he rendered assistance. Please don't hold it against him." How foolish of her to forget those whose fate she still held with her silence!

He nodded. "Whose idea was it to leave me naked?"

Naked? La Venganza had left him naked? Fire consumed her face while her imagination painted a too-vivid picture.

"Mine, of course," she lied. What else had La Venganza neglected to tell her?

"What about the square wheels?" Lucien asked. "You couldn't possibly accomplish such a feat alone."

Thank God, he didn't intend to pursue the stable incident. "Of course I could," she told him. "I simply bribed the wheelwright to tell you a tale. If you had bothered to verify his story, you would have discovered all fourteen wagons, intact, ready and able to transport the general's men home."

To her surprise, he laughed, but no humor accompanied the sound. "Well, you certainly kept us all guessing."

"They were simple jests, Major," she said. "I never intended for anyone to be harmed."

He frowned. "What about Lyncoya?"

"What about him? I didn't take the boy. Why won't you believe me?"

His sigh, full of impatience, raised the hair on her nape. "We found the note pinned to the boy's pillow."

"Major, do you have any notion how many of those notes are scattered throughout Pensacola and the Mississippi Territory?" She flung up her arms. "They're everywhere. At the Hermitage, in Mobile, even at Government House. Every time La Venganza struck, he left behind a note."

"That is my point, Marisa. Those notes make it easy for us to link you to Lyncoya's kidnapping."

"Perhaps a little too easy," she retorted. "The note you found might be years old. Did it never occur to you the true kidnapper might have saved that note from another prank? That he waited until an opportune time to take the boy and pin the blame on La Venganza?"

He arched a golden brow and his eyes flashed fire. "You were at the Hermitage before. You left one of your notes in the pocket of Mrs. Jackson's dress. I was there when she found it. Now you expect me to believe another villain slipped into the Jackson household unnoticed, left a note signed by La Venganza that he just happened to have, and then took the child to blame you? To what end? So you might hang? Tell me, Marisa, who hates you so much they'd want to see you dancing on the end of a rope?"

She shuddered, and then sighed. "You're right. I must be guilty after all. Do your duty tomorrow, Major, and *vaya con Dios.*" She waved him off. "Go now. I would spend my last hours with my memories and my prayers."

When he rose, the chair scraped the stones. The screech sizzled through her ears.

He began to walk away, but she called after him. "Major?" He turned, looked at her over one shoulder, his face etched in grim lines. "I would beg one last boon from you."

"What would that be?"

"*Tía* Rosa. I need you to put flowers on her grave for me. I promised *Tío* Miguel I would bring her roses every week until the day I died. She loved them so. If I'm to die tomorrow, I don't want *Tío* angry with me when I reach the gates of heaven."

Sorrow softened his eyes when he nodded. "I'll see to it."

She wagged a finger. "They must be roses, Major. Six red and one white. No more, no less. Promise me. Say the words. Six red, one white."

"Six red, one white," he repeated.

"Ask Santos to fetch them for you. I have dozens of rose bushes in a greenhouse behind the inn." Once more, to be certain he'd follow her directions to the letter, she insisted, "Remember, please. Six red, one white."

"Six red, one white," he said again as he strode away.

Please, God, she prayed, remember the roses.

****

When Lucien approached Santos about the roses, he gained the most cooperation he'd ever received from the bald man. With a gruff nod, Santos led him outside and to the large glass house behind the inn.

Marisa, however, miscalculated. At least a hundred rosebushes—half red, half white—flourished inside. The fragrance of so many blooms, sweet and soft, wafted reminders of the lady herself. His mind swam in a quandary. Honor or justice? Which meant more? Because clearly, within the next few hours he'd have to sacrifice at least one of his morals. Which was the right path? Where in the blazes was Kismet when he needed Her?

While he balanced the scales in his head, Santos, knife in hand, reached for a large red flower. "One dozen red?"

"No," he replied. "I need six red and one white

150

rose." She'd made him repeat the exact combination, for God's sake.

The big man's complexion turned ashen. "Marisa asked you to bring six red and one white rose to the graves?"

"Yes. Why?"

Santos swayed, crossed himself, and then mumbled, *Haz nada, haz nada, haz nada...*

Do nothing? About what? "Santos, what is it? What's wrong?"

He shook his head and quickly cut the required blooms from the nearest bushes. With a slick slide of the knife blade down the stems, he removed the outside thorns before pressing the bouquet into Lucien's hand. "You must speak to them."

Lucien blinked. "Speak to whom?"

"*Señor* and *Señora* Álvarez. Marisa always spoke to their spirits when she visited the graves. You must do the same."

Queasiness washed over his gut. "I'm not certain that's a good idea."

"Oh, but you must, Major. If Marisa asked you to take these roses to the grave, she'll expect you to speak to her *tío* and *tía*. Otherwise she would have allowed me to bring them."

The man may as well have asked him to *raise* the dead rather than talk to them. "What exactly am I going to say?"

Santos shrugged. "You must tell them who you are and why you are here."

"Oh?" He arched a brow. "As in, 'How do you do? I'm Lucien St. Clair and I'm about to have your niece hanged for kidnapping...'? Do you know how ridiculous that sounds?"

A flush crept over Santos's moon face. "I don't think you should speak those words. But it seems to me Marisa wants *Señor* and *Señora* Álvarez to meet you."

"Well, I'm going to have to disappoint them all," he retorted.

Yet, when he knelt before the headstones a short while later, the words came naturally. "How do you do? I'm Lucien St. Clair. Your niece asked me to bring you these." He placed the bouquet against Rosa's marker. "Unfortunately, Marisa cannot be here herself because I've had her imprisoned in the calaboose."

Dear God. Could he sound any more ridiculous? With a muffled curse, he leaned on his haunches. How could anyone expect him to speak to the poor couple buried here? Should he tell them that, after all the tragedies the Álvarez family had suffered, their last surviving member must suffer more? Of course no answer came to him.

He bent his head in supplication. "Forgive me. I don't know what to do."

"You can't allow them to execute her," a voice said from above him.

By the devil! His head shot up, and his gaze locked on Ramon's. A whoosh of air escaped his lungs. "Ramon, what are you doing here?"

Ramon pushed his drooping spectacles up his nose. "You mustn't let them try to hang Marisa."

Lucien shook his head. "It's not in my hands. If she tells us what she did with the general's son, I might be able to save her. As long as she continues to deny her guilt in the matter, there is nothing I can do to stop her punishment for the crime."

"Much like the Inquisition, eh?" Ramon asked bitterly. "If you throw her in water and she drowns, she's not guilty. She's dead, but at least she proclaimed her innocence before witnesses first."

Lucien folded his arms over his chest. "And you're so sure of her innocence, aren't you?"

In direct imitation, Ramon crossed arms over chest. "Of course I am. So are you."

"All I know is a young boy was kidnapped from his home and a note signed by La Venganza was found pinned to the boy's pillow."

Ramon frowned. "La Venganza will never allow you to hang Marisa. Try, and there will be blood in the streets. He's done nothing thus far because he fears for her safety, locked up as she is. But if you or your Sergeant Greene attempt to hang her tomorrow, La Venganza will kill you all. He will never let you hurt her."

Poor besotted fool. Not that Lucien blamed him. If he could protect Marisa from what Kismet had in store for her, he'd gladly do so. In an effort to comfort the old man, he patted Ramon's stooped shoulder. "You don't have to lie for her. I know Marisa is La Venganza."

Mouth set in a wide o, Ramon stepped back. "Marisa is not La Venganza."

"Of course she is," Lucien argued. "I've seen the proof with my own eyes."

"Did I not tell you Marisa is La Venganza's woman?"

Confusion rose like floodwater. "Yes, but—"

Ramon held up a hand. "The pranks were her ideas, but she had nothing to do with their accomplishment. She would tell La Venganza what to do and to whom. La Venganza followed her instructions."

Lucien's jaw dropped. No. He'd pieced the puzzle together. The timing, the letters, everything pointed to Marisa. "What about the seal? La Venganza uses the Álvarez seal on his letters."

Ramon shrugged. "Marisa gave her father's signet ring to La Venganza. The two are quite close."

A tide of anger rose, and he fisted his hands to keep from throttling Ramon. "So who is La Venganza? Pablo?"

The old man's cackle startled the birds from the

trees and sent them flapping in rapid flight. "Can you see that old bear, Pablo, taking orders from a mere slip of a woman like Marisa?"

No. "Santos then?"

"Santos is a simpleton! He is not clever enough to be La Venganza."

He scratched his temple, sharpening his brain. "But La Venganza must be well known here. Else someone would have noticed Marisa speaking to a strange man."

"*Por Dios*, Marisa owns a tavern. She and La Venganza arranged their meetings with no one ever noticing."

"How?"

Ramon pointed at the bouquet which sat so colorfully against the bleak, gray headstone. "Through the roses."

"The roses?"

"A rather ingenious idea, really." Pride strengthened the old man's voice. "When Marisa needs to speak with La Venganza, she leaves one dozen red roses atop *Tía* Rosa's grave. La Venganza replaces the red roses with one dozen white to let her know he'll come to her that evening. He appears at the inn and they speak together with no one the wiser. Six red roses left by Marisa means 'all is well.' Six white roses left by La Venganza means a prank has been accomplished and succeeded."

The conversation from earlier nagged in his brain. "Who put me in the stables?"

"La Venganza."

"Alone?"

"No." Ramon hesitated. "Santos helped."

"And Marisa?"

"Remained snug in her bed throughout the escapade." The old man grinned. "La Venganza wouldn't allow Marisa to participate, given your state of undress at the time."

Much as Lucien hated to admit his mistake, the old man made a great deal of sense. All those rosebushes, the constant visits to the graves. But most of all, Ramon's explanations confirmed his suspicion. When he'd discussed the stable incident with Marisa earlier, when he'd mentioned he'd been naked, surprise had risen in her eyes for the briefest moment. She'd masked the emotion well, but her cheeks had become rosy as she'd lied about her participation. Yes, Ramon's version of the truth definitely made more sense.

"Where is La Venganza now? Where is Lyncoya? Why won't Marisa tell me the truth about the boy?"

Ramon shook his head. "Marisa *is* telling the truth. La Venganza did not kidnap that little boy. You need only consider the timeline, *señor*, to tear the truth from this web of lies. But if you do not hurry, tomorrow you will attempt to hang an innocent woman."

"She's hardly innocent if she's La Venganza's whore."

Ramon's face suffused redder than the roses, and his relaxed stance turned rigid. "She's under his protection. She is *not* his whore."

"If she's under his protection, then where is La Venganza now? Why would he leave her to rot in the calaboose?"

"In order to release her, he would have to reveal his identity. If he does that, you'll hang them both. You've already found them guilty. Do you think La Venganza enjoys knowing Marisa sits in a prison cell? Her pain is his pain. He loves her."

"Well, he has a very strange way of showing it."

"Perhaps. But he will do what he must to save her from a hangman's noose. If you don't stop this madness before sunrise, I promise you, no matter how many soldiers stand in his way, La Venganza will save Marisa. Even if he must kill you all to do so."

He peered more closely at the old man. "Who is La Venganza?"

"I cannot tell you."

Lucien rolled his eyes heavenward. La Venganza engendered fierce loyalties. A sweep of his hand gestured to the flowers again. "You said they spoke to each other through the roses. What does one white and six red roses mean?"

"I imagine Marisa is telling La Venganza not to reveal himself to save her." He pressed a hand to his chest and sighed with dramatic flair. "She's the bravest little girl!"

Another damn message. Like the one Ramon provided. *Consider the timeline.* The full impact struck his brain with the force of lightning.

"Dear God!" Without a farewell to Ramon, Lucien raced back toward the inn. He had so few hours left.

Ramon watched until Lucien disappeared from sight. Alone, he walked from the graves and into the woods. Several moments later, he returned to replace Lucien's flowers with a bouquet of his own. Six white roses in full bloom.

"La Venganza would never allow you to hang Marisa."

*"He who learns must suffer. And even in our sleep*
*pain that cannot forget falls drop by drop upon the*
*heart, and in our own despair, against our will,*
*comes wisdom to us by the awful grace of God."*
*— Aeschylus (Agamemnon)*

## CHAPTER 20

The hinges squealed their displeasure as Captain Herrera opened the cell door. His tall shadow ducked inside and he murmured, "Forgive me, *señorita*. It is time."

Lips moving in silent prayer, Marisa rose from her knees. Fear slammed into her body.

Behind the captain, a contingent of soldiers stood in a solid line, their faces grim.

Beyond them a black-frocked priest intoned from the Bible. "...Yea, though I walk through the valley of the shadow of death, I will fear no evil; for thou art with me; thy rod and thy staff they comfort me..."

Her knees gave way, but the captain steadied her with a quick grasp at her elbow. "Be brave, *señorita*," he whispered. "It will all be over soon."

Throat clogged with unshed tears, she called up some hidden store of courage and walked out of the cell where she'd resided for three long weeks. Each footstep brought her closer to death. But she forced her legs to keep moving, down the corridor, and to the door.

Outside, the sun blinded her. She lifted a shaky hand to her forehead to shield her eyes. Still, only shadows danced in her vision. Slowly, forms took shape, and her gaze locked on the wooden scaffold that waited just for her.

"The Lord is my shepherd, I shall not want; He makes me lie down in green pastures…" the priest droned on.

Her focus honed in on the instrument of death. Marisa looked neither left nor right. She couldn't bear to see the eager faces clustered in the courtyard. Someone wept, but she didn't dare seek out the mourner for fear she'd break down herself.

Trembling fists gathered her skirts, and she ascended the stairs to meet her fate.

When she reached the top, the priest closed his black book and made the sign of the cross over her. "May God have mercy upon your immortal soul." He backed away and stood, hands clasped around his Bible.

The soldiers followed the priest to gather in a somber semi-circle in the corner of the platform.

Only Captain Herrera remained before her. "Forgive me," he whispered, and she nodded.

After tying her wrists behind her back, he dropped a scratchy woolen hood over her head. Oppressive heat and darkness cloaked her. His hand at her elbow prodded her forward, and she stumbled. A second hand grabbed her upper arm to steady her.

One step. Two… Three…

And then, nothing.

No sound reached her ears, though her mind screamed in torment. No breeze rustled the air. The world lay suspended in anticipation.

The rope smacked her shoulders as it fell, and she squeezed her eyes closed to picture her family in her mind. She saw her mother's blissful face, her father's bright eyes. All her loved ones waited outside the golden gates of heaven. Even 'Lando's perfect son, cradled in his mother's arms, reached a hand toward her.

The noose tightened, and she coughed. With no warning, her feet lost their foundation. She suspended in empty air. Her eyes popped open and bulged from her head. She would have clawed her way up, but her rope-bound hands kept her floundering. Knives of agony stabbed her chest. When would her neck snap? How long would she dangle? How long would she wheeze for breath she couldn't inhale?

Red mist floated inside the hood, and at last, a honey-rich voice whispered, "Marisa!"

The pain ebbed, replaced by a sense of peace. Bathed in warm golden light, she floated forward.

****

"Dammit, Marisa, wake up!" Lucien bent over her pallet, hands under her back as she writhed in her nightmare.

Apparently something he said reached through her panic, and she sat up. Her hands gripped his shoulders. She screamed in his ear.

By the devil! He quickly scanned the prison. Thank God, the calaboose remained empty. Captain de Vega had not yet returned from his early-hours tryst.

"Open your eyes, Marisa," he whispered. "You're safe. Open your eyes and look at me."

Her lashes fluttered against his cheek, but when she finally acceded to his demand, sleep still glazed her focus. "You can't kill me yet. I have until sunrise."

"I'm not here to kill you."

She stared past him, at the empty air behind him. "Captain Herrera promised he'd be here. He promised me a priest. I need a priest. I have to tell him what I learned."

He grabbed her bony shoulders and shook her hard. "Marisa, will you be quiet? I'm not here to kill you."

Her struggles ceased. She blinked several times. "You're not?"

Relief erupted in a sigh. "No, I'm not. I'm here to get you out. Now, do exactly as I say. We don't have much time."

Fifteen minutes at best.

Lucien had waited outside the calaboose for hours, seeking a way to free her. Finally, he'd paid a whore to entice Captain de Vega from his post. When the couple slipped out the back door, Lucien crept inside and found the guard's keys, neglected on the desk.

Fully awake now, she drew back from him, surprise in her eyes. "You're helping me escape? Why?"

"Later," he urged. "I'll explain everything later. Hurry! We have to get out of here."

She swung her legs off the pallet. "You believe me, don't you? You believe I didn't take Lyncoya."

At this rate, she'd get them both hanged. He grasped her wrist and dragged her out of the cell. "I know you didn't take Lyncoya. But now, we have to find out who did. Can you run?"

To his amazement, she laughed. "Run?" She flung her arms wide. "Right now, I could fly!"

"Running will do," he muttered and pulled her outside.

****

The fresh air of freedom filled her lungs and cleansed her dirty flesh. After weeks of breathing in despair and sorrow, she inhaled so deeply her chest shot painful reminders for release.

"Marisa!" the major hissed. "This way!"

Apparently she didn't move fast enough because his hand clamped her wrist. and he yanked her

160

forward. Her feet left earth, and then came down again hard.

"Keep low until we reach the safety of the trees," he added.

She had one quick glimpse of the cypress forest that loomed yards away before she ducked her head and bent nearer the ground. Her legs, unaccustomed to activity after her stay in the calaboose, prickled with thousands of hot needles. A stitch pierced her side, and her knees screamed with each impact. Only the major's grip on her wrist compelled her onward. His fingers, warm and strong, seeped courage into her pores.

Once beneath the cover of the massive trees, he pulled her over a deserted rock-strewn path. Her feet twisted on the uneven ground, but she bit her lip to keep the pain in check. Just when she thought she'd collapse from exhaustion, he halted. She stumbled against his back.

Whirling, he caught her in an easy embrace. Through her worn bodice, her breasts rose and fell against his chest. His heartbeat pounded a tattoo, a steady thrum that echoed hers.

Moonlight, a filtered stream from the shadowy canopy overhead, reflected in his eyes and drowned her in an ethereal ocean of molten gold. Odd. She'd once confided to *Tío* Miguel's spirit that Major St. Clair would be quite handsome if he didn't stare at her with so much hatred. Now she beheld the proof of those words. Time suspended while this golden god, all strength and virtue, sheltered her in the safe haven of his arms.

An embarrassed flush crept up her cheeks, and she quickly averted her gaze. Her eyes alit on the two horses standing near the stream. Joy rippled through her blood.

"Tormenta!" She broke from the major and raced toward her sweet, dappled mare. "Where did you come from?"

"Santos said she was yours." Major St. Clair's sultry smile turned her bones to jelly. When he arched a brow, she had to grab the horse's reins to remain upright. "He also said you don't ride a lady's saddle."

The warmth in her cheeks sparked to open flame, but she focused on Tormenta, running her hand over the beast's velvety nose. "Santos talks too much."

His laughter danced along her spine. "I've never in my life met a more laconic individual than Santos. The man behaves as though his words are rubies, each more precious than the one before. And none are shared eagerly."

For the first time in weeks, a smile graced her cheeks. The major's firm hands circled her waist, and she gasped.

His eyes glowed like sun fire. "Let me help you." In one smooth motion, he raised her into the saddle.

"Th-thank you, Major." Heat simmered across her face, nearly boiling her eyes.

"Lucien." His whisper danced down her flesh.

"Thank you, Lucien. Thank you for getting me out of that place. Thank you for believing me."

The fire in his eyes banked, and he bowed his head. "You once said there would come a day when you'd have the pleasure of seeing me beg your pardon for all the wrongs I've caused you. Your wait has come to an end, Marisa. I'm so sorry for what I've done. Can you forgive me?"

Strange how she took no comfort in his apology. Oh, she believed him sincere, but more important matters weighed on her mind. "No, Lucien."

His head shot up. "No?"

"Not until La Venganza is acquitted of the charges against him and Lyncoya is home where he belongs. Only then will justice be served."

\*\*\*\*

Less than thirty minutes elapsed before the silence overwhelmed Lucien. He turned in the saddle and found Marisa had surrendered to her fatigue. Head slumped, hands slack on the reins, she was damned lucky she hadn't tumbled to the ground.

He cursed himself for a fool. How long had he expected her to keep up their harried pace? Slowing Boreas, he allowed Tormenta to align with them. When they rode side by side, he reached an arm and scooped Marisa onto his lap.

"No," she mumbled.

Despite her weak protest, he expertly tied the mare's reins to those of Boreas. "Forgive me, but we need to press on."

Since she made no additional argument, he assumed she understood the wisdom of his words. Especially when she dropped her head against his chest and sighed.

"Sleep," he ordered in a soft voice. "I'll get us to safety."

Having her seated before him should have been no different than taking Corinne for rides around Belle Monde. They weighed about the same at this point. But Marisa was no child, and in a short time, her presence affected him in ways he hadn't anticipated. Her left hand pressed to his heart, her head nestled near his ribs. Each inhale rubbed the side of her breasts against his shirt. The other hand had dropped across the gap between his thighs. Heat settled in his core and roused desire.

In an attempt to move away from her fingers, he squirmed. Her fingers splayed and the movement burned the inside of his thigh. Gentle wisps of her fingertips branded his growing hardness. An evocative moan from her parted lips drew his gaze to her dirty face. She shivered, and a flush of shame washed over him.

Slender before her travail, she now weighed little more than a child. At her ribs and shoulders, her bones poked through the dress's thin fabric. For all the protection of the garment she'd worn since the day of her arrest, she might as well have donned spider webs. He wished he might stop, give her a chance to rest, to change her garments, at least pause long enough to wrap a blanket around her. But he didn't dare.

The more distance between them and Pensacola, the better. Unfortunately, he had no idea where to go. North? South? West? Where would they be safe? Nowhere familiar to either of them. That much he knew.

By now, someone would have noticed her disappearance. A guard would have been dispatched to the inn to inform him and Ethan of her escape. And no doubt, the sergeant would have concluded Lucien had played a part. He swallowed the distasteful lump that rose in his throat.

No regrets. He'd chosen his path.

Another moan from Marisa broke into his thoughts. Their hurried pace must have awakened her. He pulled the reins. Boreas slowed to a halt, and Tormenta, tethered behind, followed suit.

Her grip on his thigh tightened. Her fingers dug painfully into his flesh.

"Mama?" The childlike cry wrenched his heart. "Where is everyone? Juanita! *Gracias a Dios*, Juanita, you're safe. Wake up! It is over. They've gone. We must find the others."

Damn. She dreamt of Fort Mims. Suddenly, she sat bolt upright. A horrified scream ripped from her throat. Birds scattered from tree branches on raucous cries.

Boreas reared, and he struggled to keep hold of the reins while the hysterical woman thrashed in his arms. Once he had the beast calmed, he ran a hand down Marisa's hair. "Easy, *querida*. You're safe."

Eyes squeezed shut, she flung her arms around his neck and wept into his shoulder. "Don't leave me here. Please don't leave me."

"I won't leave you." He gathered her close. "Ever. I didn't come back to Pensacola merely for Lyncoya, sweetheart. I also came for you."

Her cries softened to whimpers, and then stopped altogether.

"I'll keep you safe for the rest of my days."

He lowered his head to gather the reins, and misty green eyes met his solemn gaze.

"You can't stay with me, Major."

*"That's the nature of women...not to love when we love them, and to love when we love them not."*
*—Miguel de Cervantes (Don Quixote de la Mancha)*

## CHAPTER 21

"You must return to Pensacola." Emerald fire sparked from her shimmering eyes. "Right away."

He started, back stiff. "Are you mad? By now I'd wager Captain Herrera has amassed the entire garrison to search for us."

"All the more reason for you to return." She held out her hands, palms up. "Don't you see? You saved my life, Major. I could never repay—"

"Who said anything about repayment?" he snapped.

"Would you please stop interrupting me? I'm trying to tell you something."

"Oh?" He arched a brow at her. "What do you want to say? Now that I've freed you, you have no more use for me?"

Lashes fluttered against widened eyes. "Of course not." Her deep sigh suggested she clung to the merest shred of patience. "I owe you a great debt, Major."

"Lucien," he corrected. At her sharp look, he flushed. "Sorry. Go on."

"You risked a great deal to save my life. And I won't repay your sacrifice by having you branded a traitor."

"I appreciate your concern, but I knew the consequences when I made my decision."

She cocked her head, brow furrowed. "Did you? Did you consider what might happen to your brother, his wife and their four children due to your actions?"

"Nothing will—"

"Never underestimate the law, Lucien. If your general can't find you to punish, he'll seek retribution from those he can reach."

He laughed. *Not with the debt General Jackson owes Captain Angel.* "I sincerely doubt that."

The lines in her forehead deepened. "I know the pain of losing a family," she murmured. "No one should have to bear that burden. Especially not you."

"Admirable, Marisa. But it's too late. By now, Sergeant Greene knows I'm gone. He'll assume I'm involved with your disappearance."

"Not if you return to Pensacola without me." Mischief danced over her lips. "How far away are we?"

"A few hours. But Marisa, we're not going back—"

"No, *we're* not going back. *You* are. Unless..." She arched a brow, a direct imitation of his earlier expression. "Do you have a better idea?"

Embarrassment tightened his throat. "I was thinking we might head west..."

"In other words, no." Any vestige of misery at her trials in prison had extinguished. She sat up higher, her excitement palpable. "We'll need Ramon, of course. He'll be a great help in this subterfuge."

"What subterfuge?"

She waved him off. "Later. Would you help me mount Tormenta, Lucien? We'll make faster time if we ride separately."

Advice his brother had once provided echoed in Lucien's brain. *When a headstrong woman proposes an idea, forget the argument and follow along. You're better off saving your energy to pull her out of trouble.*

Suddenly, he understood La Venganza more clearly than ever before.

****

For the first leg of their journey back, Lucien took the lead. Just after sunset, however, she broke away and urged Tormenta into a gallop through the trees.

"What the—? Marisa! Where are you going? Pensacola is the other way!"

When she passed him, she turned in the saddle. "Come this way. Follow me!"

With no choice, he pulled sharply on the gelding's reins, nudging Boreas onward in the same direction she'd urged Tormenta. "Where are we going?"

"You'll see," reverberated on a joyful laugh.

They kept pace for another mile before she finally pulled Tormenta to a halt. When he stopped beside her, he scanned the dense line of trees for any sign of civilization. Nothing. No noise. No smoke. Not so much as a broken branch. Nothing surrounded them but cypress trees and Spanish moss.

While he studied the scenery, she cupped a hand to her mouth and shouted, "*Viva La Venganza!*"

From somewhere behind the trees a man's voice replied, "*La Venganza es mía!*"

Another shout from Marisa, this one unintelligible to him as English or Spanish, followed by an equally garbled rejoinder.

She flashed Lucien a smile more brilliant than the noon sun. "We may enter."

Enter what? He would have wagered nothing but forest existed for miles. If he had, he would have lost. They'd barely traveled another twenty yards when he found himself on the edge of a small encampment. Two ramshackle cottages, a stable set between them, a patchwork vegetable garden and a hen house sat in the middle of the woods. One man, arms folded over his chest, stood waiting.

Marisa barely halted Tormenta before she leaped from the saddle and, with a squeal of joy, raced toward the man. He limped forward to meet her halfway, pushing his spectacles up higher on his nose. His wizened face split into a broad grin.

"*Montesita, querida*, you are safe?" Ramon opened his arms wide to catch her.

She flung herself into his embrace. "*Sí*, I am alive and well!"

"*Gracias a Dios!*" He gathered her close and kissed the top of her head.

"No, Ramon." She returned to where Lucien had just dismounted. "*Gracias a Major St. Clair.*"

"She is correct, as always," Ramon said and slapped Lucien's back with more than enough force for a man half his age. "*Muchas gracias*, Major. We owe you a debt that can never be repaid."

"That, Ramon," Marisa said with a frown, "is our dilemma."

"Ah." The old man's unwavering gaze landed on Lucien. "You risked a great deal to save our girl from death. We cannot allow such a sacrifice to go unrewarded." He turned to Marisa again. "You have a plan?"

She grinned. "I think so. But first, would you see to our horses, please? I'll take the major to your house. And after the horses are stabled, fetch some tequila."

With a quick head jerk, she gestured for Lucien to follow her inside the smaller of the two cottages. Inside the front room, embers glowed inside a large stone fireplace. One long battered table reigned over two benches. An oil lamp sat at one end beside an empty pewter bowl.

Cobwebs cloaked the corners, and dust lay an inch thick across the mantle. Lucien suppressed a shudder. "Who lives here?"

Marisa sat on the nearer bench. "Ramon."

He removed a handkerchief from his pocket to brush the filth from the bench. A cloud of musty dust rose to cloak the air and tickle his nose. Stifling a sneeze, he left the handkerchief crumpled on the table and sat across from her.

Her eyes glinted in the gloom as she folded her hands and leaned forward. "Tell me, Major. What convinced you I didn't take the boy?"

"First, tell me something. Who is La Venganza?"

She waved a hand. "He's of no consequence right now."

Annoyance prickled his nape like a bloodthirsty mosquito. "I beg to differ. He's at the heart of this perfidy."

Her fist slammed the table. "La Venganza would never kidnap a child!"

Palms down, he slapped the table with both hands. "Well, someone did!" She flinched, and he inhaled to release the anger from his tone. "Why do you protect your lover so steadfastly? He would have let you hang this morning."

"You almost let me hang this morning," she snapped.

"Now, now, children," Ramon drawled from the doorway. "These arguments will get us nowhere."

The old man limped inside. In his arms, he cradled a large earthenware jug and two tin cups. He settled the items on the table at Lucien's hand and eased onto the bench beside Marisa.

*Two against one. Clever.* Lucien sat up straighter, ready to battle them both—the frail old man and the angel from purgatory.

"Let's begin again," Marisa said. "What

convinced you I didn't take the boy?"

Ramon's sharp gaze drew an embarrassed flush up Lucien's throat. "Ramon reminded me to consider the time," he admitted. "You left Pensacola at the end of July. Several of the soldiers at the garrison confirmed that you were at *El Castillo de Oro* until the thirty-first of the month. But Sergeant Greene arrived at my home in mid-August. Fifteen days later. Using that time frame, without wings, you could never have reached the Hermitage to take Lyncoya and still have given Ethan enough time to get to my home in New Orleans."

She smiled, but the expression held no joy. "Which means Lyncoya was kidnapped by one of the general's own men."

The thought had lain fallow in his brain almost since the beginning. Now, with Marisa tilling the soil, the seed blossomed. And while he tried to crush the tiny flower, she encouraged more growth.

"You said the general received a ransom note from La Venganza," she reminded him. "Did it have the rose seal?"

Lucien shook his head. "I don't know. I never saw it."

"Who did?" Ramon uncorked the jug with a pop.

An excellent question. And one for which Lucien had no ready answer.

"Think, Major," Marisa pressed. "When did you first hear about the ransom note? Who told you?"

His brain flipped through the past few days to pinpoint the exact moment. "Ethan was waiting for me outside the calaboose."

"Ethan?" Marisa asked. "You mean Sergeant Greene?"

"Yes. He said the general's messenger had received a ransom request, five thousand dollars, and in retaliation, he'd ordered us to find La Venganza and threaten him with execution if he didn't reveal the boy's whereabouts."

Marisa frowned. "Did Sergeant Greene see the note?"

"I'm not sure."

"What about the messenger?" Ramon asked. "Had he seen the ransom note?"

"I never spoke to him. Ethan sent him on his way immediately after receiving the general's orders. I blistered his ears for that breach of protocol. He won't make the same mistake again."

Ramon poured amber liquid into the cups. "No, I daresay he won't."

"Ramon." Marisa's eyes narrowed. "Why don't you and Lucien share a bit of tequila?"

Revulsion rose in Lucien's throat. With the amount of filth in this place, he had no intention of eating or drinking anything set before him. "No, thank you."

Despite his gracious declination, the old man slid a cup near his hand.

"Drink it," Marisa ordered in a tone laced with steel.

He picked up the cup and stared at the liquid inside. "What is it?"

"Tequila," Ramon replied. "A liquor made from the fruit of the maguey plant."

"For your own benefit, swallow quickly," Marisa said with a smile.

Following her advice, Lucien lifted the cup to his lips and tossed his head back. The liquid scorched his throat and hurled fireballs to his eyes. He coughed and sputtered like a boy with his first dram of whiskey. A chortling Ramon pounded his back until, at last, the pain eased and Lucien inhaled cool air.

He waved a hand to stop the spinal assault, and Ramon's hands moved to refill the cups.

Lucien shook his head. "No, thank you. I'd best

keep my wits about me. This stuff might kill me."

"Drink it," Marisa ordered. "The last thing we want is for you to remain sober. That would ruin everything I've planned." She jerked her head at the cup he still held in his hand. "Drink. Then we'll talk."

Lucien lifted the cup back to his lips, a bit slower this time.

"It doesn't go down any easier if you sip," Ramon advised on a chuckle. "Swallow as quickly as you can. I promise you this time it won't burn as much."

With a suspicious frown, he did as they demanded. He didn't experience the liquid lightning sensation like the first swallow. Still, the liquor seared his tongue and burned a trail to his belly. The moment he put the cup down, Ramon refilled it again.

"Pay attention, Major," Marisa chastised. "I need you to remember what I tell you."

Lucien blinked, but she still remained fuzzy around her edges. "Perhaps you should have waited before you made me drink that fire water. I'm barely able to remember my own name right now."

"Then we're off to an excellent start," Ramon replied and lifted his cup in salute.

*"Male and female have the power to fuse into one solid, both because both are nourished in both and because soul is the same thing in all living creatures, although the body of each is different."*
*— Hippocrates (Regimen)*

## CHAPTER 22

"We must start with Sergeant Greene." Marisa pointed at Lucien. "You'll have to regain the sergeant's trust."

Lucien quirked a brow. "How? The man's not an idiot. By now he knows we're together."

"He'll know nothing of the kind if you pay attention and follow my plan." Her smile, sly yet bright, sent shivers up his spine. "First, you'll spend the rest of today here."

"Oh?" At last, her plan piqued his interest. He reached a hand to cover hers and squeezed gently, suggestively. "Here with you?"

Smoother than a silken glove, she slipped from his grasp. "Here with Ramon, drinking tequila."

He forced a frown. "My idea is better."

When she rolled her eyes as if exasperated with an errant child, he laughed.

"Laugh while you can, Major," she said. "Come tomorrow, you're going to have a raging headache."

Amusement faded.

"Ramon will take you back to *El Castillo* after midnight." Her lips twisted when he tossed another swallow of tequila down his parched throat. "Or sooner, if you've had enough before then."

His brain, wrapped in tequila-sodden wool, barely registered her words. "Had enough what?"

"Enough tequila to be convincing." When Ramon attempted to fill his cup again, she covered the rim with her hand. "Don't overdo it, Ramon. Just enough for the inn's patrons to *believe* him drunk, not enough so he's actually witless. Drunken men reveal more than they should, and we'll need the major to keep to the story I've crafted for his whereabouts today."

"And what exactly will that be?" Lucien asked through a tongue grown thick and furry.

"You've been here since yesterday evening, drinking tequila and hoping to forget the part you played in a woman's coming execution. You will have no knowledge of my escape from the calaboose until your return to *El Castillo*. You haven't seen me, haven't spoken to me, have no idea how I managed to elude the hangman's noose."

Hard to argue with her logic, but one detail niggled like a worm in an apple. "Where will you be while I'm playing the sotted fool for the patrons of *El Castillo*?"

"I'll remain here."

"Here?" He glanced around at the sunlight chinks in the walls, inches of dust, hundreds of cobwebs, and the dirt floor. "Are you mad, Marisa? You can't stay here. It isn't safe."

She waved a hand. Her fingers left colorful vapor trails in the air. "Of course it's safe. No one knows this encampment exists. Any soldiers seeking me will be searching as far from Pensacola as they believe me to be by now."

He shook his head, and tequila sloshed between his ears. "Forgive me for saying so, but you can't remain here alone."

"I won't be alone."

"Never fear, Major," Ramon added. "La Venganza will take care of her. She'll be perfectly safe."

La Venganza? Of course. Once again, she'd played him for a fool.

Rage lit a fuse inside him, and he shot up from the bench, hands fisted. "I should have realized you'd come running back to that bastard's bed."

Ramon rose almost as quickly. His fist slammed the table. "Dammit, Major, that was uncalled for!"

Palms faced outward, Marisa shook her head. "Sit, Ramon. If the major's opinion of me hasn't changed by now, your leaping to my defense will not sway him. Let's keep the discussion on the plan."

Silence ensued. Ramon's eyes blazed through his thick spectacles, hot enough to spark an inferno. Still, Lucien remained cool and unaffected.

"That will do, gentlemen." Marisa's tone was delicate calm encased in steel. "Once you've returned to *El Castillo,* Major, should you need to speak to me, use the roses. Ramon explained their significance, yes?"

Lucien nodded. While his mind heeded her words, somewhere deep inside him, a hunger grew. A hunger only she could fulfill, damn her.

"Have Santos place the flowers at *Tía* Rosa's headstone. He always tends the graves when I'm away, so no one will suspect anything amiss if he's seen there." His expression must have revealed his inner turmoil because she cocked her head, and bright pink stained her cheeks. "Are you listening to me, Major?"

"Oh, yes." His gaze lingered on her lush, parted lips. "But before I become completely inebriated on..." He pointed to the cup. "What is this again?"

"Tequila." Ramon's brow pleated with suspicion.

Lucien nodded again. He strolled toward

Marisa, casually dragging a fingertip across the scarred oaken tabletop. "Before I drink any more of your tequila, I want something in return."

"Oh?"

He took her hand and pulled her awkwardly to her feet. "I saved your life, Marisa. And since I sacrificed all I held dear for you, you owe me a great debt. A debt I intend to collect right now."

****

Trapped in his gaze like a butterfly in amber, Marisa barely breathed. Her equilibrium faltered as if she'd drunk the tequila. Flames flickered in the pit of her stomach. Her mouth and throat dried to grainy sand beneath a desert sun. "W-what do you want from me?"

She didn't have the strength to pull her hand from his grasp. Truth be told, she didn't want to pull away. His thumb slowly rubbed across her knuckles. Heat waves pulsed through her hand, straight up her arm and directly to her heart. Her eyelids fluttered as she waited for him to answer her question.

"One kiss," he said at last, and dipped his head.

His arms wrapped her waist to draw her closer. Resistance melted beneath the fire that sizzled across her flesh. Fine hairs danced on her nape, and she tilted her face toward his mouth. How would he taste? Tart and biting, like his anger? Like the tequila? Or smooth and honeyed like his apology? Like sweet claret?

As if he sensed her desires, he flicked his tongue over her lips slowly, deliberately. She shivered. A thousand delighted sprites danced across her mouth. Her heartbeat fluttered against her ribs. Sparks ignited, and her mind lost itself in a whirl of colorful fire. Her body fell from a great height, and she clutched his shoulders to remain upright. He must have sensed her tumult because he tightened his hold, keeping her safely bound to him. At this sudden closeness, her heart galloped, his seeming to echo hers in thunder and speed, a building crescendo of drums between them.

When his mouth covered hers entirely, she drank him in. She was a parched desert gaining sustenance from a sudden rain. Her soul flew into the air, through the roof, and into the heavens. He leaned into her, so close she felt his muscles tense. His breath became hers, his skin a new blanket around her. They fused together, and she lost herself in the dizzying windstorm entwining them. Like a sapling in the sun, she bent to his will, basked in his glory.

And then his tongue swept into her mouth. Confusion muddied her pleasure, and she pushed against his chest. *Dios*, what had she done? What had he done? What had they done together? In front of Ramon? Shame and disloyalty tightened her bones. With one forceful shove, she broke the major's hold and stepped away from him before he might grab her again.

Ramon's shadow fell across her, but she didn't dare see the condemnation on his face. Instead, she kept her gaze riveted on the major while she commanded her lungs to inhale air at a normal rate. At last, when she'd regained control, she nodded.

"Ex—excuse me." Before either might stop her, she turned and fled the cottage.

****

Long after Marisa disappeared, Lucien stared at the open doorway. What the hell had just occurred? His head swam. Too much tequila and too little sleep.

"Touch her again, and I'll kill you."

Lucien whirled his attention from the empty air to Ramon, who managed to look intimidating despite his stooped posture. Disapproval etched his brow above eyes narrowed to snake-like slits. His fists clenched and unclenched at his sides, as if the old man waged an inner war to hold onto his temper.

At last, Lucien voiced his confusion aloud. "She's an innocent."

On a deep exhale, Ramon visibly relaxed. "Yes, she is. And I intend to see she remains innocent until she weds. I may look infirm, but when it comes to Marisa, I've the strength of ten men. Do not test my mettle, Major."

The threat flew by, as intimidating as a dragonfly. Other more important facts required his attention. "I don't understand. How can she be...? I thought she and La Venganza—"

"Whether or not you think my wrath a detriment," Ramon said, "you should beware of La Venganza. Marisa is very precious to him."

Lucien shifted his weight to one hip. "If she's so precious, why does he involve her in his crimes?"

Ramon arched a silver brow. "Do you think any mortal man could stop her?"

No, probably not. Still... "Isn't he the least put out that she nearly died today?"

With a careless shrug, Ramon turned and poured tequila into two cups. "Why do you think I came to the graves yesterday?"

Realization pierced the fog in his brain like a shaft of sunlight in a gloomy room. "You planned it! She knew I was the only one who could save her, so she had La Venganza send you to manipulate me."

Ramon handed him the filled cup, and then picked up the second. "No, Major. Marisa knew nothing about our conversation yesterday. She was fully prepared to die for La Venganza. But La Venganza was just as determined to keep her safe, as he has these many years."

"And if I hadn't found a way to release her?"

"La Venganza was already making alternate

plans." Ramon lifted the cup in salute, a peace offering. "Instead, he now owes you a great debt."

Lucien tilted his own cup to his lips and drank. The liquor raced into his belly and burst into a meager spark, much like a flint to damp tinder. Melancholy settled around them, a dark cloud that chilled his bones and instilled a need for Marisa's bright presence.

Where the hell had she gone? His gaze strayed to the doorway again, but Ramon's voice gained his attention a second time.

"Let her be," the old man said, settling on the bench with his tequila. "She's perfectly safe here."

"Where is she?"

Ramon jerked his head toward the only window in the room. "No doubt she's planning to bathe before going to bed. I'll wager she hasn't felt clean or rested in weeks."

A twinge of guilt flared, but concern for her safety far outshone his remorse. "Perhaps I should make certain—"

Ramon's cackle raised gooseflesh on his neck. "This is La Venganza's camp. She is safer here than anywhere else in the world."

The reminder of the villain's proximity incited a furious need inside Lucien. His fists curled, ready to pound something—*or someone*—into broken bits. But he forced a calm tone and offered Ramon an expression of boredom. "Where is La Venganza? Will I ever meet this phantom face-to-face? Or will he continue to hide behind a woman's skirts?"

Ramon showed no reaction to the obvious barb. He stared into the contents of his cup and said, "La Venganza will no doubt show himself to you eventually. But not until you've proven yourself worthy."

Caught in mid-sip, Lucien sputtered. The fire water scorched a path into his lungs. "Worthy? Who the hell is this criminal who deigns to pass judgment on me?"

A brief smile twisted Ramon's lips, and then quickly disappeared. "Who he is doesn't matter. Sit, Major. I have other matters I wish to discuss with you and your present position awakens the stiffness in my neck."

Curiosity propelled Lucien to take a seat across from the old man. When he'd complied, Ramon removed his spectacles and glared with an intensity that made Lucien fight the urge to squirm like a chastised child.

"You must promise me something, Major. You must swear to me before God, you'll do nothing to defile Marisa. You now know for yourself she's as innocent as a child. I want your solemn oath you'll do nothing to change that."

The insult slapped his face as surely as if the words had been wrapped in a glove. "Did you insist La Venganza swear you such an oath?"

Ramon shook his head. "La Venganza does not need to make any such vow. He would never compromise her."

"Nor will I," Lucien ground out.

"You love her, don't you?"

Lucien nearly fell off the bench. "What makes you say that?"

"You saved her life. And you went against your principles to do so. If that's not love, what is it?"

"Justice."

Sliding the filled cup into Lucien's hand, Ramon smirked. "You're a good man, Major, but a poor liar." He waved his spectacles at Lucien. "I don't need to look through these to know a man of honor and integrity. When I first saw you in *El Castillo* I thought to myself, 'Here is a man with a backbone of steel. He will bend for no one.' I admired you for your obvious principles. Marisa, of course, did not."

"She resented me for them," Lucien swirled the amber liquid in the cup. His focus blurred, and a pleasant hum echoed in his ears. "Marisa resents anyone with honor and integrity."

Ramon frowned. "You misunderstand her. She has her own ideas of honor and integrity. You believe in the law and justice, but Marisa does not. She has seen first-hand that justice is too often blind."

So the old man thought to excuse her bad behavior because of her tragic past?

"Does she really think spiked canteens and broken crockery will somehow atone for what she endured at Fort Mims?" He took a hasty gulp of tequila, enjoyed the burn. "Did she expect General Jackson to somehow erase what happened that day because his soldiers fell on their backsides in the mud?"

"He might have at least apologized to the survivors," Ramon remarked dryly. "There's more to Marisa and La Venganza than a few childish pranks. They both despise injustice, but particularly crimes against women and children. Marisa firmly believes women and children are helpless in the eyes of the law. Thus, the responsibility of caring for the weak and helpless lies on the shoulders of those with power and means."

Unbidden, her words in the calaboose popped into Lucien's brain. *La Venganza protects the innocent. He would never take a child from his mother. That would hurt the very two people he is charged with safeguarding. Such an act goes against everything La Venganza stands for.*

Lucien shook the memories from his head. "You're making excuses for her bad behavior, Ramon."

With a sweep of his hand, Ramon pushed the jug and empty cups to the far end of the table. "Since you're in love with her, I thought you might wish to understand her better."

He stiffened. "I haven't said I was in love with her."

"You don't have to." Ramon's grin widened across his sallow cheeks. "You may not wish to admit it yet, but you love her. That's why I ask you for your promise not to compromise her. When you look at her, you may see a woman of one score and three years, but in affairs of the heart, she is still an innocent girl of sixteen."

"The tequila's addling your brain, old man."

"And I'm still waiting for your promise, Major."

At Ramon's continued sappy grin, he added, "Very well, Ramon. I promise not to compromise Marisa."

"Thank you." Resting his chin on his hands, the old man sighed. "Love is a grand thing. Love can make the frailest man strong as an ox. At the merest hint of a woman's smile, love can turn you inside out and upside down. Love changes a man for the better. Not so long ago I shared such a love with a woman I adored."

Ramon's eyes grew misty, and he turned to stare out the window once again.

"The Red Sticks destroyed my love," he murmured. "But I won't let them destroy Marisa."

*"Tis not the drinking that is to be blamed, but the excess."*
*- John Selden (Humility)*

## CHAPTER 23

Lucien awoke the next morning in the worst pain he'd ever experienced. A dozen tiny men ran inside his head, pounding hammers. His mouth, dry as dust, craved liquid, but his stomach sent urgent messages to the contrary. The light of day seared hot needles of misery into his eyes. When he rolled over onto his side, the ocean roared through his brain.

He placed a trembling hand on each side of his head and opened his mouth to groan, but couldn't form a sound. He just managed to stumble to the chamberpot in time for the eruption. If tequila tasted like lightning going down, it inflamed twice as much coming up.

Depleted, he wiped his mouth with the back of his hand and crawled back to his bed. The effort made him too dizzy to climb atop the mattress, so he remained on the floor with his swollen head in his hands.

Somewhere above him, God or the devil—who could tell?—voiced thunderous displeasure. The thunder kicked open his door. Only then did he realize what he'd assumed was some otherworldly being's anger was actually Ethan's violent demands for entrance. Rage smoldered in the air around the sergeant.

"Do you want to explain last night's behavior to me now?"

Lucien buried his head in his knees. "What behavior?"

"Where were you yesterday?"

When he shook his head, pain shot out through his eyes, and he groaned. "I spent the day drinking tequila."

"What the hell is tequila?"

"I think it's Spanish for poison." He managed to use his hands to hoist his head up and peer at Ethan through glassy eyes. "Did I behave in an unusual manner last evening?"

"You came stumbling into this inn on the arms of that old sot, Ramon, cursing and calling me a murderer!"

"I did?" A belch erupted from deep inside his gut, and he mumbled a quick apology to Ethan for his bad manners.

"Jesu, Lucien, you smell like sour wine!" The sergeant waved a hand in front of his face. "How much did you have to drink yesterday?"

He started to shake his head again, but felt something rattle inside and curled his lip instead. His lips seemed to be the only part of his body not in agony. Even the roots of his hair hurt. "I really don't recall. Ramon kept pressing a cup into my hands, and I kept drinking. No one bothered to count."

"We sent out a search party looking for you!"

"You did?" Lucien asked. "Why?"

Ethan rolled his eyes in exasperation. "By God, I never thought I'd live to see the impeccable Lucien St. Clair brought down so low. You've got two day's worth of stubble on your face, and it's a wonder you can focus those glassy eyes of yours. Just look at your uniform." He pointed at the floor with a grimace of disgust. "What's on your boots?"

"Mud."

"I'd say it was something far less pleasant than mud."

Lucien stared at his boots. He said nothing, saw nothing but stars of pain.

"Dammit, Lucien, you picked a hell of a time to get drunk. Marisa Álvarez escaped from the calaboose yesterday."

"She did?" He hoped he sounded surprised by the news. "How?"

"No one knows," Ethan retorted. "The night before her execution, Captain de Vega heard a strange noise and left the calaboose to investigate. An assailant knocked him senseless. At dawn when Captain Herrera arrived to escort Marisa to the gallows, the cell door was wide open and Marisa was gone. The only thing left behind was another one of those damned notes from La Venganza!"

"Amazing!" He tried to smile, but his cheeks cracked under the pressure so he settled for another lip curl instead. "Didn't I warn you she was clever?"

"Yes, well, for a while you were suspect in her disappearance."

He placed a hand over his chest in mock innocence. "Me? Why me?" If the demons would cease the din in his brain, he'd enjoy this game of subterfuge. Marisa was absolutely right. If you kept the lies simple enough, you could fool the world.

"When we discovered you were gone, Captain Herrera assumed you had something to do with her escape."

"Surely you wouldn't believe me capable of such a thing," he remarked.

"Of course not!"

Ethan's eyes told another tale, but Lucien couldn't react at that moment. His stomach roiled again, and he crawled back to the chamberpot.

"Go back to bed, Major." Disgust laced Ethan's

words. "When you've recovered, I'll need your help in finding where the witch may have gone."

Without another word, he spun on his heel and exited the room.

Once the door closed behind him, Lucien sat back on his haunches, smug, but still in too much pain to smile. The conversation had happened exactly as Marisa had promised it would. The entire series of events had occurred exactly as she predicted.

*Right down to the pain.*

He bent over the chamberpot yet again.

****

Another day passed before Lucien could stand erect and still another sun rose and peaked before he managed to walk down the staircase to the first floor of the inn. He finally found his way, in the early afternoon, three days after the aborted execution. By that time, sharp stomach cramps reminded him he'd had nothing to eat for quite some time.

In the quiet tavern, Santos waited with an indulgent grin, a plate of food and some thick black coffee.

"I knew we'd see you today," he said as he ushered Lucien to a chair and placed the tin plate before him. "Anita made you plátanos. Eat them slowly, Major. The sugar will absorb the tequila, but your belly might still be a bit queasy."

"*Gracias,* Santos," he told the bald man.

"*De nada.*" With a conspiratorial wink, Santos returned to the kitchen.

Lucien sipped the coffee and allowed the thick, acrid beverage a chance to rinse out any vestiges of the tequila left inside his battered body. He then turned his attention to the sugared fruit slices, which he found to be quite delicious. Although tempted to shovel the *plátanos* into his mouth as quickly as he could, he heeded Santos' advice and took his time, chewing and swallowing in a methodical manner.

After he scraped the last grains of fried sugar from his plate, he looked up. Ethan stood in the doorway. A tall, scowling man loomed behind him.

"Ah, I see you've survived your night of debauchery after all," Ethan called as he strode toward the table. "One more day, and I thought we might have to fit you for a coffin."

Lucien offered him a wry grin. "You might still get the chance." He kicked out a chair and Ethan sat, with an indication that his peevish companion do the same. "Do yourself a favor, Ethan. If anyone offers you tequila, politely decline and run as fast as you can in the opposite direction. Such cowardice might save your life."

Ethan chuckled, but his companion merely growled.

"Oh, right." Ethan waved a hand. "I don't believe you two know each other. Major Lucien St. Clair, this is Lieutenant Marcus Foster."

Lucien extended his hand. "Lieutenant."

"Major." The man squeezed Lucien's fingers tight enough to crush bone.

"The lieutenant joined the Tennessee Volunteers after you went home," Ethan added. "He's one of the general's most trusted men these days."

Lucien forced his eyes into wide surprise, but pain pounded his temples, and he lowered his lids quickly. "You don't say. How did you gain favor with the general?"

Foster leaned back in his chair. "I grew up in the same city as General John Coffee. He recommended me for service to General Jackson."

"Ah." Lucien picked up his cup. "You're from Richmond, then?"

"Yes," Foster said. "I arrived at the Hermitage in June. Of course, by then, you'd already retired and gone home to..." He cast an uncertain glance toward Ethan. "New Orleans, wasn't it?"

*Tread lightly. Don't let them suspect anything.* "Yes." With his expression hidden behind the cup's rim, Lucien sipped the last of his coffee. "When did you arrive in Pensacola?"

Foster's countenance remained bland. "Ten days ago. I was sent to witness La Venganza's execution. General Jackson demanded a full report in case she decided to confess before the rope snapped her traitorous neck. I'm sure you were as disappointed as I was with the outcome the other day."

He placed his empty cup on the table. "I wasn't disappointed, Lieutenant. A fact Ethan can attest to. I was against the execution from the start. Her disappearance, however, puts us into a quandary. I would have liked more time to question the chit."

He caught Ethan's overeager nod, but Foster ignored the sergeant, beady eyes fixed firmly on Lucien. "Do you believe her claims of innocence then, Major?"

The quiet warning whispered through Lucien again. *Tread lightly.* "Not at all, Lieutenant. But I don't believe executing La Venganza will help us find Lyncoya."

"The General seems to think it will," Ethan snapped. "And I agree with him. The fear of God will get that witch to tell us what she knows."

Judging by Ethan's sudden flinch, Foster must have kicked him under the table, but Lucien pretended not to notice. He leaned back in his chair and rubbed his eyes with his fingertips in a slow, circular motion. "Have you had any luck in locating the wench?"

"None," Foster ground out through gritted teeth. "It's as if the earth opened up and swallowed her. No one has seen her or has any idea where she might be."

"Welcome to Pensacola," he said dryly and folded his hands on the table. "La Venganza has some very loyal followers here. Gaining information is much like pushing the ocean back against the tide. For every step you take forward, you lose two more steps back. I assume no one saw anything unusual near the calaboose that night."

"No," Ethan said on a sigh of frustration. "And Captain de Vega has been no help at all. The man claims his assailant slipped up behind him while his back was turned. He never saw the perpetrator."

Lucien said nothing for a long while, and then craned his neck toward the bar. "Santos? May I have a little more coffee, please?"

"*Sí, señor.*" Santos hurried forward and whisked the cup off the table. With a bow, he backed away and disappeared through the door leading into the kitchen.

Once Santos disappeared, Lieutenant Foster leaned forward and folded his arms atop the table. "Major, we need your help. I'm certain you realize the general will be very unhappy with this turn of events."

"That's putting it mildly." Ethan dropped his chin into his cupped hand. "General Jackson will have our heads if anything happens to his damned Indian boy!"

"Lyncoya has been missing for months now," Foster continued as if Ethan hadn't spoken. "Mrs. Jackson is beside herself with worry, and the general's health is not its best. We must find the wench and make her tell us where Lyncoya is hidden before any more time passes. The problem is we have no idea where to look for her."

"*Buenos días*, Major!"

At the effusive female voice, Lucien turned. Anita bustled forward, a wide smile on her freckled face.

190

"*Cómo estás?*"

Lucien raised her hand to his lips and kissed the back like a knight with his lady fair. "Much better today, thanks to your delicious *plátanos* and coffee."

She pulled her hand away to wag a crooked finger at his nose. "You should know better than to drink with Ramon. A fine gentleman shouldn't be involved with that old drunkard."

He smiled. "Believe me, Anita, I've learned my lesson."

Lieutenant Foster sighed loudly.

Anita shot the stranger a look of disapproval then tousled Lucien's head as if he were a lad. "You should be more careful with whom you associate."

"Oh, for God's sake," Foster sputtered.

Hand held up, Lucien cut off the man's tirade. "Why don't you two go upstairs to Ethan's room and await me there? As soon as I've finished my meal, I'll join you."

"In the meantime, the lieutenant and I will discuss what our next step should be," Ethan said as he rose.

"Make a list of the places you've already searched," Lucien suggested. "We may have to revisit them. If we find nothing by nightfall, we'll spend some time with the drunks in the tavern this evening."

"The tavern?" Ethan cocked his head like a quizzical bird. "What do you hope to find in the tavern?"

He grinned. "Trust me. Under the influence of strong liquor, even the most steadfast advocate may say something he shouldn't. Never fear, gentlemen. La Venganza will not escape us for long. Together we'll find Lyncoya. We'll learn the whereabouts of Marisa Álvarez."

With an arrogant nod, Lieutenant Foster rose and gestured to Sergeant Greene. Mumbling low, the two walked away, headed upstairs.

When they disappeared, Santos returned with the coffee. "Sergeant Greene is the culprit, isn't he?" the bald man whispered.

Lucien barely nodded, and then spoke behind his hand. "And Lieutenant Foster, as well. General Coffee never lived in Richmond. Obviously, Lieutenant Foster has not been at the Hermitage."

"Marisa is never wrong."

He stared up at Santos in surprise. "Marisa suspected Ethan?"

Santos gave a quick nod. "Ramon said I was to pay close attention to anyone seen with Sergeant Greene. He said Marisa believed the sergeant would lead us to the real villains."

"When did Ramon tell you this?"

"The other evening when we carried you up to your rooms," was the low reply. "Marisa wanted you to be very careful in your dealings with the sergeant. She said to remind you he is a dangerous man."

"How did she know that?"

Santos merely shrugged and walked away. Apparently, he'd used up his allotment of words for the day.

But he still had one last important message to relate. When Lucien lifted the cup from the saucer, he discovered six white rose petals scattered beneath it.

La Venganza spoke through the roses.

*All is well...*

*"A man who exposes himself when he is intoxicated,*
*has not the art of getting drunk."*
*- George Crabbe (Inebrity)*

## CHAPTER 24

That evening, Lucien sat with the villains at his usual table when Ramon arrived. "Major! Well, I must say you look much better now than you did the other night." The old man settled into the empty chair. "I warned you tequila has a kick like an angry mule." Without waiting for a reply, Ramon turned his attention to the other two men at the table. "Sergeant Greene, is it not? *Buenas noches.* Welcome back to Pensacola."

Ethan gave a cursory nod. "Ramon. Good to see you again."

Ramon grinned and called out over the heads of the men seated with him, "Santos! I could use an ale."

"Are you paying tonight, Ramon?" Santos growled from his place behind the bar.

"Now, Santos, if Marisa were here, she'd give me ale for free."

At the mention of Marisa's name, Ethan kicked Lucien under the table. Lucien sat up in his chair and nodded. A moment later, Foster had the same reaction. Apparently, Ethan's feet were very busy.

On the other hand, Santos didn't respond as well to Marisa's name. He folded his arms over his chest and glared at the old man. "But Marisa isn't here, is she?"

"So, then you'll have to give the ale to me," Ramon called back with a chuckle. He winked at the three men at the table.

"Where did that minx get to, anyway?" a soldier called. "Has anyone seen Marisa since she escaped from the calaboose?"

"She disappeared like a puff of smoke," a man replied in a tremulous voice. "I believe it was witchcraft."

"It was not witchcraft, fool!" another shouted. "It was *Capitan* Herrera. He's always been sweet on Marisa. He let her go and then made it look like she escaped on her own."

"Bah!" someone else scoffed. "*Señora* Herrera would have his *cojones* for such a deed! It was *Capitan* de Vega."

"*Capitan* de Vega was lying on the ground outside the calaboose, knocked senseless," another voice reminded the crowd. "It was Colonel Callava."

"It was none of them. It was me," a drunken man boasted. "I took Marisa!"

"Oh, really, Enrique?" Pablo shouted. "Where did you take her?"

"I took her to heaven, *amigo*!" Enrique replied, grabbing his crotch.

The room reverberated with rumors and innuendo regarding who might have helped Marisa escape and where she might be now. Lucien shared an amused glance with Ramon while Greene and Foster seemed to swallow each tidbit of gossip as if it might have some substance of truth. Once or twice, they bent their heads together and nodded at something they thought worth consideration.

Over the cacophony, Pablo rose from his chair and added, "I heard she ran away with La Venganza. What a lucky devil!"

"If I'd known I could win Marisa for myself that way, I might have stormed the calaboose for her," another soldier shouted. "Then I would have stormed my way into her heart and under her skirts!"

Gales of laughter erupted from the crowd.

Without warning, Ramon stood. "You're all wrong," he bellowed to be heard over the raucous noise. "*I* freed Marisa from the calaboose!"

Jesu. Lucien could do nothing but stare at Ramon, slack-jawed. Had the old man lost his mind?

"So, where is she now?" Pablo asked, bushy brows arched in disbelief.

"Far away from here," Ramon retorted.

The crowd groaned and scoffed.

"Sit down, old man."

"You've gone *loco* at last, eh?"

"Comes from living alone too long."

"Or spending too much time in the sun."

"Bah!" Ramon shouted at the naysayers. "What do you know?" He thumped his chest. "I know the truth. Marisa is on her way to her home, *El Castillo de Oro*, in Alabama! I know because I sent her there."

Lucien gripped the arms of his chair to keep from falling to the floor, but Ramon only laughed in glee.

****

The soft, sweet voice haunted his dreams. "Major?"

Jolted awake, he sat up in surprise, and fumbled to gain his bearings. Where was he? What happened?

Reality came slowly. He was in his bed at *El Castillo de Plata*. A shadowy figure stood over him. His sleepy eyes drank in her angelic form, recognized every curve, even before his sleep-hazed brain pinpointed her voice.

"Marisa? What are you doing here?"

For a moment, he thought he might still be dreaming. Lately, he'd spent a great deal of time imagining this scenario in his head. He'd awaken to find she stood over him, her eyes glazed with desire and passion. Her arms would reach for him. In his dreams, he'd draw her down upon the bed and kiss every inch of her flesh while her sweet mouth explored him in much the same manner.

But now, a sliver of moonlight fell across her face and glinted in the wells of moisture that shone in her eyes.

"Wait." Lucien drew a dozen deep breaths until he managed to rein in his thunderous heartbeat and rising groin. When normalcy returned, he reached up to light the lamp on his bedside table. A flame flared over her face to illuminate her reddened eyes. Worry lines etched her forehead. "How did you get here anyway?"

"Tormenta."

*By God, did she know what she risked with such a foolhardy trip?*

"You rode that horse here in the middle of the night?" She nodded, as if she'd just admitted to choosing a dress for the day. "Have you no sense at all? Suppose someone had seen you?"

She flipped a hand. "No one saw me. I was very careful."

"How did you get into my room?"

"I climbed through the window." She pointed to the open window in the corner of the room.

"You did what?" Impotent fury leaped into his nerves, and he sat up in the bed. At the quick action, the blanket around him slipped below his waist.

"Sshh!" She whirled from the window and her gaze fixed on his bare shoulders before sliding down his broad chest. Her mouth opened in a wide 'o' at the expanse of skin revealed by the bedcovers.

Instinctively, he yanked the blanket up again.

"If you sneak into a man's bedroom at night, you'd best be prepared to see him at his worst."

"Or his best." A rosy blush suffused her cheeks.

He grinned. "Thank you."

"*De nada.*" Even after she spoke, her gaze remained fixed on his chest.

"You can stop looking now," he said pointedly.

"Sorry." She dipped her head and mumbled, "I've never seen a man without his shirt before."

He arched a brow at her confession, hoping to tease her into a happier mood. "Never?"

"Well, not since I was a child. Sometimes Papa would remove his shirt when he worked the farm. And of course, I had to put herb packets on *Tío* Miguel to ease his breathing, but..."

But even he knew there'd be no comparison between her sickly uncle and his own robust figure.

To ease her embarrassment, he folded his arms over the blanket to keep it in place. "How did you get into my room?"

Her eyes remained focused on the bedcovering for a long moment as if, by sheer will, she could stare through the fabric. Finally, she jerked her head at the window again. "I came in through there. I've been doing it for years."

"You've been coming in my window for years?"

"It's *my* window," she corrected him. "You've only been here for a month. I've lived here nearly half my life. Until *Tío* Miguel passed away, this was my room. And I've been climbing in and out that window since I was a child."

"You're lucky you never broke your pretty little neck."

"I've also managed to avoid having my pretty little neck lengthened by a hangman's noose," she retorted. "I suppose I was born under a lucky star."

"It's a little late in the evening for sarcasm, Marisa," he replied. "Would you mind telling me what you're doing here?"

A lone tear rolled down her cheek.

All thoughts of sleep and dreams scattered, forgotten in the blink of that solitary tear. "What is it? What's wrong?"

She wrung her hands. "I can't find Ramon."

Relief coursed through him, and he relaxed into the featherbed again. "Is that all? The old sot was still in the tavern when I came upstairs. No doubt he's sleeping off his drunk beneath one of the tables."

She shook her head. "He's not in the tavern. Santos said he left a few hours ago." Her lips trembled, and an agonized cry escaped. "Something has happened to him. I know it."

"What makes you think that? Because he hasn't come home yet? Don't fret, little mother. Ramon was quite into his cups tonight."

Her complexion paled. "Why do you say that? What did he do?"

He shrugged. "Nothing terrible."

"What?" she nearly shouted. "What did he do? Tell me."

"Some of the drunks were theorizing about what might have happened to you. They were all boasting they helped you slip away from the hangman. Ramon, the fool, announced he was the one behind your escape from the calaboose."

"What?!" While her hand ran down her cheek, she paced frantically at the foot of his bed. "Damn him for the stubborn ass he is! I told him not to do anything stupid. He said he'd throw them off my trail by leading them somewhere else. I told him you and I would solve this problem together." She stopped, turned to gaze at him again. "Where did Ramon say I went?"

"He said you were on your way to *El Castillo de Oro*."

"No!" She sank to her knees and tore at her hair. "Why didn't he listen to me? Now those scoundrels have him as well."

He started to rise, but remembering his state of undress, quickly pulled the blanket closer. "You don't know that for certain."

"Yes, I do." She covered her face with her hands. "If no one accosted him, he would have returned home by now. Ramon would never leave me alone at night. He knows I hate to be alone at night."

"But you're not alone. La Venganza is with you."

She didn't reply, and he cocked his head to stare at her curiously. "Marisa?"

Still, she kept her face covered. She never looked up, never uttered a sound. Suspicion crawled up his spine on centipede feet.

"Isn't that right, Marisa? La Venganza is with you at the camp, isn't he?"

Nothing.

"Marisa? Where is La Venganza?"

With a deep sigh, she removed her hands. Beneath the amber lamplight, her face reflected earnest fear. "Ramon is La Venganza."

*"Give me a young man in whom there is something of the old, and an old man with something of the young; guided so, a man may grow old in body, but never in mind."*
— *Marcus Tullius Cicero (De Senectute)*

## CHAPTER 25

Lucien laughed. Loud rumbles erupted from his chest and passed through his lips until his sides ached.

Marisa stood up, hands fisted at her sides. "It isn't funny," she shouted. "It's true."

"Forgive me, *querida*," he said through his chuckles. "But the very idea of that feeble, old man being La Venganza is too funny to consider seriously."

"Ramon is not feeble and he's not old!"

"He's eighty if he's a day," Lucien retorted. "And he's as blind as a bat."

"Ramon is not yet thirty. And he has perfect eyesight." Tears streamed down her face and she sniffed, but still they flowed. "He has perfect eyesight, perfect hearing, and a perfect face," she rambled on about Ramon's perfect assets. "He's perfect in every way. Except that he's too stubborn to do what I tell him."

All humor fled, and Lucien stared at her in dismay. It couldn't be true. He couldn't have that wrong about the man he'd befriended. Ramon was a harmless, elderly drunkard. He was a frail, old gossip. He couldn't possibly be La Venganza. The idea was ridiculous!

"No," he said.

"Yes," she insisted.

He shook his head in the negative.

She gave him an emphatic nod in response.

Lucien's mouth gaped open and closed several times, but no sound came out. This tale couldn't be true. Yet, somehow, he knew it was.

"His spectacles?" he finally croaked out.

"Clear glass," she replied.

The centipede of suspicion marched faster. "His limp and his stoop?"

"Affects."

"The white hair?"

"Powder."

A hundred tiny feet buried in his nape and tickled the fine hairs there. "Who is he?"

Hands clasped in prayer, she threw herself against the foot of the bed. "I have to find him, Lucien. He's in grave danger."

"Who is he?"

She drew back and clamped her mouth shut, her lips in a tight line.

"Who is he, Marisa?"

Her fist hit the featherbed, an inch from his ankle. "Are you going to help me find Ramon or not?"

"I'm not doing anything until I know who the man is," he said. "And the truth. No more lies."

She opened her mouth to argue, and then quickly stopped to inhale a deep breath. "As you wish."

When she rose, he folded his arms over his chest and waited. At last. He'd finally learn La Venganza's true identity.

"Go back to sleep, Lucien," she said flatly as she strode to the window. "I'm sorry I disturbed you."

With her palms flat upon the sill, she hoisted herself onto the ledge. She sat there for a moment, studying him through hooded eyes. Then, on a quick swerve of her hips, she flung her legs so they faced outside and pushed off with her hands.

"Jesu!"

Breath raced from his lungs. Lucien leaped out of the bed and sped to the window. He leaned out in time to see her dangle from a wide branch of the nearby sycamore tree.

For a long moment, she hung suspended. His heartbeat thundered in his ears. If she fell from this height, she'd easily break her neck. But she didn't fall. Instead, she swung like a pendulum until her feet touched the crook of the trunk. Once her toes settled in the tree's hollow, she released her hold on the branch. With the agility of a squirrel, she shimmied the rest of the way down until she landed on the ground.

With both feet back on earth, she ran to the knoll where Tormenta stood, tethered to a cypress tree. One graceful leap, and she vaulted into the saddle. A quick snap of the reins, and Tormenta sped into action, carrying her rider into the night.

****

Lucien managed to dress and saddle Boreas in record time. Still he lost nearly thirty minutes before he spotted her. She must have heard the sound of his hooves behind her but she never turned in the saddle. She kept her gaze fixed straight ahead even after he pulled up alongside her.

He might have been mistaken. After all, he'd drunk a great deal of tequila that night. But his senses screamed she rode in the wrong direction, away from La Venganza's secret campsite. "Where we are going?"

She lifted her chin higher in an effort to ignore him. "I don't know where you're going. I'm going home."

The delicate thread of his patience snapped at last. "Fine," he growled. "I'll take you back to the camp and then I can return to the inn, go back to bed, and forget this night ever happened."

She pulled Tormenta to a halt and stared at him. Rage sparked off her skin and crackled the air around them. "I'm not going to La Venganza's camp. I'm going home to *El Castillo de Oro*."

"Right now," he said through gritted teeth, "you'll return to La Venganza's camp. Ramon will find his way home before dawn, and you'll realize how ridiculous you're being."

Her brow steepled. "And if not?"

"If not, we'll search for Ramon together in the morning." He leaned across her to grasp Tormenta's reins and pull her with him. "Come along."

She yanked the reins out of his hand with a snap. "Don't ever touch my horse!" She pulled on the reins and gave Tormenta a nudge to start her forward again. "Go back to your soft bed, Major. I'm not being ridiculous. I know something's wrong, and I'm going after Ramon."

"You and I will both go after Ramon in the morning."

"By morning, he might be dead!" she shouted. "They already have a head start on me."

His head spun. "Who has?"

"Your friends, Greene and Foster. Who do you think waylaid him? Those heartless bastards will kill him if they discover the truth. I have to get to *El Castillo* before they do."

"Wait." He needed time. Time to understand. Time to stop her from whatever foolhardy plan she'd concocted in her addled head. "Tell me something first. Why did Ramon tell everyone you're at *El Castillo*?"

In the silent evening, her sigh rustled like crisp

autumn leaves trod underfoot. "He thinks they'll attempt to trade Lyncoya for La Venganza. That's why I must go after him."

"What about the rest of La Venganza's men? Where are they? Are they going with you?"

Marisa shook her head. "There are no others. It's always been Ramon and me. There's no one else."

He was only surprised her confession didn't shock him more. Perhaps, deep in his heart, he'd always known. But that didn't mean he'd allow her to rush headlong into danger. "You can't travel alone. It's not safe. Do you have any notion of the dangers involved? There must be hundreds of ways to die out in the wilderness. There are Indians, wild animals—"

"I'm well aware of the dangers," she interrupted. "I'm not a child. I'm a grown woman."

"A grown woman alone makes an easy target. Do you know what kind of criminals might be waiting to ambush you?"

"They couldn't be any worse than the criminals who ambushed Ramon. Don't you see?" Raw pain scraped her words. "I have to go after him. He's all I have!"

Her every emotion, the anguish and desperation in her speech, sliced his heart to ribbons. Envy stiffened his spine, hardened him to her tears.

"You love him very much, don't you?" he said gruffly.

"With all my heart," she replied.

He sighed. "Then I'll help you find him."

****

Lucien considered it a minor victory when he convinced her to stop at La Venganza's camp for a short while. "We can't ride posthaste to Alabama with nothing but the clothes on our backs. We need food, bedrolls, clothing, and supplies."

Her eyes narrowed as she considered his advice. Finally, she slumped in her saddle, an obvious signal of defeat. "Very well. But we're not remaining there until morning. We'll be on our way long before dawn."

Once they arrived at the site, she rode straight to the stables. Inside, she dismounted Tormenta and led her into one of the far stalls. With the saddle removed, she rubbed the mare down, brushed her coat until it gleamed, and gave her fresh water and oats. Never saying a word to him, she strode outside.

He watched her go with wry amusement, and then turned his attention to Boreas. He led the gelding into the stall beside Tormenta. All the necessary equipment needed to tend the horse sat stored neatly on a shelf above his head.

When Boreas was stabled and prepared for a rest, he tracked Marisa's footsteps to the larger of the two cottages, the one she'd run to after their kiss a few nights ago. Cautiously, he walked inside. His surroundings struck him dumb. The room was absolutely lovely. A large mahogany dining table with six ornately carved chairs ruled over an eclectic array of furnishings. Two settees upholstered in deep red velvet flanked a writing desk. Behind the dining table was a massive fireplace built of gray stone and what appeared to be black obsidian. Marisa had already lit the lamps on either side of the mantle, bathing the room in a soft, mellow glow.

Above the mantelpiece hung a portrait of an imposing man astride a large white stallion. The artist had captured an air of nobility in the posture of the rider seated upon the beast. The man wore a black, short-waisted jacket with a dark red shirt beneath, black breeches and black leather boots. Upon his silver head sat a wide-brimmed, black hat. In the painting he smiled, but he appeared to have a stern countenance in apple green eyes above a well-tailored beard.

"My papa," a voice said from the doorway. "Don Carlos Ramon Orlando Álvarez."

Lucien whirled. Marisa stood on the staircase. She'd changed into a dark green riding habit and carried several blankets over one arm. After she tossed the blankets on one of the settees, she walked toward the portrait. Even in the dimly lit room, she couldn't hide the glisten of tears in her eyes.

"That was painted the year I was born," she said with a nod. "Papa was such a handsome man. He seemed very gruff to outsiders, but to me he was always wonderful. He had a laugh that rumbled up from deep inside. Sometimes, I'd sit on his lap and listen to his heart beat against my ear. Eventually, I'd always drift off to sleep." A wistful smile, full of longing, creased her features. "He was so wise! Except for my cooking skills which I learned from Mama, Papa taught me everything. Languages, literature, mathematics, horsemanship, hunting. He shared all his knowledge with 'Lando and me."

A chasm split inside Lucien's chest, and he dropped his gaze to the floor. "I have only vague recollections of my father," he admitted ruefully. "You're lucky to have your memories."

"Sometimes memories are not enough," she said on a sigh. "The hardest times are evenings. That's when I miss our Shakespeare debates."

Curiosity snapped his head up. "Shakespeare debates?"

"Each night after dinner, we'd sit around the fire." She pointed to the floor. "I would sit here with Papa on my left and 'Lando on my right."

"Where would your mama sit?"

"Mama sat in a chair beside us. Papa said a queen such as Mama never sat lower than her subjects. It wasn't aristocratic."

"How exactly did you have Shakespeare

debates?"

"Every night, Papa would choose a different topic. Wealth, perhaps, or love, or royalty. And we'd each quote a line from a Shakespearean work pertaining to the topic." Her smile beamed with pride. "I always won. Papa used to say I shouldn't marry until I found a man who could best me with Shakespeare."

"Could Tomás best you?" Lucien hated himself for asking, but he needed to know.

She stared at him as if he'd suddenly grown two heads. "No one could best me, not even Papa." She kissed her fingertips and pointed them at the portrait before turning away. Sadness enveloped her again. "I can't lose Ramon. I've lost everyone else in my life. I won't lose him."

"I promise you," Lucien said fiercely. "We'll find him."

With one last look at the portrait, she sighed. "Wait here. I'll gather everything we'll need for the journey."

She left him to ponder the portrait and all he'd learned in the last few hours.

*"They would talk of nothing but high life, and high-lived company, with other fashionable topics, such as pictures, taste, Shakespeare and the musical glasses."*
— *Oliver Goldsmith (The Vicar of Wakefield)*

## CHAPTER 26

When they set off for Alabama, Lucien allowed Marisa to lead. Thus, they rode through the night and well into the next morning. She only stopped to water the horses and stretch their legs. Late in the afternoon, she pulled Tormenta to a halt beside a creek. "We'll camp here for the night."

She dismounted, and he followed suit. Her choice of locale seemed a good one. The site had a cool, running stream for water, thick, leafy trees for cover, and lush grass. While she tended to Tormenta, Lucien ran a hand over Boreas's coat from neck to legs. No injuries. He checked the gelding's shoes for stones, and then strode to the creek's edge. After pulling up handfuls of grass, he rubbed the sweat from the horse.

From the corner of his eye, he watched Marisa tend to her mare in the same manner. Finished, she sat on a flat boulder beside the creek. Legs stretched out, booted toes flexed, she leaned on her arms and stared over the water. Her dejected sighs left him no doubt about where her thoughts lay.

"How much of a start do they have on us?"

Turning, she shrugged. "Ramon left the tavern

well before midnight. If he was ambushed immediately after he left, they could be over ten miles ahead of us by now."

"That much?" He hadn't intended to sound so overwhelmed by her answer.

"Maybe not." She picked up a pebble, skipped it across the creek's surface. "Ramon's excellent at convincing others he's a frail old man who needs to rest often. If we continue our pace, we should overtake them and arrive at El Castillo long before them. Ramon will slow them down with his antics. He can be very troublesome when he wants to be."

"What's to stop them from killing him if he becomes too troublesome?" He wanted to bite off his tongue when he realized what he'd said and to whom.

But her expression never changed. "They need him to find me. Don't forget they believe *I'm* La Venganza. They have no interest in Ramon except as a means to an end. It's me they seek."

\*\*\*\*

Night fell, wrapping them in black velvet. The only noises came from the soft rustle of hidden creatures finding their beds and the occasional pops of their campfire. Marisa, ever stoical and thoughtful, sat upon her bedroll, legs folded beneath her riding skirts. In her hands she held a dead stick, which she used to draw in the dirt around her.

Lucien's bedroll lay on the opposite side, but he felt no urge to crawl into its cocoon and sleep. Instead, he sat beneath a large poplar tree to watch her.

"Santos told me you suspected Ethan was involved in the kidnapping from the start," he said. "Why?"

She looked up from her latest masterpiece, frowned. "When I was imprisoned at the calaboose, he came to see me."

"I remember." Lucien nodded. "He insisted my methods to find Lyncoya weren't working and he'd get the information from you."

"Yes, well, in his haste to get his information, he made a vital mistake," she said with a grim smile.

"Oh?" Curiosity roused inside him. He simply had to know how her clever mind worked. "What was his mistake?"

Emotions played across her face and danced beneath the light of the flames. "He described my hanging in great detail." Her forehead creased at the memory. "I think he meant to intimidate me."

Fear. Lucien saw fear in her eyes. Never in a thousand years would he have expected to see fear. And he wouldn't allow it now. "But he didn't intimidate you, did he?"

"Yes, he did," she murmured. The stick dug deeper into the ground, prying up loose stones and clods of dirt. "I tried not to show it. But I honestly don't know if he knew how much his words affected me." She looked up, eyes bright with tears. "I don't want to die, Major."

"Lucien," he corrected. "Call me Lucien."

On a deep breath, she nodded. "I told the sergeant I would pray Lyncoya was found alive and well before he could hang me. He said I shouldn't waste my time on such a useless endeavor, but pray for my immortal soul instead."

"Because he knew Lyncoya would never be found before you were hanged?" he suggested. "Because he had taken the boy?"

"Well, there was that," she agreed half-heartedly. "But there was something else. There was something in the way he spoke to me that set my mind to thinking he wasn't the man he seemed to be."

"Why?" The curiosity beast now sat on full alert, and Lucien straightened. "How did he speak to you?"

"In pure, unerring Spanish."

His jaw slammed against his chest. "You jest!"

"No, I don't. Every word of our conversation was spoken in the 'lovely tongue' Sergeant Greene speaks as well as I."

As if her confession had drained her artistic bent, she dropped the stick and stared at the glowing embers. Another deep sigh rent the air.

Had her thoughts returned to Ramon? Did she wonder if the man she loved was safe? If he didn't turn her thoughts, she'd weep. That, he wouldn't abide.

Leaning back against the tree trunk, arms folded behind his head, he looked up at the twinkling stars. Inspiration struck.

"The topic of the Shakespeare debates is the night," he announced. "I'll begin. 'How sweet the moonlight sleeps upon this bank! Here will we sit and let the sounds of music creep in our ears; soft stillness and the night becomes the touch of sweet harmony.' The Merchant of Venice."

She took up his challenge, but with little enthusiasm, the recitation monotone. "'When he shall die, take him and cut him out in little stars, and he will make the face of heaven so fine that all the world will be in love with night and pay no worship to the garish sun.' Romeo and Juliet."

"'How silver-sweet sound lovers' tongues by night, like softest music to attending ears!' Romeo and Juliet."

"'Parting is such sweet sorrow, that I shall say good night til it be morrow.' Romeo and Juliet."

Obviously, she compared Ramon to the romantic but tragic Romeo. Well, he quickly countered her dire words. "'Or in the night, imagining some fear, how easy is a bush supposed a bear!' A Midsummer Night's Dream."

"'Good-night, sweet prince: and flights of angels

sing thee to thy rest.' Hamlet."

They parried back and forth for some time. Marisa quoted tragedies and Lucien comedies until they were both exhausted from the events of the last few days and their literary efforts.

Stifling a yawn, Marisa crawled inside her bedroll. In a soft and tired voice, she ended with another quote from Hamlet. "'Tis now the very witching time of night, when churchyards yawn and hell itself breathes out contagion to this world.'"

Lucien sighed. Not only had he failed to lighten her mood, she'd managed to make him feel bereft. "You win," he told her.

"I always do," she said. They were her last words. Within moments, she'd fallen asleep.

Lucien remained under the tree awhile longer. At last, he rose and crept to where she slumbered beneath her blanket. He knelt down beside her and whispered, "'O, she doth teach the torches to burn bright! It seems she hangs upon the cheek of night like a rich jewel in an Ethiope's ear; beauty too rich for use, for earth too dear!' Your favorite work this evening; Romeo and Juliet. You may have always won against your father and brother, but you can't best me."

While satisfaction warmed his insides, he picked up his bedroll and moved it so that he lay directly next to her. "Goodnight, *montesita mia.*"

****

For days, they continued their harried pace. They followed the winding course of the Escambia River through dense forest as long as daylight allowed. Once the sun set each evening, they'd make camp, eat something Lucien trapped or caught in the river and have a Shakespeare debate.

Marisa always fell asleep first. In the mornings, the first thing she'd see was Lucien tending to the horses. Even in her barely alert state, she couldn't

212

fail to notice he was always crisply dressed and freshly shaven. Meanwhile, she'd brush the wrinkles and dust from her riding habit with the back of her hand. She resented feeling rumpled and dirty. And it certainly didn't help that she traveled with the Patron Saint of Cleanliness.

He made it look easy. After days of breakneck speeds, dense forest, and sleeping on the ground beneath oak and sycamore trees, not a wrinkle or a smudge dared land on the impeccable Major Lucien St. Clair. Not a hair lay out of place.

She, on the other hand, was filthy from head to toe. Angry red welts scratched her cheeks from the twigs that grazed her face as they rode haphazardly past boughs and branches. Her riding habit, stained with grass and mud, smelled of manure and perspiration. Her hair was hopelessly tangled and had a greasy feel to it.

On the fifth day, they halted late in the afternoon at his insistence. He dismounted first and helped her to the ground. Ever the proper gentleman...

"Are you hungry?" he asked. "I might be able to snare us a rabbit in short order."

She shook her head. "I can't eat. I'd rather press on."

Lucien's glare scanned her from head to toe, and the distaste in his eyes prickled annoyance over her overheated, over-dirty flesh. "You're exhausted. You can't keep up this pace."

"I don't need a nursemaid," she snapped. "I need to get to *El Castillo*."

"If you keep going this way, the only way you'll arrive is in a box."

Did he really think she'd allow him to lead this journey? Because he was a major or because he was a man? No matter. She'd outwitted higher ranks than majors and smarter men than Lucien St. Clair.

With a slump to her shoulders, she feigned defeat. "Very well. But forget the rabbit. I have food in my saddlebags."

She strode to where Tormenta stood and removed one of the large bags attached to her saddle. Placing the bag on the ground, she pulled out several strips of dried meat coated in berries and nuts and handed two of them to Lucien.

"What is it?" He lifted the strips to his nose and winced at the odor.

"Beef." She replaced the saddlebag and nodded at him. "Eat it."

"What's on the beef?"

On a deep sigh, she grabbed one of the strips out of his hand and took a large bite. She chewed slowly, and then swallowed with a gulp before the taste lingered on her tongue. She would've rather chewed her own boot, but the man needed to be taught a lesson. And this was a much better way.

"The beef is dried into strips and coated with a small amount of fat," she told his dubious expression. "Then rolled in berries and nuts. Seminole warriors eat these strips when on a hunt because they're filling, they don't take up much room, and keep for a long time. They aren't poison, Lucien. I admit you may need time to become accustomed to the taste, but they won't kill you."

Hesitantly, Lucien took a small bite, grimaced and gulped. "Delicious."

His lack of sincerity paired with his sudden gags brought gales of laughter. She laughed until tears came to her eyes and pain stabbed her stomach.

"It's nice to see your smile again."

She stopped, looked away. Embarrassment heated her cheeks. "If you're finished with your meal, we should press on."

"You need to rest," he said firmly.

Delight widened her lips until her cheeks hurt.

"There's an inn less than four miles from here. The rooms are small, but clean. If we press on, we could be there by dark."

Realization dawned in his narrowed eyes. "Are you saying if I'd waited, I might have had a real meal? And I wouldn't have had to eat this?" He gestured to the meat strip in his hand with a grimace.

"Perhaps next time, you'll allow me to decide when it's time to rest," she advised him with a superior air.

"Perhaps," he mumbled.

"So are we for the Black Bear, or do we continue riding?"

"The Black Bear," he announced.

*"There is a tide in the affairs of women.*
*Which, taken at the flood, leads-God knows where."*
*— Lord Byron (Don Juan)*

CHAPTER 27

The owner of the Black Bear resembled the inn itself. Small but overly wide, Elena Piñero had dark brown hair, ample hips and an even ampler bosom. When Marisa slipped out from behind Lucien inside the inn's cozy entrance, the woman's arms flung open wide.

"Marisa! What are you doing in this area in November?"

"I must see to my home." She stepped into the lady's embrace. "Has Ramon stopped here yet?"

"He's not with you?" Elena pulled back, tsking in disapproval.

"No." She tugged on Lucien's hand to draw him forward. "This is Major Lucien St. Clair. He was kind enough to accompany me. Ramon is to meet us at *El Castillo de Oro.*"

Elena's eyes grew frosty. "You're traveling alone?"

"Don't fret, Elena," Marisa said with an easy smile. "The major is my cousin."

Lucien's face didn't betray the lie as he took the woman's fingers within his own. "Madam." He bent to kiss the back of her hand.

Elena blushed from cheek to gray hairline.

"You're Marisa's cousin?"

"Yes," he replied. "Our mothers were sisters."

Elena folded her arms over her chest. "Where is Ramon?"

"He couldn't wait for me. He's traveling with the major's friends," she said. "Sergeant Greene and Lieutenant Foster. We were hoping to catch up to their party here. They must not have stopped for the night, but continued straight on."

"Did you say Lieutenant Foster?" Elena blinked. "Lieutenant Marcus Foster?"

Excitement whispered through him. "Do you know the lieutenant?"

"He was a frequent visitor here several weeks back, but I haven't seen him in quite a while. His men still visit the Black Bear. Two of them are in the tavern right now."

Marisa shot a glance in his direction, a silent message to give nothing away. "Really? What an odd coincidence."

"They've been living at the Bartlett farm," Elena continued. "Do you remember the Bartletts?" She turned to Lucien, this time her face open and without judgment. "Milton Bartlett and his wife, Cecilia, ran off and abandoned their farm during the Creek War. No one knows where they fled to, but they haven't been seen here for nearly six years now. Lieutenant Foster and his soldiers have been residing there since June. They say they're performing some task for General Jackson."

"Do you have rooms available for us?" Marisa blurted.

"Of course. *You* will have your usual room above stairs. You know the way. As for your *cousin*," she said, the icy glare reborn, "he'll be quite comfortable here on the first floor."

"*Gracias*, Elena." She placed a palm over her mouth and yawned. "I'm so very tired. I believe I'll be asleep the moment my head touches the pillow. Lucien, I wish you a pleasant night. I'm sure Elena will take excellent care of you."

Without waiting for a reply, she swept up the staircase behind him.

"Come along, Lucien," Elena led him past a charming parlor with a dying fire to the third door in the hall. "You'll sleep here." She pushed the door open and stepped back.

The room was small but clean and comfortable with a large wrought-iron bed covered by a homespun quilt in patches of green and yellow. Beside the bed sat a table holding a slender vase of fresh-cut chrysanthemums. Tired as he was, the vase could hold a fistful of weeds and he'd be happy.

"Thank you," he said. "This is quite sufficient."

Elena nodded and walked away. He barely closed the door to his room when he remembered the look on Marisa's face when she'd heard about the Bartlett farm.

Dammit! She'd made a fool of him again.

****

The Bartlett farm sat less than a mile from the Black Bear Inn. A short distance from the abandoned house, Marisa tied Tormenta to a large gnarled oak tree. She removed her special saddlebag and slung it over her arm. Years of subterfuge had taught her to be ready for any occurrence. On cat-like feet, she walked the remaining distance to the ramshackle building that had once been the cozy home of Milton and Cecilia Bartlett.

When she arrived at the structure, she clucked her tongue in dismay. Little wonder Foster's men spent their time at the Black Bear. Large holes in the roof sheltered dozens of nesting crows and barn owls. The glass long gone, only threadbare bits of cloth covered the windows, a poor defense against rain or cold.

Marisa walked around the house. She peered past the makeshift curtains to ascertain Lyncoya's whereabouts, as well as the location of any of his abductors. When she slipped to the back of the house, she caught sight of a large gum tree, which reigned over the landscape. One thick branch reached across the thatched roof and dipped into a large hole in the ceiling.

After visually mapping out her movements, she hitched the saddlebag up to her shoulder and spit on her hands for extra adhesion. On a perfect leap, she grasped the lowest branch with both hands and dangled. One deep inhale, and she swung her body until her feet reached the notch where the branch met the tree trunk. Feet firmly planted, she pulled herself up and lay flat against the branch. When she found another foothold, she scrambled into a sitting position to reach for another, higher arm of the tree. Branch by branch, she ascended until at last, she straddled the branch that loomed over the house. Scooting along on her behind, she inched her way to the rooftop.

One long look confirmed her worst fears. In such dilapidated condition, the structure would never support her weight. No matter. She'd simply have to stretch along the arm and hang her head over the side to peer into the house.

Years had passed since her tree-hanging antics with 'Lando and Timmy and the other children who lived near *El Castillo*, but she'd never lost her agility. Now she took several deep breaths to anchor her equilibrium and dipped.

She spotted him immediately, head down, seated cross-legged on the filth-covered floor in what was once the center of the Bartlett bedchamber. "Lyncoya?"

The boy looked up in surprise, but Marisa couldn't mask her own violent reaction. No one had told her General Jackson's son was an Indian—and a Creek, if her sharp eyes were not mistaken. The familiar anger roiled in her veins, hot and acidic.

Before she could tamp down the ugly reaction, a blur flew past her eye. A rock! The little savage had thrown a rock at her.

"Stop that!" She quickly pulled her head out of range, but the missiles continued to fly. With no other choice, she sat atop the branch, ducking rocks and sticks and speaking calmly to the fearful child. "My name is Marisa, Lyncoya. I want to take you home with me."

"You don't fool me!" he shouted as he hurled rocks and clumps of dirt. "You won't trick me into coming with you. I'll stay here until my papa comes to fetch me."

"Your papa sent me to fetch you," she said.

"Liar!" The rocks flew faster. One pelted her shoulder, and she drew back as far as her balance would allow.

"I'm not lying," she exclaimed. "Your papa wants me to take you home."

"How do I know you're telling the truth?"

Risking injury if not death, she poked her head into the hole and switched to the Creek language. "Because I speak your tongue."

The foreign sounds thickened over her lips, but she must not have mucked them up too badly. Lyncoya's arm stopped in mid-arc, and he gazed at her in wonder.

"You'll take me home?"

"Yes." She then switched back to English. "But first, we have to punish the men who took you."

He folded his arms over his skinny bare chest. "How?"

"If you let me come in, I'll tell you."

"Very well."

Once she gained his agreement, Marisa looked

down to clutch the branch. And froze. A man stood beneath the gum tree. Even from this height, she noted his furious expression.

"What do you think you're doing up there?" Lucien demanded from beneath the bough.

"Speaking to Lyncoya," she whispered. "Now, stay there and be silent!"

"Like hell."

Before she could stop him, he grasped the first branch to begin the steep climb up the tree to reach her.

"I hear you speaking to those men. You're one of them!" Lyncoya shrieked. Seconds later, the rocks and sticks flew again. "Stay away from me! You're trying to trick me!"

Torn between the angry man and the murderous boy, Marisa chose to deal with the child first. She dipped into the hole again. "No, Lyncoya, no. I want to help you. Please, you must listen to me."

"Liar!"

He flung a rock the size of a large pear, and as she ducked away, an arm snaked about her waist.

"Why not let me try?" Lucien said in her ear.

He sat beside her.

"How did you get up here so fast?"

"The same way you did." He nodded at the crisscross of boughs below them.

She glanced at the branches, and then up into his face, with rounded eyes. "*You* climbed a tree?"

"Why is that so unbelievable?"

"Look at you!" She gestured to his impeccable shirt and breeches. "You don't strike me as a man who has much experience at tree-climbing. You seem too fastidious for such an activity."

"I've climbed trees before. I was a mischievous young boy once, you know."

She snorted. "Hard to imagine."

"You have some very odd ideas about me."

"I have trouble picturing you as a mischievous young boy. I don't think you were ever dirty or young or mischievous. I'd wager you were born an immaculate, well-mannered adult."

He shook his head. "I assure you, madam, I came into this world in the same manner as you. And I spent quite a bit of time as a dirty, disobedient child."

She giggled. "Perhaps you and I were both born dirty and disobedient, but *I* was born a female, Lucien."

As if to punctuate her statement, a clod of dirt landed with a thud near Lucien's spotless breeches.

"I know who you are," Lyncoya shouted. "I know who you are. You don't fool me. You're with those bastards!"

Brushing the dirt from his side with a casual air, Lucien sprawled across her.

When his head fell into her lap and his chest lay across her thighs, she nearly jumped out of her skin. "What are you doing?"

"I'm speaking to Lyncoya," he said. "Now stay there and be silent!"

"Go away, you bastards!" the boy yelled.

Lucien dropped his head into the hole. "That's no way to speak to a lady, Lyncoya."

"Major Lucien? Is that you?"

The boy's tone reflected surprise.

And awe.

As if he spoke to some mysterious god.

Of course. She spoke to the child and rocks were hurled at her. The omnipotent Major St. Clair received reverence.

"Yes, Lyncoya," he replied. "And you must apologize to Miss Álvarez at once. She risked a great deal to rescue you."

A pregnant pause obliterated the air, and then finally, a more childish voice called, "I apologize,

Miss. I didn't know you were with Major Lucien."

"That's better," Lucien said. "Now, if you'll stop attacking us with your makeshift artillery, we might climb down and help you."

*"Then a spirit passed before my face; the hair of my flesh stood up."*
*— Holy Bible (Job 4:15)*

## CHAPTER 28

Lucien crouched in the corner of the darkened room, behind an opened cabinet with a mirror on the inside door. All around him lay still. Nothing sounded but his own breath, loud and harsh in the blackness.

Sudden raucous laughter heralded the return of Lyncoya's abductors from their sojourn to Elena's inn.

"Any problems with the savage tonight?" a loud bass called, his words slurred from excess drink.

"Nah," a higher tone replied from near the doorway. "He was shouting nonsense at me awhile ago, but I ignored him. After a while, he gave up and everything got quiet. I figured he went to sleep. So I did, too."

"Well, then we may as well go to our own beds," the first voice said.

The sudden loud crack of thunder nearly startled Lucien from his hiding place. Flashes of light erupted inside the bedchamber, blinding him. He heard a shout, and the sound of a fumbled key in a lock. Moments later, three men stumbled inside.

Strange sparks twinkled, flaring and then fading in different parts of the room. By these eerie lights, Lucien spotted Lyncoya in the center of the room. The boy hung from the rafters, a loop of rope wrapped around his neck. His tongue lolled as he dangled above them. The body swayed back and forth as if carried on a breeze.

Lucien's heart stopped, and he couldn't catch his breath. Until his brain reminded him the scene was staged by Marisa. Still, the vision looked so authentic.

None of the men dared to move. They merely stood, eyes agape, staring up at the gruesome scene.

"Jesu! He hanged himself," one of the men said. "What do we do now?"

"If General Jackson finds out we had something to do with this, he'll have us drawn and quartered." The second hastily made the sign of the cross.

Finally, the apparent leader of the trio croaked out, "Cut him down!"

One man took a step forward, but the rope slipped from around the beam with a hiss.

Thud! Lyncoya fell to the floor, motionless.

Then another sound echoed. A low, throaty moan built to a painful, agonizing howl.

A specter with the wispy form of a woman's face and upper torso floated toward the fallen child. Even Lucien believed her transparent. The walls of the room were clearly visible behind her. She had no limbs.

"What the hell is it?" one of the men dared ask.

The reedy voice of the specter answered, "I've come for my son."

That was Lucien's cue. Picking up the candle with its phosphorous wick, he removed the dagger from the pan of coals at his feet. Instantly, the candle ignited with no spark and the room illuminated in an eerie yellow glow.

The men, in a tight circle, inched closer to the door.

Still, the moans grew louder and angrier. "You have taken Lyncoya from his home."

"We didn't take him," the leader shouted at the ghostly figure. "Sergeant Greene and Lieutenant Foster took him. We've only been watching him."

"You must pay for your mischief," the specter called.

"W—what d—do w—we do n—now?" the smallest man sputtered.

"I don't give a whit what the rest of you do," the leader replied in a low voice. "But I'm getting the hell out of this house!"

They scrambled over each other to leave the haunted room and its ghastly view.

No one moved or made a sound until the front door opened and then slammed shut. Lyncoya sat up first. His childish glee echoed through the dark room. Rising, he loosened the slipknot Marisa had tied to hang him. He pulled the rope up over his head and tossed it on the floor.

The rope never attached to the beam. A stronger rope, dyed black, slipped inside a hole in the back of his shirt. Although invisible in the unlit room, this rope held him aloft. Lyncoya's hands, behind his back, controlled the slack of the black rope. Thus, he lowered himself to the floor as if the rope around his neck had suddenly broken free from the beam.

Threads brushed with small traces of gunpowder caused the twinkling lights. The mirror, at its current angle, reflected off the pan of hot coals and onto the wall above. When Marisa stepped in front of the mirror, her image was cast as the ghostly specter.

"That was wonderful!" Lyncoya wrapped his arms around her waist and hugged her. "Did you see how they scurried out of here like mice?"

Lucien smiled at the boy's immediate devotion to Marisa. Lyncoya's loyalty was not easily won, but once obtained, was limitless. Whether she wished it or not, Marisa now had a friend for life.

"You found that funny, did you?" she asked.

Lyncoya giggled, but then sobered as he looked up at both adults. "Will you take me home now?"

"Not yet." She knelt so they were eye to eye. "I need your help first."

Lyncoya blinked. "You need *my* help?"

"There is someone else I must rescue before I take you back to the Hermitage. I need you to come with me to my home in Alabama."

A chill tickled Lucien's spine. "Oh no," he said. "You're not going to use this innocent child for bait."

Marisa shot to her feet. "How dare you? I don't intend to use him. But if we take the time to return Lyncoya to the Hermitage, we'll never get to *El Castillo* before Greene and Foster."

"Lyncoya's been gone from the Hermitage for nearly six months," Lucien reminded her. "His parents are sick with worry over his disappearance."

"After six months, a week or two more shouldn't matter."

"Tell that to his mother!"

"Elena can send a messenger to the Hermitage to assure the general and his wife Lyncoya is safe, and we'll bring him home as soon as possible."

"It's possible to bring him home now."

Tears shimmered in Marisa's eyes, and she clasped her hands. "Please, Lucien," she whispered. "They'll kill him if I'm not there."

Pity stabbed his heart, but duty called stronger. "I must take the boy home," Lucien insisted. "I have an obligation to General and Mrs. Jackson."

Lyncoya stepped between them, his hand raised to gain their attention. "Marisa, are you worried someone will kill a friend of yours?"

"Yes." She sniffed, ran the back of her hand over her eyes. "A very dear friend."

"Did Sergeant Greene take your friend?"

"Yes."

Lyncoya shook his head. "I don't like Sergeant Greene. When he was at the Hermitage, he only pretended to be nice to me. He gained my trust, and then he took me away."

"I know," she replied. "He pretended to be nice to me also. He wanted to gain my trust."

"Did he kidnap you?"

"No, but he put me in prison and kidnapped my friend."

Lucien coughed and looked away. Truth be told, *he'd* put her in prison, not Ethan. But he wasn't about to argue that point right now.

"And you think if you take me home," Lyncoya continued, "Sergeant Greene will kill your friend?"

Posture stiff, Marisa nodded.

Lyncoya turned solemn eyes to Lucien. "Are you helping Marisa?"

"Yes, but my first obligation is to you."

The boy clucked his tongue. "I'm not a baby, Major Lucien. I'm a Creek warrior. We'll help Marisa find her friend."

Marisa nearly collapsed with relief. "Thank you, Lyncoya."

He held up his hand again. "One more question. Will we get to punish Sergeant Greene and Mr. Foster this time?" His excitement hurried the words so they fairly tripped over his tongue.

Marisa smiled. "Oh, yes," she assured him. "But we'll have to plan something much more devious for them."

Lyncoya clapped. "We will leave now."

Lucien stood stock-still, wondering when exactly he'd lost command. Neither Marisa nor Lyncoya paid him the slightest mind. With the boy's help, she gathered her magical objects into her saddlebag and hooked it over her elbow.

"Shall we go?" she said at last. "There are villains to punish and time is wasting."

"Wait!" Lyncoya exclaimed.

He raced to the bed and rifled beneath the tattered rag that served as a blanket. After several minutes, he pulled out a bow and quiver full of arrows and held them up. Then taking Marisa's hand, he linked his other arm about Lucien's elbow, still clutching his prized possessions. With infinite trust, he allowed the couple to escort him out of the dilapidated farmhouse that had been his prison for nearly six months.

****

The trio trudged through the woods hand in hand. While they walked, Lyncoya mocked the frightened antics of the men at the farmhouse.

"Where did you learn to do those tricks?" Lyncoya asked. "And why do you have all of those magical items with you?"

"I keep my magical items here." Marisa waved the saddlebag. "And I always have them ready."

"And how do you know Creek?"

Lucien gripped her upper arm, stopping her in mid-stride. "You speak the Creek language?"

"Not fluently," she murmured and stepped up her pace. "I know a few phrases of several Indian languages."

A sudden realization lit inside Lucien's head. "That's how you managed to convince those Seminoles to lock themselves in the calaboose after they set the Salinas' farm ablaze."

At last able to share her cleverness with someone besides Ramon, Marisa preened. "I could hardly convince their chief I was a ghost of their ancestors if I didn't speak the language now, could I?"

"Mr. Weatherford taught me some of my family's language when he was at the Hermitage," Lyncoya interjected.

The name sent a flaming arrow into Marisa's heart, and she laid a palm flat against her breast to keep the horrid memories at bay.

"Who taught you Creek?" the boy asked.

"Mr. Mims." Saying the poor man's name aloud nearly brought her to her knees, and she stumbled, but caught herself before she fell.

"And the sorcery? Who taught you the black arts? Are you a witch?"

"No, I'm not a witch," she said on a sigh. "Nor is it sorcery. It's merely a bit of trickery performed with smoke and mirrors."

"But where did you learn such things?"

Despite her pain, she smiled. Over the years, she'd forgotten the stubborn persistence of young boys. "When I was a child, my father took my brother and me to see a famous conjurer named Andrew Oehler. Mr. Oehler spent time in a jail in Mexico because the ruler there believed his tricks were witchcraft. When I saw him perform his tricks, I could see why superstitious people might fear him. He was wonderful! After the performance, my brother and I decided to steal some of his equipment until he divulged the secret of his tricks. We returned to see every one of his performances every day for a week, always taking something away with us. We pestered him and pestered him and finally, he told us some of his secrets." She placed a finger over her lips. "But we had to promise we wouldn't reveal his methods to anyone."

"I promise I'll never tell."

"Good! Because Mr. Oehler would be very disappointed in me if he knew I'd shared his secrets with an outsider."

"But I'm not an outsider," he argued. "We're friends now, aren't we?"

"Yes, we are," she said with a laugh. "And

friends trust each other, don't they?"

"Oh, yes," the boy exclaimed. "You may trust me!"

"And you may trust me."

"Ahem!" Lucien cleared his throat.

"We know we may trust you, as well, Major Lucien." Lyncoya waved a hand in dismissal.

As they came into the clearing where the horses waited, moonlight filtered over them like a heavenly spotlight. Marisa couldn't fight the urge to tousle the little boy's dark head, but his greasy hair upon her palm sent shudders across her flesh. Obviously, Lyncoya hadn't had a bath since before he was taken. No doubt he'd need to be washed, fed, clothed, and rested before they pressed on through the wilds of Alabama. After months in captivity, the boy wasn't prepared for the rigors of travel. Locking her gaze on Lucien's, she bent her head toward Lyncoya.

The major must have understood her because he nodded. "To the Black Bear, then?"

Lyncoya whirled, eyes round white saucers in his face. "What if Lieutenant Marcus and his soldiers return there looking for me?"

"Never fear, Lyncoya," Lucien replied. "We won't let anything happen to you. You're safe in our care until we place you back with your parents."

The boy looked up at Marisa. "Truly?"

"Of course. Didn't I tell you friends trust each other?" She untied Tormenta and vaulted into the saddle, then patted her lap. "Ride with me?"

Lyncoya nodded, and then turned to Lucien for a leg up. Once the boy sat before her, she settled him against her chest and picked up the reins.

Lyncoya tucked his head under her chin and sighed.

Marisa's heart flooded with happiness.

****

By the time they arrived at the Black Bear's

stable, Lyncoya slept against her chest. With great care, she moved her leg so she no longer sat astride Tormenta, but she never lost her hold on the boy. Lucien dismounted from Boreas and approached, arms outstretched to take the child.

"No. Don't wake him." She gathered him closer. "Help me down."

Lucien placed his hands upon her waist and lifted Marisa and Lyncoya out of the saddle in one movement. The child never stirred.

"Poor *niño*." She kissed his dirty cheek. "Would you take care of Tormenta? This little one needs me."

Upon her entrance into the inn, she found Elena seated in the kitchen next to a large tub full of steamy water. "How did you know?"

"Your cousin told me to have a hot bath waiting before he bolted out of here to follow you." Elena crossed her arms over her chest. "From the expression on his face at the time, I thought he meant to drown you in it. What devilment are you involved in now?"

She gestured to a nearby chair, and Marisa sank with Lyncoya snuggled against her. In an attempt to avoid the innkeeper's questions, she concentrated on removing the boy's filthy garments. She pried the bow and arrows out of his grip and placed them on the floor.

"Who's the boy?" Elena asked.

"General Andrew Jackson's son, Lyncoya."

"The devil, you say!"

She laughed and yanked Lyncoya's shirt off his shoulders. "No, Elena, it's true. He was kidnapped from the Hermitage by Lieutenant Foster and Sergeant Greene."

"That's why those men have been staying at the Bartlett farm?"

Marisa nodded.

"And who exactly is your cousin?"

No surprise. She could never fool Elena. "Lucien isn't my cousin. He's one of General Jackson's most trusted soldiers."

Elena's brows pinched above her nose. "Where's Ramon?"

She stifled a cry and murmured, "Greene and Foster kidnapped Ramon. Lucien and I are on our way to *El Castillo de Oro* to retrieve him."

"You've been traveling alone with a strange man? It isn't proper for you to be traveling about the country alone with a man, especially with a handsome devil like that St. Clair. Now, what are you up to? I want to know everything."

"Be at ease, Elena. Lucien is only interested in bringing Lyncoya home."

"Lucien, is it?"

Lucien, headed for the kitchen, heard his name and stopped outside the doorway.

He listened while Marisa explained to Elena about her arrest and escape from the hangman's noose, Ramon's drunken intervention, and his subsequent kidnapping.

By the time she finished her tale, the two women had stripped Lyncoya and cradled him in the tub.

Lyncoya never stirred as they washed him from his shoulders to his feet.

"After he freed me from the calaboose," Marisa's tale continued, "Lucien insisted I call him by his given name. All we had experienced together was reason enough for us to dispense with propriety."

"And just how much propriety did you dispense with?" Elena asked. "Does Ramon know about this Lucien?"

"Yes, Ramon knows all about Lucien. He says I might trust Lucien with my life." She sighed. "I already have."

"So why is Lucien still here? Why has he not taken Lyncoya back to the Jacksons?"

"I told you, Elena. He's escorting me to *El Castillo* so we can rescue Ramon."

Elena gave a very unladylike snort. "If that's what you wish to believe, I won't dissuade you. But I think you should see things as they really are and not how you think they are. There's more to your Lucien's actions than meets the eye."

Lucien stiffened. Was his affection that obvious?

"Nonsense," Marisa exclaimed, and Lucien relaxed again.

Lyncoya moaned, and he stepped forward, ready to help if needed.

"Marisa?" the boy's sleepy voice murmured.

"Yes," she replied, a maternal caress in her tone that left Lucien with a hollow ache in his core.

Apparently satisfied, Lyncoya did not speak again.

After a long silence, Elena said, "You'd make a good mama."

Lucien thought so, too.

"Perhaps," Marisa replied with little sincerity.

"Why haven't you married? Don't answer. You and Ramon have been far too busy with your vengeful pranks to think about your future. *Querida*." A gentle chastisement. "Fort Mims was a long time ago. Instead of playing games, you should marry and have dozens of children. La Venganza is ruining your life."

"No more," she said softly, to Lucien's surprise. "Once Ramon and I are together again and Lyncoya's safe with his family, La Venganza will disappear. We've risked too much for far too long. It's time for us to forget about revenge and go on with our lives."

"*Gracias a Dios!*" Elena exclaimed. "Then, at last, you'll marry and have children."

"Perhaps," Marisa repeated with the same lack of enthusiasm.

No perhaps about it, Lucien thought, as he slipped from the hall.

*"Of all actions of a man's life, his marriage does least concern other people; yet of all actions of our life, 'tis most meddled with by other people."*
*— John Selden (Table-Talk)*

## CHAPTER 29

Three days later, Marisa led their party along the wending Big Escambia Creek. Once again Lyncoya sat against her. The boy seemed completely healed from his ordeal at the Bartlett farm. He chattered endlessly about his friends and family at the Hermitage, his favorite toys, his favorite food, and anything else that popped into his mind.

Currently, he discussed his favorite subject, William Weatherford. "Mr. Weatherford promised to teach me to use my bow and arrows, but he left the Hermitage before there was time."

"Is that so?" Marisa asked for what must have been the hundredth time since they'd set out that morning.

"He was a nice man, Marisa."

Marisa doubted that. Still, she fought to keep her voice light, reminding herself Lyncoya didn't know what she knew about his hero. "Is that so?"

"He wasn't nice because I was General Jackson's son like a lot of the soldiers were. Mr. Weatherford was nice because he was nice. Do you know what I mean?"

Marisa smiled. "I think so."

"Not like Sergeant Greene, either. He pretended to be nice to me. He promised to teach me to use my bow and arrows and said we'd go hunting, but he brought me to that house instead."

"Is that so?"

"Yes. Did he pretend to be nice to you? Is that how he took your friend?"

"Yes."

"He's a mean man, fooling us like that. Do you know what I think?"

Tormenta snorted, as if to inject an equine opinion into the discussion, but Marisa simply gripped the reins a little tighter and forced her tone to remain light, conversational. "No, what do you think?"

"I think when someone pretends to be nice to you, you mustn't trust him," the boy advised her, "because he wants something from you or he wants to hurt you."

"Is that so?"

"Yes. But I know I may trust you and Major Lucien. You're not pretending to be nice to me."

Affection bloomed, and she tousled his head. "No, I'm not pretending to be nice to you. We're friends, remember?"

He looked up at her with rapt adoration. "I love you."

"I love you, too," Marisa replied.

The words surprised her. Who would have thought she'd feel so strongly about a little boy of Creek origin? Since Fort Mims, she'd despised General Andrew Jackson and the Creeks. Now she protected her enemy's son, a Creek Indian, from Americans. How odd...

"Major Lucien is nice too, don't you think?"

"Yes, Major Lucien is very nice," she answered, still distracted by her strange thoughts.

"Are you going to marry him?"

The question shook her to the core. "Why would you think that?"

"Mother doesn't approve of a man and a woman being alone together until they're married," he explained. "Last year in Nashville, Shelby Everett ran off with Alfred Gibson and they weren't married. When they came back a few months later, I overheard Mother tell Father that Alfred was a scoundrel, but Shelby would only be allowed at the Hermitage if they were wed."

Nonplussed, Marisa returned to her favorite response. "Is that so?"

"Yes. If Mother learns you and Major Lucien have been traveling together, she'll not allow you at the Hermitage until you're married. Don't you think Major Lucien would be a good husband for you?"

The idea was absurd! Oh, Lucien was handsome, considerate, and charming. She liked him a great deal and he seemed fond of her. But marriage? She hadn't thought seriously about marriage in years.

After Fort Mims, Ramon had spoken of marriage and family often. But Marisa always demurred and, after a while, he stopped discussing the topic. The young girl who dreamed of an elaborate wedding with a handsome bridegroom had perished in the fiery remnants of Fort Mims. The Marisa who survived the tragedy was quite content with her life the way it was.

At least she'd always considered herself content until Lucien St. Clair came into her life. Now every day brewed new questions. Why was Lucien helping her? Why did Ramon insist she could trust him? Why did she trust him with or without Ramon's blessing?

"You will marry him, won't you?" Lyncoya pressed.

"I—I don't know," she stammered. "Lucien hasn't asked me."

"But if he asks you, will you marry him?"

"Yes, Marisa," Lucien chimed in from behind them, not attempting to hide his delight. "Tell me. If I asked you, would you marry me?"

"Perhaps," she replied. The heat that flared in her cheeks belied her indifference.

And Lucien apparently noticed. His eyes glinted with mischief as he stroked his chin. "Is that so?"

****

Lucien spent most of the next few days in chaotic thought. He now knew Ramon's true identity, but the knowledge held little comfort. The man endangered Marisa's life time and again with his La Venganza schemes, letting her rot in the calaboose for weeks. If Lucien hadn't risked his honor, his commission to get her out of that prison cell, Ramon would have attempted some bloodbath that resulted in a double hanging. Yet, still she preferred her villain to the man who'd gladly lay down his life to keep her safe.

Too many people sought La Venganza. And all too soon, someone would discover the truth. Perhaps one of those drunken fools in Pensacola, or a member of General Jackson's army, or an angry Seminole. Any patron at the tavern—someone from England, or Spain, or Germany. No matter how careful they were, eventually someone would connect the innkeeper and her elderly friend with the culprit's escapades. The two were lucky they'd been able to escape notice for so long. But eventually, their luck would run out. And who would rescue Marisa from the hangman's noose next time?

What if he hadn't returned to Pensacola? Who would have released her from the calaboose before her neck was stretched? By God, Marisa should be on her knees, thanking him for all he'd done for her. Ramon had done nothing but cause her trouble. Lucien managed time and time again to rescue her from her own destruction. Why was she too dense to see that?

Still...as much as he wanted to hate Ramon, he couldn't. He'd discovered firsthand Marisa couldn't be controlled. She was like an untamed horse. The best any man could do was go along with her, give her her head, and keep her out of trouble until she exhausted herself. No easy task for a mere mortal.

Once again, he was reminded of his sister-in-law. Like Marisa, Antoinetta was a spirited woman with a mind of her own and a tendency to run headlong into a crisis without regard for the consequences. His brother, Darian, shared his exasperation about his wife on a regular basis. The two had fierce arguments, especially when Antoinetta took too much on herself. Yet, Darian adored Antoinetta, and she felt the same way toward him. Theirs was not always a serene marriage, but it was a loving one.

As hard as he fought against such a weakness, he envied his brother the beautiful woman he'd married. No matter what occurred, Darian knew Antoinetta loved him. Lucien, on the other hand, had no such certainty.

And worse, he'd given his word to Ramon that he'd do nothing to compromise Marisa's innocence. He couldn't touch her, couldn't kiss her again. He refused to voice his soft feelings aloud for fear of being rebuffed. It galled him to realize he'd been betrayed by his own honor.

Yet now he wondered. He'd sworn to Ramon he'd do nothing to hurt Marisa or to compromise her in any way. But was he obligated to keep such a vow to a man who'd lied to him? Was it dishonorable to call a man's bluff in affairs of the heart?

By the time they halted in the late afternoon, he'd worked himself into a fine lather. As if someone had snuffed out the boy's candle, after hours of chatter, in mid-sentence, Lyncoya stopped talking and slept against Marisa like a newborn at his mother's breast. Envy stabbed Lucien between the ribs.

"Lucien, I—" she began.

"I know," he interjected as he dismounted from Boreas. "Stay there. I'll take Lyncoya from you in a moment."

"No," she started again. "I wanted to—"

"Don't tell me you think you can alight from Tormenta without my help and without waking Lyncoya. Dammit, Marisa, will you at least be honest enough to admit you're not invincible?"

Her eyes widened in surprise. "I know I'm not invincible. I merely—"

"After everything I've done for you, you should realize I know when you need help. Even if you're too stubborn to admit it to yourself. I saved your life! And I've spent the last two weeks riding through the wilderness to help you find Ramon. I'm risking the wrath of General Jackson by delaying the return of his kidnapped son to follow you. What more do I have to do for you?"

The surprise turned to anger, and she stiffened her spine. "I didn't ask you to save my life. I didn't ask you to follow me into the wilderness. Go home if you wish. We're only a few days from *El Castillo*. Lyncoya will be safe without you. When Ramon and I are together again, he and I will escort the boy to the Hermitage."

Her easy answers shattered him. "Would it hurt you to appreciate what I've done for you? Why can't you accept what I've sacrificed to keep you safe?"

She shook her head as if to clear it. "I do appreciate what you've sacrificed."

"Oh?" He arched a brow. "So the effort means nothing to you?"

"The effort means everything to me!" she

exclaimed. "But..." She lowered her head and her voice. "...I don't understand what you want from me."

Instantly, Lucien calmed himself. Of course she didn't understand. Why should she? With a deep sigh, he reached up to take Lyncoya out of her arms. "I want nothing from you, Marisa," he whispered. "Forgive my bad humor. I suppose I'm tired of traveling."

Marisa dismounted from her mare and stared at him, utter confusion stamped on her face.

\*\*\*\*

Lyncoya awakened just as night enshrouded the forest. He sat up in his bedroll and rubbed the sleep from his eyes with fisted hands. Marisa fussed with a sputtering fire, but he didn't see Major Lucien anywhere.

Lyncoya liked to watch Marisa when she didn't know he watched her. She was so pretty and so kind, like a beautiful princess in a fairy tale. She was smart and brave too. She'd saved him from those men by outwitting them with her tricks. He knew he owed her his life and he wanted to do something to repay all of her kindness. She deserved something very special.

He rose from the bedroll and crept to where the horses were tethered. Mr. Weatherford taught him many Indian ways when he was at the Hermitage. One of his lessons included how to move quietly through a forest so as not to arouse the wildlife around you. He now used this skill to avoid Marisa.

After a thorough inspection of Tormenta's pack, he found his bow and arrows and pulled them out. He would do something special. He'd go hunting and come back with a stag or a bear. He'd slay something big—to show Marisa how much he loved her. The bigger the beast, the deeper his love. With bow in hand and arrows in the quiver on his back, he crept away from the campsite to seek out something extraordinary.

Meanwhile, Marisa finally built a roaring fire and turned to catch a glimpse of Lyncoya on her bedroll. He was gone.

"Lyncoya!"

No answer.

"Lyncoya!" she called again. Her heart nearly flew from her chest. Where could he have gone? Had she underestimated Foster and Greene? Had they found the campsite and taken the boy while her back was turned?

"Lucien!"

But Lucien had gone to do some fishing for dinner and couldn't hear her call.

Taking several deep breaths, she tried to remain calm. She'd only turned her back on the boy for a few minutes. If someone had taken him, they couldn't have gone far. She scanned the woods, but the dense forest and thick colorful foliage obscured her vision. She'd need a higher vantage point.

Of the trees around her, the tallest beckoned. Time to put her skills into action again. She grasped the branch above her head and scaled her way upward. Several feet off the ground, she stopped, pushed a branch of amber leaves away and spotted Lyncoya. He knelt in thick underbrush, his bow and arrow at the ready.

Relief poured through her on a deep sigh. She turned her attention to her descent when a movement to the right of her position caught her attention. Lucien sauntered back to the campsite with several fish hanging from his line.

Lyncoya's posture stiffened.

Oh, *Dios!* From his post in the thicket, Lyncoya heard Lucien's movement and must have assumed the man was a beast.

"No!" She launched herself from the tree, hit the

air, and then careened into Lucien.

With a whoof of expelled breath, he fell flat on his back in the dirt. The arrow whizzed past them both to land harmlessly on the ground. Breathless, she lay atop him, her face nuzzled in his neck, eyes squeezed shut.

"Marisa?" The moment she heard him speak, she struggled to rise, but he wrapped his arms about her waist and held her fast. "What happened? Where did you come from? Are you a fallen angel?"

Marisa, between gasps for air, gave him a brief explanation. "Lyncoya. He didn't mean it. He nearly killed you. I saw you both from that tree. I had to stop him. Couldn't let him hurt you."

With the flat of her hand, she pushed against his chest, but Lucien tightened his hold on her waist and drew her closer to him. "Easy, *querida*." His hot breath brushed her ear. "I've waited a long time to have you throw yourself at me. Allow me to enjoy the sensation for a moment."

*Madre de Dios*, what was she doing? Every warm breath he exhaled danced across her ear. Her breasts pressed into his chest while his hands clasped the small of her back just above her bottom. The muscles of his abdomen touched her hips, and her legs entwined between his rock-hard thighs.

Before she could break away, Lyncoya rushed out of the underbrush, his face white with fear. "Major Lucien! I didn't know it was you. I thought you were a bear." He stopped and stared at Marisa's position atop Lucien. His eyes widened and his mouth opened in a tremendous o. "Now you two *have to* get married."

Lucien burst out laughing.

Marisa burned. Perhaps it would be best for her sanity, as well as her virtue, if she taught Lyncoya how to use his bow and arrows properly. Luckily, Lucien was still too weakened by his sense of humor to stop her when she removed his hands from around her waist and got to her feet.

In three long strides, she grabbed Lyncoya's hand.

"I'm sorry!" Lyncoya wailed.

She dragged him into a clearing away from the fire and away from the major, who quickly leaped to catch up. "Come out of harm's way," she said. "I'll instruct you on the correct way to hunt with a bow and arrow."

Lyncoya stopped and dropped her hand. "You know how?"

"Yes. My papa taught me many years ago."

"Is there anything your papa couldn't do?" Lucien remarked.

"Yes," she replied solemnly. "Papa couldn't save my family from Fort Mims."

Lucien's dark flush restored her dignity. Satisfied, she turned back to Lyncoya. "The first thing you must learn is the proper stance." She nudged the boy's knees with one of her own and pointed at a sycamore tree a few hundred yards away. Halfway down the trunk, a huge bump convexed its center. "Do you see the knot in the lower part of that trunk?"

"Yes."

"That's your target. Now place your feet apart and turn your shoulder toward the target."

Lyncoya followed her lead. "Is this better?"

"Much better. Now, you must grasp the bow as if you were shaking hands with Major Lucien."

Lyncoya placed the bow handle between his thumb and forefinger. "Like this?"

"Precisely. You're an excellent student, Lyncoya."

His shoulders rose and straightened his spine. "What do I do now?"

"Take an arrow from your quiver and nock it

with the cock feather facing upwards."

"Really?" He looked up at her. Curiosity brewed in his eyes. "Facing upwards? Why upwards?"

"You'll see," she told him. She waited for him to feel comfortable with the arrow against the bow, and then pointed to the sycamore tree again. "Concentrate all your thoughts and senses on that knot. Now, keep your forefinger above the nock as you draw back the arrow."

The expression on the boy's face grew strained as he pulled back on the arrow and bowstring. "Do I release now?"

"Not yet. First, make certain your hold is correct. Your left arm should be relaxed with your right hand near your chin. Recheck your aim, but don't take your eyes off your target. Then, when you're absolutely certain, release."

Lyncoya's arrow flew through the air and landed squarely in the middle of the knot in the sycamore tree.

"I did it!" He wrapped his arms about Marisa's waist and hugged her fiercely.

"Well done, Lyncoya." She ruffled his hair. "Very well done!"

The boy's enthusiasm knew no bounds. He raced to Lucien. "Major Lucien, look! I did it." He pointed to the shaft of his arrow sticking out of the trunk. "I hit the target right in the center."

"I see that," he said. "Congratulations."

"It's because of Marisa. Isn't she wonderful?"

Lucien's gaze bored into Marisa's. Flames fanned across her cheeks. "I think she's the most extraordinary female I've ever met."

Lyncoya tugged on Lucien's sleeve. "Don't you think you should ask her to marry you? She already promised to say yes if you asked her. Go on. Ask her."

Lucien knelt and wrapped an arm about

Lyncoya's shoulders.

"When I decide to ask her, Lyncoya, it will be privately. But I promise you'll be the first to know her answer."

*"Golden slumbers kiss your eyes,*
*Smiles awake you when you rise.*
*Sleep, pretty wantons, do not cry,*
*And I will sing a lullaby.*
*Rock them, rock them, lullaby."*
*— Thomas Dekker (Patient Grissil)*

## CHAPTER 30

Before midnight, thunder rumbled.

Marisa reclined on her side, head rested on one folded arm. Lyncoya cuddled up against her, still asleep. She lifted her head from her bedroll to stare up at the sky. Beneath the waxing moon, thick ominous clouds rolled across the stars.

"Rain's coming," she announced.

At the sound of her voice, Lucien turned in his bedroll nearby. "We'd best find some place to hide before it starts."

A wise idea, but where could they possibly go? Before they made camp, they'd traveled through nothing but dense woods for miles. Familiar with the territory, she knew what lay ahead. The very same scenery.

"Are there any inns near the area?" Lucien asked.

Marisa shook her head. "Not until we reach *El Castillo*. Most of this area is still wilderness. Between here and home, we won't find so much as a lean-to."

Lucien tossed off his blanket and rose. "We'll have to find a cave or an overhang. There has to be some sort of shelter from the rain. Whatever we find will need to be large enough to accommodate the three of us and the horses."

Marisa, still beside Lyncoya, forced her eyes away from Lucien's flesh, turned silver beneath the moonlight. The sight of his bare chest brought back memories of when he'd held her earlier. She vividly recalled the strength of his arms, the hardness of his chest and stomach, the power of his thighs with her legs pinned between them.

She squeezed her eyes shut, but found no refuge there. His image was branded in her mind. And other memories of him lingered. His lips, sweetly pressed against hers when he'd kissed her in Ramon's cottage. Such a heady feeling, she'd surrendered to the pressure of his mouth devouring hers.

She remembered how he looked sitting up in his bed at the inn. Every lovely inch of him had tantalized her. Heat rose in her cheeks and somewhere deeper inside, boiling from the roots of her hair to the tips of her toes. He was absolutely beautiful. There was no other word that came to mind to describe him. Those broad shoulders, the blond hair that curled up tightly on his flesh...

The first drop of rain on her nose splashed her back to reality. She scrambled out of the bedroll, careful not to disturb Lyncoya. They had to move fast.

"Head in that direction." He pointed northward. "I'll head west. Look for anything with a cover or a canopy. But be careful. These woods are dangerous at night. Don't go too far."

Marisa nodded and headed north. She pushed through branches and weeds in search of anything they could possibly use as a shelter. By the time she spotted the cave, the rain fell steadily.

The cave was little more than an aperture set into a wall of rocks beside a waterfall. At first she worried about bears or other creatures inside, but a quick peek told her it was far too small for any ferocious creature to inhabit. It would be a tight squeeze for the three of them, but would have to do. They'd be dry tonight, but they wouldn't sleep. There was simply no room to lie down inside. And the noise from the water pounding down outside reverberated against the walls.

The path, slippery from the waterfall's splash, made the trek inside treacherous. And the entryway was narrow, too narrow for the horses. But about thirty feet away from the cave, a large overhang of granite jutted out from the top of the waterfall. If the wind didn't suddenly pick up and blow the rain in another direction, the horses would be safe and dry beneath the ledge. She hurried to the campsite to lead the others to their shelter.

Minutes later, Lucien settled the horses under the granite ledge while Marisa settled Lyncoya in the cave. Although the boy was awake when she returned to the campsite, his eyes looked heavy with the need for sleep. She didn't wait for him to argue with her as she scooped him up, still wrapped in the bedroll, and carried him to the shelter. With the boy cradled in her arms, she sidled along the narrow, slippery path toward the opening of the cave. Because of Lyncoya's lengthwise position, she had to turn sideways to slip inside, but she made it, and not a moment too soon.

Just as she sat down on the cave floor and resettled Lyncoya on her lap, a loud clap of thunder echoed throughout the cave. A shower of dust and pebbles fell upon them. A rumble of thunder clapped, followed by a streak of lightning that momentarily bathed the cave in blinding white light. The noise and the flash combined with the fallen rocks startled the boy, and he whimpered.

"Hush," she whispered softly against his neck. "It's just the storm."

But his whimpers became cries of alarm as the thunder and lightning intensified. Marisa rocked him like an infant, to no avail. Nothing soothed his terrors.

By the time Lucien inched into the cramped space, the child howled like a trapped animal. One hand shoved Lucien's dripping hair out of his face as he exchanged an uneasy glance with Marisa. He sat down against the opposite wall and nodded at the boy. "The storm?"

She shrugged and returned her attention to Lyncoya's fears. Perhaps, if she crooned softly in his ear. She began with her favorite song:

*"The angels watch over you, dear little one.*
*They sit by your bed while you sleep.*
*From setting sun to rising sun,*
*Your dreams they safely keep.*
*I will stay here beside you all night*
*And watch you as you dream.*
*From evening stars to morning light*
*And every moment in between.*
*Sleep, dear little one, sleep*
*While angels kiss your head.*
*Know that your heart is mine to keep*
*And that I am by your bed."*

While she sang to Lyncoya, her gaze strayed to Lucien. His eyes closed and his body visibly relaxed. Soon, he leaned his head against the cold, damp rocks and sighed.

Marisa smiled. Ramon always loved to hear her sing. Perhaps Lucien enjoyed it also. When Lyncoya fell asleep, Marisa continued her lullabies for the major's benefit.

*"When dawn comes, I shall fly to you*

*And on golden wings we will soar to our home.*
*We will abide one for the other,*
*And no longer will we feel the need to roam...*"
"I've heard that song before." Lucien never moved his head from the rock wall. "You sang that to Ramon on the night before I left Pensacola."

"You remember?"

Lucien lowered his head from the wall and grinned. "I remember every song you've ever sung." He leaned forward until he was on all fours and slowly crawled toward her. "I remember every word you've ever spoken. I remember every look you've ever given me. I remember every move you've ever made toward me." They were suddenly nose to nose as he added, "But most of all, I remember how you tasted the very first time I kissed you."

He placed his hands flat against the rocks behind her shoulders. Without any further warning, his lips pressed against hers. His kiss was sweet but powerful, just as she remembered.

His tongue slipped over her lower lip, slowly, silkily. Then it snaked deeper, and she clamped her teeth shut. He broke away from her, and his gaze probed her eyes.

"Open your mouth for me, *Montesita.*"

He pressed his mouth against hers again. This time, his tongue found its way into her hollow.

Marisa was uncertain what to do. She knew she should stop him. He shouldn't kiss her this way. Yet his lips filled her senses. Her head swam and her limbs melted to water. Her back arched toward him, even with the extra burden of the sleeping boy on her lap. Her lips blazed.

"I think you and Major Lucien should get married as soon as we reach your *El Castillo,*" Lyncoya told them sleepily.

Startled, she broke away from Lucien. "You should not have done that," she said, voice shaky and uncertain.

"On the contrary," Lucien replied with a lazy grin. "I think I should have done that a long time ago."

*"Believing hear, what you deserve to hear:*
*Your birthday as my own to me is dear.*
*But yours gives most; for mine did only lend*
*Me to the world; yours gave to me a friend."*
*— Marcus Valerius Martial (Epigrams)*

## CHAPTER 31

When the sun rose, Marisa awakened Lyncoya with a gentle nudge, handed him one of the chewy sticks of beef and wandered outside. Concerned, Lucien followed.

She meandered toward the waterfall and stared at the water coursing over the cliff of rocks.

Myriad white droplets splashed beneath the silver dawn. She must have known he'd followed her. But she didn't turn toward him or speak. Instead, she seemed to focus on their surroundings. She fingered a wet crimson leaf that still clung to a thin branch of a nearby tree. Once or twice, she sighed.

Lucien believed her confusion stemmed from the idea their kiss was somehow disloyal to Ramon. He might have felt guilty about the turmoil he'd instilled in her, but he'd enjoyed kissing her too much to care how it affected her afterwards. Perhaps he should allow her some time to regain her bearings.

For now, he left her with her thoughts and examined Tormenta and Boreas, pleased to see they hadn't suffered any ill effects from the storm. When the horses stood ready for the day's ride, he strode back to where she stood, still playing with the lone leaf.

"Lyncoya shall ride with me today," he said.

He expected an argument, but she merely nodded, headed for Tormenta's side, and gained her saddle. While she waited astride her mare, he returned to the cave to fetch Lyncoya.

After lifting Lyncoya onto Boreas, he mounted behind the boy. Within minutes, as they rode through the woods, he wished for a gag for Lyncoya's mouth. The boy's endless chatter nearly drove him to madness.

"...Mr. Weatherford said I might come to visit him someday."

Lucien gave the same response Marisa had spoken for days on end. "Is that so?"

The boy didn't seem to notice. "Yes," he replied. "Mr. Weatherford is a very nice man."

"Is that so?"

"Almost as nice as you and Marisa."

"You don't say."

"Yes, I do say." Lyncoya craned his neck to look up at him with narrowed eyes. "Do you suppose we might come to a town today, Major Lucien? A town with shops?"

He never blinked at the sudden turn of the subject. Lyncoya jumped from one topic to another like quicksilver. "I don't know for certain. Why do you ask?"

"I must find a nice present for Marisa."

"Oh?"

"I was hoping I could trade my bow and arrows for something pretty for her."

"Why would you wish to do that?"

"For her birthday. What are you going to give her? If you want her to say yes when you ask her to marry you, you should give her something very special for her birthday."

"Her birthday?"

"Yes, it's tomorrow. Didn't she tell you?"

Ramon! The name slammed into his brain.

He was the world's biggest fool. He'd been so smug, believing his kiss had affected her. He never considered the idea that Marisa wasn't upset about what had occurred between them, but about the fact she and that damned Ramon wouldn't be together tomorrow.

"I'm an idiot!" he mumbled.

Lyncoya grinned, but for the first time in days, said nothing.

By mid-afternoon, they'd reached the source of the Big Escambia Creek in the south of Alabama. Marisa slowed her mount and breathed an audible sigh of pleasure. She turned in her saddle and smiled at Lucien.

"Look about you." She flung her arm in a wide arc. "Isn't this the most splendid sight?"

Mother Nature had indeed painted a masterpiece for them. The scene was a wild, untouched beauty, much like the woman who led them here. When they'd started out on this trek more than three weeks ago, the area had been nothing more than swampland, muck, and mire. Now, here before them lay the most vivid array of colors he'd ever seen.

Above the clear blue waters of the slow-moving Big Escambia Creek, dark pine trees towered over white, gray, and brown walls of rock. The rays of the setting sun glinted off the rock walls to sparkle in tiny bits of silver and gold. Here and there, the deep green hills lay dotted with the reds and yellows of oak, poplar, and gum trees in autumnal splendor.

At the very end of the creek, Marisa slowed their party to a stop. "We'll camp here for the night."

"But we didn't pass a town," Lyncoya whispered.

With one wide arc of his arms, Lucien placed Lyncoya on his feet on the ground. "Sssh."

"Damn!" Lyncoya swore.

Marisa gave the boy a sharp look, and a ruddy blush crept up his bronze cheeks.

"Sorry," he mumbled.

Once she'd alit from Tormenta, she stood over Lyncoya, arms akimbo. "What's this about?"

The boy's gaze dropped to his feet and he kicked the dirt. "I wanted to get you a gift for your birthday. I was going to trade my bow and arrows to get you something special."

Marisa's stance immediately changed from confrontational to complaisance. "Oh, Lyncoya." She knelt beside the boy and embraced him. "What a generous and lovely thought!"

Lyncoya pulled away. "But now it's too late." His eyes glared daggers at Lucien, as if he blamed the major for their failure to find a place he might obtain a gift.

"It isn't too late."

Marisa placed a hand on his arm and turned his gaze her way. Good God, the boy looked up at her with the adoration of the spellbound. Was there anyone immune to the woman's charms?

"I would never allow you to trade your bow and arrows," she said. "You're just learning how to use them properly. Although I do thank you for thinking so highly of me." She leaned closer until they were dirty pink nose to dirty brown nose. "And I'll tell you a secret. Tomorrow is going to be the finest birthday I've ever had. For tomorrow, we'll be at my home."

Lyncoya's eyes opened wide. "Will your friend be there?"

"I hope so, Lyncoya," she said.

Lucien was not as thrilled. Their sojourn would end, come tomorrow. And within days, he'd once again say goodbye to Marisa. This time, forever.

"I'm going hunting," he grumbled.

"I'll go with you," Lyncoya offered, racing to collect his bow and arrows.

\*\*\*\*

Several hours later, when Lyncoya fell asleep at last, Lucien and Marisa sat before the small fire and spoke quietly. The only time they discussed anything of import was when the boy slept. While he was awake, they could barely interrupt his ever-babbling tongue.

With his legs stretched out, Lucien allowed the flames to warm him from face to feet. "How soon before we reach your family's lands?"

She laughed. "We're already on my family's lands," she said. "In fact, we're on *my* lands."

His gaze locked on hers. "Your lands?"

Her arm swept the area around them in a grand gesture. "The land we're camped on belonged to Tomás and me. I should imagine it still does. The deed was a wedding gift from my parents."

A wedding gift? "But you and Tomás never married," he said. "How could you own land together?"

She shrugged. "It was no secret Tomás wanted to marry me. He'd asked my father for my hand and received Papa's consent long before we moved to Fort Mims. Papa's only hesitation came in asking Tomás to wait until the land saw peace again."

"And your father was so sure you'd accept this marriage proposal, he acquired this land for the two of you?"

"I told you Papa was a very smart man. He knew I'd agree to the marriage. And he knew how much I loved this place. With the creek and the pasture, it's perfect for a horse farm. That's what Tomás and I planned to do, breed and raise horses. Papa bought the land and deeded it to *Señor* Tomás Esteban Ramon Marquez and his wife, the former

Marisa Isabella Cira Álvarez."

She sighed and stared up at the crescent moon above them. Lucien understood her pain, could even empathize. She'd lost so much in one violent afternoon...

"That was when Tomás and I still had a future to plan," she said softly. "Before we moved to Fort Mims, and before I became an instrument of revenge." She dropped her head, fixed him with a steely glare. "Think on it, Lucien. By now, I might have been a wife and a mother instead of a criminal and a fugitive."

A warning whispered through his brain. He was on dangerous ground here. Her emotions were all churned up by her memories. And tomorrow? Tomorrow, her birthday, spent with two people whose very backgrounds reflected those who'd stolen a happy life from her, would be agony. Perhaps he should change the subject before he wound up consoling a weepy woman all night.

"Speaking of wives," he said with a forced casual air, "the subject of tonight's Shakespeare debate shall be marriage. 'Let me not to the marriage of true minds admit impediments...'"

Marisa's expression changed from one of infinite sadness to smug satisfaction. "'I say, we will have no more marriages. Those that are married already, all but one, shall live; the rest shall keep as they are.'"

Lucien grinned. Hamlet. Oh, he'd become well accustomed to her devotion to the tragedies over the last few days. Quoting the saddest lines must have given her some perverse satisfaction. "'God the best maker of all marriages combine your hearts in one.'"

She never hesitated, never blinked, or seemed to ponder what to say next. The words flowed easily off her tongue. "'A young man married is a man that's marr'd.'"

"'Hasty marriage seldom proveth well.'"

"'If thou wilt need marry, marry a fool; for wise men know well enough what monsters you make of them.'"

"'When I said, I would die a bachelor, I did not think I should live till I were married.'"

Just as Lucien had hoped she would, Marisa quoted from the same work, *Much Ado About Nothing*. "'Here you may see Benedick the married man.'"

"'How dost thou Benedick the married man?'"

"That's cheating." She pointed her index finger in accusation. "You can't use the same words I did."

"My words are not the same," he replied with a superior air. "Your quote came from Act I, mine is from Act V."

"They're still the same words."

"Very well," he relented. Leaning forward, he trapped her in his gaze and flashed a hundred meanings through the intensity of his stare. "'I do love nothing in the world so well as you: is not that strange?'"

Marisa was either too dense or too preoccupied to understand Lucien's intentions. "Ha!" she crowed. "You lose. There's no mention of marriage in that quote."

"I wasn't quoting." He grasped her hand and pressed his lips against each of her five fingers. "Now what do you have to say in return?"

He watched the expressions dance across her face, confusion at his words, pleasure at his actions, and fear at what it all might mean. For the very first time since they began the game so many nights ago, she hesitated, as if she struggled to find something to say.

At last, she quoted Beatrice's lines from the scene in the play. "'As strange as the thing I know not.'" Her voice shook on the syllables as if she shivered from cold. "'It were as possible for me to say

I loved nothing so well as you; but believe me not, and yet I lie not; I confess nothing, nor I deny nothing.'"

Lucien smiled widely. "There now. Was that so difficult?"

She never replied.

**\*\*\*\***

Hours later, Marisa remained in a quandary. Lucien's words and actions this evening had completely wreaked havoc with her emotions. But her reaction confused her even more.

In the last few hours, nothing had changed. Ramon was still in danger. Every beat of her heart echoed his name. She didn't know what she'd do without him. He was all she had left in the world. She might have died with her family, but Ramon kept her alive. He'd found her at Fort Mims, carried her out of that hellish place and brought her to Pensacola. They'd vowed then...

Tears filled her eyes as she tried to imagine her life without him. To never hear his voice again, to never have him hold her, to never see his smile. God, no! The pain was too much to bear.

And Lord, she bore so much pain in her heart already. In a few hours they'd arrive at *El Castillo de Oro*, the lasting symbol of all the sorrows of her life. Yet, her heart wanted to fly from her breast and soar to the heavens. Because of Lucien. Because of what he'd said. Because of what he made her feel. Alive. And terrified.

Lyncoya, asleep beside her, snorted at her movements but didn't awaken. She cast a furtive glance toward Lucien's nearby bedroll. He never stirred. With as little motion as possible, she slipped out of Lyncoya's sleepy grasp. Wriggling her hips, she managed to remove her legs from the bedroll and then rose. After stretching the kinks from her back, she tiptoed away from the campsite. At the source of the creek, she sat near the edge. The water rolled slowly over the large rocks over and over and over... For centuries, the water had moved in this manner. The water didn't change. But the rocks did.

After a while, she removed her boots and hose and tossed them behind her. With her skirts in her hand, she waded into the creek until the cold water just reached the tops of her ankles. Out of part frustration and part childlike joy, she kicked her legs one at a time. Water flew. Droplets sparkled in the black night like diamonds, and then landed with tiny plops back in the stream.

Soon, the cold numbed her feet and shivers racked her bones. She waded to shore and sat on the ground. She used the hem of her skirt to dry her feet before putting her hose and boots on again, and then leaned back against the dry grass. Propped up on her elbows, she looked at the moon. It didn't hang quite so high in the sky as during the Shakespeare debate. The time was after midnight.

"It's my birthday," she announced softly to the moon.

"I know," Lucien said from behind her. "*Feliz cumpleaños, querida.*"

She stared at him aghast, eyes wide and mouth open. "How long have you been watching me?"

"Not long," he replied. "I'm sorry, sweetheart. I know this isn't how you wished to spend your birthday."

"I had no plans for my birthday, Lucien," she said flatly. "It would have been a normal day in Pensacola, swilling ale to drunken soldiers into the middle of the night. I haven't celebrated a birthday or a holiday in years."

He sat beside her and drew his knees against his chest. "Why not?"

"I have nothing to celebrate and no one to celebrate with."

"You have Ramon."

She laughed. "He's more bitter than I am! If it were not a mortal sin to do so, Ramon would have taken his life years ago. He's merely passing time here on earth until he dies."

The major's shoulders slumped. Sympathy? She didn't know.

"He told me about the loss of his wife and son," he admitted on a long sigh.

Ah, so then he did feel sympathy. But he had no right. "There's more to the tale than you know."

"What else is there?"

She shook her head.

"Marisa? What else is there to the tale?"

Her voice dropped to a whisper. "During the attack on his family, the Creeks maimed him badly. He can never be a whole man again."

"Maimed him? How?"

Heat flamed her cheeks, and she prayed the night hid her shame from him. "Ramon...is incapable of..." Her voice trailed off, and she looked away. "No. I can't tell you. It is unseemly."

"You don't have to," he said. "Ramon is incapable of coupling with a woman?"

Embarrassment choked her throat, and she nodded.

He said nothing, but picked up a pebble and tossed it into the creek where it landed with a plop to become another object altered by time and tide.

They sat in silence for a time before Marisa finally rose to head back to the camp.

"I'm sorry, Marisa," he repeated solemnly.

"Don't be sorry, Lucien," she said with no bitterness or judgment. She offered him simply a sad smile. "Your sympathy helps no one. Be happy and grateful life has been kind to you. Good night."

She returned to her bedroll and crawled inside. One arm wrapped about Lyncoya's waist. She closed her eyes against the sky and hoped to close her mind as well.

But no matter how she tried, sleep evaded her for the remainder of the night.

*"For them no more the blazing hearth shall burn,*
*Or busy housewife ply her evening care;*
*No children run to lisp their sire's return,*
*Or climb his knees the envied kiss to share."*
*— Thomas Gray (Elegy Written in a Country*
*Church-yard)*


## CHAPTER 32

"Home!" Marisa's wistful voice urged Lucien on past the crumbling house.

The well-apportioned stables, so similar to those at *El Castillo de Plata* with their large stalls and expansive, thick green pasture that surrounded them, reflected her love for horses. From the window inside the stall he acquired for Boreas, he could see the lands of *El Castillo* clearly.

Behind the stables sat a clear pond covered with water lilies and surrounded by majestic pine and ash trees. A small waterfall cascaded to a carved wooden footbridge. The farmland near the stables lay barren now, but straight lines of soil ran parallel where rows of corn and wheat once grew.

In many respects, *El Castillo de Oro* resembled a medieval castle of Europe. Built primarily of stone, it had rounded turrets on all four sides. Between these turrets, the second floor of the house lay blackened and crumbled in some areas, but reasonably intact in others. The first floor, however, was completely habitable.

He understood the name and wouldn't be surprised to see a moat and drawbridge complete with a fire-breathing dragon outside the structure. When he closed his eyes, he envisioned what this castle looked like before the Creek War. He'd always believed no place in the world compared with his home at Belle Monde. *El Castillo de Oro* might have done so in the past.

The two estates were vastly different. Belle Monde's architecture relied on French influence while *El Castillo's* was pure Spanish, including a red tiled roof still in evidence above the second floor.

"It is absolutely lovely," he told Marisa.

"This is your home?" Lyncoya said, awestruck as he gazed up at the imposing structure.

"Yes. Come in." Marisa took the boy's hand to draw him inside.

Lucien followed. "Well, I'm grateful we'll sleep with a roof over our heads tonight. I've grown tired of staring at the stars for a time."

"You're much too soft, Major Lucien," Lyncoya admonished. He puffed out his skinny, hairless chest. "Creek warriors don't need to sleep indoors."

Marisa opened the front door. With a deep bow and a sweep of her arm, she ushered them inside. *"Bienvenido al Castillo de Oro."*

In the empty foyer, her words echoed back. The moment they struck her memory, she turned wide eyes to Lucien. No doubt, she'd just realized her first words to him in Pensacola had been quite similar.

*"Muchas gracias,"* Lucien replied as he tucked her hand inside of his.

Lyncoya coughed loudly, breaking whatever spell entranced them. "Does this house have a kitchen?" His head moved up, down, left, right as he wandered into the foyer. "Creek warriors may not need to sleep indoors, but they do get tired of eating Marisa's chewy sticks of meat and berries."

She laughed. "I'll see to it at once."

Due to her annual trek here, she always kept the root cellar well stocked with dried fruits, vegetables, and herbs. She routinely raided the pantry at *El Castillo de Plata* for foods that could be stored for long periods of time at *El Castillo de Oro*. The one item in short supply was fresh meat, but that was easily remedied.

Turning to Lucien, she brushed her fingertips across his hand. "Perhaps you'd do a spot of hunting while I prepare the kitchen?"

His nod, solemn yet gentle, conveyed his own confusion at what had transpired between them. Perhaps Lyncoya had done them a favor. After so many hours forced into each other's company, time to busy themselves with the mundane of food would give them both an opportunity to sort out jumbled thoughts.

While Lucien and Lyncoya set off for dinner, Marisa readied a few sundry items in the cooking area.

With extra time on her hands, she headed for the servant's quarters behind the kitchens and found the hipbath stored in a closet. After weeks of traveling, she'd have loved a real bath, but didn't know how long Lucien and Lyncoya would be gone. So she compromised and quickly washed herself, even managing to pay attention to her filthy and matted hair. Clean again, she returned to the kitchens to chop vegetables.

Lucien and Lyncoya returned with several rabbits, and she soon had the rabbits skinned and roasting beneath a flame of the stove while a large pot of vegetable soup simmered above.

When dinner was prepared, the three sat on the floor in what was once the dining room to eat their grand meal of hearty soup and braised rabbit. Mealtime was quiet, each of them too tired or too befuddled to do more than chew and swallow.

Poor Lyncoya nearly dropped his head into his soup bowl more than once. Finally, Marisa took pity on the boy. "Let's take him upstairs and put him to bed."

Lucien rose and scooped the child into his arms. "Go. I'll follow."

She strode upstairs, but her mind flexed and swirled around thoughts of family. Not her mama and papa. Not 'Lando and Juanita, either. Oddly, she focused on Lucien carrying a sleepy child up a staircase. With her leading the way. Family.

Her foot slipped, and she grabbed the banister. Behind her, Lucien jostled, then quickly sidestepped as if to bar her flight down the stairs.

"Careful there," he murmured, his breath hot in her ear.

She shivered and righted herself to continue up to the room that had once, a long time ago, been the children's nursery.

Once they'd tucked Lyncoya into bed, they descended the staircase side by side.

At the bottom, Lucien turned to her. "Care to walk outside for a bit? I hate to sleep immediately after a meal."

Although exhaustion had already taken hold, she couldn't say no. Longing, desperate and lonely, begged to delay the dissolution of the dream.

"I'd love to," she said.

His smile made her belly flip. "Excellent. Come with me." He took her hand and led her outside.

Across the lawns, over the footbridge that spanned the creek, and straight to the stables.

"It's a little too dark for riding," she said. "Besides, I would think after riding for so long, you'd be happier on solid ground for a while."

His smile widened and sparkled white in the darkness. "Trust me."

Curious, she allowed him to lead her into the stables and, at his insistence, she climbed the ladder to the loft. In one corner, several blankets lay on the floor over layers of straw.

When Lucien followed her up, she turned to him, bewildered. "Why are we up here?"

"Because I don't want to awaken Lyncoya and set his mouth to running," Lucien replied.

"With what?"

"You'll see soon enough. Be patient."

He sat on one of the blankets and patted the space next to him. With a tired sigh, she sank down beside him. When he placed his hands on her shoulders and gently nudged her back against his chest, she leaned into him as if they fit together like puzzle pieces. He wrapped an arm about her waist and held her with her head resting at the juncture between his neck and his shoulder.

He murmured against her ear, "You smell wonderful."

Pleasure scattered like raindrops through her blood. She smiled and snuggled closer to him.

Neither spoke since night provided a symphony. Below them, horses snorted and snickered in sleep. Outside, crickets and cicadas buzzed, and the babble of the nearby creek provided a soothing backdrop. The cruel pace of the last few weeks had finally caught up to Marisa, and she closed her eyes.

"Have I ever told you how my brother managed to convince his wife to marry him?" Lucien asked at last.

Marisa smiled despite her exhaustion. "No."

"In Antoinetta's homeland, a woman is considered married after her father and her betrothed sign a marriage contract. There is no formal ceremony, no banns are posted, and no vows are spoken. At first, Darian asked Antoinetta to marry him, but she proved difficult. So he and

Antoinetta's father signed a marriage contract without her consent. She had no choice but to acquiesce to the marriage."

His chuckle irked, and she shook her head. "I don't see how that's funny. What if Antoinetta didn't really love your brother?"

"Oh, she loved him," Lucien assured her. "She was just being stubborn."

"Well, I still don't find it very funny."

He chucked her under the chin, tilting her head to gaze into his solemn eyes. "It may not seem funny to you now, but it will someday. Do you trust me?"

She stiffened. "I beg your pardon?"

"Do you trust me?" he repeated.

"Yes," she replied. "I'd trust you with my life."

"I'm not asking you to trust me with your life. I want you to trust me with your heart."

"With my heart?" Confusion swirled her in an eddy.

Lucien nodded.

"Why with my heart?"

"Because tonight I intend to make love to you."

Marisa's mouth parched dryer than the hottest desert beneath a noon sun. "You can't be serious."

He placed his hands upon her waist and turned her to face him, pinning her in his embrace. "I'm very serious."

"Wh—what if I don't want you to make love to me?"

"You said you trusted me." He drew his index finger down her cheek to her throat. "Keep faith with me a little longer. If at any time you're too frightened to continue, I promise you, I'll stop immediately."

Shame washed over her, and she lowered her head to stare at the straw. "I don't know how."

"But, I do." His whisper sent shivers down her spine. "Trust me."

He didn't give her another chance to decline. Instead, he tilted her face and rained hot, wet kisses across her forehead, her temples and her brows. While his lips brushed her face, his hands cupped her cheeks to draw her even closer to him.

She should stop him. She knew that. But his kisses made her dizzy, and her reservations faded. At last, her arms wound around his neck of their own accord.

She craned her neck, allowing him access to her throat. When his lips reached the indentation in the center of her neck, she closed her eyes and sighed. Oh, the pleasure! Sheer delight danced over her skin and left her breathless. His fingers moved from her cheeks to rake her hair above her ears then descended. He pressed soft circular motions into her nape. He kissed a languorous line from the hollow of her throat up and over her chin, then covered her mouth with his own.

This time, she didn't need to be told to open her mouth. She did so willingly. While they tasted of each other, Lucien's hands massaged her neck then moved to her shoulder blades. He never broke contact, but his fingers moved downward to open the buttons on the back of her gown.

She shrugged. The top of her gown and the strings of her chemise slid to a point just above her elbows. A wisp of cool air fluttered across her breasts when his hands tugged at the fabrics. Marisa trembled and, suddenly embarrassed at her vulnerable state, pulled away to cover herself.

"No, *querida*," he murmured as his lips kissed her flesh just above her splayed hands. "You're beautiful, and I would see all of you. Don't be afraid. Trust me."

She had to slow down. Too many new sensations made her dizzy and brainless. Boneless.

"What about you?" she asked in an attempt to

dissuade him from his actions. "Do I get to see you as well?"

Lucien shifted to his knees and quickly untied the lacing of his own shirt. Impatiently, he pulled the offensive article over his head, then returned his attention to her still covered breasts. "Better?"

Having no other choice, Marisa nodded and lowered her hands to where her gown and chemise bunched up. Lucien knelt before her and grasped her by the waist. His hands covered hers as his mouth sought out her navel. He swirled his tongue inside, and she shivered in reaction.

He glanced upwards to stare at the expression on her face. "You like that, do you?"

She could barely form the word yes since his mouth now blazed a trail from her navel to the center of her bosom. His hands clasped her belly, and then branched out in opposite directions at the bottom of her breasts.

When his thumbs brushed softly against her nipples, her breath came out in a long whoosh. She hadn't realized she'd stopped breathing, but she must have, because now, there didn't seem to be enough air in the stables to fill her lungs. She inhaled deeply, only to exhale in a gasp when Lucien's mouth fixed on one of her nipples and suckled. Sharp darts of desire pierced her breast. Then, his hand traveled back to the other nipple and rubbed insistently. Her skin hardened, melted, hardened again.

Words disappeared from her brain, leaving nothing but pictures. The first vision that came to her was fire, but she really did not burn, although her skin felt red-hot. She wasn't cold, even if she couldn't stop the tremors racking her body. She thought it might be suffocation, but she did not feel smothered, merely overwhelmed. Whatever this was, it was powerful, and she gave herself over wholly.

She arched her back toward his face, pushing her breasts closer to him. She wanted him to devour her, to lick, to suck, to bite, and to taste every inch of her flesh.

Unable to bring herself any closer to his mouth or hands without cracking her spine, she fell backwards and landed on the soft pile of blankets. Her hair spread out against the floor. The straw scratched the skin of her shoulders and her neck, a bit like crackling fire, warm and fluttery.

Lucien's lips never left her flesh as he followed her down until he crouched on all fours above her, still licking and sucking at her feverish skin.

Her head thrashed from side to side in the straw, and her hips moved in a circular motion against his knees. His hands returned to her waist and tugged her skirts. He loosened the garters at the tops of her thighs and rolled her stockings down toward her booted ankles. Running his tongue across her kneecaps, his fingers nimbly unlaced her boots.

Unaware of anything but the feel of this man's mouth on her skin, she lifted her hips higher and he stopped kissing her only long enough to pull her boots off her feet. He kicked the gown, undergarments, and shoes into a darkened corner. Now as she lay completely unveiled to his eyes, hands, and mouth, he stroked her inner thighs with whisper soft touches of his fingertips while his tongue snaked into and out of her navel.

His motions sent her into a fever of longing. But when he slipped a finger inside the juncture between her thighs, she stiffened and bucked her hips.

"Stop! Don't touch me there!"

Slowly, he withdrew the digit from her flesh, but not before brushing it across the tightened bud hidden inside.

"Oh!" she gasped. "What are you doing to me?"

"I'm loving you, *Montesita*," he told her softly.

273

"You were made for love. You were made to love me, as I was made to love you. Trust me." Again, he grazed his finger across her sensitive flesh, and she trembled violently.

"Do you want me to stop?" he asked her, still moving his finger back and forth over the tight little nub in her center.

"Yes—no!" She quickly changed her mind, and then changed it back again. "Yes!" But when he tried to slip away, she grasped at his shoulders and pulled him back down toward her. "No," she finally decided. "Don't stop. I trust you, Lucien."

He gave her a smile filled with heat and tenderness. Removing his hands from her flesh, he sat back on his haunches.

"Don't stop!" she repeated, reaching out to him blindly.

"I won't stop," he assured her as he traced a finger down her center from breasts to navel, "but things will go more smoothly if I remove the rest of my clothes."

For a brief moment, she had a flash of clarity. *Por Dios*! She was about to allow him to make love to her. She had only the barest idea of what that meant, and she didn't know if she'd like it. Her fear of the unknown increased when he peeled his breeches and drawers off and stood above her. His manhood jutted out from the center of his thighs, large, red, and ready for her.

"You can't think to put that inside me! You're too big. You'll kill me."

He knelt over her again and placed her finger in his mouth to suck upon it. He removed the digit and blew his breath upon its wet tip. A new ripple of shivers seared her spine. "While I thank you for the compliment," he drawled, "I assure you I won't kill you. I do, however, want to take you to heaven."

He pushed her back against the floor and set

one of his knees between her thighs to nudge them apart. With his weight rested on his elbows, he stretched out atop her. His finger moved rhythmically against her.

"Do you trust me, *Montesita*?" he murmured. "Do you want a real life or do you want to continue to exist in a netherworld?"

Her fears melted beneath the heat of her blood and that teasing digit. "What do I do?"

"Trust me," he repeated. Slipping just the tip of himself into her entrance, he used his thumb to open the lips of her passage a bit more and gradually slid inside her.

The pain was excruciating!

"Stop!" She rolled her head from side to side, but not with pleasure. She was impaled on a flaming dagger. "Please, Lucien. You promised me you'd stop if I didn't like it."

"Not now, *Montesita*," he told her as he kissed away the tears in the corners of her eyes.

"It hurts," she complained between sobs. "I don't like this." She tried bucking her hips to remove him, but that only implanted him deeper within her.

"No," he whispered. "Don't move. Wait and trust me."

"I don't want to wait any longer," she shouted. "You promised you would stop if I asked."

Just when she thought she could take no more, he withdrew from her and she relaxed at the idea that he'd stop. Instead, he slid out almost entirely, then slid right back in again. Oddly, his gliding motion didn't seem to hurt as much this time. And when he moved again, Marisa felt something new. A warm tickle in the pit of her belly spread through her limbs.

When he slid away for the third time, she drew her knees up against his hips to keep him inside. Deep within her, the tickle became a tingle, ebbing and flowing as Lucien's flesh sank into and out of hers. Heat bubbled from her hair to her shoulders, down her arms to her fingertips, and out through her toes, only to wash over her again.

She clutched at his shoulders, concentrated on that tingle, moved her hips to accommodate it. The tingle sparked. When she moved her hips in time with his thrusts, the spark burst into flame. His mouth possessed hers while they moved together, and the flame turned into a raging inferno.

Just as she'd wished earlier, Lucien devoured her flesh. His eyes, his mouth, his hands, and his manhood, in her and on her, caressed and consumed. Her heels dug into his hips, pulling him closer. Her mouth covered his to taste him.

With each of his thrusts, she tightened around him. She coiled herself into a tense spring, and then relaxed her body as he slid just to the edge of her threshold.

"Lucien," she cried out against his ear, terrified of the tremors that raced through her senses. "What's happening to me?"

"Don't be afraid. Let it fill you, *querida*," he advised her. "Trust me."

A moment later, she compressed the muscles in her belly. She wanted to grasp Lucien and hold him within her, yet at the same time, she burned to release them both from his sweet torment.

"Don't fight it," he murmured against her lips.

As if she could. The moment he spoke the words, she gave into her needs and convulsed. Her core erupted in a mindless frenzy of shudders, moans, and spasms. She melted against him as every fiber of her being turned to liquid and burst forth.

"Yes, *querida*, yes. Aaaahh!" Lucien stiffened within her in search of his own release. While she crested, he plunged into her fevered flesh and then finally collapsed against her heaving breasts.

Rising up on his elbows, he stared down at her face with concern. "Marisa?"

She didn't answer, couldn't answer. When he withdrew from her, she gave a soft cry. He rolled to his side and pulled her into his embrace. He kissed her lips before brushing a bit of straw out of her hair.

At last, the bliss evaporated, and she found her voice. "I told Lyncoya this would be my best birthday ever."

*"But with the morning cool repentance came."*
*— Sir Walter Scott (Rob Roy)*

## CHAPTER 33

Marisa woke upon the realization she was nude. And held in the strong arms of an equally nude man. Slowly, she sat up to glance around the loft. Cool air nipped her bare shoulders, and she shivered.

Memories of the night's activities flooded into her mind. Despair took hold. What had she been thinking? What madness had seized her? What would happen to her now?

"No regrets, *Montesita*," Lucien said as he rose on an elbow. "Unless I hurt you last night."

Embarrassment heated her cheeks, and she looked toward the far wall to avoid his gaze.

In typical male fashion, he grasped her chin and turned her gaze back to his. "Did I hurt you?"

He'd keep pressing until she answered. Too ashamed to speak, she shook her head.

"Then there are no regrets," he repeated. "I told you last evening to trust me, and you did. Don't cease to do so because the sun has risen."

"But—"

He pressed a finger to her lips. "Trust me."

With reluctance, she nodded. Regret wouldn't undo her behavior. What else could she do? She had to trust him. But if he played her false, he'd suffer La Venganza's retaliation.

"Do you remember the tale I told you last evening regarding Darian's marriage to Antoinetta?"

Understanding dawned swiftly. Oh, *por Dios*, did he honestly believe he could manipulate her in so vile a manner? She pointed a finger in his face.

But he grasped the digit with his fist, brought it to his lips, and kissed the tip.

"You've taken the decision out of my hands," she stated flatly.

"Indeed, I have," he replied.

"You don't have to sound so proud of it," she grumbled.

"I *am* proud, *Montesita*," he assured her. "I've captured a star. No small feat for a mere mortal."

Heat suffused her from head to toe, and she dropped her gaze to the floorboards. "What do we do now?"

"I suggest we dress, for a start."

When they both rose, Marisa kept her eyes averted from his naked form. She found her dress and chemise in a crumpled heap near the blankets, but her boots, stockings, and garters lay buried somewhere beneath the piles of hay. Hastily, she pulled the chemise over her head and searched on her hands and knees for her stockings.

"Do you have a bathtub in the house?"

Lucien's sudden question whirled her from her search to stare at him quizzically. "There's a bathing chamber on the second floor near my parents' bedroom. Why?"

"Because," he said, his eyes scanning down her legs, "I believe you might wish to bathe this morning."

Following his gaze, she found brown-red stains on her skin just below the hem of her chemise. "Oh!" Terror knocked her to her knees. "I knew you were much too big! Now I'm bleeding to death!"

"You're not bleeding to death. That blood is the

proof that I've breached your maidenhead. Virgins always bleed the first time they make love."

Sniffing, she looked up at him, gauged the sincerity in his eyes. "Truly?"

"Truly," he said and dropped the rest of her clothes beside her. "Finish dressing."

"I can't find my stockings."

"Leave them. We should return to the house. Lyncoya will awaken soon and our absence might distress him."

"Lyncoya!" She'd forgotten all about him.

She quickly descended the ladder from the hayloft and ran toward the house with Lucien behind her.

As they neared the front porch, he grumbled, "Every other day the boy sleeps until mid-morning, but today he awakens at sunrise."

Lyncoya waited in the doorway, his arms folded over his skinny chest as he stared at Lucien with disapproval. His black eyes moved from Marisa's disheveled appearance to Lucien and back again.

"Major Lucien?" Despite his youth, Lyncoya managed to sound like a disparaging papa.

"Lyncoya." Lucien tousled the boy's hair. "Marisa said yes."

While the boy cheered and danced around the couple, Marisa's blood chilled. Trust him? She should have known better.

"Major Lucien didn't ask me to marry him," Marisa shouted over the boy's glee. "And if he had, I would have turned him down."

Lyncoya stopped, and his smile flipped to a frown. "But...why?"

Lucien flashed an indulgent smile at the boy. "Marisa is right. I really didn't ask her. I just assumed..." Shrugging, he turned to her. "I didn't believe it necessary after last evening. But I'll ask now."

She strode past him. "I don't wish to marry you. No matter what happened between us."

His hand shot out and grasped her, stopping her ascent. "You'll marry me even if I have to drag you by your hair to a priest and press a dagger to your throat to get you to say the vows. I've risked my life and my honor for you. You're angry because I took the decision out of your hands. I can understand that." He took her fingertips inside his palm. His tone softened when he added, "You'll see. Once we're wed, we'll be blissfully happy."

She shook her head. "No, we won't. You thought because your brother took the decision out of Antoinetta's hands and forced her to the altar you could use the same foul means to win me. I won't allow that."

"I didn't use foul means—"

"You seduced me!" Lyncoya's breath came out in a sharp gasp, but she ignored him and scaled the last two steps. "You assumed I'd go along with your scheme to trap me into marriage. Well, I'm not so docile, Lucien. I'm not Antoinetta."

"I don't want you to be Antoinetta. I know you're not Antoinetta."

"You love *her*, not me."

He stared at her as if she'd lost her mind, but he didn't deny her words.

Envy pierced her heart, sharper than any dagger. She'd hoped she might be wrong about his feelings for his sister-in-law, prayed the stories he told and the way he spoke about her came from deep affection. But Lucien's silence right now gave damning evidence of the truth of the matter.

"You only want me because you can't have her," she whispered in defeat. "You're willing to settle for me because you know Antoinetta will never see you as anything more than a brother."

"That's not true—"

But his denial came too late for her peace of mind. "I won't consider marriage to a man who loves someone else."

His eyes narrowed and rage boiled the air between them. "What do you know of love, Marisa? You've spent the last seven years in a quest for revenge. You and your partner, La Venganza! You have no knowledge of what love is. You've been too busy nursing your hatred at the world."

"I don't hate the world, but I do hate you."

"That's not what you said last night," he replied.

"I didn't say I loved you. I said I trusted you. Now I'm not so certain I can do that." She turned, opened the door, and strode inside the house with Lyncoya on her heels.

"Marisa? Where are you going?"

"I need to heat some water for a bath," she said.

"Is it true, Marisa?" Hurt laced every whispered syllable. "Is your friend really La Venganza?"

Damn you, Lucien.

Regret choked her words, and she nodded.

"I thought we were friends." Through eyes blurred by tears, she saw the boy's shoulders slump. "But I could never be friends with someone who hates my papa."

****

*Thunk! Thunk! Thunk!*

The rhythmic sound woke Lucien from a deep slumber. Curious, he rose from the bedroll beside Lyncoya and peered out the window onto the lands of *El Castillo de Oro*.

By the light of a full moon, he spotted Marisa outside, dressed in a boy's shirt and breeches at least two sizes too big. Her slender form was outlined beneath the cloth. His loins instantly tightened. But her strange attire didn't keep his attention.

She was chopping firewood. Every so often, she'd drop the axe in her hands to push the sleeves of the shirt back up onto her shoulders with an impatient gesture. Then, she'd spit on her hands and grip the axe again, swinging it in a wide arc above her head to crash into the thick logs over and over.

Heaving a deep sigh, Lucien turned from the window. Oh, how he wanted to speak with her, to tell her what was truly in his heart. But her bitterness and anger kept him at a distance.

For five days after their encounter in the hayloft, Marisa avoided all contact. After her bath, she locked herself in her parents' bedroom, only leaving the quarters to prepare meals.

Three times a day for nearly a week, Lucien and Lyncoya would find a delicious repast awaiting them, but Marisa never joined them. She ate alone abovestairs.

Her coldness affected Lucien, but not as badly as Lyncoya. Devastated by her confession about Ramon's identity, the boy had crumbled, his spirit crushed. Worse, Marisa made no attempt to excuse her behavior or to appease Lyncoya's heartbreak. She simply became inaccessible.

For five nights, he listened to Lyncoya cry himself to sleep. For five days, he watched Lyncoya's face light up at the sound of her approach only to become crestfallen when she passed by without a word.

The time had come to put an end to this impasse.

He slid his feet into his boots with furious thrusts, left the room, and descended the staircase. He stalked out the front door and across the grounds. Windswept leaves crushed under his enraged footsteps.

His anger dissipated as he watched her swing the large axe over her head. She looked distracted as she chopped. Although she kept the axe moving, her eyes watched the woods around her and not the logs she split.

"Marisa? What is it? What's wrong?"

She never looked at him as she brought the axe up and slammed it into the log with an almost violent compulsion. The log splintered into pieces at the force of her blow, and he stepped back to avoid a flying chunk of wood.

"What the hell are you doing out here?" he demanded.

She dropped the axe and stared at him, her eyes filled with unshed tears. "Ramon should have been here by now. Your friends have killed him."

"How do you know that? You said Ramon would deliberately slow them down to make certain you arrived here first."

She shook her head. "Even at a snail's pace, Ramon should have reached *El Castillo* two days ago."

At her misery, his resentment melted. God, how he wanted to take her in his arms and tell her all would be well. He reached toward her, but she shook off his sympathy and returned her attention to the firewood.

"Tomorrow morning, I want you to leave *El Castillo*."

"You want us to leave here?"

She stopped in mid-swing and stared at him. Her eyes glinted like chipped granite. "If Ramon is dead, I hardly see why you should remain."

"Ramon again, is it?" Anger rose in a blood red mist. "Do you care about anyone else in this world but yourself and Ramon?"

She dropped the axe and set her hands on her hips. "You, for instance?"

He shrugged. "Why not?"

"My, my. You certainly think highly of yourself. Did you honestly believe I'd marry you because we made love in a hayloft one night? While I admit it was a pleasant enough evening, it was not so magical I've lost my senses. If I'd wanted to gain a husband in that manner, I might have done so long before you ever arrived in Pensacola. I've had many disreputable offers in the last several years."

"Mine is not a disreputable offer," he retorted. "I want to marry you."

"Well, thank you very much. But I don't want to marry you!"

"What if you're carrying my child, Marisa?"

She shook her head before grasping the axe in her hands again. "I can assure you I'm not with child."

"Perhaps not, but what of another child? What about Lyncoya?"

Her gaze quickly strayed to the woods behind her, and then returned to him. Did she think the boy might be eavesdropping? Thank God, he'd left Lyncoya blissfully sleeping, unaware of the poison Marisa spewed. Her expression grew inscrutable. She grabbed another log from the woodpile and slammed it down on the chopping block.

"What do I care about a Creek boy's feelings?" she whispered. "I despise the filthy little heathen."

He stepped back as if she'd slapped him. "You can't mean that."

"Can't I?" She pounded the axe with such ferocity, he had to strain to hear her words over the noise. "For all I know, his father murdered my family. And now this savage is living under my roof."

"Good God, I can't believe you'd say such things. The boy's an innocent."

Her lips quirked. "So was I. But you changed that for me, didn't you?"

By the devil, how could he have misjudged her so badly? On a deep sigh, he turned away from her ugly accusations. "You win, Marisa. Your bitterness is stronger than anything I could possibly offer you.

We'll leave at dawn. I hope you're happy with your decision. Prejudice and hatred make poor companions for a woman in old age."

Without waiting for a retort, he stalked away from her.

He dared one look back. Marisa sat on the chopping block, the axe at her feet, face buried in her hands. Perhaps she wept. Or perhaps it was a trick of the moonlight. Either way, he'd washed his hands of La Venganza.

*"Falsehood flies and truth comes limping after it, so that when men come to be undeceived it is too late."*
*— Jonathan Swift (The Examiner)*

## CHAPTER 34

Lucien returned to his room, his brain abuzz. He slammed the door with a bang, momentarily forgetting the little occupant slumbering inside.

"Major Lucien?" Lyncoya sat up in his bedroll.

"Yes, lad," Lucien whispered. "Go back to sleep. I'll be taking you home in the morning."

Lyncoya sat up. "What about Marisa's friend? Is he here?"

"No," Lucien admitted.

"Then we can't leave. I promised Marisa I would stay with her until her friend arrived. I must keep my promise."

Lucien was amazed at the boy's fervent loyalty to a woman who despised him. What could he possibly tell Lyncoya? How could he make the child understand they were no longer welcome here?

"You don't understand. Marisa is the one insisting you and I leave tomorrow."

Lyncoya tossed off the blankets and stood. "I don't believe you."

He placed his hands on the child's shoulders. "It's true. She doesn't wish us to stay here any longer."

"Forgive me, Major Lucien, but I want to hear

this from her. I'll ask her myself."

"That's not a good idea." In Marisa's current mood, she'd slice the boy to pieces with her hatred.

"I don't care! I want to speak to Marisa!" Lyncoya pushed Lucien out of the way to reach the door.

"Lyncoya, wait!"

The boy ignored him. "Marisaaaaaa!"

"She's outside at the woodpile," he called out.

To prevent the possibility Lyncoya might be struck by pieces of Marisa's flying debris, Lucien caught up to him before he reached the woodpile and slowed him down to a careful walk. The two stopped short in front of the chopping block. The axe lay on its side against the stack of firewood. Broken bits of log littered the ground around them.

"Where is she?"

Lucien looked about the woodpile in confusion. "She was here just a few moments ago. Perhaps she followed me indoors and sought out her bed."

Lyncoya gestured to the scattered pieces of wood. "She wouldn't have left this mess."

The boy studied the ground with an intensity ungained by most adults. After several minutes, he shook his head and looked up, misery written in his eyes. "Did she take Tormenta?"

Lucien hadn't thought to look.

Reading the answer in Lucien's shrug, Lyncoya bolted for the stables. Lucien could only follow. But Tormenta stood in her stall. The boy's face crumbled.

"It's my fault she's gone," he whined. "I told her I wouldn't be her friend anymore."

"No, Lyncoya." He placed a hand on the boy's shoulder to reassure him. "It's not your fault. Marisa's angry with me."

One clean jerk, and Lyncoya stepped away from Lucien's sympathy. Spine straight, he pointed toward the chopping block. "Go back to the woodpile.

I'll meet you there shortly."

If the situation had not seemed so desperate, he would have laughed at the boy's arrogance. Instead, he gave a crisp salute and replied, "Yes, sir!"

He watched Lyncoya head toward the house as he strode back to the woodpile. While he waited for Lyncoya's return, he bent low to study the ground around the woodpile. He could easily see Marisa's footprints. The weight of the axe and the force of her blows made deep impressions in the soft dirt. He discerned his own footprints from and to the house and the two sets of footprints he and Lyncoya made.

But when he walked behind the woodpile, he noticed the last sets of footprints. One was definitely Marisa's, but the second couldn't be. The size of the boot was too large. He followed the prints until they stopped at the edge of the forest.

"What did you find?" Lyncoya's voice came from behind him.

The boy stood with his quiver, bow and arrows strapped to his back. Pausing to hand Lucien his pistol, he bent to examine the ground more closely.

"She didn't leave us." Lyncoya pointed at the two sets of prints in the dirt. "Someone took her."

****

Marisa had waited until Lucien's broad back disappeared into the night. Assured he would not return, she rose and faced the demon hiding in the woods.

"Well done, *señorita,*" Sergeant Greene hissed in the darkness. "Very well done, indeed. Now, if you'll follow me, I'll take you to your friend."

On dejected feet, she followed Sergeant Greene through the dense woods for nearly a mile. As they walked, she kicked up a stone or tossed a bit of wood out of her pocket onto the ground. The long gave her time to review her conversation with Lucien. She'd seen the hurt look in his eyes when he'd turned toward the house. He'd believed her lies.

Why would he not? After all, she was an accomplished liar. She'd spent the last seven years of her life deceiving people. The idea she was too filled with hatred to understand love was something Lucien would never question.

Had she ever given him reason to think anything but ill of her? Even when he'd been sweet and tender, she'd behaved like a hateful, bitter harpy.

When the sergeant finally stopped, she found herself near a familiar house, the home of Timmy Pendleton and his family. Sadly, none of the Pendletons had survived Fort Mims. The farm had been unoccupied ever since.

She bit back a retort about the blackguards' penchant for abandoned farmhouses. Instead, she turned to glare at her escort, concern for Ramon uppermost in her mind. "Where is he?"

"Inside," Ethan tilted his head toward the ramshackle building.

Beyond caring what he thought, she pushed him aside with one hearty shove and scaled the steps two at a time. She swung open the front door, nearly tearing it off its rusted hinges in her haste to get to Ramon.

Racing inside the house, she came to a dead stop in the sitting room. He slumped on the floor near the fireplace, barely conscious. Even from the doorway, she saw his bruised face, bloody and swollen to twice its size. A stream of blood ran from his lip to his chin and another began somewhere near his left temple and dripped over his eye.

A large dark man stood over him, his arms folded over his chest and a smug smile on his nasty rat-like face.

"We meet at last, La Venganza," he greeted her.

Marisa ignored him. Her attention never left the

broken form on the floor. "Oh, Ramon!"

Blackened eyes opened, unfocused. *"Montesita,"* he managed to mumble through split and distended lips.

Marisa knelt beside him and cradled his head in her hands. "Hush." She smoothed a gentle finger on his brow. "Don't speak now. All will be well, I promise you."

"Forgive me. I should have listened to you."

"There's nothing to forgive, *querido,*" she whispered, kissing his forehead.

"A very moving reunion," Ethan scoffed as he strode into the sitting room. "But, shall we dispense with the remainder of this conversation for now? There'll be plenty of time for you to pledge your undying love before your necks are stretched."

Righteous anger exploded inside her, and she turned her fury on the two men who stood hale and hearty in the room. "What do you want?"

"Why, Marisa," Ethan continued in the same venomous tone. "Aren't you happy to see me again?"

"I won't be happy until I see you dead."

"Then, I fear you'll be disappointed," Foster interjected. "You're the one who will be dead shortly. General Jackson has offered a reward for your capture. Since he believes La Venganza kidnapped his son, he'll stop at nothing to see you executed for your vile deeds. Thanks to you, my dear, Ethan and I will be quite wealthy for the rest of our lives."

"Fine," she snapped. "You've caught me now. So release Ramon to return to *El Castillo.*"

"Oh no, La Venganza!" Foster shook his head. "You and your Ramon will be accompanying us to Mobile."

Too stunned to hide her reaction, she blinked. "Mobile? Why would we be going to Mobile?"

"Because the general is currently residing there," was the icy reply from Ethan. "He has instructions to pay Lyncoya's ransom at a friend's house in the city. The ransom is for his son's safe return, but that is not in the boy's future."

*Gracias a Dios.* She'd worried Sergeant Greene had overheard her discussion with Lucien about Lyncoya. Apparently, her subterfuge with the axe was enough to drown out their conversation. The two scoundrels remained unaware she'd rescued Lyncoya from the Bartlett farm.

"After the ransom monies are safely in our hands," Foster said, "Lyncoya will die. We can't release him alive lest he tell his parents the identities of the true culprits behind his disappearance."

"Once the general has received the news of his son's demise, I'll arrive in Mobile with La Venganza and her accomplice in tow, ready for execution for their vile deeds," Ethan chimed in. "I'll collect the reward money offered for your capture. While Marcus and I are spending the general's money, you, your friend, and that savage little Indian boy will all be carrion for the vultures."

If not for Ramon's broken and battered body in her lap, she'd have flown at these two villains. "You bastards!"

"Strange, Marcus," Ethan remarked dryly. "She doesn't seem excited with our plans. Or could it be that the loss of Major St. Clair has made you so distraught you don't remember your manners?"

"St. Clair is here?" Foster looked around a little too frantically.

*So he fears Lucien, does he? Good. We might use that to our advantage.*

"Where is he, Ethan?" Foster demanded.

"Gone," Ethan replied. "La Venganza gave quite an admirable performance this evening. St. Clair has been residing at *El Castillo de Oro* with her."

"So where is he now?"

Ethan shrugged. "I told Marisa to be certain he wouldn't come looking for her, and by God, she did just that. He'd sooner crawl through a swamp filled with alligators than seek out her company again."

Each word sent a dagger into her heart. But she fought back her tears and inhaled for strength. A gentle squeeze brushed her fingertips and she looked down into Ramon's eyes. But whatever he wished to communicate to her was lost at Foster's outburst.

"You let St. Clair walk away from us?" He crossed the room to grab Ethan by his shirt collar and shake him. "You fool!"

Ethan's eyes bulged as he gasped for air. His hands clawed to pry Foster's hands away. "Why not?" he rasped. "We have nothing to fear from St. Clair."

"Oh? What's to stop St. Clair from going straight to the general's camp and informing Jackson what we've been about?"

"Now who is a fool?" Ethan rejoined. "What could he possibly say? That he allowed La Venganza to escape from the calaboose and she repaid him by slipping away from him while he slept in her home? He'd be branded a laughingstock! I know the man well, Marcus. St. Clair's honor and good name mean everything to him. He is no threat to us. Let him go!"

"I don't like it," Foster grumbled.

Ethan waved off his cohort's misgivings. "Trust me, Marcus. By morning, he'll be headed to his precious Belle Monde, cursing the name of Marisa Álvarez all the way home."

*"A wind arose among the pines; it shook*
*The clinging music from their boughs, and then*
*Low, sweet, faint sounds, like the farewell of ghosts,*
*Were heard: Oh, follow, follow, follow me!"*
*— Percy Bysshe Shelley (Prometheus Unbound)*

## CHAPTER 35

Lucien plodded over a weed and vine choked ground in the dark of night. With every step he pushed away thick foliage and thin branches. Meanwhile, Lyncoya tracked Marisa's movements by nothing more than the light of the moon and a dozen stars. Lucien never thought he'd see the day when he'd allow an eight-year-old boy to lead him through a dense forest in search of answers.

But Lyncoya had been well-schooled in the fine arts of tracking and hunting prey. After all, he'd had the finest teachers in the world to show him the skills of warfare, namely his father, Major General Andrew Jackson, a Red Stick warrior named Chief Red Eagle, and, best of all, Marisa.

How foolish of him not to realize sooner she'd lied about her hatred for Lyncoya. They'd been together for weeks now, and in that time she never missed an opportunity to shower the child with affection. When she didn't instruct him with his bow and arrows or tuck him into his bedroll, she tousled his hair, sang to him, bathed him, cared for him. Those were not the actions of a woman consumed with hate.

If she despised him so much, would she have insisted he ride with her everyday? Would she have touched him so often and with so much affection? Even at night, in her sleep, she reached for him and wrapped her arm about his waist, keeping his little body close against hers. Why in the name of all that was holy had he believed her when she said she wanted Lyncoya out of her home?

He should have known better than to take Marisa's falsehoods to heart. She was an expert at illusion and misrepresentation. She'd boasted to Lucien of her ability to deceive people in word and deed. Hell, she'd even taught him how to lie.

So, if she was such an expert liar and if she'd fibbed about her feelings for Lyncoya, could it be possible she'd misstated her feelings for him as well? He certainly hoped so.

But whatever her feelings, he wanted to hear the truth from her. No, that wasn't quite right. He didn't want to hear the truth. He needed to hear it. And he'd gladly crawl through a swamp full of alligators to seek her out.

Throughout their journey now, Lyncoya remained bent at the waist. He stared at the ground, inspecting branches, twigs, and stones for any clue they might have recently been disturbed by footfalls of others traveling in the area. It was monotonous and time consuming work, but Lyncoya never faltered. Occasionally, he'd pick something up that caught his eye. He'd inspect the item, smell it, run his fingers over it carefully and then place it back where he'd found it.

They walked this way for nearly two hours with Lyncoya more and more intent upon finding any clue, no matter how small or insignificant. Finally, his exhaustive efforts and inordinate patience were rewarded.

"Major Lucien!" The boy came to a dead stop.

Instantly, Lucien halted also. "What is it? What did you find?"

"Look!"

He pointed to a small patch of blue and yellow wildflowers growing in the midst of the woods. Atop the tightly closed bud of a cornflower perched a chunk of grayish-brown tree trunk about the size of a man's thumb. A bit farther sat a second, past that a third, a fourth, and so on.

"I'll be damned," Lucien exclaimed.

"She left us a trail to follow!" the boy enthused. "She didn't leave us, Major Lucien. She knew we'd find those bits of wood here. She wants us to follow her!"

\*\*\*\*

"Get him up!" Foster ordered Marisa, pointing to Ramon. "We don't have time to dawdle, especially with St. Clair nearby."

"I will not," she informed him in a voice as cold as the underbelly of a snake. "He needs his rest."

"You and he will both be resting for eternity once we arrive in Mobile," Foster threatened. "Get him up now!"

"Ramon's a feeble old man," she shouted. *God, please, I hope they haven't learned the truth in their three-week trek through the wilderness.* "If you don't allow him a short time to rest, he'll be dead long before we reach Mobile!" Neither man gainsaid her pronouncement of Ramon's age, and she pressed her advantage. "And if Ramon should die before we reach Mobile, there's nothing to keep me cooperating with your plans."

Foster shrugged in reply. "Seems a shame to keep him healthy just so he won't die before the executioner kills him. But if that's what you want..."

"That's what I want."

"So be it. We leave at first light."

296

"I want a few cloths and some clean hot water," she demanded. "I need to wipe the dirt and blood from his wounds."

"I'm not playing nursemaid," Foster grumbled. "If you want those things, fetch them yourself. Ethan will stay by your side, no matter where you go."

"Agreed," she announced as if she controlled the situation.

Gently, she lifted Ramon's head off her lap and set him on the floor while she rose to her feet. "Do not fret, *querido*," she whispered. "All will be well."

With the sergeant behind her, she headed outdoors to the well to retrieve the water. While he watched, never offering a hand to help, she filled a bucket. Not that she'd accept help from a villain.

She lugged the filled bucket back to the house and into the kitchens, then tossed several logs into the stove and lit them. When she had a fire blazing, she placed a pot filled with some of the water atop the stove.

"I don't suppose you have a knife," she said to Greene.

He folded his arms over his chest, but said nothing.

"*Muchas gracias*," she muttered, and then went into the pantry.

She returned to the kitchen, holding an old rusted dagger. "I suppose this will have to do."

Using the dull blade, she tore strips off the sleeves of the overlarge shirt she wore. While she worked, the sergeant kept his hand on his pistol with the barrel trained between her eyes.

He never stood more than a foot away, but he remained impassive and offered no assistance.

Just as well, as far as she was concerned. She didn't wish to feel any softness for this man. Although she'd never shown him anything less than gracious hospitality, he'd repaid her kindness by

297

betraying her for money. In Marisa's eyes, there was no greater sin in the world than greed. Perhaps because greed seemed to be the catalyst for all other crimes. Some men would do anything, even commit murder, for money.

She tested the temperature of the water on the stove with an index finger. Satisfied with its warmth, she filled an old, cracked porcelain bowl. With the strips of cloth gathered, she returned to the sitting room. Her villainous shadow followed.

After setting the bowl of water and the makeshift bandages to one side, she knelt near Ramon. She picked up one of the cloths, dipped it in the water, and then dabbed it at the wound near his temple. He opened his eyes and mumbled.

"What did he say?" Ethan demanded.

Marisa's face remained blank, and she shrugged. "I don't know. I can't understand him."

Ramon continued his illogical ramblings throughout her ministrations.

"Ethan," Foster growled. "You know languages. What's he saying?"

The sergeant leaned close, listened intently, and then shook his head. "She speaks the truth. The man's delirious."

Slowly, Marisa rose. "I need more bandages and clean water."

She picked up the bowl and headed back to the kitchens. Ramon closed his eyes again and fell silent. When she returned to the sitting room, the sergeant plopped himself into the chair on the opposite side of the room while she tended to the remainder of Ramon's wounds. Finished, she brushed the hair from her patient's face and softly crooned to him.

*When dawn comes, I shall fly to you*
*And on golden wings we will soar to our home.*
*We will abide one for the other,*
*And no longer will we feel the need to roam...*

For over two hours, Marisa sang her lullabies in low tones with surprising results. All three men surrendered to the sound of her voice. While the men slept, she remained awake on the floor with Ramon's head cradled on her lap. Even if she'd been comfortable enough to sleep, her mind would never allow it.

Ramon's mumbled words reverberated in her brain as she waited and prayed Lucien would find them before dawn. Because by dawn, whether or not he'd arrived, she and Ramon would have to make their escape. She dared not risk her captors' anger by insisting they remain here another day and, once they left the Pendleton farm, no one would be able to find them.

Just as dawn lit the ragged cloth that covered the windows in the sitting room, Lucien's voice boomed from outside the house. "Time to awaken, gentlemen! Rise and meet your fate!"

Ethan stirred in his chair. "St. Clair!"

"I warned you!" Foster raced to peer out the window. "I told you he'd seek us out! St. Clair's not a man to give up easily."

Marisa also rose to peer through the window. Sure enough, Lucien stood outside, his arms folded over his chest. Her heartbeat thundered against her ribs, and she sent up a silent prayer of thanks, along with a second request for strength for the battle to come.

"I believe you have something that belongs to me," Lucien shouted. "Marisa, are you there? Are you safe?"

"Why is that man saying you belong to him, *Montesita*?" Ramon's utterance was soft and low in the room, but an icy edge clung to his tone.

"Marisa, answer me!" Lucien called again.

"I'm well, Lucien," she replied loudly.

"Lucien?" Ramon's voice thundered throughout

the tiny room as he stared at Marisa with disgust. "What is Lucien St. Clair doing here in Alabama? And since when do you call him by his given name?"

"L—Lucien traveled w—with m—me to *El Castillo*. H—he worried about my making the journey alone. He wanted to protect me from the dangers of the wilderness."

"And who was with you to protect you from the dangers of Major St. Clair?" Ramon demanded archly.

"No one," she replied. "I didn't need protection from him."

"No?" Ramon gripped her wrist and twisted.

She cried out in pain, but his eyes glared at her with a mixture of distrust and resentment.

"Why didn't you need protection from him? Did you allow him to touch you?"

Marisa kept her eyes downcast, staring at the ashes in the fireplace.

"Oh, you heartless bitch!" Ramon shouted. When he shot to his feet, he nearly pulled her arm from its socket. "How could you betray me this way?"

Ethan and Foster stared wide-eyed in disbelief at the drama unfolding before their eyes. Marisa, on the floor, cowered behind one arm while Ramon railed, her other arm clenched in his grasp.

"I trusted you! I gave you my heart and you repaid me by cavorting with that sanctimonious bastard!"

"But, Ramon—"

"Traitor!" His free hand slapped her face, and the sound crackled through the room. "How could you allow that man to take liberties with you? I loved you." He yanked her to her feet. "Well, no more!"

"Ramon, please," she begged as he dragged her across the floor. "Please let me explain."

"There is nothing to explain, harlot!"

The two men inside the sitting room were apparently so absorbed in this turn of events they forgot about Lucien waiting outside to attack them. Unfortunately for Marisa, Ramon had not forgotten.

Grabbing Marisa by her hair, he pulled her out of the house.

*"Sampson with his strong Body, had a weak Head, or he would not have laid it in a Harlot's lap."*
*— Benjamin Franklin (Poor Richard)*

## CHAPTER 36

Outrage shot through Lucien when Ramon pulled Marisa onto the porch. Ethan and Foster, both white-faced, stood in the doorway, staring at the feeble old man who dragged a grown woman as if she were made of straw.

Once outside, he pushed her down the steps while she continued to plead with him to listen to her. With a swift kick on her bottom, he propelled her forward to land at Lucien's feet in the dirt.

"There's your whore, St. Clair!" he bellowed. "Keep her or throw her to the wolves. I no longer want her near me. She's tainted goods. I wash my hands of her."

Stunned to the depths of his soul, Lucien bent to help her to her feet. He hooked his hands beneath her arms and picked her up, but her legs gave out and she fell to the ground again, sobbing and shaking. He knelt again and tried to gather her in his arms, but Ramon's words stopped him cold.

"By God! Even now, the loathsome whore cannot keep her hands off the knave who defiled her! Bah!" He spat in the dirt. "You deserve each other. One's a trollop who lost her virtue, the other's a profligate who lost his honor. You gave me your word, Major!

You swore to me you wouldn't compromise her. Yet at the very first opportunity that presented itself, you ruined your name as well as hers. Well, good riddance to you both!"

Lucien rose to face this new adversary with fisted hands. "I don't care who you really are—"

"No!" Marisa placed a hand on his chest. Tears flowed copiously down her cheeks. "Leave him be."

His heart broke at her stricken eyes, her terror. Relenting for her benefit, he knelt beside her once more. She tried to rise and this time, with Lucien's strong arms around her waist for support, she managed to stand and remain upright. In one fluid movement, she grasped his shoulders and buried her head against his neck, wailing in deep despair.

Although her hot breath tickled his earlobe, the words she murmured sent shivers down his spine. "Trust me. No regrets."

She gave him a weak smile, but her eyes glistened with tears when she pulled out of his embrace. She took several steps away from his side, her eyes locked on his face, conveying a message he couldn't understand.

A sudden cry of anguish ripped the air.

"Damn you, *Montesita*! How could you do this to me?" Ramon charged at her, his arm above his head. In his upraised hand, he held the knife she'd used to cut the bandages the evening before.

"No!" she screamed and brought her arms above her head to ward off the blow.

The blade flashed silver in the morning light for a brief moment before Ramon sank it into her chest. A froth of bright crimson liquid bubbled up from her lips and spilled out. Her mouth opened in a wide o of disbelief as she sank to her knees. Her eyelids fluttered once, and she clutched at the knife sticking out of her breast. With almost serene grace, she fell face first into the earth, still.

A cry of deep misery filled the air, quickly followed by a second. Lucien sank to his knees, his face contorted with grief, but he was not the only mourner.

Ramon threw himself over her fallen body and wept. "Forgive me. Oh, *Montesita*, I loved you so very much!"

"Jesu!" Foster's curse erupted in a harsh whisper. "La Venganza. She's dead."

He raced back into the house only to reappear in the doorway a moment later, holding Ethan's flintlock pistol in his hands.

"Marcus." Ethan pulled at the lieutenant's shirttail. "Don't do anything foolish."

"It's too late for foolish. That was our money, Ethan! Gone. It's all gone. If we don't have La Venganza, we don't have the money." Pushing past Ethan, he fled down the rickety stairs toward Ramon. He pulled the hammer to half cock with a loud click. "Prepare to die, old man."

At that moment, an arrow flew from the nearby trees, whizzed through the air, and speared itself in Foster's hand. An inhuman howl erupted from the lieutenant. He fell to his knees, and the pistol landed with a soft thud in the dirt.

Quick as a panther, Ramon reached across Marisa's back to scoop up the weapon. He placed the muzzle of the pistol against Foster's head and drew the hammer to full-cock position. "On your feet, bastard."

As Foster rose, his eyes never strayed from the arrow and the blood that poured from his hand.

Ethan, transfixed, found the energy to move—too late. Lucien trained his own pistol at the area near Ethan's heart.

"Don't move, Sergeant," he commanded. "It would give me great pleasure to kill you now."

"I didn't kill her." Ethan thrust out his hands in

supplication. "The old man killed her. You saw it."

"And what about Lyncoya?" Lucien kept his aim straight and true.

"I took him from the Hermitage," he blathered, "but Marcus was the one who thought we should blame La Venganza for the crime. I still had the note from the episode with Captain Gadsden and the striped uniforms. I pinned it to the boy's pillow and then pretended to find it there."

"Coward!" Foster growled. "You caught us, St. Clair, but to what end?" With a nod of his head, he indicated Marisa face down in the dirt. "La Venganza is dead. As for Lyncoya, we have him hidden where no one will ever find him. If we don't get our ransom, the boy will only starve to death."

"Is that so?" Lucien asked.

"Yes, it is." Foster grinned like a bobcat. "You may have won this game, but your players are dead. Your victory is hollow, indeed."

In reply, Lucien gave a shrill whistle.

A loud war whoop came from the trees as Lyncoya raced out of hiding. "Marisa!" he shouted frantically.

At the child's call, Marisa raised her head and smiled.

****

"I knew it! I knew you weren't really dead!" Lyncoya danced around Marisa as she rose and brushed the dirt off her clothing with the palm of her hand. "Did you see my arrow? I aimed it just as you taught me and it went right through his hand!"

She wrapped an arm around his shoulders, pulled him close and squeezed. "I'm so proud of you! You did very well, not only with your arrow but with your tracking as well."

"I told Major Lucien I'd find you and I did."

"Yes, you're a very clever boy!" She kissed his cheeks and laughed when she saw the red stains upon his face. Rubbing the marks only smeared them further. "I've left berry juice on your face."

"Is that what that blood in your mouth was?"

She nodded. "When I fell against Major Lucien's shoulder, I tossed the berries into my mouth. And when Ramon pretended to stab me, I bit down on them."

"And the knife?"

In reply, she picked up the knife from the dirt and showed the boy how the blade collapsed inside the handle harmlessly.

"What a wonderful trick! This was even better than the ghosts at the farmhouse. You're so clever."

"Well, thank you." She curtseyed before him.

"It was all a trick?" Ethan cried. "How can that be?"

"You made a grave error, Sergeant," Lucien answered Ethan's question with a proud grin, his eyes aglow. "You forgot how La Venganza succeeded with her antics time and again. You underestimated your adversary, and she took advantage of your weakness." He pushed the muzzle of the pistol into Ethan's shoulder blade. "Shall we go into the house now?"

With the point of his pistol to lead the way, he ushered Ethan back inside the farmhouse while Ramon used the same method to prod Foster to follow close behind.

Lyncoya remained outside with Marisa, holding her hand as if he'd never let her go. "I'm sorry I said I wouldn't be your friend anymore. I love you, Marisa. You're the very best friend I've ever had."

"I love you, too, Lyncoya." She squeezed him breathless in her arms.

Ramon returned outside after trussing up Marcus Foster in a chair in the sitting room. He approached Marisa and, with strong fingers under her chin, tilted her cheeks up to the sun. "Did I hurt you, *Montesita?*"

"Ha!" she replied with a grin. "You couldn't hurt a mosquito with that slap you gave me. If my tears and wails hadn't been so convincing, no one would have believed our ruse. You've spent so much time pretending to be a frail old man your muscles have grown weak from lack of use."

"Weak!" he retorted. He raised a fist in her direction. "I'll show you who is weak."

"Ramon?" Lucien called out from the doorway. "Before you teach Marisa a lesson, there's something I wish to discuss with you."

"Oh?" Ramon cocked his head to one side and raised an eyebrow. "What might that be?"

"I'd like to wed your sister."

*"She floats, she hesitates; in a word, she's a woman."*
— *Jean Racine (Athalie)*

## CHAPTER 37

Ramon grinned and turned his eyes back to Marisa. "And what does my sister say?"

"Your sister already gave him an answer." She folded her arms over her chest. "No."

"It seems Marisa needs convincing."

"Oh, but they must get married," Lyncoya chimed in, wringing his hands.

Ramon's gaze veered between Marisa, Lucien, and Lyncoya. "Is that so?"

"Yes, it is," Lucien announced.

At the very same moment, Marisa shouted, "No, it isn't!"

"Yes, it is!"

"No, it isn't!"

Ramon laughed. "Oh, Lucien, I do pity you! Do you really wish to wed this spitting wildcat?"

"It doesn't matter what he wishes," Marisa interjected, "since I don't wish to marry him."

"Perhaps you should have thought of that before we spent the night together in a hayloft," Lucien remarked. "Or should I inform your brother of our activities that evening?"

"Ramon knows all about that," she said with an unladylike snort. She took Lyncoya by the hand. "We're going home. Once you've taken care of those scoundrels, you may join us there."

Without waiting for a reply, she and Lyncoya plunged back into the woods to begin their walk home.

Lucien turned to Ramon who shrugged. "She told me everything last evening."

"What did she tell you?"

"She told me she was a willing participant in your seduction of her, but you used her innocence to take the decision about a marriage out of her hands. It wasn't the act of a gentleman, you know."

A hot flush crept up Lucien's neck.

"However," Ramon sighed, and then wagged his eyebrows, "I should imagine if my Juanita had been as stubborn toward my marriage proposal as my sister was toward yours, I might have resorted to nefarious means to win her hand, as well. A man in love will do strange things, won't he? Although Marisa seems to believe you're in love with your sister-in-law."

"I'm not in love with Antoinetta!"

Ramon's smile grew to full-blown laughter. "She also said you'd deny it if I called you on it. Oh, Major, she knows you too well!"

"When did she tell you all of this? And how did you manage to plan that little masquerade? I can't believe you were able to speak to each other without being overheard by those villains."

Ramon shrugged. "How do you think we managed to speak at *El Castillo de Plata* without ever being found out?"

Logic escaped Lucien, and he simply stared in confusion.

"She sings to me," Ramon said at last.

He couldn't have heard that correctly. The answer made no sense. "She what?"

"She sings to me," he repeated.

"I don't understand—"

"Marisa and I have a secret language we developed as children. To outsiders, it sounds like nonsense, but the rhythm and the pattern of the words is quite succinct. Whenever Marisa needs to speak to me, she sings a song containing a hidden message in our language. Anyone else listening assumes the words are just twaddle and ignores them. Besides, her voice is so heavenly most people are too enraptured to care what her words might mean. She sang to me for hours last night with our captors none the wiser."

And all those nights at the inn. *Marisa, sing to me. You know how I love to hear you sing...*

"By damn," Lucien exclaimed. "General Jackson could use someone half as clever as Marisa."

"Oh, my sister is a very clever wench!" Ramon rubbed his hands together with glee. "Which is why you'd never trap Marisa into marriage in the same manner your brother used to capture his wife."

Lucien's heart plummeted. "Yes, so I've guessed."

"If you want to win my sister, you'll have to outwit her." Ramon clapped a hand on his shoulder, firm and friendly.

"Thanks," Lucien retorted. "So, what do I do now?"

"Well, right now, we'll bring our friends to meet the town sheriff. But on our way home, we'll discuss how to get your spitting wildcat to take her wedding vows without scratching out your eyes."

****

"What do you mean you're leaving?" Marisa didn't take the news well at all.

They sat on the dining room floor, eating a pear tartlet she'd prepared for dessert when Lucien announced his intentions.

"There's nothing to keep me here any longer," he replied. "You and your brother have been safely reunited. Now I must take Lyncoya home to his parents and bring his kidnappers to the general. It's long past time Lyncoya went home."

"I know that," she snapped.

He seemed so calm, almost banal, about leaving her. If he loved her, wouldn't he be distressed? Shouldn't he feel sadness or melancholy at being separated from the woman he purported to love? At the moment, Lucien showed as much emotion as a boulder.

"Must you leave so soon?" Oh, she hated the plea in her voice, but couldn't squelch the panic she experienced at the thought of his departure.

He shrugged. "Captain Espinoza and his unit of soldiers took custody of the prisoners and will escort them under guard to the general. They're going by steam vessel to Mobile, leaving at first light. The captain has graciously allowed Lyncoya and I to accompany them, giving up his own cabin aboard the vessel for us. Lyncoya will be home with his family in a matter of days."

"Oh." Her reaction to the news confused her. She should be elated. The perfect, arrogant, pristine Major St. Clair would finally be out of her life. So why did the idea make her feel bereft?

She told herself it wasn't the loss of Lucien that bothered her. It was the loss of Lyncoya. And of course, Lyncoya must return home. It made perfectly good sense. Who else would take him there but Lucien?

She refused to think he planned to abandon her. After all, she didn't want him to stay. Good riddance! She wanted him to go. Lucien St. Clair could go to the devil for all she cared!

"Oh, Marisa, are you certain you won't marry Major Lucien?" Lyncoya pleaded. "If you would reconsider, you might come with us to Mobile."

But Marisa remained firm in her resolve. "No,

Lyncoya. As much as I am loath to say goodbye to you, by that very amount do I hope to never see Major Lucien again. There will be no marriage between us."

"You've stated your choice quite clearly, *Montesita*," Lucien replied in a voice as sharp as knives. "Lyncoya and I will depart within the hour." He removed his napkin from his throat and tossed it onto the floor before stalking out of the dining room.

Lyncoya and Ramon quickly followed. Marisa remained alone in the empty dining room with nothing but dirty plates and burning candles for company.

Outside the dining room, Ramon embraced Lucien. "Well done, Lucien. Now take Lyncoya and get to Mobile as fast as you can. With luck and a bit of prodding, Marisa and I shall be about a week behind you."

"Do you think you can convince her to see reason within a week?" Lucien asked him with surprise.

"The Lord God created the world in six days," he reminded Lucien with a grin.

"But the Lord God didn't have to cope with Marisa."

"Have faith, Lucien. She'll see reason within an hour," Ramon said. "But it will take her about a week to admit it."

When Lucien took Lyncoya upstairs, he prepared the boy for their departure and explained just what they were about with this sudden leavetaking.

Once fully informed of the plans, Lyncoya danced around the room. "What fun!"

"You think so?" Lucien had his doubts.

"Of course," Lyncoya replied. "Don't you see, Major Lucien? Marisa is the greatest trickster in the world. Won't it be a great victory if we're able to pull the wool over her eyes?"

Perhaps. But what if she didn't fall into line the way Ramon expected her to? Shoving his morose thoughts into the farthest corners of his mind, Lucien packed up their meager belongings.

**\*\*\*\***

One hour later, Marisa showed only the slightest emotion when it came time to say goodbye to Lyncoya. She knelt to embrace him and very nearly squeezed the breath out of the boy.

"I don't want to go, Marisa," he wheezed into her ear. "I love you!"

"Oh, Lyncoya, I love you also." She choked back sobs, pulled away, and brushed a stray tear from his cheek with the wisp of a fingertip.

"No tears, now," she chided with a shake of her wet finger. "You should be excited. You're going home. If you truly love me, you'll remember all I've taught you. Behave yourself. No more teasing your brothers and sisters, and no more wandering away from your family. Always listen to your mama and papa for they love you dearly and want what is best for you. Be devoted to your studies. But most of all, live a good life. Be happy. Make me proud of you."

"I promise, Marisa. I'll be the best boy ever!"

Satisfied with his outrageous promise, she gave him one last hug before rising to where Lucien stood before her.

"Marisa," he said flatly with a nod of deference.

"Major St. Clair," she replied in the same emotionless tone.

He grabbed her shoulders and crushed her against his chest as his mouth explored hers one final time. She melted into his arms. Hands fisted at her sides, she fought to regain control. She wouldn't give in, no matter how persuasive his kiss.

He must have felt her resistance because he tried to break down her walls with a sweep of his tongue across her lips, but she dug her nails into her palms painfully. Finally, he broke away. He shook hands with Ramon before gaining the saddle and settling Lyncoya before him. With a crack of the reins, they were gone.

Marisa watched the horizon long after his image had melted into the distance.

"Come inside, *Montesita*," her brother murmured at last, taking her by the shoulders.

She followed blindly. Tears blurred her vision.

Inside the house, she busied herself with a thousand meaningless tasks to keep the pain at bay.

The old man, Ramon, had disappeared. Orlando had removed his thick eyeglasses, then bathed and washed his hair until it gleamed. Dressed in his own clothing, he now resembled Marisa's brother again with his vivid green eyes and proud, erect carriage.

He sat in the parlor before a warming fire while she paced from one room to the other.

"'Lando?" She sat down beside him on the settee. "What say we have a Shakespeare debate? I'll even allow you to choose the topic, if you wish."

Orlando shook his head. "Not tonight, *Montesita*. It's been a long time since I've been home, and I'm for bed."

With a yawn and stretch, he rose from the settee. He offered her a quick peck on her cheek and a soft goodnight, then climbed the staircase to his room.

Long after Orlando sought his bed, Marisa sat staring off into space. Long after the fire had died and the embers had smoldered to lumps of gray-white ashes, she stared at the walls around her.

She'd never felt so lonely in all her life. Something seemed to be missing. She couldn't quite put her finger on what it was, but the house didn't feel as warm and cozy as it had just a few days ago.

It had nothing to do with the sudden departure of Lucien St. Clair. She refused to even think about that odious man. He was gone, and she was glad.

Strange, then, how she still sensed his presence here. His spirit haunted her. She heard his laughter in the air, felt his touch upon her hand, and saw his eyes glow in the darkened room.

Where was he now? No doubt, he and Lyncoya slept in their cabin aboard the steamboat that sailed up and down the Alabama River. Was he asleep? Or was he wide-awake, tormented by his thoughts of her? Did he toss and turn in his bunk, plagued by doubts and self-recrimination? Did he regret leaving her here? The idea pleased her immensely, but she refused to ponder why.

Did he wonder if he'd done the right thing when he rode away from her? Did he wish for one more opportunity to ask her to marry him? Not, of course, that she'd say yes.

Gingerly, she touched her finger to her lips and traced the area where he'd kissed her earlier. Hours later, she still felt the heat of him on her mouth. She tasted his hot breath on the tip of her tongue. If she closed her eyes, she could almost see him in this room with her. But that didn't mean she missed him.

She did not miss him.

*"Every lover is a warrior and Cupid has his camps."*
*— Ovid (Amores)*

## CHAPTER 38

"When are you headed back to Pensacola?"

Aghast, Marisa turned from the cooking stove to stare at her brother. "I'm not going back."

Seated on the lone chair in the kitchen, he cocked his head to one side. "Why not?"

"You know I've always hated living there. Besides, I can't show my face in the city since Lucien told Colonel Callava I was La Venganza. I can never return to Pensacola for fear of being arrested and hanged."

"So, where will you go? What will you do with the inn?"

"I'll give the inn to Santos and Anita."

He nodded. "A good idea. They've been loyal to us for a long time and will appreciate your gesture. Well then, what say we take a ride over to your land this afternoon? It's time to plan where your house should be built."

"My house?"

"Of course. You want to breed horses, don't you? Now that we're no longer playing our games of vengeance, I'd think you anxious to begin your new life in your own home."

She pointed to the floor. "*This* is my home!"

"No, this is *my* home," he corrected her. "But, if

you wish to remain, I'll explain to doña Isabella that my spinster sister would be too lonely to leave. I'm certain she'll understand."

"What does doña Isabella have to say about where I live?"

"Isabella will be mistress here come spring."

Her head spun. "How can that be?"

Orlando's expression turned wistful. "She's a wonderful woman, *Montesita.* You know her well. Living on the outskirts of the city as we both did, she and I became quite close. Before I left Pensacola, I asked her to be my wife, and she consented."

Marisa quirked a brow. "Does she know who you are?"

"Of course."

"You told her the truth about us?" His eyes flashed, confirming her suspicions. "How could you do such a thing? How did you know she could be trusted?"

"I love her and she loves me. With love comes trust." He glared at her disapprovingly. "You, of course, wouldn't know of such things, would you?"

"But you can't remarry!"

"Why not?"

"Well, because—" she stammered. "Because of your injury. Is she aware of your infirmity?"

"Yes, she is. And it doesn't matter to her. Isabella already has six children. She has no need for more."

"But there's more to lovemaking than the creation of children."

He chose an apple from the sideboard and took a crisp bite. "There's also more to lovemaking than satisfying maiden curiosity," he retorted. "But that didn't stop you."

Her blood chilled. "What do you mean?"

"You know exactly what I mean. Why did you allow Lucien to take liberties with you?" He didn't wait for a reply as he elaborated, "If you allowed Lucien to make love to you because you love him, then you're a fool for allowing him to ride away from you yesterday. But if you spent an evening locked in passion's embrace with a man whom you have no fondness for, you're no better than a whore."

Marisa gasped as if he'd slapped her. He'd never spoken so harshly to her before. Even when they'd feigned the argument at the Pendleton farm, she'd known his words were merely for the benefit of their audience. He hadn't meant one angry word he'd spoken. But now, there were no witnesses. He had no reason to pretend a rage he didn't feel. He really was angry with her. And although she knew why and could even understand it, sorrow filled her heart at his bitter words.

He studied the crimson skin of his apple. "Well?" he prompted. "Which is it? Are you a fool or a whore?"

She couldn't answer him. Instead, she whirled and ran from the house.

****

Marisa sat at the edge of the Big Escambia Creek and looked over the green hills and barren trees. She'd always planned to name her horse farm, *El Castillo de Cielo*, The Castle of Heaven. But without someone to share her dreams and her life, she might as well consider naming this place, *El Castillo de Infierno*. A better fit. And more suited to her mood these days. Heaven and hell...

Which was which? She didn't know anymore.

In her youth, she'd sit on this bank day after day and plan where the stables would be, which was the best pastureland for the horses, and where she and Tomás would build their house. From the time she was a child, she'd mapped out her life so clearly. A pity her life hadn't followed the trail she'd drawn.

She sighed. All her hopes and dreams, dashed

on a bright, sunny afternoon in late August when she was sixteen years old. Lord! What an innocent she'd been. In those days, her worst fear had been whether she looked her best when Tomás came to call. Before Fort Mims, she'd never fretted about the deaths of those she loved, never thought twice about those who were less fortunate. No, she spent all her time dreaming of an idyllic life that would never come to fruition. She never stopped to think how quickly life could change.

She'd lived her childhood as an indulged brat, believing if she didn't get what she wanted, she had the right to retaliate with pranks and tricks. To her deep shame, she still acted like that spoilt child who must have her way at all costs.

Perhaps Lucien was correct in his assessment of her. She'd spent so many years nursing her hatred, plotting her vengeance, and reveling in her enemies' downfalls, she'd forgotten how to love.

At sixteen, she'd known all there was to know about love. At sixteen, she'd loved Tomás Marquez and believed she would love him forever.

Seven years later, she knew nothing. And worse, she couldn't remember what Tomás looked like. When she closed her eyes and tried to picture him, all she saw was a tall form in a bright uniform. Did that mean she'd never loved him? Or did the pain of his loss close her mind to his memory?

While others become wiser as they grew older, somehow, Marisa had become more ignorant. Who was she? She had no idea. Was she the fool Orlando believed her to be? Was she a whore? Was she the heartless, vengeful Fury Lucien proclaimed her?

Hollow, she leaned across the sands to stare at her reflection in the waters of the creek. She saw her face so clearly. Her bright green eyes, her little upturned nose, her full mouth, and her tiny, pointed chin. But she didn't recognize the features of the reflection in the water. They belonged to a stranger.

She picked up a pebble and hurled it into the creek. Grim satisfaction rose when the little stone sank into the water, leaving a ring of ripples in its wake. Her reflection turned wavy and unrecognizable. She liked that image, found it more in line with her innermost feelings. And the pebble represented her heart, worn down through the years with pain and suffering, deeply buried, now untouchable.

'Lando planned to marry again. Despite the heartache of losing Juanita, despite the infirmity that kept him from sharing the ultimate joy with his bride, despite all the sorrows love could bring, Orlando would allow his heart to heal.

But not Marisa. She couldn't. The last time she'd allowed herself to fall in love, she'd known joy for such a short time. And after the momentary joy came years of anguish that time couldn't erase. She'd never fall in love again. Love brought pain, deep and incessant pain. She couldn't bear to experience that agony—that walking death—again.

She threw herself on the ground and wept for what seemed like an eternity. Devoid of tears, she remounted Tormenta and rode home with a heart as heavy as the burden of Atlas.

*"Love, then, hath every bliss in store;*
*'Tis friendship, and 'tis something more.*
*Each other every wish they give;*
*Not to know love is not to live."*
— *John Gay (Plutus, Cupid and Time)*

## CHAPTER 39

For two more days, Marisa moped about *El Castillo*, refusing to admit aloud what her heart knew to be true. She wouldn't eat, she paced the floors at night, and she barely spoke a word.

'Lando had become the most boring creature on the face of the earth. When she'd been upset over losing Ramon, Lucien had done everything in his power to keep her amused. He'd insisted on their nightly Shakespeare debates and regaled her with tales of his brother and sister-in-law's bizarre courtship, if only to keep her mind off her troubles. But not 'Lando.

Poor 'Lando. Dear, sweet, *brave* 'Lando. How else to explain his planning a new future? Without Juanita? Without their child?

'Lando was far braver than she could ever be. She'd loved Tomás deeply. And he'd died to protect her. His loss had splintered her heart into a thousand shards of broken glass. Each breath she inhaled, from that day at Fort Mims until this moment, ripped a new hole in her soul.

Tomás had barely reached the gates of the fort

on that terrible afternoon before a Red Stick club felled him. Somehow, he'd crawled on his hands and knees to the Álvarez cabin where he'd found the family brutalized. Mama and Papa were dead, Juanita with her unborn child lay dying in the dirt. But Orlando was alive, although too badly beaten to move. With the last ounce of his strength, Tomás had thrown himself over Orlando's torso and covered him from head to toe.

"Don't move," he'd whispered. "Marisa is in the woods outside the fort. Someone must survive to care for her. You're the only one left, 'Lando."

They were the last words Tomás ever spoke. Knowing his bloody body covered Orlando from the sharp eyes of the Red Sticks, Tomás had collapsed and died.

And from his death and the deaths of all the others, La Venganza was born. At first, she'd only talked of vengeance to keep moving as they walked to Pensacola. But by the time they arrived in Florida, talk had become need. A fiery drive to make someone pay for all she'd lost. Poor 'Lando had been given no choice but to become the notorious La Venganza, if only to keep her from doing the same.

Marisa's sigh of self-pity drew her brother's icy stare yet again. "So, have you decided what you are yet? Fool or whore?"

Seated on the floor near the fire in the parlor, she looked up from his boots to his face. A tremulous smile curved her lips, and she gave a little cough to clear her throat as well as her mind. "I think I'm a fool, Lando."

Tension eased from his face—as if he'd waited an eternity to hear her confession. "I think so, too."

"But I'm so afraid," she wailed.

"*Montesita*." He patted the seat beside him, and she bounded to his side. His arm slid around her, comforting and consoling. "Love doesn't always bring tragedy, you know. Most times, it brings rapture."

"Until the one you love dies." She tucked a hand under her chin and rested her elbow on her knee. "Then comes the tragedy."

"*Querida*, everyone dies eventually." He chucked her under the chin. "All the more reason why you must grasp at love while you can. Hold on tightly and suck every drop of joy from it."

The fire popped, and Marisa stared into the flames. Water wore away slowly, bit by bit, eon by eon. Fire consumed, quickly, ravenously. Was that why hatred always seemed to be portrayed as fire? Why Satan's hell was filled with it?

She didn't want to perish in the flames. She wanted to be a rock, reshaped by time and tide.

"So what do I do now?"

"You must get to Mobile as quickly as possible," Orlando said.

She whirled to him then, sadness replaced by resentment. "What about Antoinetta?"

'Lando shrugged. "What about her?"

"Lucien is in love with her."

"Lucien is in love with *you*." He rolled his eyes in exasperation. "God knows why, and I pity the man his foolish choice, but it's true. Antoinetta's his sister, and he loves her, but he's not in love with her. He loves her the way I love you."

Could it be true? Memories assailed her then. Lucien's voice, a thousand times and again. *"I do love nothing in the world so well as you: is not that strange?"*

When she finally spoke again, the words tumbled from her lips almost unintelligibly. "Will you come with me to Mobile, 'Lando?"

He pulled her into his arms and kissed the top of her head. "Of course, I will. It's my right to give the bride away."

Doubt settled over her like a wet blanket, and

she shivered. "Do you truly believe Lucien loves me?"

"I don't believe anything of the sort," he snorted.

Tears pricked her eyes, and she stared at the fire again. "Oh…"

He jerked her chin back to his grinning face. "I *know* he loves you. May God have mercy on the poor, besotted fool!"

*"Pure, as the charities above,*
*Rise the sweet sympathies of love;*
*And closer chords than those of life*
*Unite the husband to the wife."*
— *John Logan (The Lovers)*

## CHAPTER 40

As the steamboat pulled into Mobile, Marisa and Orlando stood by the rail and watched the crowds at the quay. Marisa saw Lucien before he spotted her. How he'd known she'd arrive today, she couldn't begin to fathom. But there he was, with the golden sun placed beyond his head to form a perfect halo.

The boat barely bumped the dock before Lucien climbed aboard and grasped Marisa by the hand. Ignoring the crowds of onlookers, he knelt down before her. "I love you, *Montesita*, from now until the end of time. Will you marry me?"

"Yes, Lucien," she replied without hesitation. "I love you, as well."

"Hallelujah!" To the exuberant cheers of the people on land and sea, Lucien rose and kissed her hastily on the mouth. "Let's go."

Her hand tucked in his, he turned and dragged her down the gangplank with Orlando left to follow behind. Before Marisa had time to say another word, she found herself tossed into a waiting carriage. She barely registered the ride at all. Lucien sat beside her, his hand clutching hers as if he'd never let her

325

go. Again and again, he told her he loved her, he'd always love her. And she believed him. Her heart, shattered into so many pieces for so long, began mending itself with every squeeze of his fingers, every whispered endearment that fluttered to her ears.

When the carriage finally halted and the doors opened, Marisa stared into a pair of icy blue eyes set in a golden face surrounded by a cloud of rich chestnut hair. The famous Antoinetta, at long last.

But Antoinetta's smile of welcome froze to a frown. "Blast it! Did you even let the boat stop before you dragged her here?"

"She's kept me waiting long enough," Lucien replied.

Marisa felt a soft but firm hand upon her wrist. "Well, she's going to make you wait a little longer. By Kismet, you have the Major General and Mrs. Jackson inside that church and you'd allow your bride to walk down the aisle dressed in rags! With Daya's help, I can have her more presentable in an hour. Until then, you'll have to cool your heels. And to pass the time, find something suitable for Marisa's brother to wear. You look to be about the same size. Or did your grandiose plans neglect clothing for men as well as for your bride?"

Lucien's face fell. "What in blazes do I know about a trousseau?"

"Nothing." Antoinetta flashed a quick wink in Marisa's direction. "Which is why you will leave your bride in my very capable hands for one hour. Now go. Take your soon-to-be-brother-in-law with you."

Without waiting for another argument, Antoinetta pulled Marisa out of the carriage where before them stood a set of stairs leading to a large stone church.

"This way, *Montesita*," Antoinetta murmured.

The nickname, foreign on this strange lady's

tongue, filled Marisa with warmth. She might have lost most of her family at Fort Mims, but Lucien would soon provide her with a new family. This lovely lady and her husband, as well as a family of their own. Children.

The warm glow bloomed in intensity as she considered the making of those children and the heaven she'd found that one night in a hayloft.

"Father Milton was kind enough to allow us the use of his room." Antoinetta's remark snapped her into the present.

The two ladies descended a small flight of steps and strode to the end of a dimly lit hall.

A tiny dark-haired woman stood in the last doorway, hands on her hips, a wide smile on her exotic face. "In case she didn't find time to mention it," she said, "the woman holding you is Antoinetta. I'm Daya, and we're going to make you look more presentable for today's affair."

Marisa's head spun. The last few minutes had sped by her in a blur. "H—how did you get here?"

Antoinetta laughed. The musical sound echoed off the bare walls of the priest's cell. "We received a message at Belle Monde to come to Mobile to attend your wedding. We only arrived this morning. Lucien has this church booked for every day that a steamboat arrives in Mobile. If you didn't arrive today, we'd have returned on Sunday and next Tuesday."

Annoyance pricked her temper. "What made him certain I'd come at all?"

She shrugged. "My Darian is the same way. That's why we St. Clair ladies must stick together. If we don't show our backbones every now and then, our men tend to run roughshod over us."

Marisa instantly liked this woman, liked her humor, liked her laugh, liked her spirit. Oh, yes. They would become great friends.

"I'm so glad to meet you, Antoinetta," she exclaimed.

Daya stepped between them with a length of rose-colored silk draped across her outstretched arms. "Come, come, my beauties. We must prepare the bride for her nuptials."

"But—" Marisa held up a hand.

"Daya is wonderful with a needle," Antoinetta boasted. "This gown was originally meant for her daughter, Chandra. Based on Lucien's brief description of you, we took a chance it might be altered to fit you in a hurry. Now, let's get busy. I've insisted Lucien wait one more hour. If I detain you any longer, he might carry you out of here and ravish you without the bonds of wedlock."

Joy suffused Marisa, and she easily succumbed to the women's ministrations.

When they finished an hour later, Marisa couldn't believe her eyes. The gown fit her perfectly, thanks to the numerous pins in place where the hem was too long and the bosom too large. She looked like an angel come down from heaven. The rose pink shade suited her complexion and hair beautifully. The gown seemed more like spun sugar than silk with a square cut neckline and a high Empire waist embroidered with tiny hearts in silver threads. Her hair was braided and coiled atop her head, interspersed with tiny pink rosebuds, still tightly closed to the light of day.

"Perfect!" Antoinetta finally announced. She leaned close to kiss Marisa's cheek and whispered, "I'll inform Lucien that, at long last, his wait has come to an end."

*"So dear I love him, that with him all deaths
I could endure, without him live no life."*
— *John Milton (Paradise Lost)*

## CHAPTER 41

'Lando escorted Marisa to the altar where Lucien stood beside his brother, Darian. When he placed her hand inside Lucien's, a tiny spark ran through her fingertips.

Lucien felt it, too, because he tilted his head to stare into her eyes, then smiled. "I'm guessing Kismet approves."

At last the priest pronounced them man and wife and he bent his head toward her pursed lips. His kiss aroused her passion. And when his tongue ran across her lower lip, her knees buckled. But his arm around her waist strengthened her and she walked out of the church under her own power.

Outside, 'Lando embraced his sister and kissed away the tears of joy running down her cheeks. "Remember what I told you, *Montesita*. Suck all of the love and happiness out of life you can."

"I suppose you'll be leaving here to retrieve doña Isabella from Pensacola," she noted wryly. "No doubt, your bride will be happy to be rid of me."

His face flushed and he looked at his feet, embarrassed. "Yes...well...about that. I fear I deceived you a bit."

Marisa's eyebrow arched. "You were never

329

betrothed to doña Isabella, were you? It was just a ruse to get me to come to my senses and realize how much I love Lucien. I knew you were fibbing!" She dropped her voice to a whisper and added, "I knew you wouldn't be able to marry someone with your unfortunate condition."

Orlando's feet moved rapidly across the ground and his face grew even redder. "Yes...well...er..." he began again.

"You lied about that as well? Oh, 'Lando, how could you do such a thing to me?"

"How else would I have kept you innocent all these years? You've always been so reckless. I thought if you believed I couldn't enjoy the sins of the flesh, you would commiserate with me. And you did!" He cast a glance at Lucien. "At least, you did until a certain major came along."

"So you're not maimed?"

"I assure you, I'm quite capable of functioning as a whole man."

Lyncoya, dressed as a proper young gentleman, raced to Marisa's side and wrapped his arms around her waist. "Didn't I tell you Major Lucien was the perfect husband for you, Marisa? You'll be so happy now!"

She laughed at his presumption, but her laughter died when General Andrew Jackson and his very plain, stout wife approached. His narrow face with its sharp angles held no joy.

"Well, Mrs. St. Clair," the general said in a stern voice. "May I offer you our sincerest congratulations on your nuptials? Your husband's a fine man. And yet I believe he's not fine enough to deserve such a treasure as you. That is an especially bothersome trait of these St. Clair men. They have a penchant for marrying women who are not only lovely of face and heart, but intriguing and brave, as well."

His words certainly didn't match his expression.

She looked to Lucien for guidance, and he nodded.

"Thank you, sir," she managed.

Mrs. Jackson was a bit more ebullient as she embraced Marisa tight enough to wring the blood from her veins. "My husband and I owe you our deepest gratitude for returning our son to us. Lyncoya extolled your virtues and told us how you managed to free him from his terrible captors. Surely, God sent you to rescue our child when he needed you most. And your husband informed us that if not for you, he might never have captured La Venganza."

Although utterly confused by Mrs. Jackson's mention of La Venganza's capture, Marisa's face remained serene. Still, the general must have seen some reaction in her eyes.

He frowned. "Let's not speak of such unpleasantness on this joyful day, dear wife. Leave the odious Sergeant Greene and Mr. Foster to me. They shall receive their just punishment for their vile deeds."

"Forgive me for dampening your happiness today," Rachel said softly. "But to learn that Sergeant Greene, a man whom we trusted, was the traitorous La Venganza? The idea is so distressing to me. I wouldn't have believed it to be true if your husband had not shown us the ring."

"The ring?" In a quandary, Marisa turned to Lucien.

"La Venganza's signet ring," he reminded her blandly. "I explained to the General and Mrs. Jackson how you found the ring at the Bartlett farmhouse and brought it to my attention. Without that proof, we might never have known for certain Sergeant Greene was La Venganza."

Almost too late, but Marisa finally caught on. "Well, I could hardly allow such a scoundrel to get away with kidnapping an innocent boy."

"Indeed!" Rachel Jackson embraced Marisa once more. "Thank you again, my dear. Should you ever require the services of my husband or myself in any endeavor, you shall have them."

Lyncoya shook Lucien's hand. "Treat her like a princess, Major Lucien," he said arrogantly. "She is very dear to me."

Lucien pulled her close, so close she swore his heart beat against hers. "She is dearer to me, Lyncoya. Never fear."

The Jacksons, with Lyncoya in tow, moved past the newlyweds to their carriage waiting nearby.

Once out of earshot, Marisa turned a brilliant smile to her new husband. "You gave them my ring," she said through her teeth.

Lucien lifted her hand to his lips and kissed the finger where a wedding ring now encircled her flesh. "I replaced it with another far more precious, don't you think?"

"You might have asked my permission before giving it to the Jacksons."

"Would you rather I told the Jacksons the truth?"

At his challenge, she folded her arms over her chest and quirked a brow. "And what is the truth, Lucien?"

"That I did what the General ordered me to do. I found La Venganza and have been richly rewarded for my efforts. For she is mine at last."

"'This is the very ecstasy of love,'" she quoted her Shakespeare. "Hamlet."

"'Peace! I will stop your mouth.' Much Ado About Nothing."

Any argument she might have made was stifled as his lips came down on hers in a searing kiss.

Marisa Álvarez St. Clair would remember this day the rest of her life.

## A word about the author...

Once upon a time, a fledgling author fell in love with historical romance novels and began to pen her own stories featuring heroes in breeches and heroines in petticoats. The *Kismet Series* was Katherine Brandon's result. In fact, Katherine Brandon is the pseudonym for lighthearted contemporary author Gina Ardito.

Katherine/Gina lives on Long Island with her husband of more than twenty years, their two children, a bionic dog, one cat with a foot fetish, and another cat affectionately known as "The Skitten." She is one of the co-founders and current president for Dunes & Dreams, the Eastern Long Island chapter of Romance Writers of America.

For more information on Gina or Katherine, visit Katherine's website at:

www.katherinebrandon.com

Thank you for purchasing
this Wild Rose Press publication.
For other wonderful stories of romance,
please visit our on-line bookstore at
www.thewildrosepress.com.

For questions or more information
contact us at
info@thewildrosepress.com.

The Wild Rose Press
www.TheWildRosePress.com

Breinigsville, PA USA
20 July 2010
242114BV00006B/6/P